Praise for *Dragons of a Vanished Moon*

"A must read."

— *Cinescape*

"Enjoyable fantasy written by professionals who know how to make the pages turn."

— *West County Times*

"Typical of the work of Weis & Hickman, it demands your attention once you open the cover and begin to read. . . . You will have difficulty putting it down once you have started."

— *Conacopia*

"It's safe to say the conclusion of the War of Souls sets up a new status quo for the Dragonlance saga."

— *The Storyteller's Archive*

"Mina, Galdar, Gerard and Gilthas . . . are worthy successors to the original heroes and villains of Krynn. . . . The creators of the Dragonlance world have . . . breathed new life into the series and left Krynn a much more interesting place."

— *The News-Star*

THE WAR OF SOULS

VOLUME THREE

DRAGONS OF A VANISHED MOON

Margaret Weis & Tracy Hickman

DRAGONS OF A VANISHED MOON
©2003 Wizards of the Coast, Inc.

Cover art by Matt Stawicki
Cartography by Dennis Kauth
First Printing: June 2002
First Paperback Edition: March 2003
Library of Congress Catalog Card Number: 2001092207

9 8 7 6 5 4 3

US ISBN: 0-7869-2950-2
UK ISBN: 0-7869-2951-0
620-17881-001-EN

U.S., CANADA,   EUROPEAN HEADQUARTERS
ASIA, PACIFIC, & LATIN AMERICA   Wizards of the Coast, Belgium
Wizards of the Coast, Inc.   T Hosfveld 6d
P.O. Box 707   1702 Groot-Bijgaarden
Renton, WA 98057-0707   Belgium
+1-800-324-6496   +322 467 3360

Visit our web site at **www.wizards.com**

Dedication

To those who fight the never ending battle against the darkness, this book is respectfully dedicated.

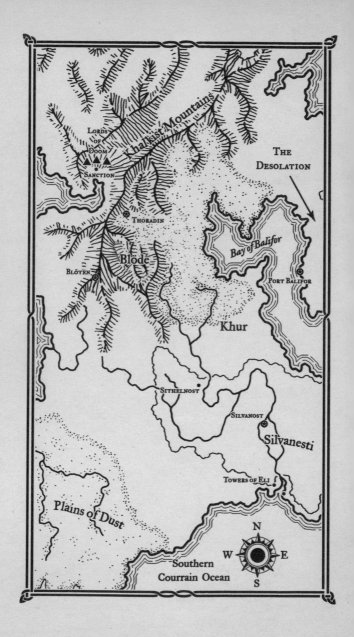

BOOK I

I

Lost Souls

In the dungeon of the Tower of High Sorcery, that had once been in Palanthas but now resided in Nightlund, the great archmagus Raistlin Majere had conjured a magical Pool of Seeing. By gazing into this pool, he was able to follow and sometimes shape events transpiring in the world. Although Raistlin Majere had been dead many long years, his magical Pool of Seeing remained in use. The wizard Dalamar, who had inherited the Tower from his *Shalafi*, maintained the magic of the pool. A veritable prisoner in the Tower that was an island in the river of the dead, Dalamar had often made use of the pool to visit in his mind those places he could not travel in his body.

Palin Majere stood now at the pool's edge, staring into the unwavering blue flame that burned in the center of the still water and was the chamber's only light. Dalamar was close beside him, his gaze fixed on

1

the same unwavering fire. Although the mages could have seen events transpiring anywhere in the world, they watched intently an event that was happening quite close to them, an event taking place at the top of the very Tower in which they stood.

Goldmoon of the Citadel of Light, and Mina, Lord of the Night, leader of the Dark Knights of Neraka, were to meet in the laboratory that had once belonged to Raistlin Majere. Goldmoon had already arrived at the strange meeting place. The laboratory was cold and dark and shadowed. Dalamar had left her a lantern, but its light was feeble and served only to emphasize the darkness that could never truly be illuminated, not if every lantern and every candle on Krynn should burst into flame. The darkness that was the soul of this dread Tower had its heart here in this chamber, which in the past had been a scene of death and pain and suffering.

In this chamber, Raistlin Majere had sought to emulate the gods and create life, only to fail utterly, bringing into the world misbegotten, shambling, pathetic beings known as the Live Ones, who had lived out their wretched existence in the room where the two wizards now stood. In the chamber, the Blue Dragonlady Kitiara had died, her death as brutal and bloody as her life. Here stood the Portal to the Abyss, a link between the realm of the mortal and realm of the dead, a link that had long ago been severed and was nothing now but a home to mice and spiders.

Goldmoon knew the dark history of this room. She must be considering that now, Palin thought, watching her image that shimmered on the surface of the pool. She stood in the laboratory, her arms clasped about her. She shivered not with the cold, but with fear. Palin was concerned. He could not remember—in all the years that he had known her—seeing Goldmoon afraid.

Perhaps it was the strange body that Goldmoon's spirit inhabited. She was over ninety. Her true body was that of an elderly woman—still vigorous, still strong for her years, but with skin marked and marred with time, a back that was starting to stoop, fingers that were gnarled, but whose touch was gentle. She had been comfortable with that body. She had never feared or regretted the passage of the years that had brought the joy of love and birth, the sorrow of love and death. That body had been taken from her the night of the great storm, and she had been given another body, a stranger's body, one that was young and beautiful, healthful and vibrant. Only the eyes were the eyes of the woman Palin had known throughout his life.

She is right, he thought, this body doesn't belong to her. It's borrowed finery. Clothing that doesn't fit.

"I should be with her," Palin muttered. He stirred, shifted, began to pace restlessly along the water's edge. The chamber was made of stone and was dark and chill, the only light the unwavering flame that burned in the heart of the dark pool, and it illuminated little and gave no warmth. "Goldmoon looks strong, but she's not. Her body may be that of someone in her twenties, but her heart is the heart of a woman whose life has spanned nine decades. The shock of seeing Mina again—especially as she is—may kill her."

"In that case, the shock of seeing you beheaded by the Dark Knights would probably do very little for her either," returned Dalamar caustically. "Which is what she would see if you were to march up there now. The Tower is surrounded by soldiers. There must be at least thirty of them out there."

"I don't think they'd kill me," said Palin.

"No? And what would they do? Tell you to go stand in a corner with your face to the wall and think what a bad boy you've been?" Dalamar scoffed.

"Speaking of corners," he added suddenly, his voice altering, "did you see that?"

"What?" Palin jerked his head, looked around in alarm.

"Not here! There!" Dalamar pointed into the pool. "A flash in the eyes of dragons that guard the Portal."

"All I see is dust," Palin said after a moment's intense gaze, "and cobwebs and mouse dung. You're imagining things."

"Am I?" Dalamar asked. His sardonic tone had softened, was unusually somber. "I wonder."

"You wonder what?"

"A great many things," said Dalamar.

Palin eyed the dark elf closely but could not read on that gaunt and drawn face a single thought stirring behind the dark eyes. In his black robes, Dalamar was indistinguishable from the darkness of the chamber. Only his hands with their delicate fingers could be seen, and they appeared to be hands that lacked a body. The long-lived elf was presumably in the prime of life, but his wasted form, consumed by the fever of frustrated ambition, might have belonged to an elder of his race.

I shouldn't be casting aspersions. What does he see when he looks at me? Palin asked himself. A shabby, middle-aged man. My face wan and wasted. My hair graying, thin. My eyes the embittered eyes of one who has not found what he was promised.

I stand on the edge of wondrous magic created by my uncle, and what have I done, except fail everyone who ever expected anything of me. Including myself. Goldmoon is just the most recent. I should be with her. A hero like my father would be with her, no matter that it meant sacrificing his freedom, perhaps his life. Yet here I am, skulking in the basement of this Tower.

"Stop fidgeting, will you?" Dalamar said irritably. "You'll slip and fall in the pool. Look there." He pointed excitedly to the water. "Mina has arrived." Dalamar rubbed his thin hands. "Now we will see and hear something to our advantage."

Palin halted on the edge of the pool, wavering in his decision. If he left immediately, walked the corridors of magic, he might yet reach Goldmoon in time to protect her. Yet, he could not pull himself away. He stared down at the pool in dread fascination.

"I can see nothing in this wizard's murk," Mina was saying loudly. "We need more light."

The light in the chamber grew brighter, so bright that it dazzled eyes accustomed to the darkness.

"I didn't know Mina was a mage," said Palin, shading his eyes with his hand.

"She's not," said Dalamar shortly. He cast Palin a strange glance. "Doesn't that tell you something?"

Palin ignored the question, concentrated on the conversation.

"You . . . you are so beautiful, Mother," Mina said softly, awed. "You look just as I imagined."

Sinking to her knees, the girl extended her hands. "Come, kiss me, Mother," she cried, tears falling.

5

"Kiss me as you used to. I am Mina. Your Mina."

"And so she was, for many years," murmured Palin, watching in sorrowful concern as Goldmoon advanced unsteadily to clasp her adopted child in her arms. "Goldmoon found Mina washed up on the shore, presumably the survivor of some terrible ship wreck, though no wreckage or bodies or any other survivors were ever discovered. They brought her to the Citadel's orphanage. Intelligent, bold, fearless, Mina charmed all, including Goldmoon, who took the child to her heart. And then, one day, at the age of fourteen, Mina ran away. We searched, but we could find no trace of her, nor could anyone say why she had gone, for she had seemed so happy. Goldmoon's heart broke, then."

"Of course, Goldmoon found her," Dalamar said. "She was meant to find her."

"What do you mean?" Palin glanced at Dalamar, but the elf's expression was enigmatic.

Dalamar shrugged, said nothing, gestured back to the dark pool.

"Mina!" Goldmoon whispered, rocking her adopted daughter. "Mina! Child . . . why did you leave us when we all loved you so much?"

"I left for love of you, Mother. I left to seek what you wanted so desperately. And I found it, Mother! I found it for you.

"Dearest Mother." Mina took hold of Goldmoon's hands and pressed them to her lips. "All that I am and all that I have done, I have done for you."

"I . . . don't understand, child," Goldmoon faltered. "You wear the symbol of evil, of darkness. . . . Where did you go? Where have you been? What has happened to you?"

6

Mina laughed. "Where I went and where I have been is not important. What happened to me along the way—that is what you must hear.

"Do you remember, Mother, the stories you used to tell me? The story about how you traveled into darkness to search for the gods? And how you found the gods and brought faith in the gods back to the people of the world?"

"Yes," said Goldmoon. She had gone so very pale that Palin determined to be with her, cost him what it might.

He began to chant the words of magic. The words that came out of his mouth, however, were not the words that had formed in his brain. Those words were rounded, smooth, flowed easily. The words he spoke were thick and square-sided, tumbled out like blocks dropped on the floor.

He halted, angry at himself, forced himself to calm down and try again. He knew the spell, could have said it backward. He might well have said it backward, for all the sense it made.

"You're doing this to me!" Palin said accusingly.

Dalamar was amused. "Me?" He waved his hand. "Go to Goldmoon, if you want. Die with her, if you want. I'm not stopping you."

"Then who is? This One God?"

Dalamar regarded him in silence a moment, then turned back to gaze down into the pool. He folded his hands in the sleeves of his robes. "There was no past, Majere. You went back in time. There was no past."

"You told me the gods were gone, Mother," Mina said. "You told me that because the gods were gone we had to rely on ourselves to find our way in the world. But I didn't believe that story, Mother.

7

"Oh"—Mina placed her hand over Goldmoon's mouth, silencing her—"I don't think you lied to me. You were mistaken, that was all. You see, I knew better. I knew there was a god for I heard the voice of the god when I was little and our boat sank and I was cast alone into the sea. You found me on the shore, do you remember, Mother? But you never knew how I came to be there, because I promised I would never tell. The others drowned, but I was saved. The god held me and supported me and sang to me when I was afraid of the loneliness and dark.

"You said there were no gods, Mother, but I knew you were wrong. So I did what you did. I went to find god and bring god back to you. And I've done that, Mother. The miracle of the storm. That is the One God. The miracle of your youth and beauty. That is the One God, Mother."

"Now do you understand, Majere?" Dalamar said softly.

"I think I am beginning to," said Palin. His broken hands clasped tightly together. The room was cold, his fingers ached with the chill. "I would add, 'the gods help us,' but that might be out of place."

"Hush!" Dalamar snapped. "I can't hear. What did she say?"

"You asked for this," Goldmoon demanded, indicating her altered body with a gesture. "This is not me. It is your vision of me. . . ."

"Aren't you pleased?" Mina continued, not hearing her or not wanting to hear. "I have so much to tell you that will please you. I've brought the miracle of healing back into the world with the power of the One God. With the blessing of the One, I felled the shield the elves had raised over Silvanesti and I killed the treacherous dragon Cyan Bloodbane. A truly monstrous green dragon, Beryl, is dead by the power of the One God. The elven nations that were corrupt and faithless have both been destroyed, their people dead."

"The elven nations destroyed!" Dalamar gasped, his eyes burning. "She lies! She cannot mean that!"

"Strange to say this, but I do not think Mina knows how to lie," Palin said.

"But in death, they will find redemption," Mina preached. "Death will lead them to the One God."

"I see blood on these hands," Goldmoon said, her voice tremulous. "The blood of thousands! This god you have found is terrible god. A god of darkness and evil!"

"The One God told me you would feel this way, Mother," Mina responded. "When the other gods departed and you thought you were left alone, you were angry and afraid. You felt betrayed, and that was only natural. For you *had* been betrayed. The gods in which you had so misguidedly placed your faith fled in fear. . . ."

"No!" Goldmoon cried out. She rose unsteadily to her feet and fell away from Mina, holding out her hand in warding. "No, Child, I don't believe it. I won't listen to you."

Mina seized Goldmoon's hand.

"You *will* listen, Mother. You must, so that you will understand. The gods fled in fear of Chaos, Mother. All except one. One god remained loyal to the people she had helped to create. One only had the courage to face the terror of the Father of All and of Nothing. The battle left her weak. Too weak to make manifest her presence in the world. Too weak to fight the strange dragons that came to take her place. But although she could not be with her people, she gave gifts to her people to help them fight the dragons. The magic that they called the wild magic, the power of healing that you know as the power of the heart . . . those were her gifts. Her gifts to you."

"If those were her gifts, then why did the dead need to steal them for her . . ." said Dalamar softly. "Look! Look there!" He pointed to the still water.

"I see." Palin breathed.

The heads of the five dragons that guarded what had once been the Portal to the Abyss began to glow with an eerie radiance, one red, one blue, one green, one white, one black.

"What fools we have been," Palin murmured.

"Kneel down," Mina commanded Goldmoon, "and offer your prayers of faith and thanksgiving to the One True God. The One God who remained faithful to her creation—"

"No, I don't believe what you are telling me!" Goldmoon said, standing fast. "You have been deceived, Child. I know this One God. I know her of old. I know her tricks and her lies and deceits."

Goldmoon looked at the five-headed dragon.

"I do not believe your lies, Takhisis!" Goldmoon said defiantly. "I will never believe that the blessed Paladine and Mishakal left us to your mercy!"

"They didn't leave, did they?" Palin said.

"No," Dalamar said. "They did not."

"You are what you have always been," Goldmoon cried. "A god of Evil who does not want worshipers, you want slaves! I will never bow down to you! I will never serve you!"

White fire flared from the eyes of the five dragons. Palin watched in horror to see Goldmoon begin to wither in the terrible heat.

"Too late," said Dalamar with terrible calm. "Too late. For her. And for us. They'll be coming for us soon. You know that."

"This chamber is hidden—" Palin began.

"From Takhisis?" Dalamar gave a mirthless laugh. "She knew of this chamber's existence long before your uncle showed it to me. How could anything be hidden from the 'One God'? The One God who stole away Krynn!"

"As I said, what fools we have been," said Palin.

"You yourself discovered the truth, Majere. You used the device to journey back to Krynn's past, yet you could go back only to the moment Chaos was defeated. Prior to that, there was no past. Why? Because in that moment, Takhisis stole the past, the present, and the future. She stole the world. The clues were there, if we'd had sense enough to read them."

"So the future Tasslehoff saw—"

"—will never come to pass. He leaped forward to the future that was supposed to have happened. He landed in the future that is now happening. Consider the facts: a strange-looking sun in the sky; one moon where there were once three; the patterns of the stars are vastly different; a red star burns in the heavens where one had never before been seen; strange dragons appear from out of nowhere. Takhisis brought the world here, to this part of the universe, wherever that may be. Thus the strange sun, the single moon, the alien dragons, and the One God, all-powerful, with no one to stop her."

"Except Tasslehoff," said Palin, thinking of the kender secreted in an upstairs chamber.

"Bah!" Dalamar snorted. "They've probably found him by now. Him and the gnome. When they do, Takhisis will do with him what we planned to do—she will send him back to die."

Palin glanced toward the door. From somewhere above came shouted orders and the sound of feet running to obey. "The fact Tasslehoff is here at all proves to me that the Dark Queen is not infallible. She could not have foreseen his coming."

"Cling to that if it makes you happy," said Dalamar. "I see no hope in any of this. Witness the evidence of the Dark Queen's power."

They continued to watch the reflections of time shimmering in the dark pool. In the laboratory, an elderly woman lay on the floor, her white hair loose and unbound around her shoulders. Youth, beauty, strength, life had all been snatched away by the vengeful goddess, angry that her generous gifts had been spurned.

Mina knelt beside the dying woman. Taking hold of Goldmoon's hands, Mina pressed them again to her lips. "Please, Mother. I can restore your youth. I can bring back your beauty. You can begin life all over again. You will walk with me, and together we will rule the world in the name of the One God. All you have to do is to come to the One God in humility and ask this favor of her, and it will be done."

Goldmoon closed her eyes. Her lips did not move.

Mina bent close. "Mother," she begged. "Mother, do this for me if not for yourself. Do this for love of me!"

"I pray," said Goldmoon in a voice so soft that Palin held his breath to hear, "I pray to Paladine and

Mishakal that they forgive me for my lack of faith. I should have known the truth," she said softly, her voice weakening as she spoke the words with her dying breath. "I pray that Paladine will hear my prayer and he will come . . . for love of Mina . . . For love of all . . ."

Goldmoon sank, lifeless, to the floor.

"Mother," said Mina, bewildered as a lost child, "I did this for you. . . ."

Palin's eyes burned with tears, but he was not sure for whom it was he wept—for Goldmoon, who had brought light into the world, or for the orphan girl, whose loving heart had been snared, tricked, deceived by the darkness.

"May Paladine hear her dying prayer," Palin said quietly.

"May I be given bat wings to flap around this chamber," Dalamar retorted. "Her soul has gone to join the river of the dead, and I fancy that our souls will not be far behind."

Footsteps clattered down the stairs, steel swords banged against the sides of the stone walls. The footsteps halted outside their door.

"I don't suppose anyone found a key?" asked a deep, rumbling voice.

"I don't like this, Galdar," said another. "This place stinks of death and magic. Let's get out of here."

"We can't get in if there's no key, sir," said a third. "We tried. It wasn't our fault we failed."

A moment's pause, then the first voice spoke, his voice firm. "Mina gave us our orders. We will break down the door."

Blows began to rain on the wooden door. The Knights started to beat on it with their fists and the hilts of their swords, but none sounded very enthusiastic.

"How long will the spell of warding hold?" Palin asked.

"Indefinitely, against this lot," said Dalamar disparagingly. "Not long at all against Her Dark Majesty."

"You are very cool about this," said Palin. "Perhaps you are not overly sorry to hear that Takhisis has returned."

"Say, rather, that she never left," Dalamar corrected with fine irony.

Palin made an impatient gesture. "You wore the black robes. You worshiped her—"

"No, I did not," said Dalamar so quietly that Palin could barely hear him over the banging and the shouting and the thundering on the door. "I worshiped Nuitari, the son, not the mother. She could never forgive me for that."

"Yet, if we believe what Mina said, Takhisis gave us both the magic—me the wild magic and you the magic of the dead. Why would she do that?"

"To make fools of us," said Dalamar. "To laugh at us, as she is undoubtedly laughing now."

The sounds of fists beating at the door suddenly ceased. Quiet descended on those outside. For a hope-filled moment, Palin thought that perhaps they had given up and departed. Then came a shuffling sound, as of feet moving hastily to clear a path. More footsteps could be heard—lighter than those before.

A single voice called out. The voice was ragged, as if it were choked by tears.

"I speak to the wizard Dalamar," called Mina. "I know you are within. Remove the magical spell you have cast on the door that we may meet together and talk of matters of mutual interest."

Dalamar's lip curled slightly. He made no response, but stood silent, impassive.

"The One God has given you many gifts, Dalamar, made you powerful, more powerful than ever," Mina resumed, after a pause to hear an answer that did not come. "The One God does not ask for thanks, only that you serve her with all your heart and all your soul. The magic of the dead will be yours. A million million souls will come to you each day to do your bidding. You will be free of this Tower, free to roam the world. You may return to your homeland, to the forests that you love and for which you long. The elven people are lost, seeking. They will embrace you as their leader, bow down before you, and worship you in my name."

Dalamar's eyes closed, as if in pain.

He has been offered the dearest wish of his heart, Palin realized. Who could turn that down?

Still, Dalamar said nothing.

"I speak now to you, Palin Majere," Mina said, and it seemed to Palin that he could see her amber eyes shining through the closed and spell-bound door. "Your uncle Raistlin Majere had the power and the courage to challenge the One God to battle. Look at you, his nephew. Hiding from the One God like a child who fears punishment. What a disappointment you have been. To your uncle, to your family, to yourself. The One God sees into your heart. The One God sees the hunger there. Serve the One God, Majere, and you will be greater than your uncle, more honored, more revered. Do you accept, Majere?"

"Had you come to me earlier, I might have believed you, Mina," Palin answered. "You have a way of speaking to the dark part of the soul. But the moment is passed. My uncle, wherever his spirit roams, is not ashamed of me. My family loves me, though I have done little to deserve it. I do thank this One God of yours for opening my eyes, for making me see that if I have done nothing else of value in this life, I have loved and been loved. And that is all that truly matters."

"A very pretty sentiment, Majere," Mina responded. "I will write that on your tomb. What of you, Dark Elf? Have you made your decision? I trust you will not be as foolish as your friend."

Dalamar spoke finally, but not to Mina. He spoke to the blue flame, burning in the center of the still pool of dark water.

"I have looked into the night sky and seen the dark moon, and I have thrilled to know that my eyes were among the few eyes that could see it. I have heard the voice of the god Nuitari and reveled in his blessed touch as I cast my spells. Long ago, the magic breathed and danced and sparkled in my blood. Now it crawls out of my fingers like maggots swarming from a carrion carcass. I would rather be that corpse than be a slave to one who so fears the living that she can trust only servants who are dead."

A single hand smote the door. The door and the spell that guarded it shattered.

Mina entered the chamber. She entered alone. The jet of flame that burned in the pool shone in her black armor, burned in her heart and in her amber eyes. Her shorn red hair glistened. She was might and power and majesty, but Palin saw that the amber eyes were red and swollen, tears stained her cheeks, grief for Goldmoon. Palin understood then the depth of the Dark Queen's perfidy, and he had never hated Takhisis so much as he hated her now. Not for what she had done or was about to do to him, but for what she had done to Mina and all the innocents like her.

Mina's Knights, fearful of the powerful wizards, hung back upon the shadowy stairs. Dalamar's voice raised in a chant, but the words were mumbled and inarticulate, and his voice faded slowly away. Palin tried desperately to summon the magic to him. The spell dissolved in his hands, ran through his fingers like grains of sand from a broken hourglass.

Mina regarded them both with a disdainful smile. "You are nothing without the magic. Look at you— two broken-down, impotent old men. Fall on your knees before the One God. Beg her to give you back the magic! She will grant your pleas."

Neither Palin nor Dalamar moved. Neither spoke.

"So be it," said Mina.

She raised her hand. Flames burned from the tips of her five fingers. Green fire, blue and red, white, and the red-black of embers lit the Chamber of Seeing. The flames merged together to form two spears forged of magic. The first spear she hurled at Dalamar.

The spear struck the elf in the breast, pinned him against the wall of the Chamber of Seeing. For a moment, he hung impaled upon the burning spear, his body writhing. Then his head sagged, his body went limp.

Mina paused. Holding the spear, she gazed at Palin.

"Beg," she said to him. "Beg the One God for your life."

Palin's lips tightened. He knew a moment's panicked fear, then pain sheared through his body. The pain was so horrific, so agonizing that it brought its own blessing. The pain made his last living thought a longing for death.

2

The Significance of the Gnome

Dalamar had said to Palin, "You do understand the significance of the gnome?"

Palin had not understood the significance at that moment, nor had Tasslehoff. The kender understood now. He sat in the small and boring room in the Tower of High Sorcery, a room that was pretty much devoid of anything interesting: sad-looking tables and some stern-backed chairs and a few knicknacks that were too big to fit in a pouch. He had nothing to do except look out a window to see nothing more interesting than an immense number of cypress trees—more trees than were absolutely necessary, or so Tas thought—and the souls of the dead wandering around among them. It was either that or watch Conundrum sort through the various pieces of the shattered Device of Time Journeying. For now Tas understood all too well the significance of the gnome.

Long ago—just how long ago Tasslehoff couldn't remember, since time had become extremely muddled for him, what with leaping forward to one future that turned out wasn't the proper future and ending up in this future, where all anyone wanted to do was send him back to the past to die—anyhow, long ago, Tasslehoff Burrfoot had, through no fault of his own (well, maybe a little) ended up quite by accident in the Abyss.

Having assumed that the Abyss would be a hideous place where all manner of perfectly horrible things went on—demons eternally torturing people, for example—Tas had been most frightfully disappointed to discover that the Abyss was, in fact, boring. Boring in the extreme. Nothing of interest happened. Nothing of disinterest happened. Nothing at all happened to anyone, ever. There was nothing to see, nothing to handle, nothing to do, nowhere to go. For a kender, it was pure hell.

Tas's one thought had been to get out. He had with him the Device of Time Journeying—this same Device of Time Journeying that he had with him now. The device had been broken—just as it was broken now. He had met a gnome—similar to the gnome now seated at the table across from him. The gnome had fixed the device—just as the gnome was busy fixing it now. The one big difference was that then Tasslehoff had *wanted* the gnome to fix the device, and now he didn't.

Because when the Device of Time Journeying was fixed, Palin and Dalamar would use it to send him— Tasslehoff Burrfoot—back in time to the point where the Father of All and of Nothing would squash him flat and turn him into the sad ghost of himself he'd seen wandering about Nightlund.

"What did you do with this device?" Conundrum muttered irritably. "Run it through a meat grinder?"

Tasslehoff closed his eyes so he wouldn't have to see the gnome, but he saw him anyway—his nut-brown face and his wispy hair that floated about his head as though he were perpetually poking his finger into one of his own inventions, perhaps the steam-powered preambulating hubble-bubble or the locomotive, self-winding rutabaga slicer. Worse, Tas could see the light of cleverness shining in the gnome's beady eyes. He'd seen that light before, and he was starting to feel dizzy. *What did you do with this device? Run it through a meat grinder?* were exactly the same words—or very close to them—that the previous gnome had said in the previous time.

To alleviate the dizzy feeling, Tasslehoff rested his head with its topknot of hair (going only a little gray here and there) on his hands on the table. Instead of going away, the uncomfortable dizzy feeling spiraled down from his head into his stomach, and spread from his stomach to the rest of his body.

A voice spoke. The same voice that he'd heard in a previous time, in a previous place, long ago. The voice was painful. The voice shriveled his insides and caused his brain to swell, so that it pressed on his skull, and made his head hurt horribly. He had heard the voice only once before, but he had never, ever wanted to hear it again. He tried to stop his ears with his hands, but the voice was inside him, so that didn't help.

You are not dead, said the voice, and the words were exactly the same words the voice had spoken so long ago, *nor were you sent here. You are not supposed to be here at all.*

"I know," said Tasslehoff, launching into his explanation. "I came from the past, and I'm supposed to be in a different future—"

A past that never was. A future that will never be.

"Is that . . . is that my fault?" Tas asked, faltering.

The voice laughed, and the laughter was horrible, for the sound was like a steel blade breaking, and the feel was of the slivers of the broken blade piercing his flesh.

Don't be a fool, kender. You are an insect. Less than an insect. A mote of dust, a speck of dirt to be flicked away with a brush of my hand. The future you are in is the future of Krynn as it was meant to be but for the meddlings of those who had neither the wit nor the vision to see how the world might be theirs. All that happened once will happen again, but this time to suit my purposes. Long ago, one died on a Tower, and his death rallied a Knighthood. Now, another dies on a Tower and her death plunges a nation into despair. Long ago, one was raised up by the miracle of the blue crystal staff. Now the one who wielded that staff will be raised up—to receive me.

"You mean Goldmoon!" Tasslehoff cried bleakly. "She used the blue crystal staff. Is Goldmoon dead?"

Laughter sliced through his flesh.

"Am I dead?" he cried. "I know you said I wasn't, but I saw my own spirit."

You are dead and you are not dead, replied the voice, *but that will soon be remedied.*

"Stop jabbering!" Conundrum demanded. "You're annoying me, and I can't work when I'm annoyed."

Tasslehoff's head came up from the table with a jerk. He stared at the gnome, who had turned from his work to glare at the kender.

"Can't you see I'm busy here? First you moan, then

22

you groan, then you start to mumble to yourself. I find it most distracting."

"I'm sorry," said Tasslehoff.

Conundrum rolled his eyes, shook his head in disgust, and went back to his perusal of the Device of Time Journeying. "I think that goes here, not there," the gnome muttered. "Yes. See? And then the chain hooks on here and wraps around like so. No, that's not quite the way. It must go . . . Wait, I see. This has to fit in there first."

Conundrum picked up one of the jewels from the Device of Time Journeying and fixed it in place. "Now I need another of these red gizmos." He began sorting through the jewels. Sorting through them now, as the other gnome, Gnimsh, had sorted through them in the past, Tasslehoff noted sadly.

The past that never was. The future that was hers.

"Maybe it was all a dream," Tas said to himself. "That stuff about Goldmoon. I think I'd know if she was dead. I think I'd feel sort of smothery around the heart if she was dead, and I don't feel that. Although it is sort of hard to breathe in here."

Tasslehoff stood up. "Don't you think it's stuffy, Conundrum? I think it's stuffy," he answered, since Conundrum wasn't paying any attention to him.

"These Towers of High Sorcery are always stuffy," Tas added, continuing to talk. Even if he was only talking to himself, hearing his own voice was far, far better than hearing that other, terrible voice. "It's all those bat wings and rat's eyeballs and moldy, old books. You'd think that with the cracks in these walls, you'd get a nice breeze, but that doesn't seem to be the case. I wonder if Dalamar would mind very much if I broke one of his windows?"

Tasslehoff glanced about for something to chuck through the windowpane. A small bronze statue of an elf maiden, who didn't seem to be doing much with her time except holding a wreath of flowers in her hands, stood on a small table. Judging by the dust, she hadn't moved from the spot for half a century or so and therefore, Tas thought, she might like a change of scenery. He picked up the statue and was just about to send the elf maiden on her journey out the window, when he heard voices outside the Tower.

Feeling thankful that the voices were coming from outside the Tower and not inside him, Tas lowered the elf maiden and peered curiously out the window.

A troop of Dark Knights had arrived on horseback, bringing with them a horse-drawn wagon with an open bed filled with straw. The Knights did not dismount but remained on their horses, glancing uneasily at the circle of dark trees that surrounded them. The horses shifted restlessly. The souls of the dead crept around the boles of the trees like a pitiful fog. Tas wondered if the riders could see the souls. He was sorry he could, and he did not look at the souls too closely, afraid he'd see himself again.

Dead but not dead.

He looked over his shoulder at Conundrum, bent almost double over his work and still mumbling to himself.

"Whoo-boy, there are a lot of Dark Knights about," Tas said loudly. "I wonder what these Dark Knights are doing here? Don't you wonder about that, Conundrum?"

The gnome muttered, but did not look up from his

work. The device was certainly going back together in a hurry.

"I'm sure your work could wait. Wouldn't you like to rest a bit and come see all these Dark Knights?" Tas asked.

"No," said Conundrum, establishing the record for the shortest gnome response in history.

Tas sighed. The kender and the gnome had arrived at the Tower of High Sorcery in company with Tas's former companion and longtime friend Goldmoon—a Goldmoon who was ninety years old if she was a day but had the body and face of a woman of twenty. Goldmoon told Dalamar that she was meeting someone at the Tower. Dalamar took Goldmoon away and told Palin to take Tasslehoff and the gnome away and put them in a room to wait—making this a waiting room. It was then Dalamar had said, *You do understand the significance of the gnome?*

Palin had left them here, after wizard-locking the door. Tas knew the door was wizard-locked, because he'd already used up his very best lockpicks without success in an effort to open it. The day lockpicks fail is a day wizards are involved, as his father had been wont to say.

Standing at the window, staring down at the Knights, who appeared to be waiting for something and not much enjoying the wait, Tasslehoff was struck by an idea. The idea struck so hard that he reached up with the hand that wasn't holding onto the bronze statue of the elf maiden to feel if he had a lump on his head. Not finding one, he glanced surreptitiously (he thought that was the word) back at the gnome. The device was almost back together. Only a few pieces remained, and those were fairly small and probably not terribly important.

Feeling much better now that he had a Plan, Tas went back to observing what was happening out the window, thinking that now he could properly enjoy it. He was rewarded by the sight of an immense minotaur emerging from the Tower of High Sorcery. Tas was about four stories up in the Tower, and he could look right down on the top of the minotaur's head. If he chucked the statue out the window now, he could bean the minotaur.

Clunking a minotaur over the head was a delightful thought, and Tas was tempted. At that moment, however, several Dark Knights trooped out of the Tower. They bore something between them—a body covered with a black cloth.

Tas stared down, pressing his nose so hard against the glass pane that he heard cartilage crunch. As the troop carrying the body moved out of the Tower, the wind sighed among the cypress trees, lifted the black cloth to reveal the face of the corpse.

Tasslehoff recognized Dalamar.

Tas's hands went numb. The statue fell to the floor with a crash.

Conundrum's head shot up. "What in the name of dual carburetors did you do that for?" he demanded. "You made me drop a screw!"

More Dark Knights appeared, carrying another body. The wind blew harder, and the black cloth that had been thrown carelessly over the corpse slid to the ground. Palin's dead face looked up at the kender. His eyes were wide open, fixed and staring. His robes were soaked in blood.

"This is my fault!" Tas cried, riven by guilt. "If I had

gone back to die, like I was supposed to, Palin and Dalamar wouldn't be dead now."

"I smell smoke," said Conundrum suddenly. He sniffed the air. "Reminds me of home," he stated and went back to his work.

Tas stared bleakly out the window. The Dark Knights had started a bonfire at the base of the Tower, stoking it with dry branches and logs from the cypress forest. The wood crackled. The smoke curled up the stone side of the Tower like some noxious vine. The Knights were building a funeral pyre.

"Conundrum," said Tasslehoff in a quiet voice, "how are you coming with the Device of Time Journeying? Have you fixed it yet?"

"Devices? No time for devices now," Conundrum said importantly. "I have this contraption about fixed."

"Good," said Tasslehoff.

Another Dark Knight came out of the Tower. She had red hair, cropped close to her head, and Tasslehoff recognized her. He'd seen her before, although he couldn't recall where.

The woman carried a body in her arms, and she moved very slowly and solemnly. At a shouted command from the minotaur, the other Knights halted their work and stood with their heads bowed.

The woman walked slowly to the wagon. Tas tried to see who it was the woman carried, but his view was blocked by the minotaur. The woman lowered the person gently into the wagon. She backed away and Tasslehoff had a clear view.

He'd assumed that the person was another Dark Knight, maybe one who'd been wounded. He was astonished to see that the person in the wagon was an old, old woman, and Tas knew immediately that the old woman was dead. He felt very sorry and wondered who she was. Some relation of the Dark Knight with the red hair, for she arranged the folds of the woman's white gown around her and then brushed out with her fingers the woman's long, flowing, silver-white hair.

"So Goldmoon used to brush out my hair, Galdar," said the woman.

Her words carried clearly in the still air. Much too clearly, as far as Tas concerned.

"Goldmoon." Tas felt a lump of sadness rise up in his throat. "She *is* dead. Caramon, Palin . . . Everyone I love is dead. And it's my fault. I'm the one who *should* be dead."

The horses drawing the wagon shifted restlessly, as if anxious to leave. Tas glanced back at Conundrum. Only two tiny jewels remained to be stuck on somewhere.

"Why did we come here, Mina?" The minotaur's booming voice could be heard clearly. "You have captured Solanthus, given the Solamnics a sound spanking and sent them running home to mama. The entire Solamnic nation is yours now. You have done what no one else has been able to do in the entire history of the world—"

"Not quite, Galdar," Mina corrected him. "We must still take Sanction, and we must take it by the time of the Festival of the Eye."

"The . . . festival?" The minotaur's forehead wrinkled. "The Festival of the Eye. By my horns, I had almost forgotten that old celebration." He grinned. "You are such a youngling, Mina, I'm surprised you know of it at all. It hasn't been celebrated since the three moons vanished."

"Goldmoon told me about the festival," said Mina, gently stroking the dead woman's wrinkled cheek. "That it was held on the night when all three moons—the red, the white, and the black—converged, forming the image of a great staring eye in the heavens. I should like to have seen that sight."

"Among humans, it was a night for riot and revelry, or so I have heard. Among my people, the night was honored and reverenced," Galdar stated, "for we believed the Eye to be the eye of Sargas, our god—*former* god," he added hastily, with a sidelong glance at Mina. "Still, what has some old festival to do with capturing Sanction? The three moons are gone, and so is the eye of the gods."

"There will be a festival, Galdar," said Mina. "The Festival of the New Eye, the One Eye. We will celebrate the festival in the Temple of Huerzyd."

"But the Temple of Huerzyd is in Sanction," Galdar protested. "We are on the other side of the continent from Sanction, not to mention the fact that Sanction is firmly in control of the Solamnic Knights. When will the festival occur?"

"At the appointed time," said Mina. "When the totem is assembled. When the red dragon falls from the skies."

"Ugh," Galdar grunted. "Then we should be marching to Sanction now and bringing with us an army. Yet we waste our time at this fell place." He cast a glance of enmity at the Tower. "Our march will be further slowed if we must cart along the body of this old woman."

The bonfire roared and crackled. The flames leaped up the stone walls of the Tower, charring them. Smoke swirled about Galdar, who batted irritably at it, and drifted in through the window. Tas coughed, covered his mouth with his hand.

"I am commanded to bring the body of Goldmoon, princess of the Qué-shu, bearer of the blue crystal staff, to Sanction, to the Temple of Huerzyd on the night of the Festival of the New Eye. There a great miracle will be performed, Galdar. Our journey will not be slowed. All will move as has been ordered. The One God will see to that."

Mina raised her hands over the body of Goldmoon and lifted up her voice in prayer. Orangish-yellow light radiated from her hands. Tas tried to look into the light to see what was happening, but the light was like tiny pieces of glass in his eyes, made them burn and hurt so that he was forced to shut them tight. Even then he could see the glare right through them.

Mina's praying ceased. The bright light slowly faded. Tasslehoff opened his eyes.

The body of Goldmoon lay enshrined in a sarcophagus of golden amber. Encased in the amber, Goldmoon's body was once again youthful, beautiful. She wore the white robes she had worn in life. Feathers adorned her hair that was gold threaded with silver—yet all now held fast in amber.

Tas felt the sick feeling in his stomach rise up into his throat. He choked and clutched the window ledge for support.

"This coffin you've created is very grand, Mina," said Galdar, and the minotaur sounded exasperated, "but what do you plan to do with her? Cart her about as a monument to this One God? Exhibit her to the populace? We are not clerics. We are soldiers. We have a war to fight."

Mina stared at Galdar in silence, a silence so large and terrible that it absorbed into itself all sound, all light, snatched away the air they breathed. The awful silence of her fury withered Galdar, who shrank visibly before it.

"I'm sorry, Mina," he mumbled. "I didn't mean—"

"Be thankful that I know you, Galdar," said Mina. "I know that you speak from your heart, without thinking. But someday, you will go too far, and on that day I will no longer be able to protect you. This woman was more than mother to me. All I have done in the name of the One God, I have done for her."

Mina turned to the sarcophagus, placed her hands upon the amber, and bent near to look at Goldmoon's calm, still face. "You told me of the gods who had been but were no more. I went in search of them—for you!"

Mina's voice trembled. "I brought the One God to you, Mother. The One God gave you back your youth and your beauty. I thought you would be pleased. What did I do wrong? I don't understand." Mina's hands stroked the amber coffin, as if smoothing out a blanket. She sounded bewildered. "You will change your mind, dear Mother. You will come to understand. . . ."

"Mina . . ." Galdar said uneasily, "I'm sorry. I didn't know. Forgive me."

Mina nodded. She did not turn her head.

Galdar cleared his throat. "What are your orders concerning the kender?"

"Kender?" Mina repeated, only half-hearing him.

"The kender and the magical artifact. You said they were in the Tower."

Mina lifted her head. Tears glistened on her

cheeks. Her face was pale, the amber eyes wide. "The kender." Her lips formed the words, but she did not speak them aloud. She frowned. "Yes, of course, go fetch him. Quickly! Make haste!"

"Do you know where he is, Mina?" Galdar asked hesitantly. "The Tower is immense, and there are many rooms."

Mina raised her head, looked directly at Tas's window, looked directly at Tas, and pointed.

"Conundrum," said Tasslehoff in a voice that didn't sound to him like his own voice but belonged to some altogether different person, a person who was well and truly scared. "We have to get out of here. Now!"

He backed precipitously away from the window.

"There, it's finished," said Conundrum, proudly displaying the device.

"Are you sure it will work?" Tas asked anxiously. He could hear footsteps on the stairs, or at least he thought he could.

"Or course," Conundrum stated, scowling. "Good as new. By the way, what did it do when it *was* new?"

Tas's heart, which had leaped quite hopefully at the first part of the gnome's statement, now sank.

"How do you know it works if you don't know what it does?" Tas demanded. He could quite definitely hear footsteps. "Never mind. Just give it to me. Quickly!"

Palin had wizard-locked the door, but Palin was . . . wasn't here anymore. Tas guessed that the wizard-lock wasn't here either. He could hear footsteps and harsh breathing. He pictured the large and heavy minotaur, tromping up all those stairs.

"I thought at first it might be a potato peeler," Conundrum was saying. He gave the device a shake that made the chain rattle. "But it's a bit small, and there's no hydraulic lift. Then I thought—"

"It's a device that sends you traveling through time. That's what I'm going to do with it, Conundrum," Tasslehoff said. "Journey back through time. I'd take you with me, but I don't think you'd much like where I'm going, which is back to the Chaos War to be stepped on by a giant. You see, it's my fault that everyone I love is dead, and if I go back, they won't be dead. I'll be dead, but that doesn't matter because I'm already dead—"

"Cheese grater," said Conundrum, regarding the device thoughtfully. "Or it could be, with a few modifications, a meat grinder, maybe, and a—"

"Never mind," said Tasslehoff, and he drew in a deep breath to give himself courage. "Just hand me the device. Thank you for fixing it. I hate to leave you here in the Tower of High Sorcery with an angry minotaur and the Dark Knights, but once I'm stepped on, they might not be here anymore. Would you please hand me the device?"

The footsteps had stopped, but not the harsh breathing. The stairs were steep and treacherous. The minotaur had been forced to halt his climb to catch his breath.

"Combination fishing rod and shoe tree?" guessed the gnome.

The minotaur's footsteps started again.

Tas gave up. One could be polite for only so long. Especially to a gnome. Tas made a grab for the device. "Give it to me!"

"You're not going to break it again?" Conundrum asked, holding it just out of the kender's reach.

"I'm not going to break it!" Tasslehoff said firmly. With a another lunge, he succeeded in nabbing the device and wrenched it out of the gnome's hand. "If you'll watch closely, I'll show you how it works. I hope," he muttered to himself.

Holding the device, Tas said a little prayer in his heart. "I know you can't hear me, Fizban . . . Or maybe you can but you're so disappointed in me that you don't want to hear me. I'm truly sorry. Truly, truly sorry." Tears crept into his eyes. "I never meant to cause all this trouble. I only wanted to speak at Caramon's funeral, to tell everyone what a good friend he was to me. I never meant for this to happen. Never! So, if you'll help me just once to go back to die, I'll stay dead. I promise."

"It's not doing anything," Conundrum grumbled. "Are you sure it's plugged in?"

Hearing the footsteps growing louder and louder, Tas held the device over his head.

"Words to the spell. I have to say the words to the spell. I know the words," the kender said, gulping. "It goes . . . It goes . . . Thy time is thine . . . Around it you journey . . . No, that can't be right. Travel. Around it you travel . . . and something, something expanses . . ."

The footsteps were so close now that he could feel the floor shake.

Sweat beaded on the kender's forehead. He gulped again and looked at the device, as if it might help him. When it didn't, he shook it.

"Now I see how it got broken in the first place," said Conundrum severely. "Is this going to take long? I think hear someone coming."

"Grasp firmly the beginning and you'll end up at the end. No, that's wrong," Tas said miserably. "All of it's wrong. I can't remember the words! What's the matter with me? I used to know it by heart. I could recite it standing on my head. I know because Fizban made me do it. . . ."

There came a thundering crash on the door, as of a heavy minotaur shoulder bashing into it.

Tas shut his eyes, so that he wouldn't hear what was going on outside the door. "Fizban made me say the spell standing on my head backwards. It was a bright, sunny day. We were in a green meadow, and the sky was blue with these little puffy white clouds, and the birds were singing, and so was Fizban until I asked him politely not to. . . ."

Another resounding crash and a sound of wood splintering.

Thy time is thy own.
Though across it you travel.
Its expanses you see.
Whirling across forever.
Obstruct not its flow.
Grasp firmly the end and the beginning.
Turn them forward upon themselves.
All that is loose shall be secure
Destiny be over your own head.

The words flooded Tasslehoff's being, as warm and bright as the sunshine on that spring day. He didn't know where they came from, and he didn't stick around to ask.

The device began to glow brightly, jewels gleaming.

The last sensation Tas felt was that of a hand clutching his. The last sound Tas heard was Conundrum's voice, crying out in panic, "Wait! There's a screw loose—"

And then all sound and sensation was lost in the wonderful and exciting rushing-wind noise of the magic.

3

The Punishment for Failure

The kender is gone, Mina," Galdar reported, emerging from the Tower.

"Gone?" Mina turned away from the amber coffin that held the body of Goldmoon to stare at the minotaur. "What do you mean? That's impossible? How could he escape—"

Mina gave a cry of anguish. Doubling over in wrenching pain, she sank to her knees, her arms clasped around her, her nails digging into her bare flesh in transports of agony.

"Mina!" Galdar cried in alarm. He hovered over her, helpless, baffled. "What has happened? Are you wounded? Tell me!"

Mina moaned and writhed upon the ground, unable to answer.

Galdar glared around at her Knights. "You were supposed to be guarding her! What enemy has done this?"

"I swear, Galdar!" cried one. "No one came near her—"

"Mina," said Galdar, bending over her, "tell me where you are hurt!"

Shuddering, in answer, she placed her hand on the black hauberk she wore, placed her hand over her heart.

"My fault!" she gasped through lips that bled. She had bitten down on them in her torment. "My fault. This . . . my punishment."

Mina remained on her knees, her head bowed, her hands clenched. Rivulets of sweat ran down her face. She shivered with fevered chills. "Forgive me!" she gasped, the words were flecked with blood. "I failed you. I forgot my duty. It will not happen again, I swear on my soul!"

The spasms of wracking pain ceased. Mina sighed, shuddering. Her body relaxed. She drew in deep breaths and rose, unsteadily, to her feet.

Her Knights gathered around her, wondering and ill at ease.

"Alarm's over," Galdar told them. "Go back to your duties."

They went, but not without many backward looks. Galdar supported Mina's unsteady steps.

"What happened to you?" he asked, eyeing her anxiously. "You spoke of punishment. Who punished you and for what?"

"The One God," said Mina. Her face was streaked with sweat and drawn with remembered agony, the amber eyes gray. "I failed in my duty. The kender was of paramount importance. I should have retrieved him first. I . . ." She licked her bloodied lips, swallowed. "I was so eager to see my mother, I forgot about him. Now he is gone, and it is my fault."

"The One God did this to you?" Galdar repeated, appalled, his voice shaking with anger. "The One God hurt you like this?"

"I deserved it, Galdar," Mina replied. "I welcome it. The pain inflicted on me is nothing compared to the pain the One God bears because of my failure."

Galdar frowned, shook his head.

"Come, Galdar," she said, her tone chiding, "didn't your father whip you as a child? Didn't your battle master beat you when you made a mistake in training? Your father did not strike you out of malice. The battle master did not hit you out of spite. Such punishment was meant for your own good."

"It isn't the same," Galdar growled. He would never forget the sight of her, who had led armies to glorious conquest, on her knees in the dirt, writhing in pain.

"Of course, it is the same," Mina said gently. "We are all children of the One God. How else are we to learn our duty?"

Galdar had no reply. Mina took his silence for agreement.

"Take some of the men and search every room in the Tower. Make certain the kender is not hiding in any of them. While you are gone, we will burn these bodies."

"Must I go back in there, Mina?" said Galdar, his voice heavy with reluctance.

"Why? What do you fear?" she asked.

"Nothing living," he replied, with a dark scowl at the Tower.

"Don't be afraid, Galdar," said Mina. She cast a careless glance at the bodies of the wizards, being dragged to the funeral pyre. "Their spirits cannot harm you. They go to serve the One God."

A bright light shone in the heavens. Distant, ethereal, the light was more radiant than the sun, made that orb seem dim and tarnished by comparison. Dalamar's mortal eyes could not look long at the sun, lest he be blinded, but he could stare at this beautiful, pure light forever, or so he imagined. Stare at it with an aching longing that rendered all that he was, all that he had been, paltry and insignificant.

As a very small child, he had once looked up in the night sky above his homeland to see the silver moon. Thinking it a bauble, just out of his reach, he wanted it to play with. He demanded his parents fetch it for him, and when they did not, he wept in anger and frustration. He felt that way now. He could have wept, but he had no eyes to weep with, no tears to fall. The bright and beautiful light was out of reach. His way to it was blocked. A barrier as thin as gossamer and strong as adamant stretched in front of him. Try as he might, he could not move past that barrier, a prison wall that surrounded a world.

He was not alone. He was one prisoner among many. The souls of the dead roamed restlessly about the prison yard of their bleak existence, all of them looking with longing at the radiant light. None of them able to attain it.

"The light is very beautiful," said a voice that was soft and beguiling. "What you see is the light of a realm beyond, the next stage of your soul's long journey. I will release you, let you travel there, but first you must bring me what I need."

He would obey. He would bring the voice whatever it wanted, so long as he could escape this prison. He had only to bring the magic. He looked at the Tower of High Sorcery and recognized it as having something to do with what he was, what he had been, but all that was gone now, behind him. The Tower was a veritable storehouse for the magic. He could see the magic glistening like streams of gold dust among the barren sand that had been his life.

The other, restless souls streamed into the Tower, now bereft of the one who had been its master. Dalamar looked at the radiant light, and his heart ached with longing. He joined the river of souls that was flowing into the Tower.

He had almost reached the entrance when a hand reached out and seized hold of him, held him fast. The voice, angry and frustrated itself, hissed at him, "Stop."

"Stop!" Mina commanded. "Halt! Do not burn the bodies. I have changed my mind."

Startled, the Knights let loose their hold. The corpses flopped limply to the ground. The Knights exchanged glances. They had never seen Mina like this, irresolute and vacillating. They didn't like it, and they didn't like to see her punished, even by this One God. The One God was far away, had little to do with them. Mina was near, and they worshiped her, idolized her.

"A good idea, Mina," said Galdar, emerging from the Tower. He glared balefully at the dead wizards. "Leave the vultures to be eaten by vultures. The kender is not in the Tower. We've searched high, and we've searched low. Let's get out of this accursed place."

Fire crackled. Smoke curled about the Tower, as the mournful dead curled about the boles of the cypress trees. The living waited in hopeful expectation, longing to leave. The dead waited patiently, they had nowhere to go. All of them wondered what Mina meant to do.

She knelt beside Dalamar's body. Clasping one hand over the medallion she wore around her neck, she placed her other hand on the mage's mortal wounds. The staring eyes looked up vacantly.

Softly, Mina began to sing.

Wake, love, for this time wake.
Your soul, my hand does take.
Leave the darkness deep.
Leave your endless sleep.

Dalamar's flesh warmed beneath Mina's hand. Blood tinged the gray cheeks, warmed the chill limbs. His lips parted, drew in breath in a shivering gasp. He quivered and stirred at her touch. Life returned to the corpse, to all but the eyes. The eyes remained vacant, empty.

Galdar watched in scowling disapproval. The Knights stared in awe. Always before, Mina had prayed over the dead, but she had never brought them back to life. The dead serve the One God, she had told them.

"Stand up," Mina ordered.

The living body with the lifeless eyes obeyed, rose to its feet.

"Go to the wagon," Mina ordered. "There await my command."

The elf's eyelids shivered. His body jerked.

"Go to the wagon," Mina repeated.

Slowly, the mage's empty eyes shifted, looked at Mina.

"You will obey me in this," said Mina, "as you will obey me in all things, else I will destroy you. Not your body. The loss of this lump of flesh would be of little consequence to you now. I will destroy your soul."

The corpse shuddered and, after a moment's hesitation, shuffled off toward the wagon. The Knights fell back before it, gave it wide berth, although a few started to grin. The shambling thing looked grotesque. One of the Knights actually laughed aloud.

Horrified and repelled, Galdar saw nothing funny in this. He had spoken glibly of leaving the corpses to the vultures, and he could have done that without a qualm—they were wizards, after all—but he didn't like this. There was something wrong with this, although he couldn't quite say what or why it should so disturb him.

"Mina, is this wise?" he asked.

Mina ignored him. Singing the same song over the second wizard, she placed her hand upon his chest. The corpse sat up.

"Go join your fellow in the wagon," she commanded.

Palin's eyes blinked. A spasm contorted his features. Slowly, the hands with their broken fingers started to raise up, reach out, as if to grab and seize hold of something only he could see.

"I will destroy you," Mina said sternly. "You will obey me."

The hands clenched. The face contorted in agony, a pain that seemed far worse than the pain of death.

"Go," said Mina, pointing.

The corpse gave up the fight. Bowing its head, it walked to the wagon. This time, none of the Knights laughed.

Mina sat back, pale, wan, exhausted. This day had been a sad one for her. The death of the woman she loved as a mother, the anger of her god. She drooped, her shoulders sagged. She seemed scarcely able to stand under her own power. Galdar was moved to pity. He longed to comfort and support her, but his duty came first.

"Mina, is this wise?" he repeated in a low voice, for her ears alone. "Bad enough we must haul a coffin about Ansalon, but now we are further burdened by these two . . . things." He didn't know what name to call them. "Why have you done this? What purpose does it serve?" He frowned. "It unsettles the men."

The amber eyes regarded him. Her face was drawn with fatigue and grief, but the eyes shone clear, undimmed, and, as always, they saw right through him.

"It unsettles you, Galdar," she said.

He grunted. His mouth twisted.

Mina turned her gaze to the corpses, sitting on the end of the wagon, staring out at nothing.

"These two wizards are tied to the kender, Galdar."

"They are hostages, then?" said Galdar, cheering up. This was something he could understand.

"Yes, Galdar, if you want to think of it that way. They are hostages. When we recover the kender and the artifact, they will explain to me to how it works."

"I'll put an extra guard on them."

"That will not be necessary," Mina said, shrugging. "Think of them not so much as prisoners, but as animated slabs of meat."

She gazed at them, her expression thoughtful. "What would you say to an army of such as these, Galdar? An army of soldiers who obey commands without question, soldiers who fight without fear, who have inordinate strength, who fall, only to rise again. Isn't that the dream of every commander? We hold their souls in thrall," she continued, musing, "and send forth their bodies to do battle. What would you say to that, Galdar?"

Galdar could think of nothing to say. Rather, he could think of too much to say. He could imagine nothing more heinous, nothing more obscene.

"Fetch my horse, Galdar," Mina ordered. "It is time we left this place of sorrow."

Galdar did as he was told, obeyed that order eagerly.

Mounting her horse, Mina took her place at the head of the mournful caravan. The Knights fell in around the wagon, forming an honor guard for the dead. The wagon's driver cracked his whip, and the heavy draft horses heaved against the harness. The wagon and its strange burden lurched forward.

The souls of the dead parted for Mina, as did the trees. A trail opened up through the thick and tangled wood that surrounded the Tower of High Sorcery. The trail was smooth, for Mina would not have the coffin jostled. She turned often in her saddle to look back to the wagon, to the amber sarcophagus.

Galdar took his customary place at Mina's side.

The bodies of the two wizards sat on the back of the wagon, feet dangling, arms flaccid, hands resting in their laps. Their eyes stared straight ahead behind them. Once, Galdar glanced back at them. He saw two wispy entities trailing after the living corpses, like silken scarves caught in the wagon wheels.

Their souls.

He looked quickly away and did not look back again.

4

The Death of Skie

The silver dragon had no idea how much time had passed since he had first entered the caverns of Skie, the mighty blue dragon. The blind silver, Mirror, had no way of judging time, for he could not see the sun. He had not seen it since the day of that strange and terrible storm, the day he'd heard the voice in the storm and recognized it, the day the voice had commanded that he bow down and worship, the day he'd been punished for his refusal, struck by the bolt that left him sightless and disfigured. That day was months past. He had wandered the world since, stumbling about in human form, because a blind human can walk, whereas a blind dragon, who cannot fly, is almost helpless.

Hidden away in this cave, Mirror knew nothing but night, felt nothing but night's cool shadows.

Mirror had no notion how long he had been here in the lair with the suffering blue dragon. It might have been a day or a year since Skie had sought to make demands of the One God. Mirror had been an unwitting witness to their encounter.

Having heard the voice in the storm and recognized it, Mirror had come seeking an answer to this strange riddle. If the voice was that of Takhisis, what was she doing in this world when all the other gods had departed? Thinking it over, Mirror had decided that Skie might be the one to provide him with information.

Mirror had always had questions about Skie. Supposedly a Krynn dragon like himself, Skie had grown larger and stronger and more powerful than any other blue dragon in the history of the world. Skie had purportedly turned on his own kind, slaying and devouring them as did the dragon overlords. Mirror had often wondered: Had Skie had truly turned upon his own kind? Or had Skie joined his own kind?

With great difficulty, Mirror had managed to find Skie's lair and enter it. He had arrived in time to witness Skie's punishment by Mina for his presumption, for his perceived disloyalty. Skie had sought to kill Mina, but the lightning bolt meant to slay her reflected off her armor, struck him. The immense blue dragon was mortally wounded.

Desperate to know the truth, Mirror had done what he could to heal Skie. He had been only partially successful. He was keeping the Blue alive, but the barbs of the gods are powerful weapons, and Mirror, though a dragon, was mortal.

Mirror left his charge only to fetch water for them both.

Skie drifted in and out of consciousness. During the times he was awake and lucid, Mirror was able to question the blue dragon about the One God, a god to whom Mirror was now able to give a name. These conversations took place over long periods of time, for Skie was rarely able to remain conscious long.

"She stole the world," Skie said at one point, shortly after he first regained his senses. "Stole it away and transported it to this part of the universe. She had long planned out her actions. All was in readiness. She awaited only the right moment."

"A moment that came during the Chaos War," Mirror said. He paused, asked quietly, "How are you feeling?"

"I am dying," Skie returned bluntly. "That's how I am feeling."

Had Mirror been human, he would have told some comforting falsehood intended to sooth the dying dragon's final moments. Mirror was not human, although he now walked in human form. Dragons are not given to telling falsehoods, not even those meant to comfort. Mirror was wise enough to know that such lies bring comfort only to the living.

Skie was a warrior dragon. A blue dragon, he had flown into battle countless times, had sent many of his foes plummeting to their deaths. He and his former rider, the infamous Kitiara uth Matar, had cut a swath of terror and destruction across half of Ansalon during the War of the Lance. After the Chaos War, Skie had been one of the few dragons in Ansalon to hold his own against the alien dragon overlords, Malys and Beryl, finally rising in power to take his place among them. He had slaughtered and gorged on other dragons, gaining in strength and power by devouring his own kind. He had built a hideous totem of the skulls of his victims.

Mirror could not see the totem, but he could sense it nearby. He heard the voices of the dead, accusing, angry, crying out for revenge. Mirror had no love for Skie. Had they met in battle, Mirror would have fought to defeat his foe and rejoiced in his destruction.

And Skie would have rejoiced in such a death. To die as a warrior, to fall from the skies with the blood of your foe wet on your talons, the taste of lightning on your tongue. That was the way Skie would have wanted to die. Not this way, not lying helpless, trapped in his lair, his life passing from him in labored, gasping breaths; his mighty wings stilled; his bloodied talons twitching and scrabbling on the rock floor.

No dragon should die this death, Mirror thought to himself. Not even my worst enemy. He regretted having used his magic to bring Skie back to life, but Mirror had to know more about this One God, he had to find out the truth. He inured himself against pity for his foe and continued asking questions. Skie did not have much time left to answer.

"You say Takhisis planned this removal," Mirror said, during another conversation. "You were part of her plan."

Skie grunted. Mirror could hear the massive body shift itself in an effort to ease the pain.

"I was the most important part, curse the eon I met the conniving bitch. I was the one who discovered the Portals. Our world, the world where I and others of my kind were born, is not like this world. We do not share our world with the short-lived, the soft-bodies. Ours is a world of dragons."

Skie was not able to say this without many pauses for breath and grunts of pain. He was determined to continue his tale. His voice was weak, but Mirror could still hear the anger, like a rumble of distant thunder.

"We roamed our world at will and fought ferocious battles for survival. These dragons you see here, this Beryl and this Malys, they seem to you enormous and powerful, but in comparison to those who ruled our world, they are small and pitiful creatures. That was one reason they came to this world. But I jump ahead of myself.

"I could see, as could others of our kind, that our world was growing stagnant. We had no future, our children had no future but to eat or be eaten. We were not advancing, we were regressing. I was not the only one to seek a way off the world, but I was the first to be successful. Using my magic, I discovered the roads that led through the ethers to worlds far beyond our own. I grew skilled at traveling these roads. Often the roads saved my life, for if I was threatened by one of the Elders, I had only to jump into the ethers to escape.

"It was while I was inside the ethers that I came upon Her Dark Majesty." Skie ground his teeth as he spoke, as if he would be glad to grind her between them. "I had never seen a god before. I had never before beheld anything so magnificent, never been in the presence of such power. I bowed before her and offered myself to her as her servant. She was fascinated by the roads through the ethers. I was not so enamored of her that I foolishly revealed their secrets to her, but I gave her enough information so that she could see how they might be of use to her.

"Takhisis brought me to her world that she called Krynn. She told me that on Krynn she was but one of many gods. She was the most powerful, she said, and because of that, the others feared her and were constantly conspiring against her. She would one day be triumphant over them, and on that day she would give me rich reward. I would rule Krynn and the soft-bodies who lived on it. This was to be my world in exchange for my services. Needless to say, she lied."

Anger stirred in Mirror, anger at the overweening ambition that gave no thought or care to any of those living on the world that was apparently little more than a bauble to Queen Takhisis. Mirror took care to keep his own anger hidden. He had to hear all that Skie had to tell. Mirror had to know what had happened. He could not change the past, but he might be able to affect the future.

"I was young then," Skie continued, "and the young of our species are the size of the blue dragons on Krynn. Queen Takhisis paired me with Kitiara—a favorite of the Dark Queen. Kitiara . . ."

Skie was silent, remembering. He gave a deep sigh, an aching sigh of longing. "Our battles together were glorious. For the first time, I learned that one could fight for more than survival—one could fight for honor, for the joy of the battle, for the glory in victory. At first, I despised the weaklings who inhabit this world: humans and the rest. I could not see why the gods permitted them to exist. Soon, I came to find them fascinating—Kitiara, especially. Courageous, bold, never doubting herself, knowing exactly what she wanted and reaching out to seize it. Ah, what a goddess *she* would have made."

Skie paused. His breath came with a painful catch. "I will see her again. I know I will. Together, we will fight . . . and ride once more to glory. . . ."

"And all this time," Mirror said, leading Skie back to the main topic, "you worked for Takhisis. You established the road that would take her here, to this part of the universe."

"I did. I made all ready for her. She had only to wait for the right time."

"But, surely, she could not have foreseen the Chaos War?" A terrible thought came to Mirror. "Or did that come about through her machinations?"

Skie snorted in disgust. "Clever Takhisis may be, but she is not that clever. Perhaps she had some inkling that Chaos was trapped inside the Graygem. If so, she had only to wait—for what is time to her, she is a god—for some fool to let him loose. If it had not been that, she would have found some other means. She was constantly watching for her chance. As it was, the Chaos War played right into her hands. All was in readiness. She made a show of fleeing the world, withdrawing her support and her power, leaving those who relied on her helpless. She had to do that, for she would need all her power for the enormous task that awaited her.

"The moment came. In the instant that Chaos was defeated, the energy released was immense. Takhisis harnessed that energy, combined it with her own power, and wrenched the world free of its moorings, brought it along the roads I had created with my magic, and set it here, in this part of the universe. All of this happened so fast that no one on the world was aware of the shift. The gods themselves, caught up in the desperate battle for survival, had no inkling of her plan, and once they realized what was happening, they were so depleted of their own power that they were helpless to stop her.

"Takhisis snatched the world away from them and hid it from their sight. All proceeded as she had planned. Bereft of the gods' blessing, stripped of their magic, the people of the world were thrown into turmoil and despair. She herself was exhausted, so weak that she was reduced to almost nothing. She needed time to heal herself, time to rest. But she wasn't worried. The longer the people were without a god, the greater their need. When she returned, they would be so thankful and relieved that they would be her abject slaves. She made one minor miscalculation."

"Malys," said Mirror. "Beryl and the rest."

"Yes. They were intrigued by this new toy that had suddenly dropped down among them. Weary of struggling to survive in their world, they were only too happy to take over this one. Takhisis was too weak to stop them. She could do nothing but watch in helpless frustration as they seized rulership of the world. Still, she lied to me and continued to promise me that someday, when she was again powerful, she would destroy the usurpers and give the world to me. I believed her for a while, but the years passed, and Malystryx and Beryl and the rest grew more powerful still. They killed the dragons of Krynn and feasted on them and built their totems, and I heard nothing from Takhisis.

"As for me, I could see this world degenerating into a world like the one I had left. I looked back with joy to my days of battle with Kitiara. I wanted nothing more to do with my kind, nothing more to do with the pathetic wretches who populated this place. I went to Takhisis and demanded payment.

"'Keep the world,' I said to her. 'I have no need of it. I do not want it. Restore Kitiara to me. We will travel the roads together. Together we will find a world where glory awaits us.' "

"She promised me she would. In a place called the Gray, I would find Kitiara's soul. I saw the Gray. I went there. Or thought I did." Skie rumbled deep in his chest. "You heard the rest. You heard Mina, the Dark Queen's new toady. You heard her tell me how I had been betrayed."

"Yet, others saw you depart. . . ."

"Others saw what she meant them to see, just as all saw what she meant them to see at the end of the Chaos War."

Skie fell silent, brooding over his wrongs. Mirror listened to the blue dragon's labored breathing. Skie might live for hours or days. Mirror had no way of knowing. He could not find out where Skie was wounded, and Skie himself would not tell him. Mirror wondered if the wound was not so much heart-deep as soul-deep.

Mirror changed the subject to turn Skie's thoughts. "Takhisis faced a new threat—the dragon overlords."

"The overlords." Skie grunted. "Yes, they were a problem. Takhisis had hoped that they would continue to fight and eventually slay each other, but the overlords agreed to a truce. Peace was declared. People began to grow complacent. Takhisis feared that soon people would start to worship the overlords, as some were already doing, and have no need of her. The Dark Queen was not yet strong enough to battle them. She had to find a way to increase her power. She had long recognized and lamented the waste of energy that passed out of the world with the souls of the dead. She conceived a way to imprison the dead within the world, and thus she was able to use them to steal away the wild magic and feed it to her. When she deemed she was strong enough to return, she came back, the night of the storm."

"Yes," said Mirror. "I heard her voice. She called to me to join her legions, to worship her as my god. I might have, but something stopped me. My heart knew that voice, if my head did not. And so I was punished. I—"

He halted. Skie had begun to stir, trying to lift his great bulk from the floor of the lair.

"What is it? What are you doing?"

"You had best hide yourself," said Skie, struggling desperately to regain his feet. "Malys is coming."

"Malys!" Mirror repeated, alarmed.

"She has heard I am dying. Those cowardly minions who used to serve me must have raced to her with the glad tidings. The great vulture comes to steal my totem. I should let her! Takhisis has usurped the totems for her own use. Malys takes her worst enemy to bed with her every night. Let the red monster come. I will fight her with my last breath—"

Skie might be raving, as Mirror truly thought he was, but the Blue's advice to hide was sound. Even had he not been blind, Mirror would have avoided a fight with the immense red dragon, much as he hated and loathed her. Mirror had seen too many of his kind caught and crushed in the mighty jaws, set ablaze by her horrific fire. Brute strength alone could not overcome this alien creature. The largest, strongest dragon ever to walk Krynn would be no match for Malystryx.

Not even a god had dared face her.

Mirror shifted back to human form. He felt very fragile and vulnerable in the soft skin, the thin and delicate bones, the paltry musculature. Yet, a blind human could manage in this world. Mirror began to grope his way around Skie's massive body. Mirror planned to retreat, move deeper into the twisting maze of corridors in the Blue's labyrinthine lair. Mirror was feeling his way about, when his hand touched something smooth and cold.

A shiver passed through his arm. Mirror could not see, but he knew immediately what he had touched— Skie's totem, made of skulls of his victims. Shuddering, Mirror snatched his hand away and almost lost his balance in his haste. He stumbled into the wall, steadied himself, used the wall to guide his steps.

"Wait," Skie's voice hissed through the dark corridors. "You did me a favor, Silver. You kept me from death by her foul hands. Because of you, I can die on my own terms, with what dignity I have left. I will do you a favor in return. The others of your kind—the Golds and Silvers—you've searched for them, and you cannot find them. True enough?"

Mirror was reluctant to admit this, even to a dying blue dragon. He made no reply but continued groping his way along the passage.

"They did not flee in fear," Skie continued. "They heard Takhisis's voice the night of the storm. Some of them recognized it, understood what it meant. They left the world to try to find the gods."

Mirror paused, turned his sightless face to the sound of Skie's voice. Outside, he could now hear what Skie had heard long before him—the beating of enormous wings.

"It was a trap," Skie said. "They left, and now they cannot return. Takhisis holds them prisoner, as she holds the souls of the dead prisoner."

"What can be done to free them?" Mirror asked.

"I have told you all I know," Skie replied. "My debt to you is paid, Silver. You had best make haste."

Moving as fast as possible, Mirror slipped and slid down the passage. He had no notion of where he was going, but guessed that he was traveling deeper into the lair. He kept his right hand on the wall, moved with the wall, never let go. Thus, he reasoned, he would be able to find his way out. When he heard Malys's voice, strident and high-pitched—an odd sound to come from such a massive creature— Mirror halted. Keeping his hand firmly against the wall, he hunkered down onto the smooth floor, shrouded in the lair's cool darkness. He quieted even his breathing, fearful that she might hear him and come seeking him.

Mirror crouched in the blue dragon's lair and awaited the outcome with dread.

Skie knew he was dying. His heart lurched and shivered in his rib cage. He fought for every breath. He longed to lie down and rest, to close his eyes, to lose himself in the past. To once more spread his wings that were the color of heaven and fly up among the clouds. To hear Kitiara's voice again, her firm commands, her mocking laughter. To feel her hands, sure and capable, on the reins, guiding him unerringly to the fiercest, hottest part of the battle. To revel again in the clash of arms and smell the blood, to feel the flesh rend beneath his talons and hear Kitiara's exultant battle cry, challenging all comers. To return to the stables, have his wounds dressed, and wait for her to come, as she always did, to sit down beside him and relive the battle. She would come to him, leaving behind those puny humans who sought to love her. Dragon and rider, they were a team—a deadly team.

"So, Skie," said a voice, a hated voice. Malys's head thrust inside the entrance to the lair, blotted out the sunlight. "I was misinformed. You're not dead yet, I see."

Skie roused himself. His dreams, his memories had been very real. This was unreality.

"No, I am not dead," he growled. His talons dug deep into the rock, fighting against the pain, forcing himself to remain standing.

Malys insinuated more of her great bulk inside his lair—her head and shoulders, front talons and neck. Her wings remained folded at her side, her hind feet and tail dangled down the cliff face. Her small, cruel eyes swept over him disdainfully. Discounting him, she searched for the reason she had come—his totem. She found it, elevated in the center of the lair, and her eyes glistened.

"Don't mind me," she said coolly. "You were dying, I believe. Please continue. I don't mean to interrupt. I just came to collect a few mementos of our time together."

Reaching out her talon, Malys began to weave a magical web around the skulls of his totem. Skie saw eyes in the skulls of the totem. He could sense his Queen's presence. Takhisis had no care for him. Not anymore. He was of no use to her now. She had eyes only for Malys. Fine. Skie wished them joy together. They deserved each other.

His legs trembled. They could not support his weight any longer, and he slumped to the floor of his lair. He was angry with himself, furious. He had to fight, to take a stand, to at least leave his mark upon Malys. He was so weak, shivering. His heart pounded as if it would burst in his chest.

"Skie, my lovely Blue!" Kitiara's voice came to him, mocking, laughing. "What, you sluggard, still asleep? Wake up! We have battles to fight this day. Death to deal. Our enemies do not slumber, you may be certain of that."

Skie opened his eyes. There she stood before him, her blue dragon armor shining in the sun. Kitiara smiled her crooked smile and, lifting her arm, she pointed.

"There stands your foe, Skie. You have one fight left in you. One more battle to go. Then you may rest."

Skie raised his head. He could not see Malys. His sight was going rapidly, draining away with his life. He could see Kitiara, though, could see where she pointed. He drew in a breath, his last breath. He had better make it a good one.

The breath mingled with the sulfur in his belly. He exhaled.

Lightning cracked and sizzled, split the air. Thunder boomed, shook the mountain. The sound was horrendous, but he could still hear Malys's shriek of rage and pain. He could not see what damage he had done to her, but he guessed it had been considerable.

Enraged, Malys attacked him. Her razor-sharp talons dug through his scales, ripped apart his flesh, tore a gaping hole in his flank.

Skie felt nothing, no more pain, no more fear.

Pleased, he let his head sink to the floor of his lair.

"Well done, my lovely Blue," came Kitiara's voice, and he was proud to feel the touch of her hand on the side of his neck. "Well done. . . ."

Skie's weak thunderbolt had caused Malys no real harm, beyond a jarring, tingling sensation that danced through her body and knocked a large chunk of scaly flesh off the joint of her upper left foreleg. She felt the pain more to her pride than to her great, bloated body, and she lashed out at the dying Skie, ripping and rending his flesh until the lair was awash with blood. Eventually, she realized she was doing nothing but maltreating an unfeeling corpse.

Her fury spent, Malys resumed her dismantling of his totem, prepared it for transport back to her lair in the new Goodlund Range, the Peak of Malys.

Gloating over her prize, eyeing with satisfaction the large number of skulls, Malys could feel her own power swell just handling them.

She had never had much use for Krynn dragons. In a world where they were the dominant species, Krynn dragons were feared and revered by the rest of the world's puny inhabitants and had thus become spoiled. Sometimes, it was true, Krynn's soft-skins had taken up arms against the dragons. Malys had heard accounts of these contests from Skie, heard him go on and on about some event known as the War of the Lance, about the thrill of battle and the bonds formed between dragonrider and dragon.

Clearly Skie had been away from his native world for too long, if he considered such childlike flailings to be true battles. Malys had gone up against a few of these dragonriders, and she'd never seen anything so amusing in her life. She thought back to her old world, where not a day went by but that some bloody fight erupted to establish hierarchy among the clan.

Survival had been a daily battle, then, one reason Malys and the others had been glad to find this fat and lazy world. She did not miss those cruel times, but she tended to look back upon them with nostalgia, like an old war veteran reliving his past. She and her kind had taught these weakling Krynn dragons a valuable lesson—those who survived. The Krynn dragons had bowed down before her, had promised to serve and worship her. And then came the night of that strange storm.

The Krynn dragons changed. Malys could not say exactly what was different. The Reds and Blacks and Blues continued to serve her, to come when summoned and answer her every beck and call, but she had the feeling they were up to something. She would often catch them in whispered conversations that broke off whenever she appeared. And, of late, several had gone missing. She'd received reports of Krynn dragons bearing dragonriders—Dark Knights of Neraka—into battle against the Solamnics at Solanthus.

Malys had no objections to the dragons killing Solamnics, but she should have been consulted first. Lord Targonne would have done so, but he had been slain, and it was in the reports of his death that Malys had first heard the most disturbing news of all—the appearance on Krynn of a god.

Malys had heard rumors of this god—the very god who had brought the world to this part of the universe. Malys had seen no signs of this god, however, and could only conclude that the god had been daunted by her arrival and had abandoned the field. The idea that the god might be lying low, building up her strength, never occurred to Malys—not surprising, for she came from a world devoid of guile, a world ruled by strength and might.

Malys began to hear reports of this One God and of
the One God's champion—a human girl-child named
Mina. Malys did not pay much attention to these,
mainly because this Mina did nothing to annoy Malys.
Mina's actions actually pleased Malys. Mina removed
the shield from over Silvanesti and destroyed the
sniveling, self-serving green dragon, Cyan Bloodbane.
The Silvanesti elves were properly cowed, crushed
beneath the boots of the Dark Knights.

Malys had not been pleased to hear that her
cousin Beryl was about to attack the land of the Qualinesti elves. Not that Malys cared anything for the
elves, but such actions broke the pact. Malys didn't
trust Beryl, didn't trust her ambition and her greed.
Malys might have been tempted to intervene and
put a stop to this, but she had been assured by Lord
Targonne, late leader of the Dark Knights, that he had
the situation under control. Too late Malys found out
that Targonne didn't even have his own situation
under control.

Beryl flew off to attack and destroy Qualinesti, and
she was successful. The Qualinesti elves were now
fleeing the wreckage of their homeland like the vermin
they were. True, Beryl managed to get herself killed in
the process, but she had always been an impulsive,
over-emotional, irrational nincompoop.

The green dragon's death was reported to Malys
by two of Beryl's minions—red dragons, who cringed
and groveled properly but who, Malys suspected,
were chortling out of the sides of their mouths.

Malys did not like the way these reds gloated over
her cousin's death. They didn't show the proper
respect. Nor did Malys like what she heard of the
reports of Beryl's death. It had the whiff of the god

about it. Beryl might have been a braying donkey of a dragon, but she was an immense and powerful beast, and Malys could not envision any circumstances under which a band of elves could have taken her down without divine assistance.

One of the Krynn dragons gave Malys the idea of seizing Beryl's totem. He had happened to mention the totem, wondered what they were going to do with it. Power radiated from the totem still, even after Beryl's death. There was some talk among her surviving human generals that they might make use of it themselves, if they could figure out how to harness the magic.

Appalled by the idea of humans laying their filthy hands on something so powerful and sacred as the totem, Malys flew immediately to claim it for herself. She used her magic to transport it to her lair, added the skulls of Beryl's victims to the skulls of her own. She drew upon the magic and felt it well up inside her, making her stronger, more powerful than ever. Then came the report from Mina that she had slain the mighty Skie.

Malys wasted no time. So much for this god. She had best creep back into whatever hole she had crawled out of. Malys wrapped Skie's totem in magic and prepared to carry it off. Pausing, she glanced at the mangled remains of the great blue dragon, and wondered if she should add his head to the totem.

"He does not deserve such distinction," Malys said, shoving aside a bit of Skie's bone and flesh with a disdainful toe. "Mad, that's what he was. Insane. His skull would likely be a curse."

She glowered at the wound on her shoulder. The bleeding had stopped, but the burned flesh stung and ached, the damage to the muscle was causing her front foreleg to stiffen. The wound would not impede her flying, however, and that was all that mattered.

Gathering up the skulls in her magical web, Malys prepared to depart. Before leaving, she sniffed the air, took one last look around. She had noticed something strange on her arrival—an odd smell. At first she'd been unable to determine the nature of the smell, but now she recognized it. Dragon. One of those Krynn dragons and, unless Malys was much mistaken, a Krynn metallic dragon.

Malys searched the chamber of Skie's lair in which his body lay, but found no trace of a metallic dragon: no golden scales lying about, no silver scrapings on the walls. At length, Malys gave up. Her wound pained her. She wanted to return to the dark and restful sanctuary of her lair and build up her totem.

Holding fast to the web-encased skulls of the totem and favoring her wounded leg, Malys wormed her massive body out of the lair of the dead Blue and flapped off eastward.

5

The Silver Dragon and the Blue

irror remained in hiding until he was certain beyond doubt that Malys was gone and that she would not return. He had heard the battle, and he'd even felt pride in Skie for standing up to the heinous red dragon, experienced a twinge of pity at Skie's death. Mirror heard Malys's furious roar of pain, heard her rip apart Skie's body. When he felt a trickle of warm liquid flow past his hand, Mirror guessed that it was Skie's blood.

Yet now that Malys was gone, Mirror wondered what he would do. He put his hand to his maimed eyes, cursed his handicap. He was in possession of important information about the true nature of the One God. He knew what had become of the metallic dragons, and he could do nothing about any of it.

Mirror realized he was going to have to do something—go in search of food and water. The odor of dragon blood was strong, but through it he could just barely detect the scent of water. He used his magic to shift back to his dragon form, for his sense of smell was better in that form than this puny human body. He invariably looked forward to the shifting, for he felt cramped and vulnerable in the frail, wingless human form, with its soft skin and fragile bones.

He flowed into the dragon's body, enjoying the sensation as a human enjoys a long, luxurious stretch. He felt more secure with his armored scales, felt better balanced on four legs than on two. He could see far more clearly, could spot a deer running through a field miles below him.

Or, rather, I could have once seen more clearly, he amended.

His sense of smell now much more acute, he was soon able to find a stream that flowed through the cavernous lair.

Mirror drank his fill and then, his thirst slaked, he next considered easing his hunger pangs. He smelled goat. Skie had brought down a mountain goat and not yet had a chance to eat it. Once he quieted the rumblings of his belly, Mirror would be able to think more clearly.

He hoped to avoid returning to the main chamber where the remnants of Skie's body lay, but his senses told him that the goat meat he sought was in that chamber. Hunger drove Mirror back.

The floor was wet and slippery with blood. The stench of blood and death hung heavy in the air. Perhaps it was this that dulled Mirror's senses or perhaps the hunger made him careless. Whatever the reason, he was startled beyond measure to hear a voice, dire and cold, echo in the chamber.

"I thought at first you must be responsible for this," said the dragon, speaking in the language of dragons.

"But now I realize that I was wrong. You could not have brought down the mighty Skie. You can barely move about this cavern without bumping into things."

Calling defensive magical spells to mind, Mirror turned his sightless head to face the unknown speaker— a blue dragon, by the sound of his voice and the faint scent of brimstone that hung about him. The blue must have flown in the main entrance to Skie's lair. Mirror had been so preoccupied with his hunger that he had not heard him.

"I did not slay Skie," said Mirror.

"Who did, then? Takhisis?"

Mirror was surprised to hear her name, then realized that he shouldn't be. He was not the only one to have recognized that voice in the storm.

"You might say that. The girl called Mina wielded the magical bolt that brought about his death. She acted in self-defense. Skie attacked her first, claiming that she had betrayed him."

"Of course she betrayed him," said the Blue. "When did she ever do anything else?"

"I am confused," said Mirror. "Are we speaking of Mina or Takhisis?"

"They are one and the same, to all intents and purposes. So what are you doing here, Silver, and why is the stench of Malys heavy about the place?"

"Malys took away Skie's totem. Skie was mortally wounded, yet he still managed to defy her. He wounded her, I think, though probably not severely. He was too weak. She did this to him in retaliation."

"Good for him," growled the Blue. "I hope gangrene sets in and she rots. But you didn't answer my first question, Silver. Why are you here?"

"I had questions," said Mirror.

"Did you receive answers?"

"I did," said Mirror.

"Were you surprised to hear these answers?"

"No, not really," Mirror admitted. "What is your name? I am called Mirror."

"Ah, the Guardian of the Citadel of Light. I am called Razor. I am"—the Blue paused and when he next spoke, his voice was heavy and tinged with grief—"I was the partner of Marshal Medan of Qualinesti. He is dead, and I am on my own now. You, being a Silver, might be interested to hear that Qualinesti has been destroyed," Razor added. "The Lake of Death, the elves call it. That is all that is left of the once-beautiful city."

Mirror was suspicious, wary. "I can't believe this!"

"Believe it," said Razor grimly. "I saw the destruction with my own eyes. I was too late to save the Marshal, but I did see the great, green dragon Beryl meet her death." His tone held grim satisfaction.

"I would be interested to hear the account," said Mirror.

The Blue chuckled. "I imagine you would. The elves of Qualinesti were warned of her coming, and they were ready for her. They stood on their rooftops and fired thousands of arrows at her. Attached to each arrow was cord that someone had strengthened with magic. The elves thought it was their magic, naturally. It wasn't. It was her magic."

"Takhisis?"

"Simply ridding herself of another rival and the elves at the same time. The thousands of strands of magical cord formed a net over Beryl, dragged her down from the skies. The elves planned to kill her as she lay helpless on the ground, but their plans went awry. The elves had worked with the dwarves, you see, to dig tunnels beneath the ground of Qualinost. Many elves managed to escape through these tunnels, but, in the end, they proved to be Qualinost's undoing. When Beryl landed on the ground, her great weight caused the tunnels to collapse, forming a huge chasm. She sank deep into the ground. The waters of the White-Rage River left their banks and flowed into the chasm, flooding Qualinost and turning it into a gigantic lake. A Lake of Death."

"Beryl dead," Mirror murmured. "Skie dead. The Qualinesti lands destroyed. One by one, Takhisis rids herself of her enemies."

"Your enemies, too, Silver," said Razor. "And mine. These overlords, as they call themselves, have slain many of our kind. You should rejoice in our Queen's victory over them. Whatever you may think of her, she is the goddess of our world, and she fights for us."

"She fights for no one but herself," Mirror retorted. "As she has always done. This is all her fault. If Takhisis had not stolen away the world, these overlords would have never found us. Those who have died would be alive today: dragons, elves, humans, kender. The great dragons murdered them, but Takhisis herself is ultimately responsible for their deaths, for she brought us here."

"Stole the world . . ." Razor repeated. His claws scratched against the rock. He shifted his tail slowly back and forth, his wings stirred restlessly. "So that is what she did."

"According to Skie, yes. So he told me."

"And why would he tell you, Silver?" Razor asked, sneering.

"Because I tried to save his life."

"He a blue dragon, your most hated enemy! And you tried to save his life!" Razor scoffed. "I am not some hatchling to swallow this kender tale."

Mirror couldn't see the Blue, but he could guess what he looked like. A veteran warrior, his blue scales would be shining clean, perhaps with a few scars of his prowess on his chest and head.

"My reasons for saving him were cold-blooded enough to satisfy even you," Mirror returned. "I came to Skie seeking answers to my questions. I could not let him die and take those answers to the grave with him. I used him. I admit it. I am not proud of myself, but at least, because of my aid, he managed to live long enough to strike a blow against Malys. For that, he thanked me."

The Blue was silent. Mirror could not tell what Razor was thinking. His claws scraped the rock, his wings brushed the blood-tainted air of the lair, his tail swished back and forth. Mirror had spells ready, should Razor decide to fight. The contest would not be equal—a seasoned, veteran Blue against a blind Silver. But at least, like Skie, Mirror would leave his mark upon his enemy.

"Takhisis stole the world." Razor spoke in thoughtful tones. "She brought us here. She is, as you say, responsible. Yet, she is our goddess as of old, and she fights to avenge us against our enemies."

"Her enemies," said Mirror coldly. "Else she would not bother."

"Tell me, Silver," Razor challenged, "what did you feel when you first heard her voice. Did you feel a stirring in your heart, in your soul? Did you feel nothing of this?"

"I felt it," Mirror admitted. "When I first heard the voice in the storm, I knew it to be the voice of a god, and I thrilled to hear it. The child whose father beats him will yet cling to that parent, not because he is a good or wise parent, but because he is the only parent the child knows. But then I began to ask questions, and my questions led me here."

"Questions," Razor said dismissively. "A good soldier never questions. He obeys."

"Then why haven't you joined her armies?" Mirror demanded. "Why are you here in Skie's lair, if not to ask questions of him?"

Razor had no response. Was he brooding, thinking things over or was he angry, planning to attack? Mirror couldn't tell, and he was suddenly tired of this conversation, tired and hungry. At the thought of food, his stomach rumbled.

"If we are going to battle," Mirror said, "I ask that we do it after I have eaten. I am famished, and unless I am mistaken, I smell fresh goat meat in the lair."

"I am not going to fight you," said Razor impatiently. "What honor is there in fighting a blind foe? The goat you seek is over to your left, about two talon-lengths away. My mate's skull is in one of those totems. Perhaps, if we had not been brought to this place, she would be alive today. Still," the Blue added moodily, slashing his tail, "Takhisis *is* my goddess."

Mirror had no help to offer the Blue. Mirror had solved his own crisis of faith. His had been relatively easy, for none of his kind had ever worshiped Takhisis. Their love and their loyalty belonged to Paladine, God of Light.

Was Paladine out there somewhere searching for his lost children? After the storm, the metallic dragons left to find the gods, or so Skie had said. They must have failed, for Takhisis remained unrivaled. Yet, Mirror believed, Paladine still exists. Somewhere the God of Light is looking for us. Takhisis shrouds us in darkness, hides us from his sight. Like castaways lost at sea, we must find a way to signal those who search the vast ocean that is the universe.

Mirror settled down to devour the goat. He did not offer to share. The Blue would be well fed, for he could see his prey. When Mirror walked the land in human form, he carried a begging bowl, lived off scraps. This was the first fresh meat he'd eaten in a long time and he meant to enjoy it. He had some notion now of what he could do, if he could only find the means to do it. First, though, he had to rid himself of this Blue, who appeared to think he had found a friend.

Blues are social dragons, and Razor was in no hurry to leave. He settled down to chat. He had seemed initially a dragon of few words, but now they poured out of him, as though he was relieved to be able to tell someone what was in his heart. He described the death of his mate, he spoke with sorrow and pride of Marshal Medan, he talked about a Dark Knight dragonrider named Gerard. Mirror listened with half his brain, the other half toying with an idea.

Fortunately, eating saved him from the necessity of replying beyond a grunt or two. By the time Mirror's hunger was assuaged, Razor had once more fallen silent. Mirror heard the dragon stir and hoped that finally the Blue was ready to leave.

Mirror was mistaken. Razor was merely shifting his bulk to obtain a more comfortable position.

If I can't get rid of him, Mirror decided dourly, I'll make use of him.

"What do you know of the dragon-skull totems?" Mirror asked cautiously.

"Enough." Razor growled. "As I said, my mate's skull adorns one of them. Why do you ask?"

"Skie said something about the totems. He said"— Mirror had to do some fancy mental shuffling to keep from revealing all Skie had said about the totems and the missing metallic dragons—"something about Takhisis having taken them over, subverted them to her own use."

"What does that mean? It's all very vague," Razor stated.

"Sorry, but he didn't say anything more. He sounded half crazy when he said it. He may have been raving."

"From what I have heard, one person alone knows the mind of Takhisis, and that is the girl Mina, the leader of the One God's armies. I have spoken to many dragons who have joined her. They say that this Mina is beloved of Takhisis and that she carries with her the goddess's blessing. If anyone knows the mystery of the totems, it would be Mina. Not that this means much to you, Silver."

"On the contrary," Mirror said thoughtfully, "it might mean more than you imagine. I knew Mina as a child."

Razor snorted, skeptical.

"I am Guardian of the Citadel, remember?" Mirror said. "She was a foundling of the Citadel. I knew her."

"Perhaps you did, but she would consider you her enemy now."

"So one would think," Mirror agreed. "But she came upon me only a few months ago. I was in human shape, blind, weak, and alone. She knew me then and spared my life. Perhaps she remembered our experiences together when she was a child. She was always asking questions—"

"She spared you out of sentimental weakness." Razor snorted. "Humans, even the best of them, all have this failing."

Mirror said nothing, carefully hid his smile. Here was a blue dragon who could grieve for his dead rider and still chide a human for being sentimentally attached to people from her youth.

"Still, in this instance, the failing could prove useful to us," Razor continued. He gave a refreshing shake, from his head to the tip of his tail, and flexed his wings. "Very well. We will confront this Mina, find out what is going on."

"Did you say 'we'?" Mirror asked, astounded. He truly thought he hadn't heard correctly, although the words "we" and "I" in the language of dragons are very distinct and easily distinguished.

"I said"—Razor lifted his voice, as though Mirror were deaf, as well as blind—"that we will go together to confront this Mina and demand to know our Queen's plans—"

"Impossible," said Mirror shortly. Whatever he himself planned, it did not involve partnering with a Blue. "You see my handicap."

"I see it," said Razor. "A grievous injury, yet it does not seem to have stopped you from doing what you needed to do. You came here, didn't you?"

Mirror couldn't very well deny that. "I travel on foot, slowly. I am forced to beg for food and shelter—"

"We don't have time for such nonsense. Begging! Of humans!" Razor shook his head so that his scales rattled. "I would think you would have much rather

75

died of starvation. You must ride with me. Time is short. Momentous events are happening in the world. We don't have time to waste trudging along at a human's pace."

Mirror didn't know what to say. The idea of a blind silver dragon riding on the back of a Blue was so utterly ludicrous as to make him sorely tempted to laugh out loud.

"If you do not come with me," Razor added, seeing that Mirror was apparently having trouble making up his mind, "I will be forced to slay you. You speak very glibly about certain information Skie gave you, yet you are vague and evasive when it comes to the rest. I think Skie told you more than you are willing to admit to me. Therefore you will either come with me where I can keep an eye on you, or I will see to it that the information dies with you."

Mirror had never more bitterly regretted his blindness than at this moment. He supposed that the noble thing to do would be to defy the Blue and die in a brief and brutal battle. Such a death would be honorable, but not very sensible. Mirror was, so far as he knew, one of two beings on Krynn who were aware of the departure of his fellow gold and silver dragons, who had flown off on the wings of magic to find the gods, only to be trapped and imprisoned by the One God. Mina was the other being who knew this, and although Mirror did not think that she would tell him anything, he would never know for certain until he had spoken to her.

"You leave me little choice," said Mirror.

"Such was my intent," Razor replied, not smug, merely matter-of-fact.

Mirror altered his form, abandoning his strong, powerful dragon body for the weak, fragile body of a human. He took on the aspect of a young man with silver hair, wearing the white robes of a mystic of the Citadel. He wore a black cloth around his hideously injured eyes.

Moving slowly on his human feet, he groped about with his human hands. His shuffling footsteps stumbled over every rock in the lair. He slipped in Skie's blood and fell to his knees, cutting the weak flesh. Mirror was thankful for one blessing—he did not have to see the look of pity on Razor's face.

The Blue was a soldier, and he made no gibes at Mirror's expense. Razor even guided Mirror's steps with a steadying talon, assisted him to crawl upon the Blue's broad back.

The stench of death was strong in the lair where lay Skie's maltreated corpse. Both Blue and Silver were glad to leave. Perched on the ledge of the cavern, Razor drew in a breath of fresh air, spread his wings and took to the clouds. Mirror held on tightly to the Blue's mane, pressed his legs into Razor's flanks.

"Hold on," Razor warned. He soared high into the air, wheeled about in a huge arc. Mirror guessed what Razor planned and held on tightly, as he'd been ordered.

Mirror felt Razor's lungs expand, felt the expulsion of breath. He smelt the brimstone and heard the sizzle and crackle of lightning. A blast and the sound of rock splitting and shattering, then the sound of tons of rock sliding down the cliff face, rumbling and roaring amidst the thunder of the lightning bolt. Razor unleashed another blast, and this time it sounded to Mirror as if the entire mountain was falling into rubble.

"Thus passes Khellendros, known as Skie," said Razor. "He was a courageous warrior and loyal to his rider, as his rider was loyal to him. Let this might be said of all of us when it comes our time to depart this world."

His duty done to the dead, Razor dipped his wings in a final salute, then wheeled and headed off in a different direction. Mirror judged by the warmth of the sun on the back of his neck that they were flying east. He held fast to Razor's mane, feeling the rush of wind strong against his face. He envisioned the trees, red and gold with the coming of autumn, like jewels set against the green velvet cloth of the grasslands. He saw in his mind the purple-gray mountains, capped by the first snows of the seasons. Far below, the blue lakes and snaking rivers with the golden blot of a village, bringing in the autumn wheat, or the gray dot of a manor house with all its fields around it.

"Why do you weep, Silver?" Razor asked.

Mirror had no answer, and Razor, after a moment's thought, did not repeat the question.

6

The Stone Fortress of the Mind

The Wilder elf known as the Lioness watched her husband with growing concern. Two weeks had passed since they had heard the terrible news of the Queen Mother's death and the destruction of the elven capital of Qualinost. Since that time, Gilthas, the Qualinesti's young king, had barely spoken a word to anyone—not to her, not to Planchet, not to the members of their escort. He slept by himself, covering himself in his blanket and rolling away from her when she tried to offer him the comfort of her presence. He ate by himself, what small amount he ate. His flesh seemed to melt from his bones, and he'd not had that much to spare. He rode by himself, silent, brooding.

His face was pale, set in grim, tight lines. He did not mourn. He had not wept since the night they'd first heard the dreadful tidings. When he spoke, it was only to ask a single question: how much farther until they reached the meeting place?

The Lioness feared that Gilthas might be slipping back into the old sickness that had plagued him during those early years of his enforced rulership of the Qualinesti people. King by title and prisoner by circumstance, he had fallen into a deep depression that left him lethargic and uncaring. He had often spent days sleeping in his bed, preferring the terrors of the dream world to those of reality. He had come out of it, fighting his way back from the dark waters in which he'd nearly drowned. He'd been a good king, using his power to aid the rebels, led by his wife, who fought the tyranny of the Dark Knights. All that he had gained seemed to have been lost, however. Lost with the news of his beloved mother's death and the destruction of the elven capital.

Planchet feared the same. His Majesty's bodyguard and valet-de-chambre, Planchet had been responsible, along with the Lioness, for luring Gilthas away from his nightmare world back to those who loved and needed him.

"He blames himself," said the Lioness, riding alongside Planchet, both gazing with concern on the lonely figure, who rode alone amidst his bodyguards, his eyes fixed unseeing on the road ahead. "He blames himself for leaving his mother there to die. He blames himself for the plan that ended up destroying the city and costing so many hundreds of lives. He cannot see that because of his plan Beryl is dead."

"But at a terrible cost," said Planchet. "He knows that his people can never return to Qualinost. Beryl may be dead, but her armies are not destroyed. True, many were lost, but according to the reports, those who remain continue to burn and ravage our beautiful land."

"What is burned can be restored. What is destroyed can be rebuilt. The Silvanesti went back to their homes to fight the dream," said the Lioness. "They took back their homeland. We can do the same."

"I'm not so sure," Planchet returned, his eyes fixed on his king. "The Silvanesti fought the dream, but look where it led them—to even greater fear of the outside world and an attempt to isolate themselves inside the shield. That proved disastrous."

"The Qualinesti have more sense," insisted the Lioness.

Planchet shook his head. Not wanting to argue with her, he let the subject drop. They rode several miles in silence, then Planchet said quietly, "You know what is truly wrong with Gilthas, don't you?"

The Lioness said nothing for long moments, then replied softly, "I think I do, yes."

"He blames himself for not being among the dead," said Planchet.

Her eyes filling with tears, the Lioness nodded.

Much as he now loathed this life, Gilthas was forced to live it. Not for his sake, for the sake of his people. Lately he began to wonder if that was reason enough to go on enduring this pain. He saw no hope for anyone, anywhere in this world. Only one thin strand tethered him to this life: the promise he had made to his mother. He had promised Laurana that he would lead the refugees, those who had managed to escape Qualinesti and who were waiting for him on the edges of the Plains of Dust. A promise made to the dead is a promise that must be fulfilled.

Still, they never rode past a river but he looked into it and imagined the peace he would find as the waters closed over his head.

Gilthas knew his wife grieved for him and worried about him. He knew or suspected that she was hurt that he had withdrawn from her, retreated to the stone-walled fortress in which he hid from the world. He would have liked to open the gates and let her come inside, but that required effort. He would have to leave the sheltered corner in which he'd taken refuge, advance into the sunlight, cross the courtyard of memory, unlock the gate to admit her sympathy, a sympathy he did not deserve. He couldn't bear it. Not yet. Maybe not ever.

Gilthas blamed himself. His plan had proven disastrous. His plan had brought destruction to Qualinesti and its defenders. His plan had caused his mother's death. He shrank from facing the refugees. They would think him a murderer—and rightly so. They would think him a coward—and rightly so. He had run away and left his people to die. Perhaps they would accuse him of having deliberately plotted the Qualinesti's downfall. He was part human, after all. In his depression, nothing was too outrageous or fantastic for him to believe.

He toyed with the idea of sending an intermediary, of avoiding facing the refugees directly.

"How very like the coward you are," Gilthas said to himself with a sneer. "Shirk that responsibility, as you've shirked others."

He would face them. He would suffer their anger and pain in silence as his due. He would relinquish the throne, would hand over everything to the Senate. They could choose another ruler. He would return to the Lake of Death, where lay the bodies of his mother and his people, and the pain would end.

Thus were the dark thoughts of the young elven king as he rode, day after day, by himself. He looked straight ahead toward a single destination—the gathering place for the refugees of Qualinost, those who had, through the gallant efforts of the dwarves of Thorbardin, escaped through tunnels that the dwarves had dug deep beneath the elven lands. There to do what he had to do. He would fulfill his promise, then he would be free to leave . . . forever.

Sunk in these musings, he heard his wife's voice speak his name.

The Lioness had two voices—one her wifely voice, as Gilthas termed it, and the other her military commander voice. She made the shift unconsciously, not aware of the difference until Gilthas had pointed it out to her long ago. The wife's voice was gentle and loving. The commander's voice could have cut down small trees, or so he teasingly claimed.

He closed his ears to the gentle and loving wife's voice, for he did not feel he deserved love, anyone's love. But he was king, and he could not shut out the voice of the military commander. He knew by the sound she brought bad news.

"Yes, what is it?" he said, turning to face her, steeling himself.

"I have received a report . . . several reports." The Lioness paused, drew in a deep breath. She dreaded telling him this, but she had no choice. He was king. "The armies of Beryl that we thought were scattered and destroyed have regrouped and reformed. We did not think this was possible, but it seems they have a new leader, a man named Samuval. He is a Dark

Knight, and he follows a new Lord of the Night, a human girl called Mina."

Gilthas gazed at his wife in silence. Some part of him heard and understood and absorbed the information. Another part crawled farther into the dark corner of his prison cell.

"This Samuval claims he serves a god known as the One God. The message he brings his soldiers is this: The One God has wrenched Qualinesti from the elves and means to give it back to the humans, to whom this land rightly belongs. Now, all who want free land have only to sign on to serve with this Captain Samuval. His army is immense, as you can imagine. Every derelict and ne'er-do-well in the human race is eager to claim his share of our beautiful land. They are on the march, Gilthas," the Lioness said in conclusion. "They are well armed and well supplied and moving swiftly to seize and secure Qualinesti. We don't have much time. We have to warn our people."

"And then do what?" he asked.

The Lioness didn't recognize his voice. It sounded muffled, as if he were speaking from behind a closed door.

"We follow our original plan," she said. "We march through the Plains of Dust to Silvanesti. Only, we must move faster than we had anticipated. I will send riders on ahead to alert the refugees—"

"No," said Gilthas. "I must be the one to tell them. I will ride day and night if need be."

"My husband . . ." The Lioness shifted to the wife voice, gentle, loving. "Your health—"

He cast her a look that silenced the words on her lips, then turned and spurred his horse. His sudden

84

departure took his bodyguard by surprise. They were forced to race their horses to catch up with him.

Sighing deeply, the Lioness followed.

The place Gilthas had chosen for the gathering of the elven refugees was located on the coast of New Sea, close enough to Thorbardin so that the dwarves could assist in the defense of the refugees, if they were attacked, but not near enough to make the dwarves nervous. The dwarves knew in their heads that the forest-loving elves would never think of living in the mighty underground fortress of Thorbardin, but in their hearts the dwarves were certain that everyone on Ansalon must secretly envy them their stronghold and would claim Thorbardin for themselves, if they could.

The elves had also to be careful not to draw the ire of the great dragon Onysablet, who had taken over what had once been New Coast. The land was now known as New Swamp, for she had used her foul magicks to alter the landscape into a treacherous bog. To avoid traveling through her territory, Gilthas was going to attempt to cross the Plains of Dust. A vast no-man's land, the plains were inhabited by tribes of barbarians, who lived in the desert and kept to themselves, taking no interest in the world outside their borders, a world that took very little interest in them.

Slowly, over several weeks, the refugees straggled into the meeting place. Some traveled in groups, streaming through the tunnels built by the dwarves and their giant dirt-devouring worms. Others came singly or by twos, escaping through the forests with the help of the Lioness's rebel forces. They left behind their homes, their possessions, their farmland, their crops, their lush forests and fragrant gardens, their beautiful city of Qualinost with its gleaming Tower of the Sun.

The elves were confident they would be able to return to their beloved homeland. The Qualinesti had always owned this land, or so it seemed to them. Looking back throughout history, they could not find a time when they had not claimed this land. Even after the elven kingdoms had split in twain following the bitter Kinslayer Wars, creating the two great elven nations, Qualinesti and Silvanesti, the Qualinesti continued to rule and inhabit land that had already been theirs.

This uprooting was temporary. Many among them still remembered how they had been forced to flee their homeland during the War of the Lance. They had survived that and returned to make their homes stronger than before. Human armies might come and go. Dragons might come and go, but the Qualinesti nation would remain. The choking smoke of burning would soon be blown away. The green shoots would shove up from underneath the black ash. They would rebuild, replant. They had done it before, they would do it again.

So confident were the elves of this, so confident were they in the defenders of their beautiful city of Qualinost, that the mood in the refugee camps, which had been dark at first, became almost merry.

True, there were losses to mourn, for Beryl had taken delight in slaughtering any elves she caught out in the open. Some of the refugees had been killed by the dragon. Others had run afoul of rampaging humans or been caught by the Dark Knights of Neraka and beaten and tortured. But the numbers of dead were surprisingly few, considering that the elves had been facing destruction and annihilation. Through the planning of their young king and the help of the dwarven nation, the Qualinesti had survived. They began to look toward the future and that future was in Qualinesti. They could not picture anything else.

The wise among the elves remained worried and troubled, for they could see certain signs that all was not well. Why had they not heard any news from the defenders of Qualinesti? Wildrunners had been stationed in the city, ready to speed swiftly to the refugee camps. They should have been here by now with either good news or bad. The fact that they had not come at all was deeply disturbing to some, shrugged off by others.

"No news is good news," was how the humans put it, or "No explosion is a step in the right direction," as the gnomes would say.

The elves pitched their tents on the sandy beaches of New Sea. Their children played in the gently lapping waters and made castles in the sand. At night they built fires of driftwood, watching the ever-changing colors of the flames and telling stories of other times the elves had been forced to flee their homeland—stories that always had a happy ending.

The weather had been beautiful, with unusually warm days for this late in the year. The seawater was the deep, blue-black color that is seen only in the autumn months and presages the coming of the winter storms. The trees were heavily laden with their harvest gifts, and food was plentiful. The elves found streams of fresh water for drinking and bathing. Elven soldiers stood guard over the people by day and by night, dwarven soldiers watched from the forests, keeping one eye alert for invading armies and one eye on the elves. The refugees waited for Gilthas, waited for him to come tell them that the dragon was defeated, that they could all go home.

"Sire," said one of the elven body guards, riding up to Gilthas, "you asked me to tell you when we were within a few hours' ride of the refugee camp. The campsite is up ahead." The elf pointed. "Beyond those foothills."

"Then we will stop here," said Gilthas, reigning in his horse. He glanced up at the sky, where the pale sun shone almost directly overhead. "We will ride again when dusk falls."

"Why do we halt, my husband?" the Lioness asked, cantering up in time to hear Gilthas give his instructions. "We have nearly broken our necks to reach our people, and, now that we are near, we stop?"

"The news I have to tell should be told only in darkness," he said, dismounting, not looking at her. "The light of neither sun nor moon will shine on our grief. I resent even the cold light of the stars. I would pry them from the skies, if I could."

"Gilthas—" she began, but he turned his face from her and walked away, vanishing into the woods.

At a sign from the Lioness, his guard accompanied him, maintaining a discreet distance, yet close enough to protect him.

"I am losing him, Planchet," she said, her voice aching with pain and sorrow, "and I don't know what to do, how to reclaim him."

"Keep loving him," Planchet advised. "That is all you can do. The rest he must do himself."

Gilthas and his retinue entered the elven refugee encampment in the early hours of darkness. Fires burned on the beach. Elven children were sprightly shadows dancing amidst the flames. To them, this was a holiday, a grand adventure. The nights spent in the dark tunnels with the gruff-voiced and fearsome looking dwarves were now distant memories. School lessons were suspended, their daily chores remitted. Gilthas watched them dance and thought of what he must tell them. The holiday would end this night. In the morning, they would begin a bitter struggle, a struggle for their very lives.

How many of these children who danced so gaily around the fire would be lost to the desert, succumbing to the heat and the lack of water, or falling prey to the evil creatures reputed to roam the Plains of Dust? How many more of his people would die? Would they survive as a race at all, or would this be forever known as the last march of the Qualinesti?

He entered the camp on foot without fanfare. Those who saw him as he passed were startled to see their king—those who recognized him as their king. Gilthas was so altered that many did not know him.

Thin and gaunt, pale and wan, Gilthas had lost almost any trace of his human heritage. His delicate elven bone-structure was more visible, more pronounced. He was, some whispered in awe, the very image of the great elven kings of antiquity, of Silvanos and Kith-Kanan.

He walked through the camp, heading for the center, where blazed a large bonfire. His retinue stayed behind, at a command from the Lioness. What Gilthas had to say, he had to say alone.

At the sight of his face, the elves silenced their laughter, ceased their storytelling, halted the dancing, and hushed their children. As word spread that the king had come among them, silent and alone, the elves gathered around him. The leaders of the Senate came hastily to greet him, clucking to themselves in irritation that he had robbed them of a chance to welcome him with proper ceremony. When they saw his face—deathlike in the firelight—they ceased their cluckings, forgot their welcoming speeches, and waited with dire foreboding to hear his words.

Against the music of the waves, rolling in one after the other, chasing each other to shore and falling back, Gilthas told the story of the downfall of Qualinesti. He told it clearly, calmly, dispassionately. He spoke of the death of his mother. He spoke of the heroism of the city's defenders. He lauded the heroism of the dwarves and humans who had died defending a land and a people not their own. He spoke of the death of the dragon.

The elves wept for their Queen Mother and for loved ones now surely dead. Their tears slid silently down their faces. They did not sob aloud lest they miss hearing what came next.

What came next was dreadful.

Gilthas spoke of the armies under this new leader. He spoke of a new god, who claimed credit for ousting the elves from their homeland and who was handing that land over to humans, already pouring into Qualinesti from the north. Hearing of the refugees, the army was moving rapidly to try to catch them and destroy them.

He told them that their only hope was to try to reach Silvanesti. The shield had fallen. Their cousins would welcome them to their land. To reach Silvanesti, however, the elves would have to march through the Plains of Dust.

"For now," Gilthas was forced to tell them, "there will be no homecoming. Perhaps, with the help of our cousins, we can form an army that will be powerful enough to sweep into our beloved land and drive the enemy from it, take back what they have stolen. But although that must be our hope, that hope is far in the future. Our first thought must be the survival of our race. The road we walk will be a hard one. We must walk that road together with one goal and one purpose in our hearts. If one of us falls out, all will perish.

"I was made your king by trickery and treachery. You know the truth of that by now. The story has been whispered among you for years. The Puppet King, you called me."

He cast a glance at Prefect Palthainon as he spoke. The prefect's face was set in a sorrowful mask, but his eyes darted this way and that, trying to see how the people were reacting.

"It would have been best if I had remained in that role," Gilthas continued, looking away from the senator and back to his people. "I tried to be your ruler, and I failed. It was my plan that destroyed Qualinesti, my plan that left our land open to invasion."

He raised his hand for silence, for the elves had begun to murmur among themselves.

"You need a strong king," Gilthas said, raising his voice that was growing hoarse from shouting. "A ruler who has the courage and the wisdom to lead you into peril and see you safely through it. I am not that person. As of now, I abdicate the throne and renounce all my rights and claims to it. I leave the succession in the hands of the Senate. I thank you for all the kindness and love that you have shown me over the years. I wish I had done better by you. I wish I was more deserving."

He wanted to leave, but the people had pressed close about him and, much as he needed to escape, he did not want to force a path through the crowd. He was forced to wait to hear what the Senate had to say. He kept his head lowered, did not look into the faces of his people, not wanting to see their hostility, their anger, their blame. He stood waiting until he was dismissed.

The elves had been shocked into silence. Too much had happened too suddenly to absorb. A lake of death where once stood their city. An enemy army behind them, a perilous journey to an uncertain future ahead of them. The king abdicating. The senators thrown into confusion. Dismayed and appalled, they stared at each other, waited for someone to speak the first word.

That word belonged to Palthainon. Cunning and conniving, he saw this disaster as a means to further his own ambition. Ordering some elves to drag up a large log, he mounted it and, clapping his hands, called the elves loudly to silence, a command that was completely unnecessary, for not even a baby's cry broke the hushed stillness.

"I know what you are feeling, my brethren," the prefect stated in sonorous tones. "I, too, am shocked and grieved to hear of the tragedy that has befallen our people. Do not be fearful. You are in good hands. I will take over the reins of leadership until such time as a new king is named."

Palthainon pointed his bony finger at Gilthas. "It is right that this young man has stepped down, for he brought this tragedy upon us—he and those who pulled his strings. Puppet King. Yes, that best describes him. Once Gilthas allowed himself to be guided by my wisdom and experience. He came to me for advice, and I was proud and happy to provide it. But there were those of his own family who worked against me. I do not name them, for it is wrong to speak ill of the dead, even though they sought continuously to reduce my influence."

Palthainon warmed to his topic. "Among those who pulled the puppet's strings was the hated and detested Marshal Medan—the true engineer of our destruction, for he seduced the son as he seduced the mother—"

Rage—white-hot—struck the fortress prison in which Gilthas had locked himself, struck it like the fiery bolt of a blue dragon. Leaping upon the log on which Palthainon stood, Gilthas hit the elf a blow on the jaw that sent him reeling. The prefect landed on his backside in the sand, his fine speech knocked clean out of his head.

Gilthas said nothing. He did not look around. He jumped off the log and started to shove his way through the crowd.

Palthainon sat up. Shaking his muzzy head, he spat out a tooth and started to sputter and point. "There! There! Did you see what he did! Arrest him! Arrest—"

"Gilthas," spoke a voice out of the crowd.

"Gilthas," spoke another voice and another and another.

They did not chant. They did not thunder his name. Each elf spoke his name calmly, quietly, as if being asked a question and giving an answer. But the name was repeated over and over throughout the crowd, so that it carried with it the quiet force of the waves breaking on the shore. The elderly spoke his name, the young spoke his name. Two senators spoke it as they assisted Palthainon to his feet.

Astonished and bewildered, Gilthas raised his head, looked around.

"You don't understand—" he began.

"We do understand," said one of the elves. His face was drawn, marked with traces of recent grief. "So do you, Your Majesty. You understand our pain and our heartache. That is why you are our king."

"That is why you have always been our king," said another, a woman, holding a baby in her arms. "Our true king. We know of the work you have done in secret for us."

"If not for you, Beryl would be wallowing in our beautiful city," said a third. "We would be dead, those of us who stand here before you."

"Our enemies have triumphed for the moment," said yet another, "but so long as we keep fast the memory of our loved nation, that nation will never perish. Some day, we will return to claim it. On that day, you will lead us, Your Majesty."

Gilthas could not speak. He looked at his people who shared his loss, and he was ashamed and chastened and humbled. He did not feel he had earned their regard—not yet. But he would try. He would spend the rest of his life trying.

Prefect Palthainon spluttered and huffed and tried to make himself heard, but no one paid any attention to him. The other senators crowded around Gilthas.

Palthainon glared at them grimly, then, seizing hold of the arm of an elf, he whispered softly, "The plan to defeat Beryl was my plan all along. Of course, I allowed His Majesty to take credit for it. As for this little dust-up between us, it was all just a misunderstanding, such as often happens between father and son. For he is like a son to me, dear to my heart."

The Lioness remained on the outskirts of the camp, her own heart too full to see or speak to him. She knew he would seek her out. Lying on the pallet she spread for both of them, on the edge of the water, near the sea, she heard his footsteps in the sand, felt his hand brush her cheek.

She put her arm around him, drew him beside her.

"Can you forgive me, beloved?" he asked, lying down with a sigh.

"Isn't that the definition of being a wife?" she asked him, smiling.

Gilthas made no answer. His eyes were closed. He was already fast asleep.

The Lioness drew the blanket over him, rested her head on his chest, listened to his beating heart until she, too, slept.

The sun would rise early, and it would rise blood red.

7

An Unexpected Journey

Following the activation of the Device of Time Journeying, Tasslehoff Burrfoot was aware of two things: impenetrable darkness and Conundrum shrieking in his left ear, all the while clutching his (Tasslehoff's) left hand so tightly that he completely lost all sense of feeling in his fingers and his thumb. The rest of Tas could feel nothing either, nothing under him, nothing over him, nothing next to him—except Conundrum. Tas couldn't tell if he was on his head or his heels or an interesting combination of both.

This entertaining state of affairs lasted an extremely long time, so long that Tas began to get a bit bored by it all. A person can stare into impenetrable darkness only so long before he thinks he might like a change. Even tumbling about in time and space (if that's what they were doing, Tas wasn't at all sure at this point) grows old after you've been doing it a long while. Eventually you decide that being stepped on by a giant is preferable to having a gnome shrieking continuously in your ear (remarkable lung capacity, gnomes) and nearly pinching your hand off at the wrist.

This state of affairs continued for a good long while until Tasslehoff and Conundrum slammed down, bump, into something that was soft and squishy and smelled strongly of mud and pine needles. The fall was not a gentle one and knocked the boredom out of the kender and the shrieks out of the gnome.

Tasslehoff lay on his back, making gasping attempts to catch what would probably be the last few breaths he would ever take. He looked up, expecting to see Chaos's enormous foot poised above him. Tas had just a few seconds in which to explain matters to Conundrum, who was about to be inadvertently squished.

"We're going to die a hero's death," said Tasslehoff with his first mouthful of air.

"What?" Conundrum shrieked with his first mouthful of air.

"We're going to die a hero's death," Tasslehoff repeated.

Then he suddenly realized that they weren't.

Absorbed in preparing both himself and the gnome for an imminent demise, Tasslehoff had not taken a close look at their surroundings. He assumed that all he would be seeing was the ugly underside of Chaos's foot. Now that he had time to notice, he saw above him not a foot, but the dripping needles of a pine tree in a rain storm.

Tasslehoff felt his head to see if he had received a severe bump, for he knew from past experience that severe bumps to the head can cause you to see the most remarkable things, although those were generally starbursts, not dripping pine needles. He could find no signs of a bump, however.

Hearing Conundrum drawing in another large breath, undoubtedly preparatory to letting loose another ear-piercing shriek, Tasslehoff raised his hand in a commanding gesture.

"Hush," he whispered tensely, "I thought I heard something."

Now, if truth be told, Tasslehoff had not heard something. Well, he had. He'd heard the rain falling off the pine needles, but he hadn't heard anything dire, which is what his tone implied. He'd only pretended that in order to shut off the gnome's shrieks. Unfortunately, as is often the way with transgressors, he was immediately punished for his sin, for the moment he pretended to hear something dire, he *did* hear something dire—the clash of steel on steel, followed by a crackling blast.

In Tas's experience as a hero, only two things made sounds like that: swords beating against swords and fireballs exploding against just about anything.

The next thing he heard was more shrieking, only this time it was not, blessedly, Conundrum. The shrieking was some distance away and had the distinct sound of dying goblin to it, a notion that was reinforced by the sickening smell of burnt goblin hair. The shrieking ended summarily, then came a crashing, as of large bodies running through a forest of dripping wet pine needles. Thinking these might be more goblins and realizing that this was an inopportune time to be running into goblins, especially those who have just been fireball-blasted, Tasslehoff squirmed his way on his belly underneath a sheltering,

low-hanging pine bough and dragged Conundrum
in after him.

"Where are we?" Conundrum demanded, lifting
up his head out of the mud in which they were lying.
"How did we get here? When are we going back?"

All perfectly sound, logical questions. Trust a gnome,
thought Tas, to go right to the heart of the matter.

"I'm sorry," said Tas, peering out through the wet
pine needles, trying to see what was going on. The
crashing sounds were growing louder, which meant
they were coming closer. "But I don't know. Any of it."

Conundrum gaped. His chin fell so far it came back
up with mud on it. "What do you mean you don't
know?" he gasped, swelling with indignation. "You
brought us here."

"No," said Tas with dignity, "I didn't. *This* brought
us here." He indicated the Device of Time Journeying
that he was holding in his hand. "When it wasn't supposed to."

Seeing Conundrum sucking in another huge breath,
Tas fixed the gnome with a withering stare. "So I guess
you didn't fix it, after all."

The breath wheezed out of Conundrum. He stared
at the device, muttered something about missing
schematics and lack of internal directives, and held
out his mud-covered hand. "Give it to me. I'll take a
look at it."

"No, thank you," said Tasslehoff, shoving the device
into a pouch and closing the flap. "I think I should
hold onto it. Now hush!" Turning back to stare out
from under the pine bough, Tas put his fingers to his
lips. "Don't let on we're here."

Contrary to most gnomes, who never see anything outside of the inside of Mount Nevermind,

Conundrum was a well-traveled gnome who'd had his share of adventures, most of which he hadn't enjoyed in the slightest. Nasty, bothersome things, adventures. Interrupted a fellow's work. But he had learned an important lesson—the best way to survive adventures was to lie hidden in some dark and uncomfortable place and keep your mouth shut. This he was good at doing.

Conundrum was so good at hiding that when Tasslehoff, who was not at all good at this sort of thing, started to get up with a glad and joyful cry to go to meet two humans who had just run out of the forest, the gnome grabbed hold of the kender with a strength borne of terror and dragged him back down.

"What in the name of all that's combustible do you think you're doing?" Conundrum gasped.

"They're not burnt goblins, like I first thought," Tas argued, pointing. "That man is a Solamnic Knight. I can tell by his armor. And the other man is a mage. I can tell by his robes. I'm just going to go say hello and introduce myself."

"If there is one thing that I have learned in my travels," said Conundrum in a smothered whisper, "it is that you never introduce yourself to anyone carrying a sword or wearing wizard's robes. Let them go their way, and you go your way."

"Did you say something?" said the strange mage, turning to his companion.

"No," said the Knight, raising his sword and looking keenly about.

"Well, somebody did," said the mage grimly. "I distinctly heard voices."

"I can't hear anything for the sound of my own heart beating." The Knight paused, listening, then shook his head. "No, I can't hear a thing. What did it sound like? Goblins?"

"No," the mage said, peering into the shadows.

The man was a Solamnic by his looks, for he had long, blond hair that he wore braided to keep out of his way. His eyes were blue, keen, and intense. He wore robes that might have started out red but were now so stained with mud, charred with smoke, and smeared with blood that their color was indistinguishable in the gray light of the rainy day. A glint of golden trim could be seen at the cuffs and on the hem.

"Look at that!" gasped Tasslehoff, agog with amazement, "He's carrying Raistlin's staff!"

"Oddly enough," the mage was saying, "it sounded like a kender."

Tasslehoff clapped his hand over his mouth. Conundrum shook his head bleakly.

"What would a kender be doing here in the middle of a battle field?" asked the Knight with a smile.

"What does a kender do anywhere?" the mage returned archly, "except cause trouble for those who have the misfortune to encounter him."

"How true," sighed Conundrum gloomily.

"How rude," muttered Tasslehoff. "Maybe I won't go introduce myself to them, after all."

"So long as it was not goblins you heard," the Knight said. He cast a glance over his shoulder. "Do you think we've stopped them?"

The Knight wore the armor of a Knight of the Crown. Tas had first taken him to be an older man, for the Knight's hair had gone quite gray, but after watching him awhile, Tas realized that the Knight was far younger than he appeared at first glance. It was his eyes that made him look older—they had a sadness about them and a weariness that should not have been seen in one so young.

"We've stopped them for the time being," the mage said. Sinking down at the foot of the tree, he cradled the staff protectively in his arms.

The staff was Raistlin's, all right. Tasslehoff knew that staff well, with its crystal ball clutched in the golden dragon's claw. He remembered the many times he'd reached out to touch it, only to have his hand smacked.

"And many times I've seen Raistlin hold the staff just like that," Tas said softly to himself. "Yet that mage is most certainly *not* Raistlin. Maybe he's stolen Raistlin's staff. If so, Raistlin will want to know who the thief is."

Tas listened with all his ears, as the old kender saying went.

"Our enemy now has a healthy fear of your sword and my magic," the mage was saying. "Unfortunately, goblins have an even healthier fear of their own commanders. The whip will soon convince them to come after us."

"It will take them time to regroup." The Knight squatted down beneath the tree. Picking up a handful of wet pine needles, he began to clean the blood off his sword. "Time enough for us to rest, then try to find our way back to our company. Or time for them to find us. They are undoubtedly out searching for us even now."

"Searching for *you*, Huma," said the mage with a wry smile. He leaned back against the tree and wearily closed his eyes. "They will not be looking very hard for me."

The Knight appeared disturbed by this. His expression grave, he concentrated on his cleaning, rubbing hard at a stubborn speck. "You have to understand them, Magius—" he began.

"Huma . . ." Tas repeated. "Magius . . ." He stared at the two, blinked in wonder. Then he stared down at the Device of Time Journeying. "Do you suppose . . . ?"

"I understand them quite well, Huma," Magius returned. "The average Solamnic Knight is an ignorant, superstitious dolt, who believes all the dark tales about wizards told to him by his nursery maid in order to frighten him into keeping quiet at night, in consequence of which he expects me to start leaping through camp naked, gibbering and ranting and transforming him into a newt with a wave of my staff. Not that I couldn't do it, mind you," Magius continued with a quirk of his brow and the twist of an infectious smile. "And don't think I haven't considered it. Spending five minutes as a newt would be an interesting change for most of them. Expand their minds, if nothing else."

"I don't think I'd much care for life as a newt," said Huma.

"You, alone, are different, my friend," Magius said, his tone softening. Reaching out his hand, he rested it on the Knight's wrist. "You are not afraid of new ideas. You are not afraid of that which you do not understand. Even as a child, you did not fear to be my friend."

"You will teach them to think better of wizards, Magius," said Huma, resting his hand over his friend's. "You will teach them to view magic and those who wield it with respect."

"*I* will not," said Magius coolly, "for I really have no care what they think of me. If anyone can change their obsolete, outdated and outmoded views, you are the one to do it. And you had best do it quickly, Huma," he added, his mocking tone now serious. "The Dark Queen's power grows daily. She is raising vast armies. Countless thousands of evil creatures flock to her standard. These goblins would never before have dared to attack a company of Knights, but you saw with what ferocity they struck us this morning. I begin to think that it is not the whip they fear, but the wrath of the Dark Queen should they fail."

"Yet she will fail. She must fail, Magius," said Huma. "She and her evil dragons must be driven from the world, sent back to the Abyss. For if she is not defeated, we will live as do these wretched goblins, live our lives in fear." Huma sighed, shook his head. "Although, I admit to you, dear friend, I do not see how that is possible. The numbers of her minions are countless, their power immense—"

"But you do defeat her!" Tasslehoff cried, unable to restrain himself any longer. Freeing himself from Conundrum's frantic grasp, Tas scrambled to his feet and burst out from underneath the pine trees.

Huma jumped up, drawing his sword in one, swift movement. Magius extended the staff with the crystal held fast in the dragon's claw, aimed the staff at the kender, and began to speak words that Tas recognized by their spidery sound as being words of magic.

Knowing that perhaps he didn't have much time before *he* was turned into a newt, Tasslehoff accelerated his conversation.

"You raise an army of heroes, and you fight the Queen of Darkness herself, and while you die, Huma, and you die, too, Magius—I'm really very sorry about that, by the way—you do send all the evil dragons back to— ulp"

Several things happened simultaneously with that "ulp." Two large, hairy, and foul-smelling goblin hands grabbed hold Conundrum, while another yellow-skinned, slavering-jawed goblin seized hold of Tasslehoff.

Before the kender had time to draw his blade, before Conundrum had time to draw his breath, a blazing arc of lightning flared from the staff and struck the goblin who had hold of Conundrum. Huma ran his sword through the goblin trying to drag off Tas.

"There are more goblins coming," said Huma grimly. "You had best take to your heels, Kender."

Flapping goblin feet could be heard crashing through the trees, their guttural voices raised in hideous howls, promising death. Huma and Magius stood back to back, Huma with his sword drawn, Magius wielding his staff.

"Don't worry!" Tasslehoff cried. "I have my knife. It's called Rabbit-slayer." Opening a pouch, he began searching among his things. "Caramon named it. You don't know him—"

"Are you mad?" Conundrum screamed, sounding like the noon whistle at Mount Nevermind, a whistle that never, on any account, goes off at noon.

A hand touched Tasslehoff on the shoulder. A voice in his ear whispered, "Not now. It is not yet time."

"I beg your pardon?" Tasslehoff turned to see who was talking.

And kept turning. And turning.

Then he was still, and the world was turning, and it was all a mass of swirling color, and he didn't know if he was on his head or his heels, and Conundrum was at his side, shrieking, and then it was all very, very dark.

In the midst of the darkness and the turning and the shrieking, Tasslehoff had one thought, one important thought, a thought so important that he made sure to hang onto it with all his brain.

"I found the past. . . ."

8

The Coming of the God

Rain fell on the Solamnic plains. The rain had been falling without letup since the Knights' crushing defeat by Mina's force at the city of Solanthus. Following the loss of the city, Mina had warned the surviving Knights that she meant next to take the city of Sanction. She had also told them to think on the power of the One God, who was responsible for the Solamnics' defeat. This done, she had bidden them ride off in safety, to spread the word of the One God.

The Knights didn't have much choice but to glumly obey the command of their conqueror. They rode for days through the rain, heading for Lord Ulrich's manor house, located about fifty miles east of Solanthus. The rain was chill and soaked everything. The Knights and what remained of their meager force were wet through, coated with mud, and shivering from the cold. The wounded they brought with them soon grew feverish, and many of them died.

Lord Nigel, Knight of the Crown, was one of the dead. He was buried beneath a rock cairn, in the hopes that at some future date his relatives would be able to remove the body and give him proper burial in his family's vault. As Gerard helped place the heavy stones over the corpse, he couldn't help but wonder if Lord Nigel's soul had gone to join the army that had defeated the Solamnic Knights—the army of the dead. In life, Lord Nigel would have shed his last drop of blood before he betrayed the Knighthood. In death, he might become their enemy.

Gerard had seen the souls of other Solamnic Knights drifting on the fearful tide of the river of souls. He guessed that the dead had no choice, they were conscripts, constrained to serve. But who or what did they serve? The girl, Mina? Or someone or something more powerful?

Lord Ulrich's manor house was constructed along simple lines. Built of stone quarried from the land on which the house stood, it was solid, massive, with square towers and thick walls. Lord Ulrich had sent his squire ahead to warn his lady wife of their coming, and there were roaring fires, fresh rushes on the floors, hot bread and mulled wine waiting for them on their arrival. The Knights ate and drank, warmed themselves and dried out their clothes. Then they met in council to try to determine what to do next.

Their first move was obvious—they sent messengers riding in haste to Sanction to warn the city that the Knights of Neraka had taken Solanthus and that they were threatening to march next on Sanction. Before the loss of Solanthus, the Knights would have scoffed at this notion. The Dark Knights of Neraka had been laying siege to Sanction for months without any success. Solamnic Knights insured that the port remained open and that supplies flowed into the city, so that while the besieged citizens didn't live well, they didn't starve either. The Solamnics had once almost broken the siege, but had been driven back by strange mischance. The siege continued, the balance held, neither side making any headway against the other.

But that had been before Solanthus had fallen to an army of dead souls, living dragons, a girl called Mina, and the One God.

These all figured large in the discussions and arguments that rang throughout the great hall of the manor house. A large, rectangular room, the hall had walls of gray stone covered with a few splendid tapestries depicting scenes illustrative of texts from the Measure. Thick, beeswax candles filled the hall with light. There were not enough chairs, so the Knights stood gathered around their leaders, who sat behind a large, ornately carved wooden table.

Every Knight was permitted his say. Lord Tasgall, Lord of the Rose and head of the Knights' Council, listened to them all in patient silence—including Odila, whose say was extremely uncomfortable to hear.

"We were defeated by a god," she told them, as they shifted and muttered and glanced askance at each other. "What other power on Krynn could hurl the souls of the dead against us?"

"Necromancers," suggested Lord Ulrich.

"Necromancers raise the bodies of the dead," Odila stated. "They drag skeletons from the ground to fight against the living. They have never had power over the souls of the dead."

The other Knights were glum, bedraggled, dour. They looked and felt defeated. By contrast, Odila was invigorated, exalted. Her wet, black hair gleamed in the firelight, her eyes sparked as she spoke of the god.

"What of death knights such as Lord Soth?" Lord Ulrich argued. The pudgy Lord Ulrich had lost considerable weight during the long, dispirited journey. Loose skin sagged around his mouth. His usually cheerful face was solemn, his bright eyes shadowed.

"You prove my point, my lord," Odila replied coolly. "Soth was cursed by the gods. Only a god has such power. And this god is powerful."

She raised her voice to be heard among the angry cries and denunciations. "You have seen that for yourself! What other force could create legions of souls and claim the loyalty of the dragons. You saw them! You saw them on the walls of Solanthus—red and white, black and green and blue. They were not there in the service of Beryl. They were not there in the service of Malys or any other of the dragon overlords. They were there in the service of Mina. And Mina is there in the service of the One God."

Odila's words were drowned out by jeers and boos, but that meant only that she'd struck a weak point in their armor. None could deny a word she said.

Lord Tasgall, the elder Knight, graying, upright, stern of bearing and countenance, shouted repeatedly for order and banged his sword hilt upon the table. Eventually order was restored. He looked at Odila, who remained standing, her head with its two thick, black braids thrown back in defiance, her face flushed.

"What is your proposal—" he began, and when one of the Knights hissed, the Lord Knight silenced him with a withering glance.

"We are a people of faith," said Odila. "We have always been people of faith. I believe that this god is trying to speak to us and that we should listen—"

The Knights thundered in anger, many shaking their fists.

"A god who brings death!" cried one, who had lost his brother in the battle.

"What of the old gods?" Odila shouted back. "*They* dropped a fiery mountain on Krynn!"

Some of the Knights were silenced by this, had no argument. Others continued to rant and rage.

"Many Solamnics lost their faith after the Cataclysm," Odila continued. "They claimed that the gods had abandoned us. Then we came to find out during the War of the Lance that we were the ones who had abandoned the gods. And after the Chaos War, when we woke to find the gods missing, we cried out again that they had left us. Perhaps again that is not the case. Perhaps this Mina is a second Goldmoon, coming to bring us the truth. How do we know until we investigate? Ask questions?"

How, indeed? Gerard asked himself, the seeds of a plan starting to take root in his mind. He couldn't help but admire Odila, even as he wanted to grab her by the shoulders and shake her until her teeth rattled. She alone had the courage to say aloud what needed to be said. Too bad she lacked the tact to say it in such a way that didn't start fistfights.

The hall erupted into chaos with people arguing for and against and Lord Tasgall banging his sword hilt with such force that chips flew from the wooden table. The wrangling continued far into the night, and eventually two resolutions were presented for consideration. A small but vocal group wanted to ride to Ergoth, where the Knights still held firm, there to lick their wounds and build up their strength. This plan was favored by many until someone sourly pointed out that if Sanction fell they might build up their strength from now until the end of forever and they wouldn't be strong enough to retake all that they had lost.

The other resolution urged the Knights to march to Sanction, there to reinforce the Knights already defending that disputed city. But, argued the minority, how do we even know they mean to go to Sanction? Why would this girl give away her plans? It is a trick, a trap. Thus they argued, back and forth. No one mentioned anything about the One God.

The council itself was divided. Lord Ulrich was in favor of riding to Sanction. Lord Siegfried, who replaced the late Lord Nigel on the council, was from Ergoth and argued that the Knights would do better to retreat.

Gerard glanced at Odila, who stood near him. She was thoughtful and very quiet, her eyes dark and shadowed. She apparently had no more arguments to present, nothing more to say. Gerard should have realized silence was a bad sign for the glib-tongued young woman. As it was, he was too absorbed in his own thoughts and plans to pay much attention to her beyond wondering what she'd expected to accomplish in the first place. When next he looked around at her, to ask her if she wanted to go get something to eat, he found that she had gone.

Lord Tasgall rose to his feet. He announced that the

council would take both matters under advisement. The three retired to discuss the matter in private.

Thinking that his own proposed plan of action might aid their decision making, Gerard left his fellows, who were still arguing, and went in search of the Lord Knights. He found them closeted in what had once been an old chapel dedicated to the worship of Kiri-Jolith, one of the old gods and one favored by the Solamnic Knights.

Retainers in the service of Lord Ulrich stood guard at the door. Gerard told them he had a matter of urgency to bring before the council and then, having been standing for hours, he sank thankfully onto a bench outside the chapel to await the Lord Knights' pleasure. While he waited, he went over his plans once more, searching for any flaw. He could find none. Confident and excited, he waited impatiently for the Knights to summon him.

At length, the guard came to him and said that they would see him now. As Gerard entered the old chapel, he realized that the council had already reached a decision. He guessed, by the way Lord Ulrich was smiling, that the decision was to march to Sanction.

Gerard was kept waiting a moment longer while Lord Siegfried conferred in a low voice with Lord Tasgall. Gerard glanced with interest around the old chapel. The walls were made of rough-hewn stone, the floor lined with wooden benches, worn smooth by years of use. The chapel was small, for it was a private chapel, intended for the family and servants. An altar stood at the front. Gerard could just barely make out the symbol of Kiri-Jolith—the head of a buffalo—carved in relief.

Gerard tried to picture in his mind what the chapel had been like all those many years ago, when the Lord Knight and his lady wife and their children, their retinue and their servants, had come to this place to worship their god. The ceiling would have been hung with bright banners. The priest—probably a stern, warrior-type—would have taken his place at the front as he prepared to read from the Measure or relate some tale of Vinas Solamnus, the founder of the Knighthood. The presence of the god would have been felt in this chapel. His people would have been comforted by that presence and would have left to go about their daily lives strengthened and renewed.

His presence was lacking now, when it was sorely needed.

"We will hear you now, Sir Gerard," said Lord Tasgall with a touch of impatience, and Gerard realized with a start that this was the second time he'd been addressed.

"I beg your pardon, my lords," said Gerard, bowing.

Receiving an invitation to advance and speak, he did so, outlining his plan. The three Knights listened in silence, giving no hint of their feelings. In conclusion, Gerard stated, "I could provide you with the answer to one question, at least, my lords— whether in truth this Mina does intend to march to Sanction or if that was a ruse to divert us from her true goal. If so, I might be able to discover the nature of that goal."

"The risk you run is very great," observed Lord Siegfried, frowning.

"'The greater the risk, the greater the glory,'" quoted Lord Ulrich, with a smile.

"I would it were so, my lord," said Gerard with a shrug, "but, in truth, I will not be in all that much danger. I am known to the Dark Knights, you see. They would have little reason to question my story."

"I do not approve of the use of spies," stated Lord Siegfried, "much less one of our own Knights acting in such a demeaning capacity. The Measure forbids it."

"The Measure forbids a lot of things," said Lord Tasgall dryly. "I, for one, tend to choose common sense over rules that have been handed down in the distant past. I do not command you to do this, Sir Gerard, but if you volunteer—"

"I do, my lord," said Gerard eagerly.

"—then I believe that you can be of inestimable help to us. The council has determined that the Knights will ride to the support of Sanction. I am convinced that this Mina does mean to attack and therefore we cannot delay. However, I would be glad to receive confirmation of this and to learn of any plans she has for the capture of the city. Even with dragons, she will find her way difficult, for there are many underground structures where armies can be safely concealed from attack."

"Then, too, her own armies may be susceptible to the dragonfear," stated Lord Ulrich. "She may use dragons against us, only to watch helplessly as her own troops flee the field in terror."

The dead won't flee in terror, thought Gerard, but he kept that thought to himself. He knew by their grim expressions and grimmer faces that the Knights understood that as well as he did.

"Good luck to you, Sir Gerard," said Lord Tasgall, rising to his feet to shake hands.

Lord Ulrich also shook hands heartily. Lord Siegfried was stiff and solemn and clearly disapproving, but he made no further argument and actually wished Gerard luck, although he did not shake hands.

"We'll say nothing of this plan to anyone, gentlemen," said Lord Tasgall, glancing around at the others.

This agreed to, Gerard was about to take his departure when the retainer entered to say that a messenger had arrived with urgent news.

Since this might have some impact on Gerard's plan, Lord Tasgall gave a sign that he was to remain. The messenger entered. Gerard was alarmed to recognize a young squire from the household of Lord Warren, commander of the outpost of Solamnic Knights that protected Solace, location of Gerard's last posting. Gerard tensed, sensing dire news. The young man was mud-spattered, his clothes travel-worn. He strode forward, came to stand in front of Lord Tasgall. Bowing, he held out a sealed scrollcase.

Lord Tasgall opened the scrollcase, drew out the scroll, and began to read. His countenance changed markedly, his eyebrows raised. He looked up, amazed.

"Do you know what this contains?" Lord Tasgall asked.

"Yes, my lord," answered the squire. "In case the message was lost, I committed it to memory to relate to you."

"Then do so," said Lord Tasgall, leaning on the table. "I want these gentlemen to hear. I want to hear myself," he added in a low voice, "for I can scarce believe what I have read."

"My lords," said the squire, facing them, "three weeks ago, the dragon Beryl launched an attack against the elven nation of Qualinesti."

The Knights nodded. None were surprised. Such an attack had been long foreseen. The messenger paused to draw breath and consider what he would say next. Gerard, in a fever of impatience to hear news of his friends in Qualinesti, was forced to clench his fists to keep from dragging the information out of the man's throat.

"My lord Warren regrets to report that the city of Qualinost was completely destroyed in the attack. If the reports we have received are to be believed, Qualinost has disappeared off the face of Ansalon. A great body of water covers the city."

The Knights stared, astounded.

"The elves did manage to take their enemy down with them. The dragon overlord, Beryl, is dead."

"Excellent news!" said Lord Ulrich.

"Perhaps there is a god, after all," said Lord Siegfried, making a weak joke at which no one laughed.

Gerard bounded across the room. Grasping the startled messenger by the collar, Gerard nearly lifted the young man off the floor. "What of the elves, damn you? The Queen Mother, the young king? What of them? What has happened to them?"

"Please, sir—" the messenger exclaimed, rattled.

Gerard dropped the gasping young man. "I beg your pardon, sir, my lords," he said, lowering his strident tones, "but I have recently been in Qualinesti, as you know, and I came to care deeply for these people."

"Certainly, we understand, Sir Gerard," said Lord Tasgall. "What news do you have of the king and the royal family?"

"According to the survivors who managed to reach Solace, the Queen Mother was killed in the battle with the dragon," said the messenger, eyeing Gerard distrustfully and keeping out of his reach. "She is being proclaimed a hero. The king is reported to have escaped safely and is said to be joining the rest of his people, who fled the dragon's wrath."

"At least with the dragon dead, the elves can now go back to Qualinesti," said Gerard, his heart heavy.

"I am afraid that is not the case, my lord," the messenger replied grimly. "For although the dragon is dead and her armies dispersed, a new commander arrived very shortly afterward to take control. He is a Knight of Neraka and claims he was present during the attack on Solanthus. He has rallied what was left of Beryl's armies and overrun Qualinesti. Thousands flock to his standard for he has promised wealth and free land to all who join him."

"What of Solace?" asked Lord Tasgall anxiously.

"For the moment, we are safe. Haven is free. Beryl's forces who held control of that city abandoned their posts and traveled south to be in on the looting of the elven nation. But my lord believes that once this Lord Samuval, as he calls himself, has a firm grip on Qualinesti, he will next turn his gaze upon Abanasinia. Thus does my lord request reinforcements. . . ."

The messenger paused, looked from one lord Knight to another. None met the man's pleading gaze. They looked at each other and then looked away. There were no reinforcements to send.

Gerard was so shaken that he did not immediately recognize the name Samuval and call to mind the man who had escorted him through Mina's camp. He would remember that only when he was on the road to Solanthus. For now, all he could think about was Laurana, dying in battle against the great dragon, and his friend and enemy, the Dark Knight commander, Marshal Medan. True, the Solamnics would never mention him or name Medan a hero, but Gerard guessed that if Laurana had died, the gallant Marshal had preceded her in death.

Gerard's heart went out to the young king, who must now lead his people in exile. Gilthas was so young to have such terrible responsibility thrust upon him, young and untried. Would he be up to the task? Could anyone, no matter how old and experienced, be up to that task?

"Sir Gerard . . ."

"Yes, my lord."

"You have leave to go. I suggest that you depart tonight. In all the turmoil, no one will think to question your disappearance. Do you have everything you need?"

"I need to make arrangements with the one who is to carry my messages, my lord." Gerard had no more luxury for sorrow. Someday, he hoped to have the chance to avenge the dead. But, for now, he had to make certain that he did not join them. "Once that is accomplished, I am ready to depart on the instant."

"My squire, Richard Kent, is young, but sensible, and an expert horseman," said Lord Tasgall. "I will appoint him to be your messenger. Would that be satisfactory?"

"Yes, my lord," said Gerard.

Richard was summoned. Gerard had seen the young man before and been impressed with him. The two soon settled where Richard was to wait to hear from Gerard and how they were going to communicate. Gerard saluted the Knights of the council, then departed.

Leaving the chapel of Kiri-Jolith, Gerard entered the sodden wet courtyard, ducked his head to keep the rain out of his eyes. His first thought was to find Odila, to see how she was faring. His second and better thought convinced him to leave her alone. She would ask questions about where he was going and what he was planning, and he'd been ordered to tell no one. Rather than lie to her, he decided it would be easier to not speak to her at all.

Taking a circuitous route to avoid the possibility of bumping into her or anyone else, he went to gather up what he needed. He did not take his armor, nor even his sword. Going to the kitchen, he packed some food in a saddlebag, snagged some water, and a thick cape that had been hung in front of the fire to dry. The cape was still damp in places and smelled strongly of wet sheep that had been baked in an oven, but it was ideal for his purpose. Clad only in his shirt and breeches, he wrapped himself in the cape and headed for the stables.

He had a long ride ahead of him—long, wet, and lonely.

9

The Plains of Dust

The rain that drenched the northlands of Ansalon and was such a misery to the Solamnic Knights would have been welcome to the elves in the south, who were just starting their journey through the Plains of Dust. The Qualinesti elves had always gloried in the sun. Their Tower was the Tower of the Sun; their king, the Speaker of the Sun. The sun's light banished the darkness and terrors of the night, brought life to the roses and warmth to their houses. The elves had loved even the new sun, that had appeared after the Chaos War, for though its light seemed feeble, pale, and sickly at times, it continued to bring life to their land.

In the Plains of Dust, the sun did not bring life. The sun brought death.

Never before had any elf cursed the sun. Now, after only a few days' travel through the empty, harsh land under the strange, glaring eye of this sun—an eye that was no longer pale and sickly but fierce and unforgiving as the eye of a vengeful goddess—the elves grew to hate the sun and cursed it bleakly as it rose with malevolent vindictiveness every morning.

The elves had done what they could to prepare for their journey, but none, except the runners, had ever traveled so far from their homeland, and they had no idea what to expect. Not even the runners, who maintained contact with Alhana Starbreeze of the Silvanesti, had ever crossed the Plains of Dust. Their routes took them north through the swamp land of the dragon overlord Onysablet. Gilthas had actually considered trying to travel these routes, but rejected the idea almost immediately. While one or two could creep through the swamps undetected by the dragon or the evil creatures who served her, an entire populace could not escape her notice. The runners reported that the swamp grew darker and more dangerous, as the dragon extended her control over the land, so that few who ventured into it these days came out alive.

The rebel elves—most of them Wilder elves, who were accustomed to living out-of-doors—had a better idea of what the people would face. Although none of them had ever ventured out into the desert, they knew that their lives might well depend on being able to flee at a moment's notice, and they knew better than to burden themselves with objects that are precious in life, but have no value to the dead.

The majority of the refugees had yet to learn this hard lesson. The Qualinesti elves had fled their homes, made a dangerous journey through dwarven tunnels or traveled by night under the shelter of the trees. Even so, many had managed to bring along bags and boxes filled with silken gowns, thick woolen robes, jewels and jewel boxes, books containing family histories, toys and dolls for the children, heirlooms of all types and varieties. Such objects held sweet remembrances of their past, represented their hope for the future.

Acting on the advice of his wife, Gilthas tried to convince the people that they should leave their heirlooms and jewels and family histories behind. He insisted that every person carry as much water as he or she could possibly manage, along with food enough for a week's journey. If that meant an elf maiden could no longer carry her dancing shoes, so be it. Most thought this stricture harsh in the extreme and grumbled incessantly. Someone came up with the idea of building a litter that could be dragged along behind and soon many of the elves began lashing together tree limbs to haul their goods. Gilthas watched and shook his head.

"You will never force them to abandon their treasures, my love," said the Lioness. "Do not try, lest they come to hate you."

"But they will never make it alive through the desert!" Gilthas gestured to an elven lord who had brought along most of his household possessions, including a small striking clock. "Don't they understand that?"

"No," the Lioness said bluntly, "but they will. Each person must make the decision to leave his past behind or die with it hanging about his neck. Not even his king can make that decision for him." Reaching out, she rested her hand over his. "Remember this, Gilthas, there are some who would *rather* die. You must steel yourself to face that."

Gilthas thought of her words as he trudged over the windswept rock that flowed like a harsh, hard, and barren red-orange sea to the blue horizon. Looking back across the land that shimmered in the hot sun, he saw his people straggling along behind. Distorted by the waves of heat rising from the rock, they appeared to waver in his vision, to lengthen and recede as he watched. He had placed the strongest at the rear of the group to assist those who were having difficulty, and he set the Wilder elves to keep watch along the flanks.

The first few days of their march, he had feared being attacked by the human armies rampaging through Qualinesti, but after traveling in the desert, he soon realized that here they were safe—safe because no one in his right mind would ever waste his energy chasing after them. Let the desert kill them, his enemies would say. Indeed, that seemed likely.

"We're not going to make it," Gilthas realized.

The elves did not know how to dress for the desert. They discarded their clothes in the heat and many were terribly burned by the sun. The litters now served a useful purpose—carrying those too burned or sick to walk. The heat sapped strength and energy, so that feet stumbled and heads bowed. As the Lioness had predicted, the elves began to divest themselves of their past. Although they left no mark on the rock, the tale of their passage could be read in the abandoned sacks and broken chests dumped off the litters or thrown down by weary arms.

Their pace was slow—heartbreakingly slow. According to the maps, they would have to cross two hundred and fifty miles of desert before they reached the remnants of the old King's Highway that led into

Silvanesti. Managing only a few miles a day, they would run out of both food and water long before they reached the midpoint. Gilthas had heard that there were places in the desert where one could find water, but these were not marked on the maps, and he didn't know how to locate them.

He had one hope—the hope that had led him to dare to make this treacherous journey. He must try to find the Plainspeople who made their homes in this forbidding, desolate land. Without their help, the Qualinesti nation would perish.

Gilthas had naively supposed that traveling the Plains of Dust was similar to traveling in other parts of Ansalon, where one could find villages or towns within a day's journey along the route. He had been told that there was a village of Plainspeople at a place called Duntol. The map showed Duntol to be due east from Thorbardin. The elves traveled east, walking straight into the morning sun, but they saw no signs of a village. Gazing across the empty expanse of glistening red rock, Gilthas could see for miles in all directions and in all directions he saw no sign of anything except more rock.

The people were drinking too much water. He ordered that waterskins be collected by the Wilder elves and rationed. The same with the food.

At the loss of their precious water, the elves became angry and afraid. Some fought, others pleaded with tears in their eyes. Gilthas had to be harsh and stern, and some of the elves turned from cursing the sun to cursing their king. Fortunately for Gilthas—his one single stroke of luck—Prefect Palthainon was so badly sunburned that he was too sick to cause trouble.

"When the water runs out, we can bleed the horses and live off their blood for a few days," said the Lioness.

"What happens when the horses die?" he asked.

She shrugged.

The next day, two of the sunburn victims died. The elves could not bury them, for no tool they owned would break through the solid rock. They could find no stones on the windswept plains to cover the bodies. They finally wrapped them in woolen capes and lowered the bodies with ropes into deep crevices in the rock.

Light-headed from walking in the blazing sun, Gilthas listened to the keening of those who mourned the dead. He stared down into the crevice and thought dazedly how blissfully cool it must be at the bottom. He felt a touch on his arm.

"We have company," said the Lioness, pointing north.

Gilthas shaded his eyes, tried to see against the harsh glare. In the distance, wavering in the heat, he could make out three riders on horseback. He could not discern any details—they were shapeless lumps of darkness. He stared until his eyes watered, hoping to see the riders approaching, but they did not move. He waved his arms and shouted until his parched throat was hoarse, but the riders simply stood there.

Unwilling to lose any more time, Gilthas gave the order for the people to start walking.

"Now the watchers are on the move," said the Lioness.

"But not toward us," said Gilthas, sick with disappointment.

The riders traveled parallel to the elves, sometimes vanishing from sight among the rocks, but always reappearing. They made their presence known, made the elves aware that they were being watched. The strange riders did not appear threatening, but they had no need to threaten. If they viewed the elves as an enemy, the blazing sun was the only weapon they required.

Hearing the wailing of children in his ears and the moans of the ill and dying, Gilthas could bear it no longer.

"You're going to talk to them," the Lioness said, her voice cracking from lack of water.

He nodded. His mouth was too parched to waste words.

"If they are Plainspeople, they have no love for strangers trespassing in their territory," she warned. "They might kill you."

He nodded again and took hold of her hand, raised it to his lips, kissed it. Turning his horse's head, he rode off toward the north, toward the strange riders. The Lioness called a halt to the march. The elves sank down on the burning rock. Some watched their young king ride off, but most were too tired and dispirited to care what happened to him or them.

The strange riders did not gallop forth to meet Gilthas, nor did they gallop off. They waited for him to come to them. He could still make out very few details, and as he drew closer, he could see why. The strangers were enveloped in white garments that covered them from head to toe, protecting them from the sun and the heat. He could also see that they carried swords at their sides.

Dark eyes, narrowed against the sun, stared at him from the shadows cast by the folds of cloth swathed

127

around their heads. The eyes were cold, dispassionate, gave no indication of the thoughts behind them.

One rider urged his horse forward, putting himself forth as the leader. Gilthas took note of him, but he kept glancing at a rider who kept slightly apart from the rest. This rider was extremely tall, towered over the heads of the others, and, although Gilthas could not say why, instinct led him to believe that the tall man was the person in charge.

The lead rider drew his sword, held it out before him and shouted out a command.

Gilthas did not understand the words. The gesture spoke for itself, and he halted. He raised his own sunburned hands to show that he carried no weapons.

"Bin'on du'auth," he said, as best he could talk for his cracked lips. "I give you greeting."

The stranger answered with a swarm of unfamiliar words that buzzed about the king's ears, all of them sounding alike, none making any sense.

"I am sorry," Gilthas said, flushing and shifting to Common, "but that is all I know of your language." Speaking was painful. His throat was raw.

Waving the sword, the stranger spurred his horse and rode straight at Gilthas. The king did not move, did not flinch. The sword whistled harmlessly past his head. The stranger wheeled, galloped back, bringing his horse to a halt in a flurry of sand and a fine display of riding skill.

He was about to speak, but the tall man raised his hand in a gesture of command. Riding forward, he eyed Gilthas approvingly.

"You have courage," he said, speaking Common.

"No," Gilthas returned. "I am simply too tired to move."

The tall man laughed aloud at this, but his laughter was short and abrupt. He motioned for his comrade to sheathe his sword, then turned back to Gilthas.

"Why do the elves, who should be living on their fat land, leave their fat land to invade ours?"

Gilthas found himself staring at the waterskin the man carried, a waterskin that was swollen and beaded with drops of cool water. He tore his gaze away and looked back at the stranger.

"We do not invade your land," he said, licking his dry lips. "We are trying to cross it. We are bound for the land of our cousins, the Silvanesti."

"You do not plan to take up residence in the Plains of Dust?" the tall man asked. He was not wasteful of his words, spoke only what was needful, no more, no less. Gilthas guessed that he was not one to waste anything on anyone, including sympathy.

"Trust me, no, we do not," said Gilthas fervently. "We are a people of green trees and cold, rushing water." As he spoke these words, a homesickness welled up inside him so that he could have wept. He had no tears. They had been burned away by the sun. "We must return to our forests, or else we will die."

"Why do you flee your green land and cold water?" the tall man asked.

Gilthas swayed in the saddle. He had to pause to try to gather enough moisture in his throat to continue speaking. He failed. His words came out a harsh whisper.

"The dragon, Beryl, attacked our land. The dragon is dead, but the capital city, Qualinost, was destroyed in the battle. The lives of many elves, humans, and dwarves were lost defending it. The Dark Knights now overrun our land. They seek our total annihilation. We are not strong enough to fight them, so we must—"

The next thing Gilthas knew, he was flat on his back on the ground, staring up at the unwinking eye of the vengeful sun. The tall man, wrapped in his robes, squatted comfortably at his side, while one of his comrades dribbled water into Gilthas's lips.

The tall man shook his head. "I do not know which is greater—the courage of the elves or their ignorance. Traveling in the heat of the day, without the proper clothing . . ." He shook his head again.

Gilthas struggled to sit up. The man giving him water shoved him back down.

"Unless I am much mistaken," the tall man continued, "you are Gilthas, son of Lauralanthalasa and Tanis Half-elven."

Gilthas stared, amazed. "How did you know?"

"I am Wanderer," said the tall man, "son of Riverwind and Goldmoon. These are my comrades." He did not name them, apparently leaving it up to them to introduce themselves, something they did not seem disposed to do. Obviously a people of few words. "We will help you," he added, "if only to speed you through our land."

The offer was not very gracious, but Gilthas took what he could get and was grateful for it.

"If you must know," Wanderer continued, "you have my mother to thank for your salvation. She sent me to search for you."

Gilthas could not understand this in the slightest, could only suppose that Goldmoon had received a vision of their plight.

"How is . . . your mother?" he asked, savoring the cool drops of tepid water that tasted of goat, yet were better to him than the finest wine.

"Dead," said Wanderer, gazing far off over the plains.

Gilthas was taken aback by his matter-of-fact tone. He was about to mumble something consoling, but the tall man interrupted him.

"My mother's spirit came to me the night before last, and told me to travel south. I did not know why, and she did not say. I thought perhaps I might find her body on this journey, for she told me that she lies unburied, but her spirit disappeared before she could tell me where."

Gilthas again began to stammer his regrets, but Wanderer paid no heed to his words.

"Instead," Wanderer said quietly, "I find you and your people. Perhaps you know how to find my mother?"

Before Gilthas could answer, Wanderer continued on. "I was told she fled the Citadel before it was attacked by the dragon, but no one knows where she went. They said that she was in the grip of some sort of madness, perhaps the scattered wits that come to the very old. She did not seem mad to me when I saw her spirit. She seemed a prisoner."

Gilthas thought privately that if Goldmoon was not mad, her son certainly was—all this talk of spirits and unburied bodies. Still, Wanderer's vision had saved their lives, and Gilthas could not very well argue against it. He answered only that he had no idea where Goldmoon was, or if she was dead or alive. His heart ached, for he thought of his own mother, lying unburied at the bottom of a new-formed lake. A great weariness and lethargy came over him. He wished he could lie here for days, with the taste of cool water on his lips. He had his people to think of, however. Resisting all admonitions to remain prone, Gilthas staggered to his feet.

"We are trying to reach Duntol," he said.

Wanderer rose with him. "You are too far south. You will find an oasis near here. There your people may rest for a few days and build up their strength before you continue your journey. I will send my comrades to Duntol for food and supplies."

"We have money to pay for it," Gilthas began. He swallowed the words when he saw Wanderer's face darken in anger. "We will find some way to repay you," he amended lamely.

"Leave our land," Wanderer reiterated sternly. "With the dragon seizing ever more land to the north, our resources are stretched as it is."

"We intend to," said Gilthas, wearily. "As I have said, we travel to Silvanesti."

Wanderer gazed long at him, seemed about to say more, but then apparently thought better of it. He turned to his companions and spoke to them in the language of the Plainspeople. Gilthas wondered what Wanderer had been about to say, but his curiosity evaporated as he concentrated on just remaining upright. He was glad to find that they had given his horse water.

Wanderer's two companions galloped off. Wanderer offered to ride with Gilthas.

"I will show you how to dress yourselves to protect your fair skin from the sun and to keep out the heat," Wanderer said. "You must travel in the cool of the night and the early morning, sleep during the heat of the day. My people will treat your sick and show you how to build shelters from the sun. I will guide you as far as the old King's Highway, which you will be able to follow to Silvanesti. You will take that road and leave our land and not return."

"Why do you keep harping on this?" Gilthas demanded. "I mean no offense, Wanderer, but I cannot imagine anyone in his right mind wanting to live in a place like this. Not even the Abyss could be more empty and desolate."

Gilthas feared his outburst might have angered the Plainsman and was about to apologize, when he heard what sounded like a smothered chuckle come from behind the cloth that covered Wanderer's face. Gilthas remembered Riverwind only dimly, when he and Goldmoon had visited his parents long ago, but he was suddenly reminded of the tall, stern-faced hunter.

"The desert has its own beauty," said Wanderer. "After a rain, flowers burst into life, scenting the air with their sweetness. The red of the rock against the blue of the sky, the flow of the cloud shadows over the rippling sand, the swirling dustdevils and the rolling tumbleweed, the sharp scent of sage. I miss these when I am gone from them, as you miss the thick canopy of incessantly dripping leaves, the continuous rain, the vines that tangle the feet, and the smell of mildew that clogs the lungs."

"One man's Abyss is another man's Paradise, it seems," said Gilthas, smiling. "You may keep your Paradise, Wanderer, and you are welcome to it. I will keep my trees and cool water."

"I hope you will," said Wanderer, "but I would not count upon it."

"Why?" Gilthas asked, alarmed. "What do you know?"

"Nothing for certain," said Wanderer. Checking his horse, he turned to face Gilthas. "I was of two minds whether to tell you this or not. These days, rumors drift upon the wind like the cottonwood seeds."

"Yet, obviously, you give this rumor credence," Gilthas said.

When Wanderer still did not speak, Gilthas added, "We intend to go to Silvanesti no matter what has happened. I assure you, we have no plans to remain any longer in the desert than is necessary for us to cross it."

Wanderer gazed out across the sand to the mass of elves, bright spots of color that had blossomed among the rocks without benefit of life-giving rain.

"The rumors say that Silvanesti has fallen to the Dark Knights." Wanderer turned his dark eyes to Gilthas. "You've heard nothing of this?"

"No," replied Gilthas. "I have not."

"I wish I could give you more details, but, needless to say, your people do not confide in us. Do you believe it?"

Even as Gilthas shook his head firmly in the negative, his heart sank. He might speak confidently before this stranger and before his people, but the truth was that he had heard nothing from the exiled Silvanesti queen, Alhana Starbreeze, in many weeks, not since before the fall of Qualinost. Alhana Starbreeze had been waging a concerted fight to reenter Silvanesti, to destroy the shield that surrounded it. The last Gilthas had heard, the shield had fallen and she and her forces were poised on the border, ready to enter her former homeland. One might argue that Alhana's messengers would have a difficult time finding him, since he'd been on the move, but the Silvanesti Wildrunners were friends with the eagles and the hawks and all whose sight was keen. If they had wanted to find him, they could have. Alhana had sent no runners, and perhaps this explained why.

Here was yet another burden to bear. If this was true, they were not fleeing danger, they were running headlong toward it. Yet, they could not stay in the desert.

At least if I have to die, let it be under a shade tree, Gilthas thought.

He straightened in the saddle. "I thank you for this information, Wanderer. Forewarned is forearmed. Now I should no longer delay telling my people that help is coming. How many days will take us to reach the King's Highway?"

"That depends on your courage," said Wanderer. Gilthas could not see the man's lips, due to the folds of cloth that swathed his face, but he saw the dark eyes warm with a smile. "If all your people are like you, I should not think the journey will take long at all."

Gilthas was grateful for the compliment. He wished he had earned it. What is taken for courage might only be exhaustion, after all.

10

Breaking Into Prison

Gerard planned to enter Solanthus on foot. He stabled the animal at a roadhouse about two miles from the city—a roadhouse recommended by young Richard. Taking the opportunity to eat a hot meal (about the best that could be said for it), Gerard caught up on the local gossip. He put out that he was a sell-sword, wondered if there might be work in the great city.

He was immediately told all he needed and more than he wanted to know about the disastrous rout of the Solamnic Knights and the takeover of the city by the Dark Knights of Neraka. There had not been many travelers after the fall of Solanthus several weeks ago, but the inn's mistress was hopeful that business would soon improve. Reports coming from Solanthus indicated that the citizens were not being tortured and slaughtered in droves as many had feared, but that they were well treated and encouraged to go about their daily lives as though nothing had happened.

Oh, certainly, a few people had been hauled off to prison, but they had probably deserved it. The person in charge of the Knights, who was said to be a slip of a girl, was not lopping off heads, but was preaching to the people of a new god, who had come to take care of them. She had gone so far as to order an old temple of Paladine cleaned out and restored, to be dedicated to this new god. She went about the city healing the sick and performing other miracles. The people of Solanthus were becoming enamored of her.

Trade routes between Solanthus and Palanthas, long closed, had now been reopened, which made the merchants happy. All in all, the innkeeper stated, things could be worse.

"I heard there were evil dragons about," Gerard said, dunking his stale bread in the congealing gravy, the only way to make either palatable. "And worse than that." He lowered his voice. "I heard that the dead walked in Solanthus!"

The woman sniffed. She'd heard something along these lines, but she'd seen nothing of any dragons herself, and no ghost had come to the roadhouse asking for food. Chuckling at her own humor, she went bustling off to provide indigestion to some other unsuspecting guest, leaving Gerard to feed the rest of his meal to the roadhouse dog and ponder what he'd heard.

He knew the truth of the matter. He'd seen the red and blue dragons flying above the city, and he'd seen the souls of the dead surrounding the city's walls. The hair still rose on the back of his neck whenever he thought about that army of empty eyes and gaping mouths, wispy hands with ragged fingers that stretched out to him over the gulf of death. No, that had been very real. Inexplicable, but real.

He was startled to hear that the people of Solanthus were being so well treated, but not much surprised to hear that they had apparently taken Mina to their hearts. He'd had only a brief talk with the charismatic leader of the Dark Knights, and yet he retained a vivid picture of her: he could see the fell, amber eyes, hear the timbre of her voice, recall every word she'd spoken. Did the fact that she was treating the Solanthians well make his job easier or more difficult? He argued one way and the other and at length came to the conclusion that the only way to find out was to go there and see for himself.

Paying for his meal and for the stabling of the horse for a week, Gerard set out for Solanthus on foot.

Coming within sight of the city walls, he did not immediately enter. He sat down in a grove of trees, where he could see but not be seen. He needed more information on the city, and he needed that information from a certain type of person. He had been sitting there for about thirty minutes when a wicket at the main gate opened up and several small bodies shot out, as though forcibly propelled from behind.

The small bodies picked themselves up, dusted themselves off as though this were nothing out of the ordinary, and, after shaking hands all round, set off upon their separate ways.

One of the small bodies happened to pass quite close to Gerard. He called out, accompanying his call with a friendly gesture, and the small body, which belonged to a kender, immediately came over to chat.

Reminding himself that this was for a worthy cause, Gerard braced himself, smiled in a friendly manner at the kender, and invited him to be seated.

"Goatweed Tangleknot," said the kender, by way of introduction. "My goodness, but you're ugly," he added cheerfully, peering up into Gerard's pock-marked face, admiring his corn-yellow and recalcitrant hair. "You're probably one of the ugliest humans I've ever met."

The Measure promised that all who made the supreme sacrifice for the sake of their country would be rewarded in the afterlife. Gerard figured that this particular experience should gain him a suite of rooms in some celestial palace. Gritting his teeth, he said he knew he wouldn't win any prizes as queen of the May dance.

"And you have *very* blue eyes," said Goatweed. "Uncomfortably blue, if you don't mind my saying so. Would you like to see what I have in my pouches?"

Before Gerard could answer, the kender dumped out the contents of several pouches and began happily to sort through them.

"You just left Solanthus," Gerard said, interrupting Goatweed in the middle of a story about how he'd come by a hammer that had once belonged to some unfortunate tinker. "What's it like inside there? I heard that it had been taken over by Dark Knights?"

Goatweed nodded vigorously. "It's about the same as usual. The guards round us up and throw us out. Except that now they take us first to this place that used to belong to the Mystics, and before that it was a temple of some old god or other. They brought in a group of Mystics from the Citadel of Light and talked to them. That was fun to watch, I tell you! A girl stood up in front of them, dressed up like a knight. She had very strange eyes. Very strange. Stranger than your eyes. She stood in front of the Mystics and told them all about the One God, and she showed them a pretty lady stored up in an amber box and told them that the One God had already performed one miracle and given the pretty lady her youth and beauty and the One God was going to perform another miracle and bring the pretty lady back to life.

"The Mystics stared at the pretty lady, and some of them began to cry. The girl asked the Mystics if they wanted to know more about this One God, and those who said they did were marched off one way, and those who said that they didn't were marched off another, including some old man called the Starmaster or something like that. And then the girl came to us and asked us lots of questions, and then she told *us* all about this new god who has come to Krynn. And then she asked us if we'd like to worship this new god and serve the new god."

"And what did you say?" Gerard was curious.

"Why, I said 'yes,' of course," said Goatweed, astonished that he could suppose otherwise. "It would be rude *not* to, don't you think? Since this new god has taken all this trouble to come here and everything, shouldn't we do what we can to be encouraging?"

"Don't you think it might be dangerous to worship a god you don't know anything about?"

"Oh, I know a lot about this god," Goatweed assured him. "At least, as much as seems important. This god has a great liking for kender, the girl told us. A very great liking. So great that this god is searching for one very special kender in particular. If any of us find this kender, we're supposed to bring him to the girl and she'll give us a huge reward. We all promised we would, and that's the very thing I'm off to do. Find this kender. You haven't seen him, by any chance?"

"You're the first kender I've seen in days," said Gerard. And hopefully the last, he added mentally. "How do you manage to get into the city without—"

"His name," said Goatweed, fixated on his quest, "is The Tasslehoff Burrfoot, and he—"

"Eh?" Gerard exclaimed, astonished. "What did you say?"

"Which time? There was what I said about Solanthus and what I said about the girl and what I said about the new god—"

"The kender. The special kender. You said his name was Burrfoot? Tasslehoff Burrfoot?"

"*The* Tasslehoff Burrfoot," Goatweed corrected. "The 'The' is very important because he can't be just any Tasslehoff Burrfoot."

"No, I guess he couldn't be," said Gerard, thinking back to the kender who had started this entire adventure by managing to get himself locked inside the Tomb of Heroes in Solace.

"Although, to make sure," Goatweed continued, "we're supposed to bring any Tasslehoff Burrfoot we find to Sanction for the girl to have a look at."

"You mean Solanthus," said Gerard.

Goatweed was absorbed in examining with interest a bit of broken blue glass. Holding it up, he asked eagerly, "Do you think that's a sapphire?"

"No," said Gerard. "It's a piece of broken blue glass. You said you were supposed to take this Burrfoot to

Sanction. You mean Solanthus. The girl and her army are in Solanthus, not Sanction."

"Did I say Sanction?" Goatweed scratched his head. After some thought, he nodded. "Yes, I said Sanction, and I meant Sanction. The girl told us that she wasn't going to be in Solanthus long. She and her army were all heading off to Sanction, where the new god was going to establish a huge temple, and it was in Sanction where she wanted to see Burrfoot."

That answers one of my questions, Gerard thought to himself.

"I think it's a sapphire," Goatweed added, and slid the broken glass back into his pouch.

"I once knew a Tasslehoff Burrfoot—" Gerard began hesitantly.

"Did you?" Goatweed leaped to his feet and began to skip around Gerard in excitement. "Where is he? How do I find him?"

"I haven't seen him for a long time," Gerard said, motioning the kender to calm down. "It's just that I was wondering what makes this Burrfoot so special."

"I don't think the girl said, but I may be mistaken. I'm afraid I dozed off for a bit at about that point. The girl kept us sitting there a very long time, and when one of us tried to get up to leave, a soldier stuck us with a sword, which isn't as exciting as it sounds like it might be. What was the question?"

Patiently, Gerard repeated it.

Goatweed frowned, a practice that is commonly known to aid the mental process, then said, "All I can remember is that he is very special to the One God. If you see this Tasslehoff friend of yours, will you be sure to tell him the One God is looking for him? And please mention my name."

"I promise," said Gerard. "And now, you can do me a favor. Say that a fellow had a very good reason for *not* entering Solanthus through the front gate, what's another way a fellow could get inside?"

Goatweed eyed Gerard shrewdly. "A fellow about your size?"

"About," said Gerard, shrugging.

"What would this information be worth to a fellow about your size?" Goatweed asked.

Gerard had foreseen this, and he brought forth a pouch containing an assortment of interesting and curious objects he'd appropriated from the manor house of Lord Ulrich.

"Take your pick," he said.

Gerard regretted this immediately, for Goatweed was thrown into an agony of indecision, dithering over the lot, finally ending up torn between a rusty caltrop and an old boot missing its heel.

"Take them both," Gerard said.

Struck by such generosity, Goatweed described a great many places whereby one could sneak unnoticed into Solanthus. Unfortunately, the kender's descriptions were more confusing than helpful, for he often jumped forward to add details about one he hadn't described yet or fell backward to correct information about one he'd described fifteen minutes earlier.

Eventually, Gerard pinned Goatweed down and made him go over each in detail—a time-consuming and frustrating process, during which Gerard came perilously close to strangling Goatweed. At length, Gerard had three locations in mind: one he deemed most suitable to his needs and the other two as backup. Goatweed required Gerard to swear on his yellow hair that he would never, never divulge the location of the sites to anyone. Gerard did so, wondering if Goatweed himself had taken that very same vow and considering it highly likely.

After this came the hard part. Gerard had to rid himself of the kender, who had by now decided that they were best friends, if not brothers or maybe cousins. The loyal Goatweed was quite prepared to travel with Gerard for the rest of his days. Gerard said that was fine with him, he was going to lounge about here for a good long while. Maybe take a nap. Goatweed was free to wait.

Fifteen minutes passed, during which the kender developed the fidgets and Gerard snoozed with one eye open to see that he didn't lose anything of value. Finally Goatweed could stand the strain no longer. He packed up his treasure and departed, coming back several times to remind Gerard that if he saw The Tasslehoff Burrfoot, he was to send him straight to the One God and mention that his friend Goatweed was to receive the reward. Gerard promised and finally managed to rid himself of the kender. He had several hours to wait until darkness, and he whiled away his time trying to figure out what Mina wanted with Tasslehoff Burrfoot.

Gerard couldn't imagine that Mina had any great love for kender. The magical Device of Time Journeying the kender carried was probably the prize the girl was after.

"Which means," said Gerard to himself, "that if the kender can be found, we should be the ones to find him."

He made a mental note to tell the Solamnic Knights to be on the lookout for any kender calling himself Tasslehoff Burrfoot and to seize and hold said kender for safekeeping and, above all, not let him fall into the hands of the Dark Knights. This settled, Gerard waited for nightfall.

II

The Prison House of Death

erard had no difficulty slipping unobserved into the city. Although his first choice had been blocked up—showing that the Dark Knights were working to stop up all the "rat holes"—they had not yet found the second. True to his vow, Gerard never revealed the location of the entrance site.

The streets of Solanthus were dark and empty. According to the innkeeper, a curfew had been imposed on the city. Patrols marched through the streets, forcing Gerard to duck and dodge to avoid them, sliding into a shadowed doorway, ducking behind piles of rubbish in an alleyway.

What with hiding from the patrols and an imperfect knowledge of the streets, Gerard spent a good two hours roaming about the city before he finally saw what he'd been looking for—the walls of the prison house.

He huddled inside a doorway, keeping watch and wondering how he was going to manage to sneak inside. This had always been the weak point of his plan. Breaking into a prison was proving just as difficult as breaking out.

A patrol marched into the courtyard, escorting several curfew violators. Listening as the guard made his report, Gerard found out that all the taverns had been shut down by order of the Dark Knights. A tavern owner, trying to cut his losses, had secretly opened his doors to a few regular customers. The private party had turned rowdy, drawing the attention of the patrols, and now the customers and the proprietor were all being incarcerated.

One of the prisoners was singing at the top of his lungs. The proprietor wrung his hands and demanded to know how he was supposed to feed his family if they took away his livelihood. Another prisoner was sick on the pavement. The patrol wanted to rid themselves of their onerous burden as quickly as possible, and they beat on the door, yelling for the gaoler.

He arrived, but he didn't look pleased. He protested that the jail cells were filled to overflowing, and he didn't have room for any more. While he and the patrol leader argued, Gerard slid out of his doorway, darted across the street, and took his place at the back of the group of prisoners.

He pulled the hood of his cloak over his head, hunched his shoulders, and crowded as close to the others as possible. One of the prisoners glanced at him, and his eyes blinked. Gerard held his breath, but after staring at him a moment, the man broke into a drunken grin, leaned his head on Gerard's shoulder, and burst into tears.

The patrol leader threatened to march away and leave the prisoners in the street, adding that he would most certainly report this obstruction of his duty to his superiors. Cowed, the gaoler flung open the door of the prison and shouted for the prison guards. The prisoners were handed over, and the patrol marched off.

The guards herded Gerard and the others into the cell block.

The moment the gaoler came in sight, the prisoners began shouting. The gaoler paid no attention to them. Shoving his prisoners into any cell that could accommodate them, the gaoler and his guards left with all haste.

The cell in which they stuffed Gerard was already so packed that he didn't dare sit down for fear of being trampled. Adjoining cells were just as bad, some filled with men, others with women, all of them clamoring to be set free. The stench of unwashed bodies, vomit, and waste was intolerable. Gerard retched and clamped his hand over his nose and mouth, trying desperately and unsuccessfully to filter the smell through his fingers.

Gerard shoved his way through the mass of bodies toward the back of the cell, as far from the overflowing slop bucket as he could manage. He had feared he and his clothes might look too clean for what he planned, but he no longer had to worry about that. A few hours in here and the stench would cling to him so that he doubted if he could ever be free of it. After a brief time spent convincing himself that he was not going to throw up, he noticed that a neighboring cell—one that was large and spacious— appeared to be empty.

Nudging one of his cellmates in the ribs, Gerard jerked a thumb in that direction.

"Why don't they put some of us in there?" he asked.

"You can go in there if you want to," said the prisoner, with a dark glance. "Me, I'll stay here."

"But it's empty," Gerard protested.

"No, it ain't. You just can't see 'em. Good thing, too." The man grimaced. "Bad enough lookin' at 'em by daylight."

"What are they?" asked Gerard, curious.

"Wizards," the man grunted. "At least, that's what they was. I ain't sure what they are now."

"Why? What's wrong with them?"

"You'll see," the man predicted dourly. "Now let me get some sleep, will you?"

Squatting down on the floor, the man closed his eyes. Gerard figured he should try to rest, too, although he guessed gloomily it would be impossible.

He was pleasantly amazed to wake up some hours later to find daylight struggling to make its way inside the slit windows. Rubbing the sleep from his eyes, he looked with interest at the occupants of the neighboring cell, wondering what made the wizards so very formidable.

Startled, Gerard pressed his face against the bars that separated the two cells.

"Palin?" Gerard called out in a low voice. "Is that you?"

He honestly wasn't certain. The mage looked like Palin. But if this was Palin, the usually conscientious mage had not bathed or shaved or combed his hair or taken any care of his appearance for weeks. He sat on a cot, staring at nothing, eyes empty, his face expressionless.

Another mage sat on another cot. This mage was an elf, so emaciated that he might have been a corpse. He had dark hair, unusual in the elves, who tended to be fair, and his skin was the color of bleached bone. He wore robes that might have started out black in color, but grime and dust had turned them gray. The elf sat still and lifeless as Palin, the same expression that was no expression on his face.

Gerard called Palin's name again, this time slightly louder so that it could be heard over the coughing, hacking, wheezing, shouting, and complaining of his fellow prisoners. He was about to call again when he was distracted by a tickling sensation on his neck.

"Damn fleas," he muttered, slapping at it.

The mage lifted his head, looked up.

"Palin! What are you doing here? What's happened to you? Are you hurt? Drat these fleas!" Gerard scrubbed viciously at his neck, wriggled about in his clothes.

Palin stared vacantly at Gerard for long moments, as if waiting for him to do something or say something more. When Gerard only repeated his earlier questions, Palin shifted his eyes away and once more stared at nothing.

Gerard tried several more times but finally gave up and concentrated on ridding himself of the itching vermin. He managed to do so at last, or so he assumed, for the tickling sensation ceased.

"What happened to those two?" Gerard asked his cellmate.

"Dunno," was the answer. "They were like that when I was brought here, and that was three days ago. Every day, someone comes in and gives 'em food and water and sees that they eat it. All day, they just sit like that. Gives a fellow the horrors, don't it."

Yes, Gerard thought, indeed it did. He wondered what had happened to Palin. Seeing splotches of what appeared to be dried blood on his robes, Gerard concluded that the mage had been beaten or tortured so much that his wits had left him. His heart heavy with pity, Gerard scratched absently at his neck, then turned away. He couldn't do anything to help Palin now, but, if all went as he planned, he might be able to do something in the future.

He squatted down in the cell, keeping his distance from a loathsome-looking straw mattress. He had no doubt that's where he'd picked up the fleas.

"Well, that was a waste of time," remarked Dalamar.

The elf's spirit lingered near the prison's single window. Even in this twilight world that he was forced to inhabit—neither dead nor alive—he felt as if he were suffocating inside the stone walls. He found it comforting at least to imagine he was breathing fresh air.

"What were you trying to accomplish?" he asked. "I take it you weren't indulging in a practical joke."

"No, no joke," said Palin's spirit quietly. "If you must know, I was hoping to be able to contact the man, to speak to him."

"Bah!" Dalamar snorted. "I would have thought you had more sense. He cares nothing for us. None of them do. Who is he, anyhow?"

"His name is Gerard. He's a Solamnic Knight. I knew him in Qualinesti. We were friends . . . well, maybe not friends. I don't think he liked me. You know how Solamnics feel about mages, and I wasn't very pleasant company, I have to admit. Still"—Palin remembered what it was to sigh—"I thought perhaps I might be able to communicate with him, just as my father was able to communicate with me."

"Your father loved you, and he had something of importance to relate to you," said Dalamar. "Besides, Caramon was quite thoroughly dead. We are not, at least I must suppose we are not. Perhaps that has something to do with it. What were you hoping he could do for you, anyhow?"

Palin was silent.

"Come now," said Dalamar. "We are hardly in a position to keep secrets from one another."

If that is true, Palin thought, then what do you do on those solitary rambles of yours? And don't tell me you are lingering beneath the pine trees to enjoy nature. Where do *you* go and why?

For a long time after their return from death, the mages' spirits remained tethered to the bodies they had once inhabited, as a prisoner is chained to a wall. Dalamar, restless, searching for a way back to life, was the first to discover that their bonds were self-created. Perhaps because they were not wholly dead, their spirits were not enslaved to Takhisis, as were the souls caught up in the river of the dead. Dalamar was able to sever the link that bound body and soul together. His spirit left its jail, left Solanthus, or so he told Palin, although he didn't say where he had gone. Yet, even though he could leave, the mage was always forced to return.

Their spirits tended to be as jealous of their bodies as any miser of the chest that holds his wealth. Palin had tried venturing out into the sad world of the

other imprisoned souls only to be consumed by fear
that something might happen to his body in his
absence. He flitted back to find it still sitting there,
staring at nothing. He knew he should feel glad, and
part of him was, but another part was bitterly disappointed. After that, he did not leave his body. He
could not join with the dead souls, who neither saw
nor heard him. He did not like to be around the living
for the same reason.

Dalamar was often away from his body, though
never for long. Palin was convinced that Dalamar
was meeting with Mina, trying to bargain with her
for the return of his life. He could not prove it, but he
was certain it was so.

"If you must know," said Palin, "I was hoping to
persuade Gerard to kill me."

"It would never work," said Dalamar. "Don't you
think I've already considered it?"

"It might," Palin insisted. "The body lives. The
wounds we suffered are healed. Killing the body again
might sever the cord that binds us."

"And once again, Takhisis would bring us back to
this charade of life. Haven't you figured out why?
Why does our Queen feed us and watch over us as
the *Shalafi* once fed and cared for those poor wretches
he termed the Live Ones? We are her experiment, as
they were his. The time will come when she will
determine if her experiment has succeeded or failed.
She will determine it. We will not. Don't you think
I've tried?"

He spoke the last bitterly, confirming Palin's sus-
picions.

"First," Palin said, "Takhisis is not my queen, so
don't include me in your thinking. Second, what do

you mean—experiment? She's obviously keeping us around to make use of the magical Device of Time Journeying, should she ever get hold of it."

"In the beginning that was true. But now that we've done so well—thrived, so to speak—she's starting to have other ideas. Why waste good flesh and bone by letting it rot in the ground when it could be animated and put to use? She already has an army of souls. She plans to augment her forces by creating an army of corpses to go along with it."

"You sound very certain."

"I am," said Dalamar. "One might say I've heard it from the horse's mouth."

"All the more reason for us to end this," said Palin firmly. "I—"

Dalamar's spirit made a sudden move, darted quickly back to be near the body.

"We are about to have visitors," he warned.

Guards entered the cells, dragging along several kender, tied together with ropes around their waists. The guards marched the kender through the cells to the clamorous amusement of the other prisoners. Then jeering and insults ceased abruptly. The prison grew hushed, quiet.

Mina walked along the rows of cells. She glanced neither to the right nor the left, took no interest in those behind the bars. Some of the prisoners looked at her with fear, some shrank from her. Others reached out their hands in wordless pleading. She ignored them all.

Halting in front of the cell in which the bodies of the two mages were incarcerated, Mina took hold the rope and dragged the assorted kender forward.

"Every one of them claims to be Tasslehoff Burrfoot,"

she said, speaking to the corpses. "Is one of these the kender I seek? Do either of you recognize him?"

Dalamar's corpse responded with a shake of the head.

"Palin Majere?" she asked. "Do you recognize any of these kender?"

Palin could tell at a glance that none of them were Tasslehoff, but he refused to answer. If Mina imagined she had the kender, let her waste her time finding out otherwise. He sat there, did nothing.

Mina was not been pleased at his show of defiance.

"Answer me," she commanded. "You see the shining light, the realms beyond?"

Palin saw them. They were his constant hope, his constant torment.

"If you have any thought of freedom, of obtaining your soul's wish to leave this world, you will answer me."

When he did not, she clasped her hand around the medallion she wore at her throat.

"Just tell her!" Dalamar hissed at him. "What does it matter? A simple search of the kender will reveal that they don't have the device. Save your defiance for something truly important."

Palin's corpse shook its head.

Mina released her hold on the medallion. The kender, most of them protesting that they were too The Tasslehoff Burrfoot, were marched away.

Watching them go, Palin wondered how Tasslehoff—the real one—had managed to evade capture for so long. Mina and her God were both growing increasingly frustrated.

Tasslehoff and his device were the bedbugs keeping the Queen from having a really good night's sleep. The knowledge of her vulnerability must nip at her constantly, for no matter how powerful she grew, the kender was out there when and where he should not be.

If anything happened to him—and what kender ever lived to a ripe old age?—Her Dark Majesty's grand schemes and plans would come to naught. That might be a comforting thought, but for the fact that Krynn and its people would come to naught, as well.

"All the more reason to remain alive," Dalamar stated with vehemence, speaking to Palin's thoughts. "Once you join that river of death, you will drown and be forever at the mercy of the tide, as are those poor souls who are out there now. We still have a modicum of free will, as you just discovered. That is the flaw in the experiment, the flaw that Takhisis has yet to correct. She has never liked the concept of freedom, you know. Our ability to think and act for ourselves has always been her greatest enemy. Unless she somehow finds a way to deprive us of that, we must cling to our one strength, keep fast hold of it. Our chance will come, and we must be ready to seize it."

Our chance or yours? Palin wondered. He was half-amused by Dalamar, half-angry at him, and on reflection, wholly ashamed of himself.

As usual, he thought, I've been sitting around feeling sorry for myself while my self-serving, ambitious colleague has been out and doing. No more. I will be just as selfish, just as ambitious as any two Dalamars. I may be lost in a foreign country, hobbled hand and foot, where no one speaks my language and they are all deaf, dumb, and blind to boot. Yet, some way, some how, I will find someone who sees me, who hears me, who understands me.

Your experiment will fail, Takhisis, Palin vowed. The experiment itself will see to that.

12

In the Presence of the God

The day Gerard spent in the cell was the worst day of his life. He hoped he would grow used to the smell, but that proved impossible, and he caught himself seriously wondering if breathing was actually worth it. The guards tossed food inside and brought buckets of water for drinking, but the water tasted like the smell, and he gagged as he swallowed. He was gloomily pleased to note that the day gaoler, who appeared none too intelligent, was, if possible, more harassed and confused than the night man.

Late in the afternoon, Gerard began to think that he'd miscalculated, that his plan wasn't as good as he'd thought and that there was every possibility he would spend the rest of his life in this cell. He'd been caught by surprise when Mina had entered the cells, accompanying the kender. She was the last person he wanted to see. He kept his face hidden, remained crouched on the floor until she had gone.

After a few more hours, when it appeared that no one else was likely to come, Gerard was beginning to have second thoughts about this mission. Suppose no one came? He was reflecting that he wasn't nearly as smart as he'd thought he was, when he heard a sound that improved his spirits immensely—the rattle of steel, the clank of a sword.

Prison guards carried clubs, not swords. Gerard leaped to his feet. Two members of the Dark Knights of Neraka entered the prison cells. They wore their helmets with the visors lowered (probably to keep out the smell), cuirasses over woolen shirts, leather breeches, and boots. They kept their swords sheathed but their hands on the hilts.

Immediately the prisoners set up a clamor, some demanding to be freed, others pleading to be able to talk to someone about the terrible mistake that had been made. The Dark Knights ignored them. They headed for the cell where the two mages sat staring at the walls, oblivious to the uproar.

Lunging forward, Gerard managed to thrust his arm between the bars and seize hold of the sleeve of one of the Dark Knights. The man whipped around. His companion drew his sword, and Gerard might have lost his hand had he not snatched it away.

"Captain Samuval!" Gerard shouted. "I must see Captain Samuval."

The Knight's eyes were glints of light in the shadow of his helm. He lifted his visor to get a better view of Gerard.

"How do you know Captain Samuval?" he demanded.

"I'm one of you!" Gerard said desperately. "The Solamnics captured me and locked me up in here. I've been trying to convince the great oaf who runs this place to set me free, but he won't listen. Just bring Captain Samuval here, will you? He'll recognize me."

The Knight stared at Gerard a moment longer, then snapped his visor shut and walked over to the cell that held the mages. Gerard could do nothing more but hope that the man would tell someone, would not leave him here to die of the stink.

The Dark Knights escorted Palin and his fellow mage out of the cellblock. The prisoners fell back as the mages shuffled past, not wanting anything to do with them. The mages were gone for more than an hour. Gerard spent the time wondering if the Knight would tell someone. Hopefully, the name of Captain Samuval would spur the Knight to action.

The clanking of swords announced the Knights' return. They deposited their catatonic charges back on their cots. Gerard hastened forward to try to talk to the Dark Knight again. The prisoners were banging on the cell bars and shrieking for the guards when the commotion suddenly ceased, some swallowing their cries so fast that they choked.

A minotaur entered the cells. The beast-man, who had the face of a bull made even more ferocious by the intelligent eyes that looked out of the mass of shaggy brown fur, was so tall that he was forced to walk with his head bowed to avoid raking his sharp horns against the low ceiling. He wore a leather harness that left bare his muscular torso. He was armed with numerous weapons, among them a heavy sword that Gerard doubted he could have lifted with two hands. Gerard guessed rightly that the minotaur was coming to see him, and he didn't know whether to be worried or thankful.

As the minotaur approached his cell, the other prisoners scrambled to see who could reach the back fastest. Gerard had the front of the cell all to himself. He tried desperately to remember the minotaur's name, but it eluded him.

"Thank goodness, sir," he said, making do. "I was beginning to think I'd rot in here. Where's Captain Samuval?"

"He is where he is," the minotaur rumbled. His small, bovine eyes fixed on Gerard. "What do you want with him?"

"I want him to vouch for me," said Gerard. "He'll remember me, I'm sure. You might remember me, too, sir. I was in your camp just prior to the attack on Solanthus. I had a prisoner—a female Solamnic Knight."

"I remember," said the minotaur. The eyes narrowed. "The Solamnic escaped. She had help. Yours."

"No, sir, no!" Gerard protested indignantly. "You've got it all wrong! Whoever helped her, it wasn't me. When I found out she was gone, I chased after her. I caught her, too, but we were close to the Solamnic lines. She shouted, and before I could shut her up"— he drew his hand across his throat—"the Solamnics came to her rescue. They took me prisoner, and I've been locked here ever since."

"Our people checked to see if there were any Knights being held prisoner after the battle," said the minotaur.

"I tried to tell them then," said Gerard, aggrieved. "I've been telling them ever since! No one believes me!"

The minotaur said nothing in reply, just stood staring. Gerard had no way of knowing what the beastman was thinking beneath those horns.

"Look, sir," said Gerard, exasperated, "would I be in this stinking hole if my story wasn't true?"

The minotaur stared at Gerard a moment longer. Turning on his heel, he stalked off to the end of the corridor to confer with the gaoler. Gerard saw the jailer peer at him and then shake his head and fling up his hands helplessly.

"Let him out," ordered the minotaur.

The gaoler hurried to obey. Fitting the key in the lock, he opened the cell door. Gerard walked out to the tune of muttered curses and threats from his fellow prisoners. He didn't care. At that moment, he could have hugged the minotaur, but he thought his reaction should be one of indignation, not relief. He flung a few curses himself and glowered at the gaoler.

The minotaur laid a heavy hand on Gerard's shoulder. The hand was not there in the spirit of friendship. The minotaur's nails dug painfully into Gerard's shoulder.

"I will take you to Mina," said the minotaur.

"I plan to pay my respects to Lord of the Night Mina," said Gerard, "but I can't appear before her like this. Give me some time to wash up and find some decent clothes—"

"She will see you as you are," said the minotaur, adding, as an afterthought, "She sees all of us as we are."

This being precisely what he feared, Gerard was not in the least eager to be interviewed by Mina. He had hoped to be able to retrieve his knightly accoutrements (he knew the storehouse where the Solamnics had stashed them) and blend in with the crowd, hang about the barracks with the other Knights and soldiers, pick up the latest gossip, discover who'd been given orders to do what, then leave to make his report.

There was no help for it, however. The minotaur (whose name was Galdar, Gerard finally remembered), marched Gerard out of the prison. Gerard cast a last glance at Palin as he left. The mage had not moved.

Shaking his head, feeling a shiver run through him, Gerard accompanied the minotaur through the streets of Solanthus.

If anyone would know Mina's plans, it was Galdar. The minotaur was not the talkative type, however. Gerard mentioned Sanction a couple of times, but the minotaur answered only with a cold, dark glower. Gerard gave up and concentrated on seeing what he could of life in Solanthus. People were out in the streets, going about their daily routine, but they did so in a fearful and hurried manner, keeping their heads down, not wanting to meet the eyes of the numerous patrols.

All the taverns were closed, their doors ceremoniously sealed by a band of black cloth that had been stretched across them. Gerard had always heard the saying about courage being found at the bottom of a jug of dwarf spirits, and he supposed that was why the taverns had been shut down. The black cloth was stretched across other shops, as well—most notably mageware shops and shops that sold weapons.

They came within sight of the Great Hall, where Gerard had been brought to trial. Memories came back to him forcibly, particularly memories of Odila. She was his closest friend, his only friend, really, for he was not the type to make friends easily. He was sorry now that he hadn't said good-bye to her and at least given her some hint of what he planned.

Galdar steered Gerard past the Great Hall. The building teemed with soldiers and Knights, for it had apparently been taken over as a barracks. Gerard thought they might stop here, but Galdar led him to the old temples that stood near the hall.

These temples had been formerly dedicated to the gods most favored by the Knights—Paladine and Kiri-Jolith. The temple of Kiri-Jolith was the older of the two and slightly larger, for Kiri-Jolith was considered the Solamnics' special patron. Paladine's temple, constructed of white marble, drew the eye with its simple but elegant design. Four white columns adorned the front. Marble steps, rounded so that they resembled waves, flowed down from the portico.

The two temples were attached by a courtyard and a rose garden. Here grew the white roses, the symbol of the Knighthood. Even after the departure of the gods and, subsequently, the priests, the Solamnics had kept up the temples and tended the rose gardens. The Knights had used the temples for study or for meditation. The citizens of Solanthus found them havens of peace and tranquility and could often be seen walking here with their families.

"Not surprising this One God looks on them with covetous eyes," Gerard said to himself. "I'd move here in a minute if I were out wandering the universe, searching for a home."

A large number of the citizens stood gathered around the outer doors of the temple of Paladine. The doors were closed, and the crowd appeared to be awaiting admittance.

"What's going on, sir?" Gerard asked. "What are all these people doing here? They aren't threatening to attack, are they?"

A tiny smile creased the minotaur's muzzle. He almost chuckled. "These people have come to hear about the One God. Mina speaks to crowds like this every day. She heals the sick and performs other miracles. You will find many residents of Solanthus worshiping in the temple."

Gerard had no idea what to say to this. Anything that came to mind would only land him in trouble and so he kept his mouth shut. They were walking past the rose garden when a brilliant flash of sunlight reflecting off amber caught his eye. He blinked, stared, then stopped so suddenly that Galdar, irritated, almost yanked off his arm.

"Wait!" Gerard cried, appalled. "Wait a minute." He pointed. "What is that?"

"The sarcophagus of Goldmoon," said Galdar. "She was once the head of the Mystics of the Citadel of Light. She was also the mother of Mina—her adopted mother," he felt compelled to add. "She was an old, old woman. Over ninety, so they say. Look at her. She is young and beautiful again. Thus does the One God grant favor to the faithful."

"A lot of good that does her if she's dead," Gerard muttered, his heart aching, as he looked at the body encased in amber. He remembered Goldmoon vividly, remembered her beautiful, golden hair that seemed spun with silver moonbeams, remembered her face, strong and compassionate and lost, searching. He couldn't find the Goldmoon he had known, though. Her face, seen beneath the amber, was the face of no one, anyone. Her gold and silver hair was amber-colored. Her white robes amber. She'd been caught in the resin, like all the rest of the insects.

"She will be granted life again," said Galdar. "The One God has promised to perform a great miracle."

Gerard heard an odd tone in Galdar's voice and he glanced, startled, at the minotaur. Disapproving? That was hard to be believe. Still, as Gerard thought back over what he knew of the minotaur race, he had always heard them described as devout followers of their former god, Sargonnas, who was himself a minotaur. Perhaps Galdar was having second thoughts about this One God. Gerard marked that down as a hunch he might be able to make use of later.

The minotaur gave Gerard a shove, and he had to continue walking. He looked back at the sarcophagus. Many of the citizenry were standing around the amber coffin, gaping at the body inside and sighing and ooohing and aahing. Some were on their knees in prayer. Gerard kept twisting his head to look around, forgot to watch where he was going, and tripped over the temple stairs. Galdar growled at him, and Gerard realized he had better keep his mind on his own business or he'd end up in a coffin himself. And the One God wasn't likely to perform any miracle on him.

The temple doors opened for Galdar, then shut behind him, to the great disappointment of those waiting outside.

"Mina!" they called out, chanting her name. "Mina! Mina!"

Inside, the temple was shadowed and cool. The pale light of the sun, that seemed to have to work hard to shine through the stained glass windows, formed weak and watery patterns of blue, white, green, and red on the floor, criss-crossed with black bars. The altar had been covered with a cloth of white velvet. A single person knelt there. At the sound of their foot-falls in the still temple, the girl raised her head and glanced over her shoulder.

"I am sorry to disturb you in your prayers, Mina," said Galdar in a subdued voice that echoed eerily in the still temple, "but this is a matter of importance. I found this man in the prison cells. You may remember him. He—"

"Sir Gerard," said Mina. Rising, she moved away from the altar, walked down the central aisle. "Gerard uth Mondar. You brought that young Solamnic Knight to us. Odila was her name. She escaped."

Gerard had his story all ready, but his tongue stuck firmly to the roof of his mouth. He had not thought he could ever forget those amber eyes, but he had forgot-ten the powerful spell they could cast over any person caught in their depths. He had the feeling that she knew all about him, knew everything he had done since they last parted, knew exactly why he was here. He could lie to her, but he would be wasting his time.

Still, he had to try, futile as it might be. He stumbled through his tale, thinking all the while that he sounded exactly like a guilty child lying to avoid the strap and the woodshed.

Mina listened to him with grave attention. He ended by saying that he hoped that he would be per-mitted to serve her, since he understood that his former commander, Marshal Medan, had died in the battle of Qualinesti.

"You grieve for the Marshal and for the Queen Mother, Laurana," said Mina.

Gerard stared at her, dumbfounded.

She smiled, the amber eyes shone. "Do not grieve for them. They serve the One God in death as they both unwittingly served the One God in life. So do we all serve the One God, whether we will or no. The rewards are greater for those who serve the One God knowingly, however. Do you serve the One God, Gerard?"

Mina came nearer to him. He saw himself small and insignificant in her amber eyes, and he suddenly wanted very much to do something to make her proud of him, to win her favor.

He could do so by swearing to serve the One God, yet in this, if in nothing else, he must speak the truth. He looked at the altar, and he listened to the stillness, and it was then he knew for a certainty that he was in the presence of a god and that this god saw through to his very heart.

"I . . . I know so little of this One God," he stammered evasively. "I cannot give you the answer you want, Lady. I am sorry."

"Would you be willing to learn?" she asked him.

"Yes" was all he needed to say to remain in her service, yet the truth was that he didn't want to know anything at all about this One God. Gerard had always done very well without the gods. He didn't feel comfortable in the presence of this one.

He mumbled something unintelligible, even to himself. Mina seemed to hear what she wanted to hear from him, however. She smiled.

"Very well. I take you into my service, Gerard uth Mondar. The One God takes you into service, as well."

At this, the minotaur made a disgruntled rumbling sound.

"Galdar thinks you are a spy," said Mina. "He wants to kill you. If you are a spy, I have nothing to hide. I will tell you my plans freely. In two days time, an army of soldiers and Knights from Palanthas will join us, adding another five thousand to our number. With that army and the army of souls, we will march on Sanction. And we will take it. Then we will rule all of the northern part of Ansalon, well on our way to ruling all of this continent. Do you have any questions?"

Gerard ventured a feeble protest. "Lady, I am not—"

Mina turned from him. "Open the doors, Galdar," she ordered. "I will speak to the people now." Glancing back at Gerard, she added, "You should stay to hear the sermon, Sir Gerard. You might find my words instructive."

Gerard could do nothing but acquiesce. He glanced sidelong at Galdar, caught the minotaur glowering back at him. Clearly, Galdar knew him for what he was. Gerard must take care to keep out of the minotaur's way. He supposed he should be thankful, for he'd accomplished his mission. He knew Mina's plans—always provided she was telling the truth—and he had only to hang about for a couple of days to see if the army from Palanthas showed up to confirm it. His heart was no longer in his mission, however. Mina had killed his spirit, as effectively as she might have killed his body.

We fight against a god. What does it matter what we do?

Galdar flung wide the temple doors. The people streamed inside. Kneeling before Mina, they pleaded with her to touch them, to heal them, to heal their children, to take away their pain. Gerard kept an eye on Galdar. The minotaur watched a moment, then walked out.

Gerard was about to sidle out the door when he saw a troop of Knights marching up the stairs. They had with them a prisoner, a Solamnic, to judge by the armor. The prisoner's arms were bound with bow-strings, but she walked with her head held high, her face set in grim determination.

Gerard knew that face, knew the expression on that face. He groaned softly, swore vehemently, and hastily drew back into the deepest shadows, covering his face with his hands as though overcome by reverence.

"We captured this Solamnic trying to enter the city, Mina," said one of the Knights.

"She's a bold one," said another. "Walked right in the front gate wearing her armor and carrying her sword."

"Surrendered her sword without a fight," added the first. "A fool and a coward, like all of them."

"I am no coward," said Odila with dignity. "I chose not to fight. I came here of my own accord."

"Free her," said Mina, and her voice was cold and stern. "She may be our enemy, but she is a Knight and deserves to be treated with dignity, not like a common thief!"

Chastened, the Knights swiftly removed the bindings from Odila's arms. Gerard had stepped into the shadows, afraid that if she looked around and saw him, she might give him away. He soon realized he could spare himself the worry. Odila had no eyes for anyone except Mina.

"Why have you come all this way and risked so much to see me, Odila?" Mina asked gently.

Odila sank to her knees, clasped her hands.

"I want to serve the One God," she said.

Mina bent down, kissed Odila on the forehead.

"The One God is pleased with you."

Mina removed the medallion she wore on her breast, fastened the medallion around Odila's neck.

"You are my cleric, Odila," said Mina. "Rise and know the blessings of the One God."

Odila rose, her eyes shining with exaltation. Walking to the altar, she joined the other worshipers, knelt in prayer to the One God. Gerard, a bitter taste in his mouth, walked out.

"Now what in the Abyss do I do?" he wondered.

13

The Convert

Absorbed into the main body of the Dark Knights of Neraka, Gerard was assigned to patrol duty. Every day, he and his small band of soldiers marched through their assigned portion of Solanthus, keeping the populace in check. His task was not difficult. The Dark Knights under Mina's command had acted swiftly to round up any members of the community who might have given them trouble. Gerard had seen most of them inside the prison.

As for the rest, the people of Solanthus appeared to be in a state of shock, stunned by the recent, disastrous turn of events. One day they were living in the only free city in Solamnia, and the next day their city was occupied by their most hated enemy. Too much had happened too quickly for them to comprehend. Given time, they might organize and become dangerous.

Or they might not.

Always a devout people, the Solamnics had grieved over the absence of their gods. Feeling an absence and a lacking in their lives, they were interested in hearing about this One God, even if they didn't plan on believing what they heard. The adage goes that while elves strive to be worthy of their gods, humans require that their gods be worthy of them. The citizens of Solanthus were naturally skeptical.

Every day, the sick and the wounded came or were carried to the former temple of Paladine, now the temple of the One God. The lines for miracles were long and the lines waiting to view the miracle maker were longer still. The elves of far-off Silvanesti, so Mina had told them, had bowed down to the One God and proclaimed their devotion. By contrast, the humans of Solanthus started fistfights, as those who believed in the miracles took umbrage with those who claimed they were tricks. After two days of patrol duty, Gerard was ordered to cease walking the streets (where nothing happened) and to start breaking up fights in the temple.

Gerard didn't know if he was glad for this change in assignment or not. He'd spent the last two days trying to decide if he should confront Odila and try to talk some sense into her or if he should continue to avoid her. He didn't think she'd give him away, but he wasn't certain. He couldn't understand her sudden religious fervor and therefore no longer trusted her.

Gerard had never really been given the choice of worshiping the gods, so he hadn't wasted much thought on the matter. The presence or absence of the gods had never made much difference to his parents. The only change that had occurred in their lives when the gods left was that one day they said prayers at the table and the next day they didn't. Now Gerard was being forced to think about it, and in his heart he could sympathize with those who started the fights. He wanted to punch someone, too.

Gerard sent off his report to Richard, who was waiting for it at the roadhouse. He gave the Knights' Council all the information he'd gleaned, confirming that Mina planned to march to Sanction.

Counting the reinforcements expected to arrive from Palanthas, Mina had over five thousand soldiers and Knights under her command. A small force, yet with this force she planned to take the walled city that had held out against double that number of troops for over a year. Gerard might have laughed at the notion, except that she'd taken Solanthus—a city considered impregnable—with far fewer troops than that. She'd taken Solanthus using dragons and the army of souls, and she spoke of using dragons and the army of souls to take Sanction. Recalling the terror of that night he'd fought the dead, Gerard was convinced that nothing could withstand them. He said as much to the Knights' Council, although they hadn't asked for his opinion.

His assignment now completed, he could have left Solanthus, returned to the bosom of the Solamnic Knighthood. He stayed on, however, at risk of his life, he supposed, for Galdar considered him a spy. If that was true, no one paid much attention to him. No one watched him. He was not restricted in his movements. He could go anywhere, talk to anyone. He was not admitted to Mina's inner circle, but he didn't lose by that, for apparently Mina had no secrets. She freely told everyone who asked what she and the One God meant to do. Gerard was forced to concede that such supreme confidence was impressive.

He stayed in Solanthus, telling himself that he would remain to see if Mina and her troops actually marched out, headed east. In truth, he was staying because of Odila, and the day he took up his duties at the temple was the day he finally admitted as much to himself.

Gerard stationed himself at the foot of the temple steps, where he could keep a watchful eye on the crowd, who had gathered to hear Mina speak. He posted his men at intervals around the courtyard, trusting that the sight of armed soldiers would intimidate most of the troublemakers. He wore his helmet, for there were those in Solanthus who might recognize him.

Mina's own Knights, under the command of the minotaur, surrounded her, kept watch over her, guarding her not so much from those who would do her harm, but from those who would have adored her to death. Her speech concluded, Mina walked among the crowd, lifting up children in her arms, curing the sick, telling them all of the One God. The skeptical watched and jeered, the faithful wept and tried to fling themselves at Mina's feet. Gerard's men broke up a few fights, hauled the combatants off to the already crowded prisons.

When Mina's steps began to falter, the minotaur stepped in and called a halt. The people still waiting for their share of the miracles groaned and wailed, but he told them to come back tomorrow.

"Wait a moment, Galdar," said Mina, her voice carrying clearly over the tumult. "I have good news to tell the people of Solanthus."

"Silence!" Galdar shouted, but the effort was needless. The crowd immediately hushed, leaned forward eagerly to hear her words.

"People of Solanthus," Mina cried. "I have just received word that the dragon overlord, Khellendros, also known as Skie, is dead. Only a few days earlier, I told you that the dragon overlord, Beryl, was dead, as well as the wicked dragon known as Cyan Bloodbane."

Mina raised her arms and her eyes to the heavens. "Behold, in their defeat, the power of the One God!"

"Khellendros dead?" The whisper went through the crowd, as each person turned to his neighbors to see what their reaction was to such astonishing news.

Khellendros had long ruled over much of the old nation of Solamnia, exacting tribute from the citizens of Palanthas, using the Dark Knights to keep the people in line and the steel flowing into the dragon's coffers. Now Khellendros was dead.

"So when does this One God go after Malys?" someone yelled.

Gerard was appalled to find that the someone was himself.

He'd had no idea he was going to shout those words. They'd burst out before he could stop them. He cursed himself for a fool, for the last thing he wanted to do was draw attention to himself. Snapping shut the visor of his helm, he glared around, as if searching for the person who had spoken. He did not fool Mina, however. Her amber gaze pierced the eyeslits of his helmet with unerring accuracy.

"After I have taken Sanction," Mina said coolly, "then I will deal with Malys."

She acknowledged the cheers of the crowd with a gesture toward heaven, indicating that their praise belonged to the One God, not to her. Turning, she disappeared inside the temple.

Gerard's skin burned so hot it was a wonder that his steel helm didn't melt around his ears. He expected to feel the heavy hand of the minotaur close around his neck any moment, and when someone touched his shoulder, he nearly crawled out of his armor.

"Gerard?" came a puzzled voice. "Is that you in there?"

"Odila!" he gasped in relief, uncertain whether to hug her or hit her.

"So now you're back to being a Dark Knight," she said. "I must concede that drawing your pay from two coffers is a good way to make a living, but don't you find yourself getting confused? Do you flip a coin? 'Which armor do I put on this morning? Heads Dark Knight, tails Solamnic—'"

"Just shut up, will you," Gerard growled. Grabbing her by the arm, he glanced around to see if anyone had been listening, then hauled her off to a secluded part of the rose garden. "Apparently finding religion hasn't caused you to lose your twisted sense of humor."

He yanked off his helm, glared at her. "You know perfectly well why I'm here."

She eyed him, frowning. "You didn't come after me, did you?"

"No," he answered, which was truth enough.

"Good," she said, her face clearing.

"But now that you mention it—" Gerard began.

Her frown returned.

"Listen to me, Odila," he said earnestly, "I came at the behest of the Knights' Council. They sent me to find out if Mina's threat to attack Sanction is real—"

"It is," said Odila coolly.

"I know that now," said Gerard. "I'm on an intelligence-gathering mission—"

"So am I," she said, interrupting, "and my mission is far more important than yours. You are here to gain information about the enemy. You are here to listen at keyholes and count the numbers of troops and how many siege engines they have."

She paused. Her gaze shifted to the temple. "I am here to find out about this god."

Gerard made a sound.

She looked back at him. "We Solamnics can't ignore this, Gerard, just because it makes us uncomfortable. We can't deny this god because the god came to an orphan girl and not to the Lord of the Rose. We have to ask questions. It is only in the asking that we find answers."

"And what have you found out?" Gerard asked unwillingly.

"Mina was raised by Goldmoon at the Citadel of Light. Yes, I was surprised to hear that myself. Goldmoon told Mina stories of the old gods, how she—Goldmoon—brought knowledge of the gods back to the people of Ansalon when everyone thought the gods had left the world in anger. Goldmoon showed them that it was not the gods who had left mankind but mankind who had left the gods. Mina asked if that might be what was happening now, but Goldmoon told her no, that this time the gods had gone, for there were those who spoke to Paladine and the other gods before they left and who were told that the gods departed the world to spare the world the wrath of Chaos.

"Mina didn't believe this. She knew in her heart that Goldmoon was wrong, that there was a god on this world. It was up to Mina to find the god, as Goldmoon had once found the gods. Mina ran away. She searched for the gods, always keeping her heart open to hear the voice of the gods. And, one day, she heard it.

"Three years, Mina spent in the presence of the One God, learning the One God's plans for the world, plans for us, learning how to put those plans in motion. When the time was right and Mina was strong enough to bear the burden of the task given to her, she was sent to lead us and tell us of the One God."

"That answers some of the questions about Mina," said Gerard, "but what about this One God? So far all I've seen is that this god is a sort of press-gang for the dead."

"I asked Mina about that," Odila said, her face growing solemn at the memory of that terrible night she and Gerard had fought the dead souls. "Mina says that the souls of the dead serve the One God willingly, joyfully. They are glad to remain among the living in the world they love."

Gerard snorted. "They didn't look glad to me."

"The dead do no harm to the living," Odila said sharply. "If they seem threatening, it is only because they are so eager to bring the knowledge of the One God to us."

"So that was proselytizing?" Gerard said. "While the souls preach to us of the One God, Mina and her soldiers fly red dragons into Solanthus. They kill a few hundred people in the process, but I suppose that's just more evangelical work. More souls for the One God."

"You saw the miracles of healing Mina performed," said Odila, her gaze clear and level. "You heard her tell of the deaths of two of the dragon overlords who have long terrorized this world. There *is* a god in this world, and all your gibes and snide comments won't change that."

She thrust a finger accusingly into his chest. "You're afraid. You're afraid to find out that maybe you're *not* in control of your own destiny. That maybe the One God has a plan for you and for all of us."

"If you're saying I'm afraid to find out I'm a slave to this One God, then you're right!" Gerard returned. "I make my own decisions. I don't want any god making them for me."

"You've done so well so far," Odila said caustically.

"Do you know what *I* think?" Gerard returned, jabbing his finger in her chest with a force that shoved her backward a step. "I think you made a mess of your life, and now you're hoping this god will come along and fix everything."

Odila stared at him, then she rounded on her heel, started to walk away. Gerard leaped after her, caught hold of her by the arm.

"I'm sorry, Odila. I had no right to say that. I was just angry because I don't understand this. Any of it. And, well, you're right. It does frighten me."

Odila kept her head turned away, her face averted, but she didn't try to break loose from his grip.

"We're both in a tough situation here," Gerard said, lowering his voice. "We're both in danger. We can't afford to quarrel. Friends?"

He let go her arm, held out his hand.

"Friends," Odila said grudgingly, turning around to shake hands. "But I don't think we're in any danger. I honestly believe that the entire Solamnic army could walk in here and Mina would welcome them with open arms."

"And a sword in each hand," Gerard muttered beneath his breath.

"What did you say?"

"Nothing important. Listen, there's something you can do for me. A favor—"

"I won't spy on Mina," Odila stated firmly.

"No, no, nothing like that," Gerard said. "I saw a friend of mine in the dungeon. His name is Palin Majere. He's a wizard. He doesn't look well, and I was wondering if maybe Mina could . . . er . . . heal him. Don't tell her I said anything," he added hurriedly. "Just say that you saw him and you were thinking . . . I mean, it should sound like your idea. . . ."

"I understand," Odila said, smiling. "You really do believe that Mina has god-given powers. This proves it."

"Yes, well, maybe," said Gerard, not wanting to start another argument. "Oh, and one thing more. I hear that Mina is searching for Tasslehoff Burrfoot, the kender who was with me. You remember him?"

"Of course." Odila's eyes were suddenly alert and focused, intent on Gerard's face. "Why? Have you seen him?"

"Look, I have to ask—what does this One God want with Tasslehoff Burrfoot. Is this some sort of joke?"

"Far from it," said Odila. "This kender is not supposed to be here."

"Since when is a kender supposed to be anywhere?"

"I'm serious. This is very important, Gerard. Have you seen him?"

"No," said Gerard, thankful he didn't have to lie to her. "Remember about Palin, will you? Palin Majere? In the prison?"

"I'll remember. And you keep watch for the kender."

"I will. Where can we meet?"

"I am always here," Odila said, gesturing toward the Temple.

"Yeah, I guess you are. Do you . . . um . . . pray to this One God?" Gerard asked uncomfortably.

"Yes," said Odila.

"Have your prayers been answered?"

"You're here, aren't you?" Odila said. She wasn't being glib. She was serious. With a smile and a wave, she walked back toward the temple.

Gerard gaped at her, speechless. Finally, he found his tongue. "I'm not . . ." he shouted after her. "I didn't . . . You didn't . . . Your god didn't . . . Oh, what's the use!"

Figuring that he was confused enough for one day, Gerard turned on his heel and stalked off.

The minotaur, Galdar, saw the two Solamnics deep in discussion. Convinced that both of them were spies, he sauntered their direction in hopes of hearing something of their conversation. One drawback to being a minotaur in a city of humans was that he could never blend in with his surroundings. The two stood near the amber sarcophagus of Goldmoon, and using that as cover, he edged near. All he could hear was a low murmur, until at one point they forgot themselves and their voices rose.

"You're afraid," he heard the the female Solamnic say in accusing tones. "You're afraid to find out that maybe you're *not* in control of your own destiny. That maybe the One God has a plan for you and for all of us."

"If you're saying I'm afraid to find out I'm a slave to this One God, then you're right!" the Knight returned angrily. "I make my own decisions. I don't want any god making them for me."

At that point their voices dropped again. Even though they were talking theology, not sedition, Galdar was still troubled. He remained standing in the shadow of the sarcophagus until long after they had both gone, one returning to the temple and the other heading back to his quarters. The Knight's face was red with anger and frustration. He muttered to himself as he walked and was so absorbed in his thoughts that he passed within a foot of the enormous minotaur and never noticed him.

Solamnics and minotaurs have always had much in common—more in common than not, although, throughout history, it was the "not" that divided them. Both the Solamnics and the minotaurs place high emphasis on personal honor. Both value duty and loyalty. Both admire courage. Both reverenced their gods when they had gods to worship. Both gods were gods of honor, loyalty and courage, albeit one god fought for the side of light and the other for the side of darkness.

Or was it truly that? Might not it be said that one god, Kiri-Jolith, fought for the side of the humans and that Sargonnas fought for the minotaurs? Was it race that divided them, not daylight and night shadow? Humans and minotaurs both told tales of the famous Kaz, a minotaur who had been a friend of the great Solamnic Knight, Huma.

But because one had horns and a snout and was covered with fur and the other had soft skin and a puny lump of a nose, the friendship between Kaz and Huma was considered an anomaly. The two races had been taught to hate and distrust each other for centuries. Now the gulf between them was so deep and wide and ugly that neither could cross.

In the absence of the gods, both races were deteriorating. Galdar had heard rumors of strange doings in the minotaur homeland—rumors of murder, treachery, deceit. As for the Solamnics, few young men and women in this modern age wanted to endure the rigors and constraints and responsibilities of the Knighthood. Their numbers were dwindling, their backs were to the wall. And they had a new enemy—a new god.

Galdar had seen in Mina the end of his quest. He had seen in Mina a sense of duty, honor, loyalty, and courage—the ways of old. Yet, certain things Mina had said and done had begun to trouble Galdar. The foremost of these was the horrible rebirth of the two wizards.

Galdar had no use for wizards. He could have watched these two being tortured without a qualm, could have slain them with his own hand and never given the matter another thought. But the sight of their lifeless bodies being used as mindless slaves gave him a sick feeling in the pit of his stomach. He could not look at the two shambling corpses without feeling his gorge rise.

Worst was the One God's punishment of Mina for losing the kender. Recalling the sacrifices Mina had made, the physical pain she had endured, the torment, the exhaustion, thirst, and starvation, all in the name of the One God, then to see her suffering like that, Galdar was outraged.

Galdar honored Mina. He was loyal to Mina. His duty lay with Mina. But he was beginning to have doubts about this One God.

The Solamnic's words echoed in Galdar's mind. *If you're saying I'm afraid to find out I'm a slave to this One God, then you're right! I make my own decisions. I don't want any god making them for me.*

Galdar did not like thinking of himself as a slave to the will of this One God or any god. More important, he didn't like seeing Mina as a slave to this One God, a slave to be whipped if she failed to do the god's bidding.

Galdar decided to do what he should have done long ago. He needed to find out more about this One God. He could not speak of this to Mina, but he could speak of it to this Solamnic female.

And perhaps kill two with one blow, as the saying went among minotaurs, in reference to the well-known tale of the thieving kender and the minotaur blacksmith.

14

Faith in the One God

Over a thousand Knights and soldiers from Palanthas entered the city of Solanthus. Their entry was triumphant. Flags bearing the emblems of the Dark Knights as well as flags belonging to individual Knights whipped in the wind. The Dark Knights who served in Palanthas had grown wealthy, for although much of the tribute had gone to the late dragon Khellendros and still more had been sent to the late Lord of the Night Targonne, the high-ranking Knights of Palanthas had done all right for themselves. They were in a good mood, albeit a bit concerned over rumors that had reached them concerning the new, self-proclaimed Lord of the Night—a teen-age girl.

These officers could not imagine how any right-thinking veteran soldier could take orders from a chit who should be dreaming of dancing around the May-pole, not leading men into battle. They had discussed this on the march to Solanthus and had privately agreed among themselves that there must be some shadowy figure working behind the scenes—this minotaur, who was said never to stir far from Mina's side. He must be the true leader. The girl was a front, for humans would never follow a minotaur. There were some who pointed out that few men would follow a slip of a girl into battle, either, but others replied knowingly that she performed tricks and illusions to entertain the ignorant, dupe them into fighting for her.

No one could argue with her success, and so long as it worked, they had no intention of destroying those illusions. Of course, as intelligent men, they would not be fooled.

As had others before them, the officers of the Palanthas Knighthood met Mina with boisterous bravado, preparing to hear her with outward composure, inward chuckles. They came away pale and shaken, quiet and subdued, every one them trapped in the resin of the amber eyes.

Gerard faithfully recorded their numbers in a coded message to the Knighthood. This was his most important missive yet, for this confirmed that Mina meant to attack Sanction and she meant to march soon. Every blacksmith and weaponsmith in the city was pressed into duty, working day and night, making repairs on old weapons and armor and turning out new ones.

Her army would move slowly. It would take weeks, maybe months, to march through the woods and trek across the grasslands and into the mountains that surrounded Sanction. Watching the preparations and thinking of this prolonged march, Gerard developed a plan of attack that he included along with his report. He had little hope that the plan would be adopted, for it involved fighting by stealth, hitting the flanks of the army as it crawled across the ground, striking their supply trains, attacking swiftly, then disappearing, only to strike again when least expected.

Thus, he wrote, *did the Wilder elves of Qualinesti succeed in doing great damage to the Dark Knights who occupied that land. I realize that this is not an accepted means of fighting for the Knighthood, for it is certainly not chivalric nor honorable nor even particularly fair. However, it is effective, not only in reducing the numbers of the enemy but in destroying the morale of the troops.*

Lord Tasgall was a sensible man, and Gerard actually thought that he might toss aside the Measure and act upon it. Unfortunately, Gerard couldn't find any way of delivering the message to Richard, who'd been instructed to return to the roadhouse on a weekly basis to see if Gerard had more information.

Gerard was now being watched day and night, and he had a good idea who was to blame. Not Mina. The minotaur, Galdar.

Too late Gerard had noticed the minotaur eavesdropping on his conversation with Odila. That night, Gerard discovered Galdar was having him watched.

No matter where Gerard went, he was certain to see the horns of the minotaur looming over the crowd. When he left his lodging, he found one of Mina's Knights loitering about in the street outside. The next day, one of his patrol members fell mysteriously ill and was replaced. Gerard had no doubt that the replacement was one of Galdar's spies.

He had no one to blame but himself. He should have left Solanthus days ago instead of hanging about. Now he had not only placed himself in danger, he'd imperiled the very mission he'd been sent to accomplish.

During the next two days, Gerard continued to perform his duties. He went to the temple as usual. He had not seen Odila since the day they'd spoken and was startled to see her standing alongside Mina today. Odila searched the crowd until she found Gerard. She made a small gesture, a slight beckoning motion. When Mina left, and the supplicants and idlers had departed, Gerard hung around outside, waiting.

Odila emerged from the temple. She shook her head slightly, indicating he was not to speak to her, and walked past him without a glance.

As she passed, she whispered, "Come to the temple tonight an hour before midnight."

Gerard sat gloomily on his bed, waiting for the hour Odila had set. He whiled away the time, by staring in frustration at the scrollcase containing the message that should have been in the hands of his superiors by now. Gerard's quarters were in the same hall once used to house the Solamnic Knights. He had at first been assigned a room already occupied by two other Knights, but he'd used some of the money he'd earned from the Dark Knights to buy his way into a private chamber. The chamber was, in reality, little more than a windowless storage room located on the first level. By the lingering smell, it had once been used to store onions.

Restless, he was glad to leave it. He walked openly into the streets, pausing only long enough to lace up his boot and to catch a glimpse of a shadow detaching itself from a nearby doorway. Resuming his pace, he heard light footfalls behind him.

Gerard had a momentary impulse to whirl around and confront his shadow. He resisted the impulse, kept walking. Going straight to the temple, he entered and found a seat on a stone bench in a corner of the building.

The temple's interior was dark, lit by five candles that stood on the altar. Outside, the sky was clouded over. Gerard could smell rain in the air, and within a few moments, the first drops began to fall. He hoped his shadow got soaked to the skin.

The flames of the candles wavered in a sudden gust stirred up by the storm. A robed figure entered the temple from a door in the rear. Pausing at the altar, she fussed with the candles for a moment, then, turning, walked down the aisle. Gerard could see her silhouetted against the candlelight, and although he could not see her face, he knew Odila by her upright bearing and the tilt of her head.

She sat down beside him, slid closer to him. He shifted on the stone bench, moved nearer to her. They were the only two in the temple, but they kept their voices low.

"Just so you know, I'm being followed," he whispered.

Alarmed, Odila turned to stare at him. Her face was pale against the candle-lit darkness. Her eyes were smudges of shadow. Reaching out her hand, she fumbled for Gerard's, found it, and clasped hold tightly. He was astonished, both at the fact that she was seeking comfort and by the fact that her hand was cold and trembling.

"Odila, what is it? What's wrong?" he asked.

"I found out about your wizard friend, Palin," she said in a smothered voice, as if she found it hard to draw breath. "Galdar told me."

Odila's shoulders straightened. She turned to him, looked him in the eyes. "Gerard, I've been a fool! Such a fool!"

"We're a pair of them, then," he said, patting her hand clumsily.

He felt her stiff and shivering, not comforted by his touch. She didn't seem to hear his words. When she spoke, her voice was muffled.

"I came here hoping to find a god who could guide me, care for me, comfort me. Instead I've found—" She broke off, said abruptly. "Gerard, Palin's dead."

"I'm not surprised," Gerard said, with a sigh. "He didn't look well—"

"No, Gerard!" Odila shook her head. "He was dead when you saw him."

"He wasn't dead," Gerard protested. "He was sitting on his cot. After that, I saw him get up and walk out."

"And I'm telling you that he was dead," she said, turning to face him. "I don't blame you for not believing me. I didn't believe it myself. But I . . . Galdar took me to see him. . . ."

He eyed her suspiciously.

"Are you drunk?"

"I wish I were!" Odila returned, but with sudden, savage vehemence. "I don't think there's enough dwarf spirits in the world to make me forget what I've seen. I'm cold sober, Gerard. I swear it."

He looked at her closely. Her eyes were focused, her voice shaking but clear, her words coherent.

"I believe you," he said slowly, "but I don't understand. How could Palin be dead when I saw him sitting and standing and walking?"

"He and the other wizard were both killed in the Tower of High Sorcery. Galdar was there. He told me the whole story. They died, and then Mina and Galdar found out that this kender they were searching for was in the Tower. They went to find him, only they lost him. The One God punished Mina for losing the kender. Mina said that she needed the wizards' help to find him, and . . . and she . . . she gave them back their lives."

"If she did, they didn't look any too pleased by it," Gerard said, thinking of Palin's empty eyes, his vacant stare.

"There's a reason for that," Odila returned, her voice hollow. "She gave them their lives, but she didn't give them their souls. The One God holds their souls in thrall. They have no will to think or act on their own. They are nothing more than puppets, and the One God holds the strings. Galdar says that when the kender is captured, the wizards will know how to deal with him and the device he carries."

"And you think he's telling the truth?"

"I *know* he is. I went to see your friend, Palin. His body lives, but there is no life in his eyes. They're both corpses, Gerard. Walking corpses. They have no will of their own. They do whatever Mina tells them to do. Didn't you think it was strange the way they both just sit there, staring at nothing?"

"They're wizards," Gerard said lamely, by way of excuse.

Now that he looked back, he wondered he hadn't guessed something was wrong. He felt sickened at the thought.

Odila moistened her lips. "There's something else," she said, dropping her voice so that it was little more than a breath. Gerard had to strain to hear her. "Galdar told me that the One God is so pleased by this that she has ordered Mina to use the dead in battle. Not just the souls, Gerard. She is supposed to give life back to the bodies."

Gerard stared at her, aghast.

"It doesn't matter that Mina plans to attack Sanction with a ridiculously small army," Odila continued relentlessly. "None of her soldiers will ever die. If they do, Mina will just raise them up and send them right back into battle—"

"Odila," said Gerard, his voice urgent, "we have to leave here. Both of us. You don't want to stay, do you?" he asked suddenly, uncertain.

"No," she answered emphatically. "No, not after this. I am sorry I ever sought out this One God."

"Why did you?" Gerard asked.

She shook her head. "You wouldn't understand."

"I might. Why do you think I wouldn't?"

"You're so . . . self-reliant. You don't need anyone or anything. You know your own mind. You know who you are."

"Cornbread," he said, recalling her disparaging nickname for him. He had hoped to make her smile, but she didn't even seem to have heard him. Speaking of his feelings like this wasn't easy for him. "I'm looking for answers," he said awkwardly, "just like you. Just like everyone. Like you said, in order to find the answers, you have to ask questions." He gestured outside the temple, to the steps where the worshipers congregated every day. "That's what's the matter with half these people around here. They're like starving dogs. They are so hungry to believe in something that they take the first handout that's offered and gulp it down, never dreaming that the meat might be poisoned."

"I gulped," said Odila, sighing. "I wanted what everyone claimed they had in the old days. You were right when you said I hoped that the One God would fix my life. Make everything better. Take away the loneliness and the fear—" She halted, embarrassed to have revealed so much.

"I don't think even the old gods did that, at least from what I've been told," Gerard said. "Paladine certainly didn't solve all Huma's problems. If anything, he heaped more on him."

"Unless you believe that Huma chose to do what he did," said Odila softly, "and that Paladine gave him strength to do it." She paused, then added, in bleak despair, "We can't do anything to this god, Gerard. I've seen the mind of this god! I've seen the immense power this god wields. How can such a powerful god be stopped?"

Odila covered her face with her hands.

"I've made such a mess of things. I've dragged you into danger. I know the reason you've stayed around Solanthus, so don't try to deny it. You could have left days ago. You *should* have. You stayed around because you were worried about me."

"Nothing matters now because both of us are going to leave," Gerard said firmly. "Tomorrow, when the troops march out, Mina and Galdar will be preoccupied with their own duties. There will be such confusion that no one will miss us."

"I want to get out of here," Odila said emphatically. She jumped to her feet. "Let's leave now. I don't want to spend another minute in this terrible place. Everyone's asleep. No one will miss me. We'll go back to your quarters—"

"We'll have to leave separately. I'm being followed. You go first. I'll keep watch."

Reaching out impulsively, Odila took hold of his

hand, clasped it tightly. "I appreciate all you've done for me, Gerard. You are a true and loyal friend."

"Go on," he said. "Quickly. I'll keep watch."

Releasing his hand with a parting squeeze, she started walking toward the temple doors, which were never locked, for worshipers of the One God were encouraged to come to the temple at any time, day or night. Odila gave the doors an impatient push and they opened silently on well-oiled hinges. Gerard was about to follow when he heard a noise by the altar. He glanced swiftly in that direction, saw nothing. The candle flames burned steadily. No one had entered. Yet he was positive he'd heard something. He was still staring at the altar, when he heard Odila give a strangled gasp.

Gerard whipped around, his hand on his sword. Expecting to find that she had been accosted by some guard, he was surprised to see her standing in the open doorway, alone.

"Now what's the matter?" He didn't dare go to her. The person following him would be watching for him. "Just walk out the damn door, will you?"

Odila turned to stare at him. Her face glimmered so white in the darkness, that he was reminded uncomfortably of the souls of the dead.

She spoke in a harsh whisper that carried clearly in the still night. "I can't leave!"

Gerard swore beneath his breath. Keeping a tight grip on his sword, he sidled over to the wall, hoping to remain unseen. Reaching a point near the door, he glared at Odila.

"What do you mean you won't leave?" he demanded in low and angry tones. "I risked my neck coming here, and I'll be damned if I'm going to leave without you. If I have to carry you—"

"I didn't say I won't leave!" Odila said, her breath coming in gasps. "I said I *can't!*"

She took a step toward the door, her hands outstretched. As she came nearer the door, her movements grew sluggish, as if she were wading into a river, trying to move against a swift-flowing current. Finally, she came to a halt and shook her head.

"I . . . can't!" she said, her voice choked.

Gerard stared in perplexity. Odila was trying her best, that much was clear. Something was obviously preventing her from leaving.

His gaze went from her terrified face to the medallion she wore around her neck.

He pointed at it. "The medallion! Take it off!"

Odila raised her hand to the medallion. She snatched back her fingers with a pain-filled cry.

Gerard grabbed the medallion, intending to rip it off her.

A jolting shock sent him staggering back against the doors. His hand burned and throbbed. He stared helplessly at Odila. She stared just as helplessly back.

"I don't understand—" she began.

"And yet," said a gentle voice, "the answer is simplicity itself."

Hand on his sword hilt, Gerard turned to find Mina standing in the doorway.

"I want to leave," Odila said, managing with a great effort to keep her voice firm and steady. "You have to let me go. You can't keep me here against my will."

"I am not keeping you here, Odila," said Mina.

Odila tried again to walk through the door. Her jaw clenched, and she strained every muscle. "You are lying!" she cried. "You have cast some sort of evil spell on me!"

"I am no wizard," said Mina, spreading her hands. "You know that. You know, too, what binds you to this place."

Odila shook her head in violent negation.

"Your faith," said Mina.

Odila stared, baffled. "I don't—"

"But you do. You believe in the One God. You said so yourself. 'I've seen the mind of this god! I've seen the immense power this god wields.' You have placed your faith in the One God, Odila, and in return, the One God claims your service."

"Faith shouldn't make anyone a prisoner," Gerard said angrily.

Mina turned her eyes on him, and he saw with dismay the images of thousands of people frozen in their amber depths. He had the terrible feeling that if he looked long enough, he would see himself there.

"Describe to me a faithful servant," said Mina, "or, better yet, a faithful knight. One who is faithful to his Order. What must he do to be termed 'faithful'?"

Gerard stubbornly kept silent, but that didn't matter, because Mina answered her own question.

Her tone was fervent, her eyes glowed with an inner light. "A faithful servant performs loyally and without question all the duties his master asks of him. In return, the master clothes him and feeds him and protects him from harm. If the servant is disloyal, if he rebels against his master, he is punished. Just so the faithful knight who is duty-bound to obey his superior. If he fails in his duty or rebels against authority, what happens to him? He is punished for his oath breaking. Even the Solamnics would punish such a knight, wouldn't they, Sir Gerard?"

She is the faithful servant, Gerard realized. She is the faithful knight. And this makes her dangerous, perhaps the most dangerous person to have ever lived on Krynn.

Her argument was flawed. He knew that, in some deep part of him, but he couldn't think why. Not while staring into those amber eyes.

Mina smiled gently at him. Because he had no answer, she assumed she had won. She turned the amber eyes back to Odila.

"Deny your belief in the One God, Odila," Mina said to her, "and you will be free to go."

"You know I cannot," Odila said.

"Then the One God's faithful servant will remain here to perform her duties. Return to your quarters, Odila. The hour is late. You will need your rest, for we have much to do tomorrow to prepare for the battle that will see the fall of Sanction."

Odila bowed her head, started to obey.

"Odila!" Gerard risked calling.

She kept walking. She did not look back at him.

Mina watched her depart, then turned to Gerard. "Will we see you among the ranks of our Knights as we march in triumph to Sanction, Sir Gerard? Or do you have other duties that call you away? If you do, you may go. You have my blessing and that of the One God."

She knows! Gerard realized. She knows I'm a spy, yet she does nothing. She even offers me the chance to leave! Why doesn't she have me arrested? Tortured? Killed? He wished suddenly that she would. Even death would be better than the notion in the back of his mind that she was using him, allowing him to think he was acting of his own free will, when all the time, whatever he did, he was carrying out the will of the One God.

"I'll ride with you," Gerard said grimly and stalked past her through the door.

On the steps of the temple he halted, stared in the darkness, and announced in a loud voice, "I'm going back to my quarters! Try to keep up, will you?"

Entering his room, Gerard lit a candle, then went to his desk and stood staring for long moments at the scrollcase. He opened it, removed the paper that detailed his plans to defeat Mina's army. Deliberately, grimly, he ripped the paper into small pieces. That done, he fed the pieces, one by one, to the candle's flame.

15

The Lame and the Blind

ina's army left Solanthus the next day. Not all the army marched, for she was forced to leave behind troops enough to occupy what was presumably a hostile city. Its hostility was largely a myth, judging by the number of Solanthians who turned out to cheer her and wish her well and press gifts upon her—so many that they would have filled the wagon that contained the amber sarcophagus, had Mina permitted it. She told them instead to give the gifts to the poor in the name of the One God. Weeping, the people of Solanthus blessed her name.

Gerard could have wept, too, but for different reasons. He'd spent the night wondering what to do, whether to go or stay. He decided finally to remain with the army, ride with them to Sanction. He told himself it was because of Odila.

She rode with the army. She sat in the wagon with the corpse of Goldmoon, imprisoned in amber, and the corpses of the two wizards, imprisoned in their own flesh. Viewing the wretched, ambulating corpses, Gerard wondered that he had not known the truth the moment he saw Palin, with his staring, vacant eyes. Odila did not glance at Gerard as the wagon rumbled past.

Galdar looked at him, dark eyes baleful. Gerard stared back. The minotaur's displeasure gave Gerard one consolation. The fact that he was accompanying Mina's army so obviously angered the minotaur that Gerard felt he must be doing something right.

As he cantered out the gates, taking up a position in the rear, as far from Mina as he could get and still be part of her army, his horse nearly ran down two beggars, who scrambled hastily to get out of his way.

"I'm sorry, gentlemen," said Gerard, reigning in his horse. "Are you hurt, either of you?"

One beggar was an older man, human, with gray hair and a gray, grizzled beard. His face was seamed with wrinkles and browned from the sun. His eyes were a keen, glittering blue, the color of new-made steel. Although he limped and leaned upon a crutch, he had the air and bearing of a military man. This was borne out by the fact that he wore what appeared to be the faded, tattered remnants of some sort of military uniform.

The other beggar was blind, his wounded eyes wrapped in a black bandage. He walked with one hand resting on the shoulder of his comrade, who guided him along his way. This man had white hair that shone silver in the sun. He was young, much younger than the other beggar, and he lifted his sightless head at the sound of Gerard's voice.

"No, sir," said the first beggar gruffly. "You did but startle us, that is all."

"Where is this army bound?" the second beggar asked.

"Sanction," said Gerard. "Take my advice, sirs, keep clear of the temple of the One God. Even though they could heal you, I doubt it's worth the price."

Tossing each beggar a few coins, he turned his horse's head, galloped off down the road, and was soon enveloped in a cloud of dust raised by the army.

The citizens of Solanthus watched until Mina was long out of sight, then they turned back to their city, which seemed bleak and empty now that she was gone.

"Mina marches on Sanction," said the blind beggar.

"This confirms the information we received last night," said the lame beggar. "Everywhere we go, we hear the same thing. Mina marches on Sanction. Are you satisfied now, at last?"

"Yes, Razor, I am satisfied," the blind man replied.

"About time," Razor muttered. He hurled the coins Gerard had given him at the blind man's feet. "No more begging! I have never been so humiliated."

"Yet, as you have seen, this disguise permits us to go where we will and talk to whom we want, from thief to knight to nobleman," Mirror said mildly. "No one has any clue that we are more than we seem. The question now is, what do we do? Do we confront Mina now?"

"And what would you say to her, Silver?" Razor raised his voice to a mocking lilt. "'Where, oh where, are the pretty gold dragons? Where, oh where, can they be?'"

Mirror kept silent, not liking how close Razor had come to the mark.

"I say we wait," Razor continued. "Confront her in Sanction."

"Wait until Sanction has fallen to your Queen, you mean," Mirror stated coldly.

"And I suppose you're going to stop her, Silver? Alone, blind?" Razor snorted.

"You would have me walk into Sanction, alone and blind," said Mirror.

"Don't worry, I won't let anything happen to you. Skie told you more than you've let on. I intend to be there when you have your conversation with Mina."

"Then I suggest you pick up that money, for we will need it," said Mirror. "These disguises that have worked well thus far will aid us all the more in Sanction. What better excuse to speak to Mina than to come before her as two seeking miracles?"

Mirror could not see the expression on Razor's face, but he could imagine it—defiant at first, then glum, as he realized that what Mirror said made sense.

He heard the scrape of the coins being snatched irritably from the ground.

"I believe you are enjoying this, Silver," Razor said.

"You're right," Mirror returned. "I can't think when I've had this much fun."

16

An Unexpected Meeting

ike leaves flung from out the center of the cyclone, the gnome and the kender fluttered to the ground. That is, the kender—with his gaily colored clothes—fluttered. The gnome landed heavily, resulting in a subsequent cessation of breathing for a few heart-stopping minutes. Lack of breath also resulted in a cessation of the gnome's shrieking, which, considering where they found themselves, was undeniably a good thing.

Not that they knew right away where they were. All Tasslehoff knew, as he looked about, was where he wasn't, which was anywhere he'd been up to this point in his life. He was standing—and Conundrum was lying—in a corridor made of enormous blocks of black marble that had been polished to a high gloss. The corridor was lit sporadically with torches, whose orange light gave a soft and eerie glow to the corridor. The torches burned clean, for no whisper of air stirred.

The light did nothing to remove the gloom from the corridor. The light only made the shadows all that much darker by contrast.

No whisper, no sound at all came from anywhere, though Tas listened with all his might. Tas made no sound either, and he hushed Conundrum as he helped the gnome to his feet. Tas had been adventuring most of his life, and he knew his corridors, and without doubt, this corridor had the smothery feeling of a place where you want to be quiet, very quiet.

"Goblins!" was the first word Conundrum gasped.

"No, not goblins," said Tasslehoff in a quiet tone that was meant to be reassuring. He rather spoiled by it by adding cheerfully, "Probably worse things than goblins down here."

"What do you mean?" Conundrum wheezed and clutched at his hair distractedly. "Worse than goblins! What could be worse than goblins? Where are we anyway?"

"Well, there's lots worse than goblins," whispered Tas upon reflection. "Draconians, for instance. And dragons. And owlbears. Did I ever tell you the story about the Uncle Trapspringer and the owlbear? It all began—"

It all ended when Conundrum doubled up his fist and punched Tasslehoff in the stomach.

"Owlbears! Who cares about owlbears or your blasted relations? I could tell you stories about my cousin Strontiumninety that would make your hair fall out. Your teeth, too. Why did you bring us here, and where is here, anyway?"

"*I* didn't bring us anywhere," returned Tasslehoff in irritable tones when he could speak again. Being

struck soundly and unexpectedly in the stomach
tended to make a fellow irritable. "The device brought
us here. And I don't know where 'here' is anymore
than you do. I— Hush! Someone's coming."

When in a dark and smothery feeling corridor, it
is always a good idea to see who is coming before
giving them a chance to see you. That's the maxim
Uncle Trapspringer had always taught his nephew,
and Tas had found that, in general, it was a good
plan. For one thing, it allowed you to leap out of
the darkness and give the person a grand surprise.
Tasslehoff took hold of the collar of Conundrum's
shirt and dragged the gnome behind a black,
marble pillar.

A single figure walked the corridor. The figure
was robed in black and was not easily distinguish-
able from either the darkness of the corridor or the
black, marble walls. Tasslehoff had his first good
view of the figure as it passed beneath one of the
torches. Even in the darkness, able to see only the
dimmest, shadowiest outline of the figure, Tasslehoff
had the strange and squirmy feeling in his stomach
(probably left over from being struck) that he knew
this person. There was something about the walk
that was slow and halting, something about the way
the person leaned upon the staff he was carrying,
something about the staff that gave off a very soft,
white light.

"Raistlin!" Tasslehoff breathed, awed.

He was about to repeat the name in a much louder
voice, accompanied by a whoop and a shout and a
rushing forward to give his friend, whom he hadn't
seen in a long time and presumed to be dead, an enormous hug.

A hand grasped his shoulder, and a voice said softly, "No. Leave him be."

"But he's my friend," Tas said to Conundrum. "Not counting the time he murdered another friend of mine, who was a gnome, by the way."

Conundrum's eyes opened wide. He clutched at Tas nervously. "This friend of yours. He doesn't make it a practice of . . . of m-m-murdering gnomes, does he?"

Tas missed this because he was staring at Conundrum, noting that the gnome had hold of Tasslehoff's sleeve with one hand and his shirt front with the other. This accounted for two hands and, so far as Tas knew, gnomes came with only two hands. Which meant there was a hand left over, and that hand was holding Tasslehoff firmly by the shoulder. Tasslehoff twisted and squirmed to see who had hold of him, but the pillar behind which they were standing cast a dark shadow, and all he could see behind him was more darkness.

Tas looked round at the other hand—the hand that was on his shoulder—but the hand wasn't there. Or at least, it was there because he could feel it, but it wasn't there because he couldn't see it.

Finding this all very strange, Tasslehoff looked back at Raistlin. Knowing Raistlin as he did, Tas was forced to admit that there were times when the mage had not been at all friendly to the kender. And there was the fact that Raistlin *did* murder gnomes. Or at least, he had murdered one gnome for fixing the Device of Time Journeying. This very device, although not this very gnome. Raistlin wore the black robes now, and he had been wearing black robes then, and while Tasslehoff found Conundrum extremely annoying at times, he didn't want to see the gnome murdered. Tasslehoff decided that for Conundrum's sake he would keep silent and not jump out at Raistlin, and he would forgo the big hug.

Raistlin passed very near the kender and the gnome. Conundrum was, thank goodness, speechless with terror. Through a heroic effort on his part, Tasslehoff kept silent, though the absent gods alone knew what this cost him. He was rewarded with an approving squeeze by the hand on his shoulder that wasn't there, which, all in all, didn't make him feel as good as it might have under the circumstances.

Raistlin was apparently deep in thought, for his head was bowed, his walk slow and abstracted. He stopped once to cough, a racking cough that so weakened him he was forced to lean against the wall. He choked and gagged, his face grew deathly pale. Blood flecked his lips. Tas was alarmed, for he'd seen Raistlin have these attacks before but never one this bad.

"Caramon had a tea he used to fix for him," Tas said, starting forward.

The hand pressed him back.

Raistlin raised his head. His golden eyes shone in the torchlight. He looked about, up and down the corridor.

"Who spoke?" he said in his whispering voice. "Who spoke that name? Caramon? Who spoke, I say?"

The hand dug into Tasslehoff's shoulder. He had no need of its caution, however. Raistlin looked so very strange and his expression was so very terrible that the kender would have kept silent, regardless.

"No one," said Raistlin, at last able to draw a ragged breath. "I am imagining things." He mopped his brow with the hem of his black velvet sleeve, then smiled sardonically. "Perhaps it was my own guilty conscience. Caramon is dead. They are all dead, drowned in the Blood Sea. And they were all so shocked when I used the dragon orb and departed, leaving them to their fate. Amazed that I would not meekly share in their doom."

Recovering his strength, Raistlin drew away from the wall. He steadied himself with the staff, but did not immediately resume his walk. Perhaps he was still too weak.

"I can see the look on Caramon's face now. I can hear his blubbering." Raistlin pitched his voice high, spoke through his nose. "'But . . . Raist—'" He ground his teeth, then smiled again, a most unpleasant smile. "And Tanis, that self-righteous hypocrite! His illicit love for my dear sister led him to betray his friends, and yet he has the temerity to accuse *me* of being faithless! I can see them all—Goldmoon, Riverwind, Tanis, my brother—all staring at me with great cow eyes."

Again, his voice rose to mimic. "'At least save your brother . . .'" The voice resumed its bitter monologue. "Save him for what? A lawn ornament? His ambition takes him no further than the bed of his latest conquest. All my life, he has been the manacles that bound my hands and shackled my feet. You might as well ask me to leave my prison but take along my chains. . . ."

He resumed his walk, moving slowly down the corridor.

"You know, Conundrum," whispered Tasslehoff, "I said he was my friend, but it takes a lot of work to like Raistlin. Sometimes I'm not sure it's worth

the effort. He's talking about Caramon and the rest
drowning in the Blood Sea, but they didn't drown.
They were rescued by sea elves. I know because
Caramon told me the whole story. And Raistlin
knows they weren't drowned because he saw them
again. But if he thinks that they're drowned, then
obviously he doesn't yet know that they weren't,
which means that he must be somewhere between
the time he thought they drowned and the time he
finds that they didn't. Which means," Tas continued,
awed and excited, "that I've found another part of
the past."

Hearing this, Conundrum eyed the kender suspiciously and backed up a few steps. "You haven't *met*
my cousin, Stroniumninety, have you?"

Tas was about to say that he hadn't had the pleasure when the sound of footsteps rang through the corridor. The footsteps were not those of the mage, who
barely made any noise at all beyond the occasional
rasping cough and the rustle of his robes. These footsteps were large and imposing, thunderous, filling the
corridor with noise.

The hand that wasn't on Tasslehoff's shoulder
pulled him back deeper into the shadows, cautioning
him with renewed pressure to keep quiet. The gnome,
with finely honed instincts for survival so long as
steam-powered pistons weren't in the offing, had
already pressed himself so far into the wall that he
might have been taken for the artistic renderings of
some primitive tribe.

A man as large as his footfalls filled the corridor
with sound and motion and life. He was tall and
brawny, wore heavy, ornately designed armor that
seemed a part of his anatomy for all that it slowed him

down. He carried under his arm the horned helm of a Dragon Highlord. An enormous sword clanked at his side. He was obviously on his way somewhere with a purpose in mind, for he walked rapidly and with intent, looking neither to the right nor the left. Thus he very nearly ran down Raistlin, who was forced to fall back against the wall at the man's coming or be crushed.

The Dragon Highlord saw the mage, acknowledged his presence with no more than a sharp glance. Raistlin bowed. The Dragon Highlord continued on his way. Raistlin started to go his, when suddenly the Highlord halted, spun round on his heel.

"Majere," boomed the voice.

Raistlin halted, turned. "My Lord Ariakas."

"How do you find things here in Neraka? Your quarters comfortable?"

"Yes, my lord. Quite adequate for my simple needs," Raistlin replied. The light of the crystal ball atop his staff glimmered ever so slightly. "Thank you for asking."

Ariakas frowned. Raistlin's response was polite, servile, as the Dragon Highlord had a right to respect. Ariakas was not a man to note subtleties, but apparently even he had heard the sardonic tone in the mage's raspy voice. The Highlord could not very well rebuke a man for a tone, however, so he continued.

"Your sister Kitiara says that I am to treat you well," said Ariakas gruffly. "You have her to thank for your post here."

"I owe my sister a great deal," Raistlin replied.

"You owe me more," said Ariakas grimly.

"Indeed," said Raistlin with another bow.

Ariakas was plainly not pleased. "You are a cool

one. Most men cringe and cower when I speak to them. Does nothing impress you?"

"*Should* anything impress me, my lord?" Raistlin returned.

"By our Queen," Ariakas cried, laying his hand on the hilt of his sword, "I could strike off your head for that remark!"

"You could try, my lord," said Raistlin. He bowed again, this time more deeply than before. "Forgive me, sir, I did not mean the words the way they sounded. Of course, I find you impressive. I find the magnificence of this city impressive. But just because I am impressed does not mean I am fearful. You do not admire fearful men, do you, my lord?"

"No," said Ariakas. He stared at Raistlin intently. "You are right. I do not."

"I would have you admire me, my lord," said Raistlin.

Ariakas continued to stare at the mage. Then, suddenly, the Highlord burst out laughing. His laughter was enormous. It rolled and crashed through the corridor, smashed the gnome up against the wall. Tasslehoff felt dazed by it, as though he'd been struck in the head by a large rock. Raistlin winced slightly, but held his ground.

"I don't admire you yet, mage," said Ariakas, when he had regained control of himself. "But someday, Majere, when you have proven yourself, maybe I will."

Turning on his heel, still chuckling, he continued on his way down the corridor.

When his footfalls had died away and all was once again silent, Raistlin said softly, "Someday, when I have proven myself, my lord, you will do more than admire me. You will fear me."

Raistlin turned and walked away, and Tasslehoff turned to try to see who it was who didn't have hold of his shoulder, and he turned and turned and kept on turning. . . .

BOOK 2

I

Meeting of the Gods

The gods of Krynn met in council, as they had done many times since the world had been stolen away from them. The gods of light stood opposite the gods of darkness, as day stands opposite night, with the gods of neutrality divided evenly in between. The children of the gods stood together, as they always did.

These council sessions had accomplished little in the past except to sometimes soothe raging tempers and cheer crushed spirits. One by one, each of the gods came forth to tell of searching that had been done in vain. Many were the journeys taken by each god and goddess to try to find what was lost. Long and dangerous were some of these treks through the planes of existence, but one and all ended in failure. Not even Zivilyn, the all-seeing, who existed in all times and in all lands, had been able to find the world. He could see the path Krynn and its people

217

would have taken into the future, but that path was populated now by the ghosts of might-have-beens. The gods were close to concluding sorrowfully that the world was lost to them forever.

When each had spoken, Paladine appeared to them in his radiance.

"I bring glad tidings," he said. "I have heard a voice cry out to me, the voice of one of the children of the world. Her prayer rang through the heavens, and its music was sweet to hear. Our people need us, for as we had suspected, Queen Takhisis now rules the world unchallenged."

"Where is the world?" Sargonnas demanded. Of all the gods of darkness, he was the most enraged, the most embittered, for Queen Takhisis had been his consort, and he felt doubly betrayed. "Tell us and we will go there immediately and give her the punishment she so richly deserves."

"I do not know," Paladine replied. "Goldmoon's voice was cut off. Death took her and Takhisis holds her soul in thrall. Yet, we now know the world exists. We must continue to search for it."

Nuitari stepped forth. The god of the magic of darkness, he was clad all in black. His face, that of a gibbous moon, was white as wax.

"I have a soul who begs an audience," he said.

"Do you sponsor this?" Paladine asked.

"I do," Nuitari answered.

"And so do I." Lunitari came forward in her red robes.

"And so do I." Solinari came forth in his silver robes.

"Very well, we will hear this soul," Paladine agreed. "Let this soul come forward."

The soul entered and took his place among them. Paladine frowned at the sight, as did most of the other gods, light and darkness alike, for none trusted this soul, who had once tried to become a god himself.

"Raistlin Majere has nothing to say that I want to hear," Sargonnas stated with a snarl and turned to depart.

The others grumbled their agreement—all but one.

"I think we should listen to him," Mishakal said.

The other gods turned to look at her in surprise, for she was the consort of Paladine, a loving goddess of healing and compassion. She knew better than most the harm and suffering and sorrow that this man had brought upon those who loved and trusted him.

"He made reparation for his crimes," Mishakal continued, "and he was forgiven."

"Then why has his soul not departed with the rest?" Sargonnas demanded. "Why does he linger here, except to take advantage of our weakness?"

"Why does your soul remain, Raistlin Majere," Paladine asked sternly, "when you were free to move on?"

"Because half of me is missing," returned Raistlin, facing the god, meeting his eyes. "Together, my brother and I came into this world. Together, we will leave it. We walked apart for much of our lives. The fault was mine. If I can help it, we will not be separated in death."

"Your loyalty is commendable," said Paladine dryly, "if a bit belated. But I do not understand what business you have with us."

"I have found the world," said Raistlin.

Sargonnas snorted. The other gods stared at Raistlin in troubled silence.

"Did you hear Goldmoon's prayer as well?" Paladine asked.

"No," Raistlin responded. "I could hardly be expected to, could I? I did hear something else, though—a voice chanting words of magic. Words I recognized, as perhaps none other could. I recognized, as well, the voice that spoke them. It belonged to a kender, Tasslehoff Burrfoot."

"That is impossible," said Paladine. "Tasslehoff Burrfoot is dead."

"He is and he isn't, but I will come to that later," Raistlin said. "His soul remains unaccounted for." He turned to Zivilyn. "In the future that was, where did the kender's soul go after his death?"

"He joined his friend Flint Fireforge," said Zivilyn readily.

"Is his soul there now? Or does the grumbling dwarf wait for him still?"

Zivilyn hesitated, then said, "Flint is alone."

"A pity you did not notice this earlier," Sargonnas growled at Zivilyn. The minotaur god turned his glare at Raistlin. "Suppose this blasted kender *is* alive. What was he doing speaking words of magic? I never had much use for you mages, but at least you had sense enough to keep kender from using magic. This story of yours smells of yesterday's fish to me."

"As for the magic words he spoke," Raistlin replied, unperturbed by the minotaur god's gibe, "they were taught to him by an old friend of his, Fizban, when he gave into his hands the Device of Time Journeying."

The gods of darkness raised a clamor. The gods of magic looked grave.

"It has long been decreed that none of the Gray Gemstone races should ever be given the opportunity to travel through time," said Lunitari accusingly. "We should have been consulted in this matter."

"In truth, I gave him the device," said Paladine with a fond smile. "He wanted to attend the funeral of his friend Caramon Majere to do him honor. Quite logically assuming that he would die long before Caramon, Tasslehoff asked for the device so that he could go forward into the future to speak at the funeral. I thought this a noble and generous impulse, and thus I permitted it."

"Whether that was wise or not, you know best, Great One," Raistlin said. "I can affirm that Tasslehoff did travel forward in time once, but he missed, arriving at the funeral too late. He came back, thinking he would go again. As for what happened after that, the following is surmise, but since we know kender, I believe we can all agree that the premise I put forth is logical.

"One thing came up, then another, and Tasslehoff forgot all about traveling to Caramon's funeral until he was just about to be crushed by Chaos. At that moment, with only a few seconds of life left, Tas happened to recall this piece of unfinished business. He activated the device, which carried him forward in time. He arrived in the future, as he intended, except that it was a different future. Quite by mischance, the kender found the world. And I have found the kender."

For long moments, no one spoke. The gods of magic glanced at one another, their thoughts in perfect accord.

"Then take us there," said Gilean, the keeper of the book of knowledge.

"I would not advise it," Raistlin returned. "Queen Takhisis is extraordinarily powerful now. She is

221

watchful. She would be aware of your coming far in advance, and she has made preparations to receive you. Should you return now, weak and unprepared to face her, she might well destroy you."

Sargonnas rumbled deep in his chest. The thunder of his ire echoed through the heavens. The other gods were scornful, suspicious, or solemn, depending on the nature of each.

"You have another problem," Raistlin continued. "The people of the world believe that you abandoned them in their hour of greatest need. If you enter the world now, you will not find many who will welcome you."

"My people know I did not abandon them!" Sargonnas cried, clenching his fist.

Raistlin bowed, made no reply. He kept his gaze upon Paladine, who looked troubled.

"There is something in what you say," said Paladine at last. "We know how the people turned against us after the Cataclysm. Two hundred years passed before they were ready to accept us back. Takhisis knows this, and she would gladly use the distrust and anger of the people against us. We must proceed slowly and cautiously, as we did then."

"If I might suggest a plan," Raistlin said.

He detailed his idea. The gods listened, most of them. When he concluded, Paladine glanced around the circle.

"What say you all?"

"We approve," said the gods of magic, speaking together with one voice.

"I do not," said Sargonnas in anger.

The other gods remained silent, some doubtful, others disapproving.

Raistlin looked at each of them in turn, then said quietly, "You do not have an eternity to mull this over and debate among yourselves. You may not even have one second. Is it possible that you do not see the danger?"

"From a kender?" Sargonnas laughed.

"From a kender," said Nuitari. "Because Burrfoot did not die when he was supposed to have died, the moment of his death hangs suspended in time."

Solinari caught up his cousin's words, so that they seemed to come from the same throat. "If the kender dies in a time and place that is not his own, Tasslehoff will not defeat Chaos. The Father of All and Nothing will be victorious, and he will carry out his threat to destroy us *and* the world."

"The kender must be discovered and returned to the time and place of his death," Lunitari added, her voice stern. "Tasslehoff Burrfoot must die when and where he was supposed to die or we all face annihilation."

The three voices that were distinct and separate and yet seemed one voice fell silent.

Raistlin glanced around again. "I take it I have leave to go?"

Sargonnas muttered and grumbled, but in the end he fell silent.

The other gods looked to Paladine.

At length, he nodded.

"Then I bid you farewell," said Raistlin.

When the mage had departed, Sargonnas confronted Paladine. "You heap folly upon folly," the minotaur stated accusingly. "First you give a powerful magical artifact into the hands of a kender, then you send this twisted mage to fight Takhisis. If we are doomed, you have doomed us."

"Nothing done out of love is ever folly," Paladine returned. "If we face great peril, we now do so with hope." He turned to Zivilyn. "What do you see?"

Zivilyn looked into eternity.

"Nothing," he replied. "Nothing but darkness."

2

The Song of the Desert

ina's army moved east, heading for Sanction. The army traveled rapidly, for the skies were clear, the air cool and crisp, and they met no opposition. Blue dragons flew above them, guarding their march and scouting out the lands ahead. Rumor of their coming spread. Those along their route of march quaked in fear when they heard that they lay in the path of this conquering army. Many fled into the hills. Those who could not flee or had nowhere to go waited fearfully for destruction.

Their fears proved groundless. The army marched through villages and past farms, camped outside of towns. Mina kept her soldiers under strict control. Supplies they could have taken by force, they paid for. In some cases, when they came to an impoverished house or village, the army gave of what they had. Manor houses and castles they could have razed, they let stand. Everywhere along their route, Mina spoke

225

to the people of the One God. All they did, they did in the name of the One God.

Mina spoke to the high born and the low, to the peasant and the farmer, the blacksmith and the inn-keeper, the bard and the tinker, the noble lord and lady. She brought healing to the sick, food to the hungry, comfort to the unhappy. She told them how the old gods had abandoned them, left them to the scourge of these alien dragons. But this new god, the One God, was here to take care of them.

Odila was often at Mina's side. She took no part in the proceedings, but she watched and listened and fingered the amulet around her neck. The touch no longer seemed to cause her pain.

Gerard rode in the rear, as far as possible from the minotaur, who was always in the front ranks with Mina. Gerard guessed that Galdar had been ordered to leave him alone. Still, there was always the possibility of an "accident." Galdar could not be faulted if a poi-sonous snake happened to crawl into Gerard's bedroll or a broken tree branch came crashing down on his head. Those few times when the two were forced by circumstance to meet, Gerard saw by the look in the minotaur's eyes that Gerard was alive only because Mina willed it.

Unfortunately, riding in the rear meant that Gerard was back among those who guarded the wagon car-rying the sarcophagus of Goldmoon and the two wiz-ards. The phrase, "More dead than alive" came to Gerard's mind as he looked at them, and he looked at them often. He didn't like to. He couldn't stand the sight of them, sitting on the end of the wagon, bodies swaying to and fro with the motion of the bumpy ride, feet and arms dangling, heads drooping. Every time he watched them, he rode away sickened, vowing that was the last time he would have anything to do with them. The next day he was drawn to stare at them, fascinated, repulsed.

Mina's army marched toward Sanction, leaving behind not fire and smoke and blood, but cheering crowds, who tossed garlands at Mina's feet and sang praises of the One God.

Another group marched east, traveling almost parallel to Mina's army, separated by only a few hundred miles. Their march was slower because it was not as organized and the land through which they traveled was not as hospitable. The same sun that shone brightly on Mina seared the elves of Qualinesti as they struggled across the Plains of Dust, heading for what they hoped would be safe sanctuary in the land of their kin, the Silvanesti. Every day, Gilthas blessed Wanderer and the people of the plains, for without their help, not a single elf would have crossed the desert alive.

The Plainspeople gave the elves enveloping, protective clothing that kept out the heat of the day and held body warmth for the cold nights. The Plainspeople gave the elves food, which Gilthas suspected they could ill afford to share. Whenever he questioned them about this, the proud Plainspeople would either ignore him or cast him such cold glances that he knew that to continue to ask questions would offend them. They taught the elves that they should march during the cool parts of the morning and night and seek shelter against the sweltering heat of the afternoon. Finally, Wanderer and his comrades offered to accompany the elves and serve as guides. Gilthas knew, if the rest of the elves did not, that Wanderer had a twofold purpose. One was beneficent—to make certain the elves survived the crossing of the desert. The other was self-serving—to make certain the elves crossed.

The elves had come to look very much like the Plainspeople, dressing in baggy trousers and long tunics and wrapping themselves in many layers of soft wool that protected them from the desert sun by day and the desert chill by night. They kept their faces muffled against the stinging sand, kept delicate skin shielded from exposure. Having lived close to nature, with a respect for nature, the elves soon adapted to the desert and lost no more of their people. They could never love the desert, but they came to understand it and to honor its ways.

Gilthas could tell that Wanderer was uneasy at how swiftly the elves were adapting to this hard life. Gilthas tried his best to convince the Plainsman that the elves were a people of forests and gardens, a people who could look on the red and orange striated rock formations that broke the miles of endless sand dunes and see no beauty, as did the Plainspeople, but only death.

One night, when they were nearing the end of their long journey, the elves arrived at an oasis in the dark hours before the dawn. Wanderer had decreed that here the elves could rest this night and throughout the day tomorrow, drinking their fill and renewing their strength before they once more took up their weary journey. The elves made camp, set the watch, then gave themselves to sleep.

Gilthas tried to sleep. He was weary from the long walk, but sleep would not come. He had fought his way out of the depression that had plagued him. The need to be active and responsible for his people had been beneficial. He had a great many cares and worries still, not the least of which was the reception they might receive in Silvanesti. He was thinking of these matters, and restless, he left his bedroll, taking care not to wake his slumbering wife. He walked into the night to stare up at the myriad stars. He had not known there were so many. He was awed and even dismayed by their number. He was staring thus, when Wanderer found him.

"You should be sleeping," said Wanderer.

His voice was stern, he was giving a command, not making idle conversation. He had not changed from the day Gilthas had first met him. Taciturn, quiet, he never spoke when a gesture would serve him instead. His face was like the desert rock, formed of sharp angles marred by dark creases. He smiled, never laughed, and his smile was only in his dark eyes.

Gilthas shook his head. "My body yearns for sleep, but my mind prevents it."

"Perhaps the voices keep you awake," said Wanderer.

"I've heard you speak of them before," Gilthas replied, intrigued. "The voices of the desert. I have listened, but I cannot hear them."

"I hear them now," said Wanderer. "The sighing of the wind among the rocks, the whispering of the sand floes. Even in the silence of the night, there is a voice that we know to be the voice of the stars. You cannot see the stars in your land or, if you can, they are caught and held prisoner by the tree branches. Here"—Wanderer waved his hand to the vast vault of star-studded sky that stretched from horizon to horizon—"the stars are free, and their song is loud."

"I hear the wind among the rocks," said Gilthas, "but to me it is the sound of a dying breath whistling through gaping teeth. Yet," he added, pausing to look around him, "now that I have traveled through this land, I must admit that there is a beauty to your night. The stars are so close and so numerous that sometimes I *do* think I might hear them sing." He shrugged. "If I did not feel so small and insignificant among them, that is."

"That is what truly bothers you, Gilthas," said Wanderer, reaching out his hand and touching Gilthas on his breast, above his heart. "You elves rule the land in which you live. The trees form the walls of your houses and provide you shelter. The orchids and the roses grow at your behest. The desert will not be ruled. The desert will not be subjugated. The desert cares nothing about you, will do nothing for you except one thing. The desert will always be here. Your land changes. Trees die and forests burn, but the desert is eternal. Our home has always been, and it will always be. That is the gift it gives us, the gift of surety."

"We thought our world would never change," said Gilthas quietly. "We were wrong. I wish you a better fate."

Returning to his tent, Gilthas felt exhaustion overcome him. His wife did not waken, but she was sleepily aware of his return, for she reached out her arms and drew him close. He listened to the voice of her heart beating steadily against his. Comforted, he slept.

Wanderer did not sleep. He looked up at the stars and thought over the words of the young elf. And it seemed to Wanderer that the song of the stars was, for the first time since he'd heard it, mournful and off-key.

The elves continued their trek, their progress slow but steady. Then came the morning the Lioness shook her husband awake.

"What?" Gilthas asked, fear jolting him from sleep. "What is it? What is wrong?"

"For a change, nothing," she said, smiling at him through her rampant, golden curls. She sniffed the air. "What do you smell?"

"Sand," said Gilthas, rubbing his nose, that always seemed clogged with grit. "Why? What do you smell?"

"Water," said the Lioness. "Not the muddy water of some oasis but water that runs swift and fast and cold. There is a river nearby. . . ." Her eyes filled with tears, her voice failed her. "We have done it, my husband. We have crossed the Plains of Dust!"

A river it was, yet no river such as the Qualinesti had ever before seen. The elves gathered on its banks and stared in some dismay at the water, that flowed red as blood. The Plainspeople assured them that the water was fresh and untainted, the red color came from the rocks through which the river ran. The elves might have still hesitated, but the children broke free of their parents' grasp and rushed forward to splash in the water that bubbled around the roots of giant cottonwood and willow trees. Soon what remained of the Qualinesti nation was laughing and splashing and rollicking in the River Torath.

"Here we leave you," said Wanderer. "You can ford the river at this point. Beyond, only a few miles distant, you will come upon the remains of the King's Highway that will take you to Silvanesti. The river runs along the highway for many miles, so you will have water in abundance. The foraging is good, for the trees that grow along the river give of their fruits at this time of year."

Wanderer held out his hand to Gilthas. "I wish you good fortune and success at your journey's end. And I wish for you that someday you will hear the song of the stars."

"May their song never fall silent for you, my friend," said Gilthas, pressing the man's hand warmly. "I can never thank you enough for what you and your people have done—"

He stopped speaking, for he was talking to Wanderer's back. Having said all that was needed, the Plainsman motioned to his comrades, led them back into the desert.

"A strange people," said the Lioness. "They are rude and uncouth and in love with rocks, which is something I will never understand, but I find that I admire them."

"I admire them, too," said Gilthas. "They saved our lives, saved the Qualinesti nation. I hope that they never have reason to regret what they have done for us."

"Why should they?" the Lioness asked, startled.

"I don't know, my love," Gilthas replied. "I can't say. Just a feeling I have."

He walked away, heading for the river, leaving his wife to gaze after him with a look of concern and consternation.

3

The Lie

Alhana Starbreeze sat alone in the shelter that had been shaped for her by those elves who still had some magical power remaining to them, at least enough to command the trees to provide a safe haven for the exiled elven queen. As it turned out, the elves did not need their magic, for the trees, which have always loved the elves, seeing their queen sorrowful and weary to the point of collapse, bent their branches of their own accord. Their limbs hung protectively over her, their leaves twined together to keep out the rain and the wind. The grass formed a thick, soft carpet for her bed. The birds sang softly to ease her pain.

The time was evening, one of the few quiet times in Alhana's unquiet life. These were busy times, for she and her forces were living in the wilderness, fighting a hit-and-run war against the Dark Knights: raiding prison camps, attacking supply ships, making

233

daring forays into the city itself to rescue elves in peril. For the moment, though, all was peaceful. The evening meal had been served. The Silvanesti elves under her command were settling down for the night. For the moment, no one needed her, no one demanded that she make decisions that would cost more elven lives, shed more elven blood. Alhana sometimes dreamed of swimming in a river of blood, a dream from which she could never escape, except by drowning.

Some might say—and some elves did—that the Dark Knights of Neraka had done Alhana Starbreeze a favor. She had once been deemed a dark elf, exiled from her homeland for daring to try to bring about peace between the Silvanesti and their Qualinesti cousins, for daring to marry a Qualinesti in order to unite their two squabbling realms.

Now, in their time of greatest trouble, Alhana Starbreeze had been accepted back by her people. The sentence of exile had been lifted from her formally by the Heads of House who remained alive after the Dark Knights had completed their occupation of the capital, Silvanost. Alhana's people now embraced her. Kneeling at her feet, they were loud in their lamentations for the "misunderstanding." Never mind that they had tried to have her assassinated. In the very next breath, they cried to her, "Save us! Queen Alhana, save us!"

Samar was furious with her, with her people. The Silvanesti had invited the Dark Knights into their city and turned away Alhana Starbreeze. Not so many weeks before, they had fallen on their knees before the leader of the Dark Knights, a human girl called Mina. The Silvanesti had been warned of Mina's treachery, but they had been blinded by the miracles she performed in the name of the One God. Samar had been among those who had warned them that they were fools to put their trust in humans—miracles or not. The elves had been all astonishment and shock and horror when the Dark Knights had turned on them, set up their slave camps and prisons, killed any who opposed them.

Samar was grimly pleased that the Silvanesti had at last come to revere Alhana Starbreeze, the one person who had remained loyal to them and fought for them when they had reviled her. He was less pleased with his queen's response, which was forgiving, magnanimous, patient. He would have seen them cringe and grovel to obtain her favor.

"I cannot punish them, Samar," Alhana said to him on the evening on which the sentence of exile had been lifted. She was now free to return to her homeland—a homeland ruled over by the Dark Knights of Neraka, a homeland she was going to have to fight to reclaim. "You know why."

He knew why: All she did was for her son, Silvanoshei, who was the king of Silvanesti. An unworthy son, as far as Samar was concerned. Silvanoshei had been the person responsible for admitting the Knights of Neraka into the city of Silvanost. Enamored of the human girl, Mina, Silvanoshei was the cause of the downfall of the Silvanesti people.

Yet the people adored him and still claimed him as their king. Because of him, they followed his mother. Because of Silvanoshei, Samar was on a perilous journey, forced to leave his queen at the most desperate time in the ancient history of Silvanesti, forced to go chasing over Ansalon after this very son. Although few knew it, Silvanoshei, the king of the Silvanesti, had run away the very night Samar and other elves had risked their lives to rescue him from the Dark Knights.

Few knew he was gone, because Alhana refused to admit it, either to her people or to herself. Those elves who had been with them the night of his departure knew, but she had sworn them to secrecy. Long loyal to her, loving her, they had readily agreed. Now Alhana kept up the pretense that Silvanoshei was ill and that he was forced to remain in seclusion until he had healed.

Meantime, Alhana was confident he would return. "He is off sulking somewhere," she told Samar. "He will get over this infatuation and come to his senses. He will come back to me, to his people."

Samar did not believe it. He tried to point out to Alhana the evidence of the tracks of horse's hooves. The elves had brought no horses with them. This animal was magical, had been sent for Silvanoshei. He wasn't coming back. Not then, not ever. At first Alhana had refused even to listen to him. She had forbidden him to speak of it. But as the days passed and Silvanoshei did not return, she was forced to admit, with a breaking heart, that Samar might be right.

Samar had been gone long weeks now. During this time, Alhana had kept up the pretense that Silvanoshei was with them, sick and confined to his tent. She even went so far as to maintain his tent, pretend to go visit him. She would sit on his empty bed and talk to him, as if he were there. He would come back, and when he did, he would find her waiting for him, with all in readiness as if he had never left.

Alone in her bower, Alhana read and reread her latest message from Samar, a message carried by a hawk, for these birds had long served as messengers between the two. The message was brief—Samar not being one to waste words—and it brought both joy and sorrow to the anxious mother, dismay and despair to the queen.

I have picked up his trail at last. He took a ship from Abanasinia, sailed north to Solamnia. There he traveled to Solanthus in search of this female, but she had already marched eastward with her army. Silvanoshei followed her.

Other news I have heard. The city of Qualinost has been utterly destroyed. A lake of death now covers what remains of Qualinost. The Dark Knights now ravage the countryside, seizing land and making it their own. It is rumored that many Qualinesti escaped, including Laurana's son, Gilthas, but where they are or what has happened to them is unknown. I spoke to a survivor, who said that it is certain that Lauranalanthalasa was slain in the battle, along with many hundreds of Qualinesti, as well as dwarves of Thorbardin and some humans who fought alongside them. They died heroes. The evil dragon Beryl was killed.

I am on the trail of your son. I will report when I can.
Your faithful servant,
Samar

Alhana whispered a prayer for the soul of Laurana and the souls of all those who had perished in the battle. The prayer was to the old gods, the departed gods, who were no longer there to heed it. The beautiful words eased her grief, even if she knew in her heart that they held no meaning. She prayed, too, for the Qualinesti exiles, hoping that the rumor of their escape was true. Then, concern for her son banished all other thoughts from her mind.

"What witchery has this girl worked on you, my son?" she said softly, absently smoothing the vellum on which Samar had written his note. "What foul witchery . . ."

A voice spoke from outside her shelter, calling her name. The voice belonged to one of her elite guard, a woman who had served her long, through many difficult and dangerous times. She was known to Alhana to be stoic, reserved, never showing any emotion, and the queen was startled and alarmed now to hear a tremor in the woman's voice.

Fears of all kinds and sorts crowded around Alhana. She had to steel herself to react calmly. Crumpling the vellum in her hand, she thrust it into the bosom of her chemise, then ducked out of the sheltering vines and branches to face the woman. She saw with her a strange elf, someone unknown to her.

Or was he unknown? Or simply forgotten? Alhana stared at him closely. She knew this young man, she realized. Knew the lines of his face, knew the eyes that held in them a sadness and care and crushing responsibility to mirror her own. She could not place him, probably due to the foreign garb he wore—the long and enveloping robes of the barbarians who roamed the desert.

She looked to her guard for answers.

"The scouts came across him, my queen," said the woman. "He will not give his name, but he claims to be related to you through your honored husband, Porthios. He is Qualinesti, beneath all these layers of wool. He does not come armed into our lands. Since he may be what he claimed, we brought him to you."

"I know you, sir," Alhana said. "Forgive me, I cannot give you a name."

"That is understandable," he replied with a smile. "Many years and many trials separate us. Yet"—his voice softened, his eyes were warm with admiration—"I remember you, the great lady so wrongfully imprisoned by her people—"

Alhana gave a glad cry, flung herself into his arms. Even as she embraced him, she remembered the mother he had lost, who would never more put her arms around her son. Alhana kissed him tenderly, for her sake and that of Laurana's, then she stepped back to look at him.

"Those trials of which you speak have aged you more than the corresponding years. Gilthas of the House of Solostaran, I am pleased beyond measure to see you safe and well, for I just heard the sad news concerning your people. I hoped that what I heard was rumor and gossip and that it would prove false, but, alas, I see the truth in your eyes."

"If you have heard that my mother is dead and that Qualinost is destroyed, then you have heard the truth," Gilthas said.

"I am sorry beyond measure," Alhana said, taking his hand in her own and holding it fast. "Please, come inside, where you may be comfortable, for I see the weariness of many weeks of travel lie on you. I will have food and water brought to you."

Gilthas accompanied Alhana into the shelter. He ate the food that was offered, though Alhana could see he did so out of politeness rather than hunger.

He drank the water with a relish he could not disguise, drank long and deep, as if he could never get enough.

"You have no idea how good this water tastes to me," he said, smiling. He glanced around. "But when am I going to have a chance to greet my cousin, Silvanoshei? We have never met, he and I. We heard the sad rumor that he had been slain by ogres and were glad to receive news that this was not true. I am eager to embrace him."

"I regret to say that Silvanoshei is not well, Gilthas," said Alhana. "He was brutally beaten by the Dark Knights when they seized Silvanost and barely escaped with his life. He keeps to his tent on the order of the healers and is not permitted to have any company."

She had told this lie so often that she was able to tell it now without a break in her voice. She could meet the young man's eyes and never falter. He believed her, for his face took on a look of concern.

"I am sorry to hear this. Please accept my wishes for his swift recovery."

Alhana smiled and changed the subject. "You have traveled far and on dangerous roads. Your journey must have been a hard and perilous one. What can I do for you, Nephew? May I call you that, although I am only your aunt by marriage?"

"I would be honored," said Gilthas, his voice warm. "You are all the family I have left now. You and Silvanoshei."

Alhana's eyes filled with sudden tears. He was all the family she had, at this moment, with Silvanoshei lost to her. She clasped his hand, and he held fast to hers. She was reminded of his father, Tanis Half-Elven.

The memory was heartening, for the times in which they had known each other had been fraught with peril, yet they had overcome their foes and gone on to find peace, even if only for a short while.

"I come to ask a great boon of you, Aunt Alhana," he said. He gazed at her steadfastly. "I ask that you receive my people."

Alhana stared at him, bewildered, not understanding.

Gilthas gestured to the west. "Three days' ride from here, on the border of Silvanesti, a thousand exiles from Qualinesti wait to receive your permission to enter the land of our cousins. Our home is destroyed. The enemy occupies it. We lack the numbers to fight them. Someday," he said, his chin lifting and pride lighting his eyes, "we will return and drive the Dark Knights from our land and reclaim what is ours.

"But that day is not today," he continued, the light fading, darkened by shadow. "Nor is it tomorrow. We have traveled across the Plains of Dust. We would have died there but for the help of the people who call that terrible land home. We are weary and desperate. Our children look to us for comfort, and we have none to give them. We are exiles. We have nowhere to go. Humbly we come to you, who left so long ago, and humbly we ask that you take us in."

Alhana looked long at him. The tears that had burned in her eyes now slid unchecked down her cheeks.

"You weep for us," he said brokenly. "I am sorry to have brought this trouble to you."

"I weep for us all, Gilthas," Alhana said. "For the Qualinesti people, who have lost their homeland,

and for the Silvanesti, who are fighting for ours. You will not find peace and sanctuary here in these forests, my poor nephew. You find us at war, battling for our very survival. You did not know this when you set out, did you?"

Gilthas shook his head.

"You know this now?" she asked.

"I know," he said. "I heard the news from the Plainspeople. I had hoped they exaggerated—"

"I doubt it. They are a people who see far and speak bluntly. I will tell you what is happening, and then you can decide if you want to join us."

Gilthas would have spoken, but Alhana raised her hand, silenced him. "Hear me out, Nephew." She hesitated a moment, underwent some inward struggle, then said, "You will hear from some of our people that my son was bewitched by this human girl, Mina, the leader of the Dark Knights. He was not the only Silvanesti to fall under her fatal spell. Our people sang songs of praise to her as she walked through the streets. She performed miracles of healing, but there was a price—not in coin but in souls. The One God wanted the souls of the elves to torment and enslave and devour. This One God is not a loving god, as some of our people mistakenly thought, but a god of deceit and vengeance and pain. Those elves who served the One God were taken away. We have no idea where. Those elves who refuse to serve the One God were killed outright or enslaved by the Dark Knights.

"The city of Silvanost is completely under the control of the Dark Knights. Their forces are not yet large enough to extend that control, and so we are able to maintain our existence here in the forests.

We do what we can to fight against this dread foe, and we have saved many hundreds of our people from torture and death. We raid the prison camps and free the slaves. We harass the patrols. They fear our archers so much that no Dark Knight now dares set foot outside the city walls. All this we do, but it is not enough. We lack the forces needed to retake the city, and every day the Dark Knights add to its fortifications."

"Then our warriors will be a welcome addition," said Gilthas quietly.

Alhana lowered her eyes, shook her head. "No," she said, ashamed. "How could we ask that of you? The Silvanesti have treated you and your people with contempt and disdain all these years? How could we ask you to give your lives for our country?"

"You forget," said Gilthas, "that our people have no country. Our city lies in ruins. The same foe that rules your land rules ours." His fist clenched, his eyes flashed. "We are eager to take retribution. We will take back your land, then combine our forces to take back our own."

He leaned forward, his face alight. "Don't you see, Alhana? This may be the impetus we need to heal the old wounds, to once more unite our two nations."

"You are so young," Alhana said. "Too young to know that old wounds can fester so that the infection strikes to the very heart, turning it sick and putrid. You do not know that there are some who would see all of us fall rather than one of us rise. I tried to unite our people. I failed and this is what has come of my failure. I think it is too late. I think that nothing can save our people."

He gazed at her in consternation, clearly disturbed by her words.

Alhana rested her hand on his. "Maybe I am wrong. Perhaps your young eyes see more clearly. Bring your people into the safety of the forest. Then you must go before the Silvanesti and tell them of your plight and ask them to admit you into their lands."

"Ask them? Or do you mean beg them?" Gilthas rose, his expression cool. "We do not come before the Silvanesti as beggars."

"There, you see," Alhana said sadly. "You have been infected. Already, you jump to conclusions. You should ask the Silvanesti because it is politic to ask. That is all I meant." She sighed. "We corrupt our young, and thus perishes hope for anything better."

"You are sorrowful and weary and worried for your son. When he is well, he and I— Alhana," Gilthas said, alarmed, for she had sunk down upon a cushion and begun weeping bitterly. "What is wrong? Should I call someone? One of your ladies?"

"Kiryn," Alhana said in a choked voice. "Send for Kiryn."

Gilthas had no notion who this Kiryn was, but he ducked outside the shelter and informed one of the guards, who dispatched a runner. Gilthas went back inside the shelter, stood ill at ease, not knowing what to do or say to ease such wrenching grief.

A young elf entered the dwelling. He looked first at Alhana, who was struggling to regain her composure, then at Gilthas. Kiryn's face flushed with anger.

"Who are you? What have you said—"

"No, Kiryn!" Alhana raised her tearstained face. "He has done nothing. This is my nephew, Gilthas, Speaker of the Sun of the Qualinesti."

"I beg your pardon, Your Majesty," said Kiryn, bowing low. "I had no way of knowing. When I saw my queen—"

"I understand," said Gilthas. "Aunt Alhana, if I inadvertently said or did anything to cause you such pain—"

"Tell him, Kiryn," Alhana ordered in a tone that was low and terrible to hear. "Tell him the truth. He has a right . . . a need to know."

"My queen," said Kiryn, glancing at Gilthas uncertainly, "are you certain?"

Alhana closed her eyes, as if she would thankfully close them upon this world. "He has brought his people across the desert. They came to us for succor, for their capital city is destroyed, their land ravaged by the Dark Knights."

"Blessed E'li!" exclaimed Kiryn, calling, in his astonishment, upon the absent god Paladine or E'li, as the elves know him.

"Tell him," said Alhana, sitting with her face averted from them, hidden behind her hand.

Kiryn motioned Gilthas to draw near. "I tell you, Your Majesty, what only a few others know, and they have taken vows of secrecy. My cousin, Silvanoshei, is not wounded. He does not lie in his tent. He is gone."

"Gone?" Gilthas was puzzled. "Where has he gone? Has he been captured? Taken prisoner?"

"Yes," said Kiryn gravely, "but not the way you mean. He has become obsessed with a human girl, a leader of the Dark Knights called Mina. We believe that he has run off to join her."

"You *believe?*" Gilthas repeated. "You do not know for sure?"

Kiryn shrugged, helpless. "We know nothing for certain. We rescued him from the Dark Knights, who were going to put him to death. We were escaping into the wilderness when a magical sleep came over us. When we awoke, Silvanoshei was gone. We found the tracks of a horse's hooves. We tried to follow the hoofprints, but they entered the Than-Thalas River, and although we searched upstream and down, we could not find any more tracks. It was as if the horse had wings."

Alhana spoke, her voice muffled. "I have sent my most trusted friend and advisor after my son, to bring him back. I have told the Silvanesti people nothing about this. I ask you to say nothing of this to anyone."

Gilthas was troubled. "I don't understand. Why do you keep his disappearance secret?"

Alhana lifted her head. Her eyes were swollen with her grief, red-rimmed. "Because the Silvanesti people have taken him to their hearts. He is their king, and they follow him, when they would not willingly follow me. All I do, I do in his name."

"You mean you make the hard decisions and face the danger, while your son, who should be sharing your burden, chases after a petticoat," Gilthas began sternly.

"Do not criticize him!" Alhana flared. "What do you know of what he has endured? This female is a witch. She has ensorcelled him. He does not know what he is doing."

"Silvanoshei was a good king until he had the misfortune to meet Mina," said Kiryn defensively. "The people came to love and respect him. He will be a good king when this spell is broken."

"I thought you should know the truth, Gilthas," Alhana said stiffly, "since you have responsibilities of your own you must bear, decisions you must make. I ask only that you do as Kiryn does, respect my wishes and say nothing of this to anyone. Pretend, as we pretend, that Silvanoshei is here with us."

Her tone was cold, her eyes beseeching. Gilthas would have given much to have been able to ease her pain, to lift her burdens. But, as she said, he bore burdens himself. He had responsibilities, and they were to his people.

"I have never yet lied to the Qualinesti, Aunt Alhana," he said, as gently as he could. "I will not start now. They left their homeland on my word, they followed me into the desert. They have given their lives and the lives of their children into my hands. They trust me, and I will not betray that trust. Not even for you, whom I love and honor."

Alhana rose to her feet, her fists clenched at her sides. "If you do this, you will destroy all that I have worked for. We might as well surrender to the Dark Knights now." Her fists unclenched, and he saw that her hands trembled. "Give me some time, Nephew. That is all I ask. My son will return soon. I know it!"

Gilthas shifted his gaze from her to Kiryn, looked long and intently at the young elf. Kiryn said nothing, but his eyes flickered. He was clearly uncomfortable.

Alhana saw Gilthas's dilemma.

"He is too kind, too polite, too mindful of my pain to speak the words that must be burning on his tongue," she said herself. "If he could, he would say to me, *This is not my doing. I am not at fault. This is your son's doing. Silvanoshei has failed his people. I will not follow in those same footsteps.*"

Alhana was angry with Gilthas, jealous of him and proud of him, all in the same scalding moment. She envied Laurana suddenly, envied her death that brought blessed silence to the turmoil, an end to pain, an end to despair. Laurana had died a hero's death, fighting to save her people and her country. She had left behind a legacy of which she could be proud, a son she could honor.

"I tried to do what was right," Alhana said to herself in misery, "but it all has ended up so terribly wrong."

Her loved husband Porthios had vanished and was presumed to be dead. Her son, her hope for the future, had run away to leave her to face that future alone. She might tell herself he had been ensorcelled, but deep in her heart, she knew better. He was spoiled, selfish, too easily swayed by passions she had never had the heart to check. She had failed her husband, she had failed her son. Her pride refused to let her admit it.

Pride would be her downfall. Her pride had been wounded when her people turned against her. Her pride had caused her to attack the shield, to try to reenter a land that didn't want her. Now her pride forced her to lie to her people.

Samar and Kiryn had both counseled against it. Both had urged her to tell the truth, but her pride could not stomach it. Not her pride as a queen, but her pride as a mother. She had failed as a mother and now all would see that failure. She could not bear for people to regard her with pity. That, more than anything else, was the true reason she had lied.

She had hoped that Silvanoshei would come back, admit that he had been wrong, ask to be forgiven. If that had happened, she could have overlooked his downfall. She knew now after reading Samar's letter that Silvanoshei would never come back to her, not of his own free will. Samar would have to drag him back like an errant schoolboy.

She looked up to find Gilthas looking at her, his expression sympathetic, grave. In that moment, he was his father. Tanis Half-Elven had often looked at her with that same expression as she underwent some inward battle, fought against her pride.

"I will keep your secret, Aunt Alhana," Gilthas said. His voice was cool, he was clearly unhappy with what he was doing. "As long as I can."

"Thank you, Gilthas," she said, grateful and ashamed for having to be grateful. Her pride! Her damnable pride. "Silvanoshei will return. He will hear of our plight and come back. Perhaps he is already on his way."

She pressed her hand over her bosom, over Samar's letter that said entirely the opposite. Lying had become so easy, so very easy.

"I hope so," said Gilthas somberly.

He took her hand in his own, kissed it respectfully. "I am sorry for your trouble, Aunt Alhana. I am sorry to have added to your trouble. But if this brings about the reunification of our two nations, then someday we will look back upon the heartbreak and turmoil and say that it was worth it."

She tried to smile, but the stiffness of her lips made her mouth twitch. She said nothing, and so in silence they parted.

"Go with him," she told Kiryn, who remained behind. "See to it that he and his people are made welcome."

"Your Majesty—" Kiryn began uneasily.

"I know what you are going to say, Kiryn. Do not say it. All will be well. You will see."

After both had left, she stood in the doorway of the shelter, thinking of Gilthas.

"Such pretty dreams," she said softly. "The dreams of youth. Once I had pretty dreams. Now, like my pretty gowns, they hang about me in rags and in tatters. May yours fit better, Gilthas, and last longer."

4

Waiting and Waiting

General Dogah, leader of the Dark Knights in Silvanost, was having his own problems. The Dark Knights used blue dragons as scouts, patrolling the skies above the thick and tangled forests. If the dragons caught sight of movement on the ground, they swooped down and, with their lightning breath, laid waste to entire tracts of forest land.

These dragon scouts saw the large gathering of people in the desert but had no idea they were Qualinesti. The scouts thought them the barbarians, the Plainspeople, fleeing the onslaught of the dragon overlord Sable. General Dogah wondered what to do about this migration. He had no orders concerning the Plainspeople. His forces were limited, his hold on Silvanost tenuous at best. He did not want to start war on another front. He dispatched a courier on dragonback with an urgent message for Mina, telling her about the situation and asking for orders.

The courier had some difficulty locating Mina, for he flew first to Solanthus, only to find that her army had left there and was on the march for Sanction.

After another day's flying, the courier located her. He sped back with this reply, short and terse.

General Dogah
These are not Plainspeople. They are Qualinesti exiles. Destroy them.

In the name of the One God,

Mina

Dogah sent off his dragonriders to do just that, only to find that in the interim the Qualinesti had disappeared. No trace of them could be found anywhere. He received this report with a bitter curse, for he knew what it meant. The Qualinesti had managed to escape into the forests of Silvanesti and were now beyond his reach.

Here were yet more elves to attack his patrols and fire flaming arrows at his supply ships. To add to his woes, the dragons began bringing reports that the ogres, long enraged at the Knights for stealing their land, were massing on the northern Silvanesti border that adjoined Blöde, undoubtedly hoping to seize some elven land in return.

And to make matters worse, Dogah was having morale trouble. So long as Mina had been around to enchant them and entrance them, the soldiers were committed to her cause, dedicated and enthusiastic followers. But Mina had been gone many long weeks now. The soldiers and the Knights who commanded them were isolated in the middle of a strange and unfriendly realm, where enemies lurked in every shadow—and Silvanesti was a land of shadows. Arrows came out of the skies to slay them. Even the vegetation seemed intent on trying to kill them. Tree roots tripped them, dead limbs dropped on their heads, forests lured them into tangles from which few ever returned.

Not a single supply ship had sailed down the river in the past week. The elves set fire to those that made the attempt. The soldiers had no food other than what the elves ate, and no human could subsist on leaves and grass for long. The meat-hungry humans dared not enter the woods to hunt, for, as they soon discovered, every creature in the forest was a spy for the elves.

The elves of the city of Silvanost, seemingly cowed by the might of the Dark Knights, were growing bolder. None of Dogah's men dared venture into the city alone lest they risk being found dead in an alley. The men began to grouse and grumble.

Dogah issued orders to torture more elves, but such entertainment could keep his troops occupied for only so long. He was fortunate in that there were no desertions. This was not due to loyalty, as he well knew, but to the fact that the men were too terrified of the elves and the forest that sheltered them to flee.

Now, with the knowledge that a thousand more elves had joined those already in the forest, the mutinous rumblings grew loud as thunder, so that Dogah could not remain deaf to them. He himself began to doubt. When he could not see himself reassuringly reflected in her amber eyes, his trust in Mina started to wane.

He dispatched another urgent message to Mina, telling her that the Qualinesti had escaped his best efforts to destroy them, that morale was in the privies, and that unless something happened to change the situation, he would have no choice but to pull out of Silvanesti or face mutiny.

Dark-bearded and, these days, dark-faced and gloomy, the short, stocky Dogah sat alone (he had very little trust even in his own bodyguards these days) in his quarters, drank elven wine that he wished mightily was a liquor far stronger, and waited for Mina's reply.

The Qualinesti entered the forest to be coolly welcomed by their long-estranged cousins, the Silvanesti. A polite cousinly kiss of greeting was exchanged, and then spears and arrows were thrust into Qualinesti hands. If they were going to relocate to Silvanesti, they had better be prepared to fight for it.

The Qualinesti were only too happy to oblige. They saw this as a chance to avenge themselves on those who had seized their own realm and were now laying waste to it.

"When do we attack?" they demanded eagerly.

"Any day now," was the response from the Silvanesti. "We are waiting for the right time."

"Waiting for the right time?" the Lioness asked her husband. "For what 'right time' do we wait? I have talked to the scouts and spies. We outnumber the Dark Knights who are bottled up in Silvanost. Their morale sinks faster than a shipwrecked dwarf in full battle armor. Now is the opportune time to attack them!"

The two spoke in the shelter that had been provided for them—a hutch made of woven willow branches on the side of a bubbling stream. The space was small and cramped, but they were luckier than most of the elves, for they had a place of their own (due to Gilthas's royal rank) and some privacy. Most of the elves slept in the boughs of living trees or the hollowed-out boles of dead ones, inside caves or simply lying in the grass under the stars. The Qualinesti had no complaints. After their trek through the desert, they asked for nothing more than to sleep on crisp-smelling pine needles, lulled by the gentle murmur of the falling rain.

"You tell me nothing that I don't already know," said Gilthas morosely. He had taken to wearing clothing more typical of his people—the long, belted tunic, woollen shirt, and stockings in woodland colors. But he had folded neatly and put away safely the coverings of the desert.

"There are problems, however. The Silvanesti are spread out all over the land. Some are stationed along the river to disrupt the Dark Knights' supply lines. Others hide near the city of Silvanost, to make certain that any patrol that has nerve enough to leave the city does not return intact. Still others are scattered along the borders . . ."

"The wind, the hawk, the squirrel carry messages," returned the Lioness. "If the orders were sent now, most of the Silvanesti could be gathered outside Silvanost in a week's time. Days go by, and the orders are not given. We must skulk about in the forest and wait. Wait for what?"

Gilthas knew, but he could not answer. He kept silent, was forced let his wife fume.

"We know what will happen if the opportunity is missed! Thus did the Dark Knights take over our homeland during the Chaos War. The same will be true of the Silvanesti, if we don't act now. Is it your cousin, Silvanoshei, who holds back? He is young.

255

Probably he doesn't understand. You must speak to him, Gilthas, explain to him—"

She knew her husband well. At the look on her face, the words clotted on her tongue.

The Lioness eyed him narrowly. "What is it, Gilthas? What's wrong? Something about Silvanoshei, isn't it?"

Gilthas looked at her ruefully. "Am I so transparent? Kings should be cloaked in inscrutability and mystery."

"My husband," said the Lioness, unable to keep from laughing, "you are inscrutable and mysterious as a crystal goblet. The truth inside you is plain for all the world to see."

"The truth . . ." Gilthas made a wry face. "The truth is, my dear, that Silvanoshei could not lead his people in a three-legged race, much less lead them to war. He is nowhere near here, nowhere near Silvanesti. I promised Alhana I would say nothing, but now a fortnight has passed and it seems to me that the time for lying has come to an end. Although"—Gilthas shook his head—"I fear that the truth will do more harm than good. The Silvanesti follow Alhana now only because she speaks in the name of her son. Some still view her with suspicion, see her as a 'dark elf.' If they find out the truth, that she has been lying to them, I fear they will never believe her again, never listen to her."

The Lioness looked into her husband's eyes. "That leaves you, Gilthas."

Now it was his turn to laugh. "I am everything that they despise, my dear. A Qualinesti with human blood thrown in. They will not follow me."

"Then you must persuade Alhana to tell her people the truth."

"I don't believe she can. She has told the lie so long that, for her, the lie has become the truth."

"So what do we do?" the Lioness demanded. "Live here in the forest until we take root along with the trees? We Qualinesti could attack the Dark Knights—"

"No, my dear," said Gilthas firmly. "The Silvanesti have permitted us to enter their homeland, that much is true, but they view us with suspicion, nonetheless. There are those who think we are here to usurp their homeland. For the Qualinesti to attack Silvanost—"

"The Qualinesti are *not* attacking Silvanost. The Qualinesti are attacking the Dark Knights *in* Silvanost," argued the Lioness.

"That is not how the Silvanesti will view it. You know that as well as I do."

"So we sit and do nothing."

"I do not know what else we can do," said Gilthas somberly. "The one person who could have united and rallied his people has been lured away. Now the only people left to lead the elves are a dark elf queen and a half-human king."

"Yet sooner or later someone must take the lead," the Lioness said. "We must follow someone."

"And where would that someone lead them?" Gilthas asked somberly, "except to our own destruction."

General Dogah drank his way through several barrels of wine. His problems increased daily. Six soldiers ordered to stand guard on the battlements refused to obey. Their officer threatened them with the lash. They attacked him, beat him severely, and ran off, hoping to lose themselves in the streets of Silvanost. Dogah sent his troops after the deserters, intending to string them up to serve as examples to the rest.

The elves saved him the cost of rope. The bodies of the six were delivered to the castle. Each had died in some gruesome, grotesque manner. A note found on one, scrawled in Common, read, *A gift for the One God*.

That night, Dogah sent another messenger to Mina, pleading for either reinforcements or permission to withdraw. Although, he thought glumly, he had no idea where he would withdraw to. Everywhere he looked, he saw enemies.

Two days later, the messenger finally returned.

General Dogah
Hold your ground. Help is on the way.

In the name of the One God.

Mina

That wasn't much comfort.

Every day, Dogah cautiously mounted·the walls of Silvanost, peered out to the north, the south, the east, and the west. The elves were out there. They had him surrounded. Every day, he expected the elves to attack.

Days passed, and the elves did nothing.

5

The Hedge Maze

Tasslehoff Burrfoot was, at that moment in time feeling extremely put-out, put-upon, dizzy, and sick to his stomach. Of the three feelings, the dizzy feeling predominated, so that he was finding it hard to think clearly. Plain, wooden floors and good, hard ground had once seemed mundane objects as far as he was concerned, but now Tasslehoff thought fondly, wistfully, longingly of ground or floor or any solid surface beneath his feet.

He also thought longingly of his feet returning to their proper place as feet and not thinking themselves his head, which they were continually doing, for he always looked for them below and found them above. The only good thing to happen to Tasslehoff was that Conundrum had screamed himself hoarse and could now make only feeble croaking sounds.

Tas blamed everything on the Device of Time Journeying. He wondered sadly if this whirling and turning and dropping in on various points of time was going to go on eternally, and he was a bit daunted at the prospect. Then it occurred to him that sooner or later, the device was bound to land him back in the time where he'd be stepped on by Chaos. All in all, not a bright prospect.

Such thoughts ran through his head, which was constantly whirling and twirling through time. He thought them through as best he could, given the dizzy feeling, and suddenly a fresh thought popped in. Perhaps the owner of the voice that he heard in his ear and the hand that he felt on his shoulder could do something about this endless whirling. He made up his mind that the moment they landed again, he would do everything in his power to see the hand's owner.

Which he did. The very minute he felt firm ground (blessed ground!) beneath his feet, he stumbled around (rather wobbly) to look behind him.

He saw Conundrum and Conundrum's hand, but that was the wrong hand. No one else was about, and Tas immediately knew why. He and the gnome were standing in what appeared to be a field blackened by fire. Some distance away, crystal buildings caught the last glow of evening, glimmered orange or purple or gold as the dying rays of the sun painted them. The air was still tainted with the smell of burning, although the fire that had consumed the vegetation had been put out some time ago. He could hear voices, but they were far distant. From somewhere came the sweet and piercing music of a flute.

Tasslehoff had the vague notion that he'd been here before. Or maybe he'd been here after before. What with all the time jumping, he wasn't certain about anything anymore. The place looked familiar, and he was about to set off in search of someone who could tell him where he was, when Conundrum gave a wheezing gasp.

"The Hedge Maze!"

Tas looked down and looked sideways, and he realized that Conundrum was right. They were standing in what remained of the Hedge Maze after the red dragons had destroyed it with their fiery breath. The walls of leaves were burnt down to the ground. The paths that wound and twisted between them—leading those who walked the paths deeper into the maze—were laid bare. The maze was a maze no longer. Tas could see the pattern clearly, the white paths standing out starkly against the black. He could see every twist, every turning, every whorl, every jog, every dead end. He saw the way to the heart of the Hedge Maze and he saw the way out. The silver stair stood naked, exposed. He could see plainly now that it led up and up to nowhere, and with a queasy flutter of the stomach, he remembered his leap off the top and his dive into the smoke and the flame.

"Oh, my!" whispered Conundrum, and Tas remembered that mapping the Hedge Maze had been the gnome's Life Quest.

"Conundrum," said Tas somberly. "I—"

"You can see everything," said the gnome.

"I know," said Tas, patting the gnome's hand. "And I—"

"I could walk from one end to the other," said Conundrum, "and never get lost."

"Maybe you could find some other line of work," Tas suggested, wanting to be helpful. "Although I'd stay away from the repair of magical devices—"

"It's perfect!" Conundrum breathed. His eyes filled with happy tears.

"What?" Tas asked, startled. "What's perfect?"

"Where's my parchment?" Conundrum demanded. "Where's my ink bottle and my brush?"

"I don't have an ink bottle—"

Conundrum glared at him. "Then what good are you? Never mind," he added huffily. "Ah ha! Charcoal! That'll do."

He plopped down on the burnt ground. Spreading out the hem of his brown robes, he picked up a charred stick and began slowly and laboriously tracing the route of the burnt Hedge Maze on the fabric.

"This is so much easier," he muttered to himself. "I don't know why I didn't think of it sooner."

Tasslehoff felt the familiar touch of the hand on his shoulder. The jewels of the Device of Time Journeying began to sparkle and glitter with golden and purple light, a reflection of the setting sun.

"Goodbye, Conundrum," Tas called, as the paths of the Hedge Maze began to swirl in his vision.

The gnome didn't look up. He was concentrating on his map.

6

The Strange Passenger

At a small port in southern Estwilde, the strange passenger disembarked from the ship on which he had sailed across New Sea. The captain was relieved to be rid of his mysterious passenger and more relieved to be rid of the passenger's fiery-tempered horse. Neither the captain nor any of the crew knew anything about the passenger. No one ever saw his face, which he kept hidden beneath the hood of his cloak.

Such seclusion had raised much speculation among the crew about the nature of their passenger, most of it wild and all of it wrong. Some guessed the passenger was a woman, disguised as a man, for the cabin boy had once caught a glimpse of a hand that, according to him, was slender and delicate in appearance. Others suspected him to be a wizard of some sort for no other reason than that wizards were known to wear hooded cloaks and that they were always mysterious and never to be trusted. Only one sailor stated that he believed the passenger to be an elf, hiding his face because he knew that the humans aboard ship would not take kindly to one of his race.

The other sailors scoffed at this notion and, since the conversation was being held at dinner, they threw weevily biscuits at the head of the man who made it. He offered his hunch as a wager, and everyone took him up on it. He became a wealthy man, relatively speaking, at the end of the voyage, when a gust of wind blew back the passenger's hood as he was leading his horse down the gangplank to reveal that he was, indeed, an elf.

No one bothered to ask the elf what brought him to this part of Ansalon. The sailors didn't care where the elf had been or where he was going. They were only too happy to have him off their ship, it being well known among seafarers that the sea elves—those who purportedly make their homes in the watery deeps—will try to scuttle any ship carrying one of their land-bound brethren in order to persuade them to live the remainder of their lives below the sea.

As for Silvanoshei, he never looked back, once he had set foot on land. He had no care for the ship or the sailors, although both had sped him across New Sea at a truly remarkable rate of speed. The wind had blown fair from the day they set forth, never ceasing. There had been no storms—a miracle this late in the season. Yet no matter how fast the ship sailed, it had not sailed fast enough for Silvanoshei.

He was overjoyed when he first set foot on land, for this was the land on which Mina walked. Every step brought him closer to that loved face, that adored voice. He had no idea where she was, but the horse knew.

Her horse, which she had sent for him. The moment he set foot on shore, Silvanoshei mounted Foxfire, and they galloped off so fast that he never knew the name of the small port in which they'd landed.

They traveled northwest. Silvanoshei would have ridden day and night, if he could, but the horse (miraculous animal though it was) was a mortal horse and required food and rest, as did Silvanoshei himself. At first he bitterly grudged the time they must spend resting, but he was rewarded for his sacrifice. The very first night away from the ship, Silvanoshei fell in with a merchant caravan bound for the very same port town he'd recently left.

Many humans would have shunned a lone elf met by chance on the road, but merchants view every person as a potential customer and thus they tend not to be prejudiced against any race (except kender). Elven coin being just as good (or oftentimes better) than human, they cordially invited the young elf, whose clothing, though travel-stained, was of fine quality, to share their repast. Silvanoshei was on the verge of loftily refusing—he wanted to do nothing but sit by himself and dream of amber eyes—when he heard one of them speak the name, "Mina."

"I thank you gentlemen and ladies for your hospitality," said Silvanoshei, hurrying over to sit by their roaring fire. He even accepted the tin plate of dubious stew they offered him, although he didn't eat it, but surreptitiously dumped it in the bushes behind him.

He still wore the cloak he had worn on board ship, for the weather this time of year was cool. He removed the hood, however, and the humans were lost in admiration for this handsome youth, with his wine-colored eyes, charming smile and a voice that was sweet and melodious. Seeing that he'd eaten his stew quickly, one of the women offered him more.

"You're as thin as last year's mattress," she said, filling a plate, which he politely declined.

"You mentioned the name 'Mina,' " Silvanoshei said, trying to sound casual, though his heart beat wildly. "I know someone of that name. She wouldn't be an elf maid, by chance?"

At this they all laughed heartily. "Not unless elf maids wear armor these days," said one.

"I heard tell of an elf maid who wore armor," protested another, who seemed of an argumentative nature. "I recall my grandfather singing a song about her. Back in the days of the War of the Lance, it was."

"Bah! Your grandfather was an old souse," said a third. "He never went anywhere, but lived and died in the bars of Flotsam."

"Still, he's right," said one of the merchant's wives. "There was an elf maid who fought in the great war. Her name was Loony-tarry."

"Lunitari was the old goddess of magic, my dear," said her friend, another one of the wives, with a nudge of her elbow. "The ones who went away and left us to the mercy of these huge, monstrous dragons."

"No, I'm sure it wasn't," said the first wife, offended. "It was Loony-tarry, and she slew one of the foul beasts with a gnomish device called a dragonlunch. So called because she rammed it down the beast's gullet. And I wish another such would come and do the same to these new dragons."

"Well, from what we hear, this Mina plans to do just that," said the first merchant, trying to make peace between the two women, who were muttering huffily at each other.

"Have you seen her?" Silvanoshei asked, his heart on his lips. "Have you seen this Mina?"

"No, but she's all anyone's talking about in the towns we've passed through."

"Where is she?" Silvanoshei asked. "Is she close by?"

"She's marching along the road to Sanction. You can't miss her. She rides with an army of Dark Knights," answered the argumentative man dourly.

"Don't you take that amiss, young sir," said one of the wives. "Mina may wear black armor, but from what we hear, she has a heart of pure gold."

"Everywhere we go, we see some child she's healed or some cripple she's made to walk," said her friend.

"She's going to break the siege of Sanction," added the merchant, "and give us our port back. Then we can quit trekking halfway across the continent to sell our wares."

"And none of you think this is wrong?" said the argumentative man angrily. "Our own Solamnic Knights are in Sanction, trying to hang onto it, and you're cheering on this leader of our enemies."

This precipitated a lively discussion, which led at last to the majority of the group being in favor of whichever side would at last open up the ports to shipping once again. The Solamnics had tried to break out of Sanction and failed. Let this Mina and her Dark Knights see what they could do.

Shocked and horrified to think of Mina placing herself in such danger, Silvanoshei slipped away to lie awake half the night sick with fear for her. She must not attack Sanction! She must be dissuaded from such a dangerous course of action.

He was up and away with the first light of dawn. He had no need to urge the horse. Foxfire was as anxious to return to his mistress as was his rider. The two pushed themselves to the limit, the name "Mina" sounding with every hoofbeat, every beat of Silvanoshei's heart.

Several days after their encounter with Silvanoshei, the merchant caravan arrived in a port town. Leaving their husbands to set up camp, the two women went to visit the marketplace, where they were stopped by another elf, who was loitering about the stalls, accosting all new-comers.

This elf was an "uppity" elf, as one of the wives stated. He spoke to them, as one said, "like we were a bit of something that dropped in the dog's dish."

Still, they took the elf's money readily enough and told him what he wanted to know in exchange for it.

Yes, they had run into a young elf dressed like a fine gentleman on the road. A polite, well-spoken young man. Not like *some,* said the merchant's wife with a telling look. She could not recall where he said he'd been going, but she did remember that they had talked about Sanction. Yes, she supposed it was possible that he might be going to Sanction, but she thought it just as possible he might be going to the moon, for all she knew of the matter.

The older elf, whose face was grim and manner chill, paid them off and left them, traveling the same road as Silvanoshei.

The two wives knew immediately what to make of it.

"That young man was his son and has run away from home," said the first, nodding sagely.

"I don't blame him," said the second, looking after the elf irately. "Such a sour-faced old puss as that."

"I wish now I'd thrown him off the trail," said the first. "It would have served him right."

"You did what you thought was best, my dear," said her friend, craning her neck to see how many silver coins had been taken in. "It's not up to us to get involved in the affairs of the likes of such outlandish folk."

Linking arms, the two headed for the nearest tavern to spend the elf's money.

7

Faith's Convicts

ina's forces moved relentlessly, inexorably toward Sanction. They continued to march unopposed, met no resistance on the way. Mina did not ride with her legions but traveled on ahead of them, entering cities, villages, and towns to work her miracles, spread the word of the One God, and round up all the kender. Many wondered at this last. Most assumed she meant to slay the kender (and few would have been sorry), but she only questioned them, each and every one, asking about a particular kender who called himself Tasslehoff Burrfoot.

Many Tasslehoffs presented themselves to her, but none was ever The Tasslehoff Burrfoot. Once they had all been questioned, Mina would then release the kender and send them on their way, with promise of rich reward should they find this Burrfoot.

Every day, kender arrived at the camp in droves, bringing with them Tasslehoff Burrfoots of every shape and description in hopes of receiving the reward. These Tasslehoffs included not only kender but dogs, pigs, a donkey, a goat, and once an extremely irate and hung-over dwarf. Trussed and bound, he was dragged into camp by ten kender, who proclaimed he was The Tasslehoff Burrfoot trying to disguise himself in a false beard.

The humans and the kender of Solamnia and Throt and Eastwilde were as enchanted with Mina as the elves of Silvanesti had been. They viewed her with deep suspicion when she rode in and followed after her with prayers and songs when she left. Castle after castle, town after town fell to Mina's charm, not her might.

Gerard had long ago given up hoping that the Solamnic Knights would attack. He guessed that Lord Tasgall intended to concentrate his efforts in Sanction rather than try to halt Mina along the way. Gerard could have told them they were wasting their time. Every day, Mina's army grew larger, as more and more men and women flocked to her standard and the worship of the One God. Although the pace her officers set was fast and the troops were forced to be up with the dawn and march until nightfall, morale was high. The march had more the feeling of a wedding procession, hastening forward to joyous celebration, rather than marching toward battle, carnage, and death.

Gerard still did not see much of Odila. She traveled in Mina's retinue and was often away from the main body of the force. Either she went by consent or she was forced to go, Gerard could not be sure, for she carefully avoided any contact with him. He knew that she did this for his own safety, but he had no one else to talk to, and he felt he would have risked the danger just for the chance to share his thoughts—dark and pessimistic as they were—with someone who would understand.

One day Gerard's contemplations were interrupted by the minotaur, Galdar. Discovering Gerard riding in the rear, the minotaur tersely ordered him to take his place at the front with the rest of the Knights. Gerard had no choice but to obey, and he spent the rest of the march traveling under the minotaur's watchful eye.

Why Galdar didn't kill him was a mystery to Gerard, but then Galdar himself was a mystery. Gerard felt Galdar's beady eyes on him often, but the look in them was not so much sinister as it was speculative.

Gerard kept to himself, rebuffing the attempts by his "comrades" to make friends. He could not very well share the cheerful mood of the Dark Knights nor participate in discussions of how many Solamnics they were going to gut or how many Solamnic heads they were going to mount on pikes.

Because of his morose silence and perverse nature, Gerard soon acquired the reputation as a dour, unsociable man, who was little liked by his "fellow" Knights. He didn't care. He was glad to be left alone.

Or perhaps not so alone. Whenever he roamed off by himself, he would often look up to find Galdar shadowing him.

The days stretched into weeks. The army traveled through Estwilde, wound north through Throt, entered the Khalkist Mountains through the Throtyl

Gap, then headed due south for Sanction. As they left
the more populated lands behind, Mina returned to
the army, riding in the vanguard with Galdar, who
now paid far more attention to Mina than he did to
Gerard, for which Gerard was grateful.

Odila also returned, but she rode in the rear, in the
wagon carrying the amber sarcophagus. Gerard would
have liked to have found a way to talk to her, but the
one time he lagged behind, hoping he wouldn't be
missed, Galdar sought him out and ordered him to
maintain his position in the ranks.

Then the day came that a mountain range appeared
on the horizon. They saw it first as a dark blue
smudge, which Gerard mistook for a bank of dark
blue storm clouds. As the army drew closer, he could
see plumes of smoke drifting from the summits. He
looked upon the active volcanoes known as the Lords
of Doom—the guardians of Sanction.

"Not long now," he thought, and his heart ached
for the defenders of Sanction, watching and waiting.
They would be confident, certain their defenses
would hold. They had held for over a year now; why
should they expect anything different?

He wondered if they'd heard rumors about the
horrific army of the dead that had attacked Solanthus. Even if they had, would they believe what they
heard? Gerard doubted it. He would not have believed
such tales himself. He wasn't certain, thinking back
on it, that he believed it even now. The entire battle
had the unreal disconnection of a fever dream. Did
the army of the dead march with Mina? Gerard sometimes tried to catch a glimpse of them, but, if the
dead were with them, this fell ally traveled silently
and unseen.

Mina's army entered the foothills of the Khalkists and began the climb that would lead them to the pass through the Lords of Doom. In a valley, Mina halted their march, telling them they would remain here for several days. She had a journey to make, she said, and, in her absence, the army would prepare for the push through the mountains. Everyone was ordered to have armor and weapons in good condition, ready for battle. The blacksmith set up his forge, and he and his assistants spent the days mending and making. Hunting parties were sent out to bring in fresh meat.

They had only just set up camp on the first day when the elf prisoner was captured.

He was dragged into camp by several of the outriders who patrolled the army's flanks, scouring the area for any sign of the enemy.

Gerard was at the smith's, having his sword mended and finding it strange to think that the very enemy who might soon be spitted on that sword was now working hard to fix it. He had determined that he would take the opportunity of Mina's absence to try to convince Odila to escape with him. If she refused, he would ride off for Sanction alone, to take the news to them of the approaching enemy. He had no idea how he was going to manage this, how he was going to elude Galdar or, once he reached Sanction, how he was going to pass through the hordes of the enemy who had the city surrounded, but he figured he would deal with all that later.

Bored with waiting, tired of his own gloomy thoughts, he heard a commotion and walked over to see what was going on.

The elf was mounted on a red horse of fiery temper and disposition, for no one was able to get near the beast. The elf himself seemed uneasy on his mount, for when he reached down a hand to try to sooth the animal, the horse flung his head about and bit at him. The elf snatched his hand back and made no further move to touch the horse.

A crowd had gathered around the elf. Some knew him, apparently, for they began to jeer, bowing before him mockingly, saluting the "king of Silvanesti" with raucous laughter. Gerard eyed the elf curiously. He was dressed in finery that might have suited a king, though his cloak of fine wool was travel-stained and his silken hose were torn, his gold-embroidered doublet worn and frayed. He paid no attention to his detractors. He searched the camp for someone, as did the horse.

The crowd parted, as it always did whenever Mina walked among them. At the sight of her, the eyes of both horse and rider fixed on her with rapt attention.

The horse whinnied and shook his head. Mina came to Foxfire, laid her head against his, ran her hand over his muzzle. He draped his head over her shoulder and closed his eyes. His journey ended, his duty done, he was home, and he was content. Mina patted the horse and looked up at the elf.

"Mina," said the young man, and her name, as he spoke it, was red with his heart's blood. He slid down off the horse's back, stood before her. "Mina, you sent for me. I am here."

Such aching pain and love was in the elf's voice that Gerard was embarrassed for the young man. That his love was not reciprocated was obvious. Mina paid no attention to the elf, continued to lavished her attention on the horse. Her disregard for the young man did not go unnoticed. Mina's Knights grinned at one another. Bawdy jests were whispered about. One man laughed out loud, but his laughter ceased abruptly when Mina shifted her amber eyes to him. Ducking his head, his face red, he slunk away.

Mina finally acknowledged the elf's presence. "You are welcome, Your Majesty. All is in readiness for your arrival. A tent for you has been prepared next to mine. You have come in good time. Soon we march on Sanction to lay claim to that sacred city in the name of the One God. You will be witness to our triumph."

"You can't go to Sanction, Mina!" said the elf. "It's too dangerous . . ." His words faltered. Glancing around the crowd of black-armored humans, he seemed to have only just now realized that he had ridden into a camp of his enemies.

Mina saw and understood his unease. She cast a stern look around the crowd, quelled the jokes and silenced the laughter.

"Let it be known throughout the army that the king of the elves of the land of Silvanesti is my guest. He is to be treated with the same respect with which you treat me. I make each and every one of you responsible for his safety and well being."

Mina's gaze went searchingly about the camp and, to Gerard's great discomfiture, halted when it reached him.

"Sir Gerard, come forward," Mina ordered.

Aware that every man and woman in camp was staring at him, Gerard felt the hot blood suffuse his face, even as a cold qualm gripped his gut. He had no idea why he was being singled out. He had no choice but to obey.

Saluting, he kept quiet, waited.

"Sir Gerard," said Mina gravely, "I appoint you as special bodyguard for the elven king. His care and comfort are your responsibility. I choose you because you have had considerable experience dealing with elves. As I recall, you served in Qualinesti before coming to us."

Gerard could not speak, he was so astonished, primarily at Mina's cursed cleverness. He was her avowed enemy, a Solamnic Knight come to spy on her. She knew that. And because he was a Solamnic Knight, he was the only person in her army to whom she could entrust the life of the young elven king. Set a prisoner to guard a prisoner. A unique concept, yet one that must work in Gerard's case.

"I am sorry, but I fear that this duty will keep you out of the battle for Sanction, Sir Gerard," Mina continued. "It would never do for His Majesty to be exposed to that danger, and so you will remain with him in the rear, with the baggage train. But there will be other battles for you, Sir Gerard. Of that, I am certain."

Gerard could do nothing but salute again. Mina turned her back, walked away. The elf stood staring after her, his face bleak and pale. Many in the army remained to stare and, now that Mina had departed, resume their gibes at the elf's expense. Some started to grow downright nasty.

"Come on," said Gerard and, seeing that the elf was not going to move unless prompted, he grabbed hold of the elf's arm and hauled him off bodily. Gerard marched the elf through the camp toward the area where Mina had raised her tent. Sure enough, another tent had been set up a short distance from hers. The tent was empty, awaiting the arrival of this strange guest.

"What is your name?" Gerard asked grumpily, not feeling kindly disposed toward this elf, who had further complicated his life.

The elf didn't hear at first. He kept looking about, trying to find Mina.

Gerard asked again, this time raising his voice.

"My name is Silvanoshei," the elf replied. He spoke Common fluently, though his accent was so thick it was hard to understand him. The elf looked directly at Gerard, the first time he'd done so since Gerard had been put in charge of him.

"I don't recognize you. You weren't with her in Silvanesti, were you?"

No need to specify which "her" he was talking about. Gerard could see plainly that for this young man, there was only one "her" in the world.

"No," said Gerard shortly. "I wasn't."

"Where has she gone now? What is she doing?" Silvanoshei asked, looking about again. "When will she come back?"

Mina's tent and those of her bodyguards stood apart from the main camp, off to themselves. The noise of the camp faded behind them. The show was over. The Knights and soldiers went back to the business of making ready for war.

"Are you really king of the Silvanesti elves?" Gerard asked.

"Yes," said Silvanoshei absently, preoccupied by his search, "I am."

"Then what in the Abyss are you doing here?" Gerard demanded bluntly.

At that moment, Silvanoshei saw Mina. She was far distant, galloping on Foxfire across the valley. The two were alone, happy together, racing the wind with wild abandon. Seeing the pain in the young man's eyes, Gerard answered his own question.

"What did you say?" Silvanoshei asked, sighing

and turning around. Mina had ranged out of sight. "I didn't hear you."

"Who's ruling your people in your absence, Your Majesty?" Gerard asked accusingly. He was thinking of another elven king—Gilthas—who had sacrificed so much to save his people. Not run away from them.

"My mother," said Silvanoshei. He shrugged. "It's what she's always wanted."

"Your mother rules," said Gerard skeptically. "Or the Dark Knights of Neraka? I hear they've taken over Silvanesti."

"Mother will fight them," said Silvanoshei. "She enjoys fighting. She has always enjoyed it, you know. The battle and the danger. It's what she lives for. I hate it. Our people, dying and suffering. Dying for her. Always dying for her. She drinks their blood, and it keeps her beautiful. But it poisoned me."

Gerard stared at him in perplexity. Even though the elf had been speaking Common, Gerard had no idea what he was talking about. He might have asked, but at that moment, Odila emerged from a tent that was set up next to Mina's. She stopped at the sight of Gerard, flushed self-consciously, then turned swiftly and walked off.

"I will fetch you some hot water, Your Majesty," Gerard offered, keeping an eye on her. "You'll want to freshen up and clean away the dust of the road. And I'll bring food and drink. You look as if you could use it."

That much was true. Elves were always thin, but this young elf was emaciated. Apparently he was trying to live on love. Gerard's anger started to fade. He was beginning to feel sorry for this young man, who was as much a prisoner as any of them.

"As you wish," said Silvanoshei, not caring. "When do you think Mina will return?"

"Soon, Your Majesty," said Gerard, almost shoving the young man into the tent. "Soon. You should be rested."

Having rid himself of his responsibility, at least for the moment, he hurried after Odila, who was walking through the camp.

"You've been avoiding me," he said in an undertone, catching up to her.

"For your own good," she replied, still walking. "You should leave, take word to the Knights in Sanction."

"I was planning to." He jerked his thumb back over his shoulder. "Now I have this besotted young elf king on my hands. I've been assigned duty as his bodyguard."

Odila halted, stared at him. "Truly?"

"Truly."

"Mina's idea?"

"Who else?"

"How clever," Odila remarked, continuing on.

"My thoughts exactly," said Gerard. "You don't happen to know what she plans to do with him, do you? I can't think she's romantically inclined."

"Of course not," said Odila. "She told me all about him. He may not look it at the moment, but he has the potential to be a strong and charismatic leader of the elven nation. Mina saw the threat and acted to remove it. I don't know much about elven politics, but I gather that the Silvanesti will not willingly follow anyone but him."

"Why doesn't she just kill him?" Gerard asked. "Death would be more merciful that what she's doing to him now."

"His death makes him a martyr, gives his people a cause for which they would fight. Now they do nothing but sit and twiddle their thumbs, waiting for him to come back. There's Galdar watching us," she said suddenly. "I should go on alone. Don't come with me."

"But where are you going?"

She did not look at him. "It is my task to take food to the two wizards. Force them to eat."

"Odila," said Gerard, holding her back, "you still believe in the power of this One God, don't you?"

"Yes," she said, casting him a swift and defiant glance.

"Even though you know it's an evil power?"

"An evil power that heals the sick and brings peace and comfort to hundreds," Odila returned.

"And restores hideous life to the dead!"

"Something only a god could do." Odila faced him squarely. "I believe in this god, Gerard, and, what's more, so do you. That's the real reason you're here."

Gerard tried to come up with a glib rejoinder, but found he couldn't. Was this what the voice in his heart was trying to tell him? Was he here of his own free will, or was he just one more prisoner?

Seeing he had no response, Odila turned and left him.

Gerard stood in troubled silence, watched her make her way through the bustling camp.

8

Knight of the Black Rose

The journey this time was brief. Tas had barely started to grow annoyed with the tumbling about when he was suddenly right side up and standing solidly on his own two feet. Time, once again, stopped.

He exhaled in relief and looked around.

The Hedge Maze was gone. Conundrum was gone. Tas stood alone in what must have once been a beautiful rose garden. The garden was beautiful no longer, for everything in it had died. Dried rose blossoms, that had once been red, were now dark as sorrow. Their heads hung drooping on the stems that were brown and withered. Dead leaves from years that knew nothing but winter lay in piles beneath a crumbling stone wall. A path made of broken flagstones led from the dead garden into a manor house, its walls charred and blackened by long-dead flames. Tall cypress trees surrounded the manor house, their enormous limbs cutting off any vestige of sunlight, so that if night fell, it came only as a deepening of day's shadows.

Tasslehoff thought that he had never in his life seen any place that made him feel so unutterably sad.

"What are you doing here?"

A shadow fell over the kender. A voice spoke, a voice that was fell and cold. A knight, clad in ancient armor, stood over him. The knight was dead. He had been dead for many centuries. The body inside the armor had long ago rotted away. The armor was the body now, flesh and bone, muscle and sinew, tarnished and blackened with age, charred by the fires of war, stained with the blood of his victims. Red eyes, the only light in an eternal darkness, were visible through the slit visor of the helm. The red eyes flicked like flame over Tasslehoff. Their gaze was painful, and the kender flinched.

Tasslehoff stared at the apparition before him, and a most unpleasant feeling stole over him, a feeling he had forgotten because it was such a horrible feeling that he didn't like to remember it. His mouth filled with a bitter taste that stung his tongue. His heart lurched about in his chest as though it were trying to run away, but couldn't. His stomach curled up in a ball and searched for some place to hide.

He tried to answer the question, but the words wouldn't come out. He knew this knight. A death knight, Lord Soth had taught the kender fear, a sensation that Tasslehoff had not liked in the least. The thought came that perhaps Lord Soth might not remember him, and it occurred to Tas that it might be a good thing if Lord Soth didn't, for their last meeting hadn't been all that friendly. That notion was quickly dispelled by the words that bit at the kender like winter's bitter wind.

"I don't like to repeat myself. What are you doing here?"

Tas had been asked that question a lot in his long life, although never quite with this shade of meaning. Most of the time the question was: "What are you doing *here?*" said in tones that implied the questioner would be glad if whatever he was doing *here* he would do it someplace else. Other times, the question was: "What are you *doing* here?" which really meant stop *doing* that immediately. Lord Soth had placed the emphasis on the "you" making it "What are *you* doing here?" which meant that he was referring to Tasslehoff Burrfoot directly. Which meant that he recognized him.

Tasslehoff made several attempts to answer, none of which were successful, for all that came out of his mouth was a gargle, not words.

"Twice I asked you a question," said the death knight. "And while my time in this world is eternal, my patience is not."

"I'm trying to answer, sir," returned Tas meekly, "but you cause the words to get all squeezed up inside of me. I know that this is impolite, but I'm going to have to ask you a question before I can answer yours. When you say 'here', what exactly do you mean by that?" He mopped sweat from his forehead with the sleeve of his hand and tried to look anywhere except into those red eyes. "I've been to lots of 'heres,' and I'm a bit muddled as to where your 'here' is."

Soth's red eyes shifted from Tasslehoff to the Device of Time Journeying, clutched in the kender's stiff fingers. Tas followed the death knight's gaze.

"Oh, uh, this," Tas said, gulping. "Pretty, isn't it? I came across it on my . . . er . . . last trip. Someone dropped it. I plan on returning it. Isn't it lucky I found it? If you don't mind, I'll just put it away—" He tried to open one of his pouches, but his hands wouldn't quit shaking.

"Don't worry," said Soth. "I won't take it from you. I have no desire for a device that would carry me backward in time. Unless"—he paused, the red eyes grew shadowed—"unless it would take me back to undo what I did. Perhaps then I might make use of it."

Tas knew full well that he could never stop Lord Soth from taking the device if he wanted it, but he meant to give it a good try. The courage that is true courage and not merely the absence of fear rose up in Tasslehoff, and he fumbled for the knife, Rabbit Slayer, that he wore on his belt. He didn't know what good his little knife could do against a death knight, but Tas was a Hero of the Lance. He had to try.

Fortunately, his courage was not tested.

"But what would be the use?" said Lord Soth. "If I had it to do over again, the outcome would be the same. I would make the same decisions, commit the same heinous acts. For that was the man I was."

The red eyes flickered. "If I could go back, knowing what I know, maybe then my actions would be different. But our souls can never go back. They can only go forward. And some of us are not even permitted to do that. Not until we have learned the hard lessons life— and death—teach us."

His voice, already cold, grew colder still, so that Tas stopped sweating and began to shiver.

"And now we are no longer given the chance to do that."

The red eyes flared again. "To answer your question, kender, you are in the Fifth Age, the so-called 'Age of Mortals'." The helmed head shifted. He lifted his hand. The tattered cape he wore stirred with his motion. "You stand in the garden of what was once my dwelling place and is now my prison."

"Are you going to kill me?" Tas asked, more because it was a question he might be expected to ask than because he felt threatened. A person has to take notice of you in order to threaten you, and Tas had the distinct impression that he was of less interest to this undead lord than the withered stems or the dried-up rose petals.

"Why should I kill you, kender?" Soth asked. "Why should I bother?"

Tas gave the matter considerable thought. In truth, he could find no real reason why Soth should kill him, other than one.

"You're a death knight, my lord," Tas said. "Isn't killing people your job?"

"Death was not my job," Soth replied tonelessly. "Death was my joy. And death was my torment. My body has died, but my soul remains alive. As the torture victim suffers in agony when he feels the red-hot brand sear his flesh, so I suffer daily, my soul seared with my rage, my shame, my guilt. I have sought to end it, sought to drown the pain in blood, ease the pain with ambition. I was promised that the pain would end. I was promised that if I helped my goddess achieve her reward, I would be given my reward. My pain would end, and my soul would be freed. These promises were not kept."

The red eyes flicked over Tasslehoff, then roved restlessly to the withered and blackened roses.

"Once I killed out of ambition, for pleasure and for spite. No more. None of that has any meaning to me now. None of that drowned the pain.

"Besides," Soth added off-handedly, "in your case, why should I bother to kill you? You are already dead. You died in the Fourth Age, in the last second of the Fourth Age. That is why I ask, why are you here? How did you find this place, when even the gods cannot see where it is hidden?"

"So I *am* dead," Tas said to himself with a little sigh. "I guess that settles it."

He was thinking it strange that he and Lord Soth should have something in common, when a voice, a living voice, called out, "My lord! Lord Soth! I seek an audience with you!"

A hand closed over the kender's mouth. Another strong hand wrapped around him, and he was suddenly enveloped in the folds of soft black robes, as if night had taken on shape and form and dropped over his head. He could see nothing. He could not speak, could barely breathe, for the hand was positioned right over his nose and mouth. All he could smell— oddly enough—was rose-petals.

Tas might have strongly protested this rude behavior, but he recognized the living voice that had called out to Lord Soth, and he was suddenly quite glad that he had the strange hand to help him keep quiet, for even though sometimes he meant to be very quiet, words had a tendency to leap out of his throat before he could stop them.

Tas wriggled a bit to try to free up his nose for breathing, which—dead or not—his body required him to do. This accomplished, he held perfectly still.

Lord Soth did not immediately answer the call. He, too, recognized the person who had called out, although he had never before met her or seen her. He knew her because the two of them were bound together by the same chain, served the same master. He knew why she had come to him, knew what she meant to ask of him. He did not know what his answer would be, however. He knew what he wanted it to be, yet doubted if he had the courage.

Courage. He smiled bitterly. Once he'd imagined himself afraid of nothing. Over time, he'd come to realize he'd been afraid of everything. He had lived his life in fear: fear of failure, fear of weakness, fear that people would despise him if they truly knew him. Most of all, he had feared she would despise him, once she found out that the man she adored was just an ordinary man, not the paragon of virtue and courage she believed him.

He had been given knowledge by the gods that might have prevented the Cataclysm. He had been riding to Istar when he had been confronted by a group of elven women, misguided followers of the Kingpriest. They told him lies about his wife, told him she had been unfaithful to him and that the child she carried was not his. His fear caused him to believe their stories, and he had turned back from the path that might have been his salvation. Fear had stopped his ears to his wife's protestations of innocence. Fear had made him murder that which he truly loved.

He stood thinking of this, remembering it all yet again, as he had been doomed to remember so many, many times.

Once more he stood in the blooming garden where she tended the roses with her own hands, not trusting the gardener he had hired to do the work for her. He looked with concern at her hands, her fair skin torn and scratched, marred with drops of blood.

"Is it worth it?" he asked her. "The roses cause you so much pain."

"The pain lasts for but a moment," she told him. "The joy of their beauty lasts for days."

"Yet with winter's chill breath, they wither and die."

"But I have the memory of them, my love, and that brings me joy."

Not joy, he thought. Not joy, but torment. Memory of her smile, her laughter. Memory of the sorrow in her eyes as the life faded from them, taken by my hand. Memory of her curse.

Or was it a curse? I thought so then, but now I wonder. Perhaps it was, in truth, her blessing on me.

Leaving the garden of dead roses, he entered the manor house that had stood for centuries, a monument to death and fear. He took his seat in the chair that was covered with the dust of ages, dust that his incorporeal body never disturbed. He sat in that chair and stared, as he had stared for hour after hour after hour, at the bloodstain upon the floor.

There she fell.

There she died.

For eons he had been doomed to hear the recital of his wrongs sung to him by the spirits of those elven women who had been his undoing and who were cursed to live a life that was no life, an existence of torment and regret. He had not heard their voices since the Fifth Age began. How many years that was he did not know, for time had no meaning to him. The voices were part of the Fourth Age, and they had remained with the Fourth Age.

Forgiven, at last. Granted permission to leave.

He sought forgiveness, but it was denied him. He was angry at the denial, as his queen had known he would be. His anger snared him. Thus Takhisis caught him in her trap and bound him fast and carried him here to continue on his wretched existence, waiting for her call.

The call had come. Finally.

Footsteps of the living brought him out of his dark reverie. He looked up to see this representative of Her Dark Majesty and saw a child clad in armor, or so he first thought. Then he saw that what he had mistaken for a child was a girl on the edge of womanhood. He was reminded of Kitiara, the only being who had, for a brief time, been able to ease his torment. Kitiara, who never knew fear except once, at the very end of her life, when she looked up to see him coming for her. It was then, when he gazed into her terror-stricken eyes, that he understood himself. She had given him that much, at least.

Kitiara was gone now, too, her soul moving on to wherever it needed to go. Was this to be another? Another Kitiara, sent to seduce him?

No, he realized, looking into the amber eyes of the girl who stood before him. This was not Kitiara, who had done what she did for her own reasons, who had served no one but herself. This girl did all for glory— the glory of the god. Kitiara had never willingly sacrificed anything in order to achieve her goals. This girl had sacrificed everything, emptied herself, left herself a vessel to be filled by the god.

Soth saw the tiny figures of thousands of beings held fast in the amber eyes. He felt the warm amber slide over him, try to capture and hold him, just another insect.

He shook his helmed head. "Don't bother, Mina," he told the girl. "I know too much. I know the truth."

"And what is that truth?" Mina asked. The amber eyes tried again to seize hold of him. She was not one to give up, this woman-child.

"That your mistress will use you and then abandon you," Soth said. "She will betray you, as she has betrayed everyone who ever served her. I know her of old, you see."

He felt the stirrings of his queen's anger, but he chose to ignore it. Not now, he told her. You cannot use that against me now.

Mina was not angry. She seemed saddened by his response. "How can you say that of her when she went to such trouble to bring you with her? You are the only one so honored. All the rest . . ." She waved her hand to indicate the chamber, empty of its ghosts, or so it must seem to her. To him, the chamber was crowded. "All the rest were banished to oblivion. You alone were granted the privilege of remaining with this world."

"Oblivion is it? Once I believed that. Once I feared the darkness, and thus she kept her hold on me. Now I know differently. Death is not oblivion. Death frees the soul to travel onward."

Mina smiled, pitying his ignorance. "You are the one who has been deceived. The souls of the dead went nowhere. They vanished into the mist, wasted, forgotten. The One God now takes the souls of the dead unto her and gives them the opportunity to remain in this world and continue to act for the good of the world."

"For the good of the god, you mean," said Soth. He stirred in his chair, which gave him no comfort. "Let us say I find myself grateful to this god for the privilege of remaining in the world. Knowing this god as I do of old, I know that she expects my gratitude to take on a tangible form. What is it she requires of me?"

"Within a few days time, armies of both the living and the dead will sweep down on Sanction. The city will fall to my might." Mina did not speak with bravado. She stated a fact, nothing more. "At that time, the One God will perform a great miracle. She will enter the world as she was long meant to do, join the realms of the mortal and the immortal. When she exists in both realms, she will conquer the world, rid it of such vermin as the elves, and establish herself as the ruler of Krynn. I am to be made captain of the army of the living. The One God offers you the captaincy of the army of the dead."

"She 'offers' me this?" Soth asked.

"Offers it. Yes, of course," said Mina.

"Then she will not be offended if I turn down her offer," said Soth.

"She would not be offended," Mina replied, "but she would be deeply grieved at your ingratitude, after all that she has done for you."

"All she has done for me." Soth smiled. "So this is why she brought me here. I am to be a slave leading an army of slaves. My answer to this generous offer is 'no.'

"You made a mistake, my queen," called Soth, speaking to the shadows, where he knew she lay coiled, waiting. "You used my anger to keep your talons in me, and you dragged me here so that you could make use of me still. But you left me alone too long. You left me to the silence in which I could once more hear my wife's beloved voice. You left me to the darkness that became my light, for I could once more see my wife's beloved face. I could see myself, and I saw a man consumed by his fear. And it was then I saw you for what you are.

"I fought for you, Queen Takhisis. I believed your cause was mine. The silence taught me that it was you who fed my fear, raising around me a ring of fire from which I could never escape. The fire has gone out now, my queen. All around me is nothing but ashes."

"Beware, my lord," said Mina, and her tone was dire. "If you refuse this, you risk the god's anger."

Lord Soth rose to his feet. He pointed to a stain upon the stone floor.

"Do you see that?"

"I see nothing," said Mina, with an indifferent glance, "nothing except the cold, gray rock."

"I see a pool of blood," said Lord Soth. "I see my beloved wife lying in her blood. I see the blood of all those who perished because my fear kept me from accepting the blessing the gods offered to me. Long have I been forced to stare at that stain, and long have I loathed the very sight of it. Now, I kneel on it," he said, bending his knees on the stone, "I kneel in her blood and the blood of all who died because I was afraid. I beg her to forgive me for the wrong I did to her. I beg them all to forgive me."

"There can be no forgiveness," said Mina sternly. "You are cursed. The One God will cast your soul into the darkness of unending pain and torment. Is this what you choose?"

"Death is what I choose," said Lord Soth. Reaching beneath the breast plate of his armor, he drew forth a rose. The rose was long dead, but its vibrant color had not faded. The rose was red as her lips, red as her blood. "If death brings unending torment, then I accept that as my fitting punishment."

Lord Soth saw Mina reflected in the red fire of his soul. "Your god has lost her hold on me. I am no longer afraid."

Mina's amber eyes hardened in anger. Turning on her heel, she left him kneeling on the cold stone, his head bowed, his hands clasped over the thorns and dried leaves and crumpled petals of the red rose. Mina's footfalls reverberated through the manor house, shook the floor on which he knelt, shook the charred and broken walls, shook the blackened beams.

He felt pain, physical pain, and he looked in wonder at his hand. The accursed armor was gone. The thorns of the dead rose pierced his flesh. A tiny drop of blood gleamed on his skin, more red than the petals.

A beam above him gave way and crashed down beside him. Shards of splintered wood flew from the shattered beam, punctured his flesh. He gritted his teeth against the pain of his wounds. This was the Dark Queen's last, desperate attempt to keep her hold on him. He had been given back his mortal body.

She would never know, but she had, in her ignorance, granted him a final blessing.

She lay coiled in the shadows, certain of her triumph, waiting for his fear to once more bind him to her, waiting for him to cry out that he had been wrong, waiting for him to plead and grovel for her to spare him.

Lord Soth lifted the rose to his lips. He kissed the petals, then scattered them over the blood that stained the gray stone red. He cast off the helm that had been his flesh and bone for so many empty years. He tore off the breastplate and hurled it far from him, so that it struck the wall with a clank and a clatter.

Another beam fell, hurled by a vengeful hand. The beam struck him, crushed his body, drove him to the floor. His blood flowed freely, mingled with his dear wife's blood. He did not cry out. The pain of dying was agony, but it was an agony that would soon end. He could bear the pain for her sake, for the pain her soul had born for him.

She would not be waiting for him. She had long ago made her own journey, carrying in her arms their son. He would make his solitary way after them, lost, alone, seeking.

He might never find them, the two he had so wronged, but he would dedicate eternity to the search.

In that search, he would be redeemed.

Mina stalked through the rose garden. Her face was livid and cold as a face carved of marble. She did not look back to see the final destruction of Dargaard Keep.

Tasslehoff, peeping out from behind a fold of blackness, saw her leave. He did not see where she went, for at that moment the massive structure collapsed, falling in upon itself with a thunderous crash that sent clouds of dust and debris roiling up into the air.

A gigantic block of stone smashed down into the rose garden. He was extremely surprised to find that he wasn't underneath it, for it fell right where he'd been standing, but, like thistledown, he floated on the winds of ruin and death and was lifted above them into the pure, chill blue of a cloudless, sunlit sky.

9

The Attack on Sanction

The city of Sanction had been besieged for months. The Dark Knights threw everything they had against it. Countless numbers died in the shadows of Sanction's walls, on both sides of Sanction's walls, died for no reason, for the siege could not be broken. When Mina's army marched into view, Sanction's defenders laughed to see it, for how could such pitifully small numbers of men make any difference?

They did not laugh long. The city of Sanction fell to the army of souls in a single day.

Nothing could halt the advance of the dead. The moats of sluggish, hot lava flowing from the Lords of Doom that kept the living at bay, were no barrier to the souls. The newly built and strengthened earthwork fortifications against which the army of the Dark Knights had thrown themselves time and again without success now stood as monuments to futility. The thick, gray mist of hapless souls flowed down the sides of the mountains, filled the valleys like a rising tide, and boiled up and over the fortifications. Besieger and besieged alike fled before the terrifying dead.

Mina's sappers had no need to batter down the gates that led into the city or breach the walls. Her troops had only to wait until the gates were flung open from within by the panic-stricken defenders. Fleeing the army of the dead, they soon joined their ranks. Mina's Knights, hidden among the ghastly mist, cut down the living without mercy. Led by Galdar, the army stormed through the gates to do battle in the city.

Mina fought her battles in the foothills around Sanction, doing what she could to quell the panic of the army of besiegers, who were just as terrified as their enemy. She rode among them, halting their flight, urging them back to battle.

She seemed to be everywhere upon the battlefield, galloping swiftly on her red horse to wherever she was needed. She rode without care for her own safety, often leaving her bodyguards far behind, spurring their steeds frantically to keep up.

Gerard did not take part in the battle. True to her word, Mina posted him and his prisoner, the elf king, atop a ridgeline overlooking the city.

Along with the elf, Gerard and four other Dark Knights guarded the wagon carrying the amber sarcophagus of Goldmoon and the two dead wizards. Odila rode with the wagon. Like Gerard, her gaze was fixed on the battle in which she could take no part. Frustrated, helpless to do anything to aid his fellow Knights, Gerard followed the battle from his detested safe vantage point. Mina shone with a pale, fey light that made her a rallying point anywhere on the field.

"What is that strange fog that fills the valley?" Silvanoshei asked, staring down from his horse in wonder.

"That strange fog is not fog, Your Majesty. That is an army of dead souls," Gerard answered grimly.

"Even the dead adore her," Silvanoshei said. "They come to fight for her."

Gerard glanced at the wagon, carrying the bodies of the two dead mages. He wondered if Palin's soul was on that battlefield, fighting for Mina. He guessed how much Palin "adored" her. He could have pointed this out to the besotted young elf, but he kept quiet. The young man wouldn't listen, anyway. Gerard sat his horse in grim silence.

The din of battle, the cries of the dying, rose up from the mist of souls that grew thicker by the moment. Gerard suddenly saw it all in a blood-drenched haze, and he determined to ride down to join that desperate battle, though he knew from the outset that he could do no good and would only die in the attempt.

"Gerard!" Odila called out.

"You can't stop me!" he cried angrily, and then, when the red haze cleared a bit, he saw she wasn't trying to stop him. She was trying to warn him.

Four of Mina's Knights, who were supposed to be guarding the elf, spurred their horses, surrounded him.

He had no idea how they had divined his intention, but he drew his sword, fiercely glad to have this chance to do battle. Their first words astonished him.

"Ride off, Gerard," said one, a man named Clorant. "This is not your fight. We mean you no harm."

"It is my fight, you bloody bastards—" Gerard began. His words of defiance sputtered out.

They were not staring at him. Their hate-filled eyes stared behind him, at the elf. Gerard remembered the jeers and catcalls he'd heard when the elven king rode into camp. He glanced over his shoulder. Silvanoshei was not armed. He would be defenseless against these four.

"What happens to the pointy-ear is none of your concern, Gerard," Clorant said. His tone was dire. He was in deadly earnest. "Ride on, and don't look back."

Gerard had to grapple with himself, squelch his rage, force himself to think calmly and rationally. All the while, he cursed Mina for seeing into his heart.

"You boys have got yourselves all turned around," Gerard said. Trying his best to sound casual, he edged his horse so that it was between Clorant and the young elf. Gerard pointed. "The fight's in that direction. Behind you."

"You won't get into trouble with Mina, Gerard," Clorant promised. "We have our story all thought out. We're going to tell her we were attacked by an enemy patrol that had been lurking up in the mountains. We drove them off, but in the confusion the elf was killed."

"We'll drag a couple of bodies up here," added another. "Bloody ourselves up some. Make it look real."

"I'll be happy to bloody any one of you," said Gerard, "but it's not going to come to that. This elf's not worth it. He's no threat to anybody."

"He's a threat to Mina," said Clorant. "He tried to kill her when we were in Silvanesti. The One God brought her back to us, but the next time the bastard might succeed."

"If he did try to kill her, let Mina deal with him," said Gerard.

"She can't see through his tricks and deceits," said Clorant. "We have to protect her from herself."

He's a jealous lover, Gerard realized. Clorant is in love with Mina himself. Every one of them is in love with her. That's the real reason they want to kill this elf.

"Give me a sword. I can fight my own battles," declared Silvanoshei, riding up alongside Gerard. The elf cast him a proud and scornful glance. "I don't need you to fight them for me."

"You young fool," Gerard growled out of the side of his mouth. "Shut up, and let me handle this!"

Aloud he said, "Mina ordered me to guard him, and I'm bound to obey. I took an oath to obey, the same as you. There's a concept floating around called honor. Maybe you boys have heard of it?"

"Honor!" Clorant spat on the ground. "You talk like a cursed Solamnic. You have a choice, Gerard. You can either ride off and let us deal with the elf, in which case we'll see to it that you don't get into trouble, or you can be one of the corpses we leave on the field to prove our story. Don't worry," he sneered. "We'll tell Mina that you died 'with honor.' "

Gerard didn't wait for them to come at him. He didn't even wait for Clorant to finish his speech but spurred his horse toward him. Their swords clanged together on the word, "honor."

"I'll deal with this bastard," shouted Clorant. "The rest of you kill the elf!"

Leaving Clorant to take care of Gerard, the other three galloped toward the elf. Gerard heard Silvanoshei shout in Elvish, heard one of the Knights curse, and then a thud and a clatter of metal. Risking a glance, Gerard saw to his amazement that Silvanoshei, with no weapon but his own hands, had thrown himself bodily on one of the armored Knights, carried him off his horse and onto the ground. The two floundered, grappling for the Knight's loose sword. The Knight's comrades circled around the combatants, waiting a chance to strike the elf, not wanting to risk hitting their friend.

Gerard had his own problems. Fighting an armed foe on horseback is not so much a matter of skilled thrust and parry between two swordsmen as a bludgeoning, slashing battle to try to unseat your foe.

Their horses snorted and churned up the ground with their hooves. Clorant and Gerard circled each other, swords swinging wildly, striking any part of the body that came into view, neither making much headway. Gerard's fist smashed into Clorant's jaw, his sword sliced through the chain mail of the man's upper arm. Gerard himself was not wounded, but he was the one at a disadvantage. Clorant had only to defend himself, keep Gerard occupied so that he could not save the elf.

Another glance showed Gerard that Silvanoshei had managed to grab the fallen Knight's sword. Taking up a defensive position, Silvanoshei grimly eyed his foes, two of whom were still mounted and still armed. The fallen Knight was staggering to his feet.

Raising his sword, one Knight sent his horse at a gallop straight at Silvanoshei, intending to behead him with a slashing downward stroke. Desperate, Gerard turned his back on Clorant. Gerard was leaving himself wide open, but he had no other recourse if he wanted to save the elf's life. Gerard spurred his horse, so that the startled animal leaped ahead, his intent being to gallop between the two combatants, putting himself between the elf and his attacker.

Clorant struck Gerard from behind. His sword thunked against Gerard's helm, setting his ears to ringing and scattering his wits. Then Clorant was at Gerard's side. A sword flashed in the sunlight.

"Stop this!" a woman shouted, her voice shaking with fury. "In the name of the One God, stop this madness!"

The Knight galloping down on the elf pulled so hard on the reins that his horse reared and practically upended both of them. Gerard had to rein in his steed swiftly or crash into the floundering animal. He heard Clorant suck in his breath, heard him try to check his horse.

Gerard lowered his sword, looked about to see who had spoken. He could tell by Clorant's wild-eyed stare and guilty expression that he thought the voice was Mina's. Gerard knew it wasn't. He recognized the voice. He could only hope that Odila had the nerve to pull this off.

Her face livid, her robes whipping about her ankles, Odila marched into the midst of the sweating, bleeding, deadly fray. She thrust aside a sword with her bare hand.

Glaring around at them, her eyes burning, she looked directly at Clorant. "What is the meaning of this? Did you not hear Mina's command that this elf was to be treated with the same respect you show her?" Odila sent a flashing glance at each one of them in turn, not excluding Gerard. "Put away your weapons! All of you!"

She was taking a great risk. Did these men view her as a true cleric, a representative of the One God, someone as sacred as Mina herself? Or did they see her as nothing more than a follower, no different from themselves?

The men hesitated, glanced uncertainly at each other. Gerard kept quiet, tried to look as guilty and dismayed at the rest. He cast one warning glance at the elf, but Silvanoshei had the sense to keep his mouth shut. He panted, gasping for breath, kept wary watch on his enemies.

Odila's gaze hardened, her eyes narrowed. "In the name of the One God put down your weapons," she ordered again, and this time she pointed at Clorant, "lest your sword hand wither with my displeasure and fall from your arm!"

"Will you tell Mina about this?" Clorant asked sullenly.

"I know that you did what you did out of misguided care for Mina," said Odila, her voice softening. "You have no need to protect her. The One God holds Mina in the palm of her hand. The One God knows what is best for Mina and for us all. This elf lives only because the One God wills it." Odila pointed in the direction of Sanction. "Return to the battle. Your true foe lies down there."

"Will you tell Mina?" Clorant persisted, and there was fear in his voice.

"I won't," said Odila, "but you will. You will confess to her what you have done and seek her forgiveness."

Clorant lowered his sword and, after a moment's hesitation, thrust it into his sheath. He made a motion for his comrades to do the same. Then, casting a final, loathing glance at the elf, he turned his horse's head and galloped down the hill, heading for Sanction. His friends rode after him.

Exhaling a great sigh of relief, Gerard slid down from his horse.

"Are you all right?" he asked Silvanoshei, looking him over. He saw a few splashes of blood on his clothes but nothing serious.

Silvanoshei drew away from him, stared at him suspiciously. "You—a Dark Knight—risked your life to save mine. You fought your own comrades. Why?"

Gerard could not very well tell him the truth. "I didn't do it for you," he said gruffly. "I did it for Mina. She ordered me to guard you, remember?"

Silvanoshei's face smoothed. "That makes sense. Thank you."

"Thank Mina," muttered Gerard ungraciously.

His movements stiff and painful, he limped over to Odila. "Well acted," he said in low tone. "That was quite a performance. Though, I'm curious—what would have happened if Clorant had called your bluff? I thought he was going to for a minute there. What would you have done then?"

"It's strange," Odila said. Her gaze was abstracted, her voice soft and introspective. "At the moment I made the threat, I knew I had the power to carry it out. I could have withered his hand. I could have."

"Odila—" he began to remonstrate with her.

"It doesn't matter if you believe me or not," Odila said bleakly. "Nothing can stop the One God."

Clasping the medallion she wore around her neck, she walked back to the wagon.

"Nothing can stop the One," Odila repeated. "Nothing."

10

City of Ghosts

Riding in the vanguard of the triumphant army as they entered, unopposed, Sanction's West Gate and marched victorious along the famous Shipmaker's Road, Gerard looked at the city and saw nothing but ghosts: ghosts of the past, ghosts of the present, ghosts of prosperity, ghosts of war.

He remembered what he'd heard of Sanction, remembered—as if it had happened to someone else and not to him—talking to Caramon Majere about hoping to be sent to Sanction. *Someplace where there is real fighting going on,* he had said or, if he had not said it, he had thought it. He looked back on that ghost of himself and saw a callow youth who didn't have sense enough to know when he was well off.

What must Caramon have thought of me? Gerard flushed as he remembered some of his foolish spoutings. Caramon Majere had fought in many wars. He knew the truth about glory—that it was nothing more than a bloodstained and rusted old sword hanging on the wall of an old man's memory. Riding past the bodies of those who had defended Sanction, Gerard saw the true glory of war: the carrion birds flapping down to pluck out eyeballs, the flies that filled the air with their horrid buzzing, the burial crews laughing and joking as they filled wheelbarrows with bodies and dumped them into mass graves.

War was a thief who dared accost Death, robbing that majestic noble of his dignity, stripping him bare, tossing him in a pit, and covering him with lime to stop the stench.

Gerard was grateful for one blessing: The dead were laid to rest. At the end of the battle, Mina—her armor covered with blood, herself unscathed—knelt beside the first of the hastily dug trenches meant to receive the dead and prayed over them. Gerard watched in stomach-clenching horror, more than half expecting the bloodied corpses to rise up, seize their weapons, and fall into ranks at Mina's command.

Fortunately, that did not happen. Mina commended the spirits to the One God, urged them all to serve the One God well. Gerard glanced at Odila, who stood not far from him. Her head was bowed, her hands clasped.

Gerard was angry at her and angry at himself for being angry. Odila had done nothing more than speak the truth. This One God was all-seeing, all-knowing, all-powerful. There was nothing they could do to stop the One. He was loath to face the truth. That was all. Loath to admit defeat.

After the ceremony for the dead ended, Mina mounted her horse and rode into the city, which was, for the most part, deserted.

During the War of the Lance, Sanction had been an armed camp dedicated to the Queen of Darkness, headquarters for her armies. The draconians had been born in the temple of Luerkhisis. Lord Ariakas had his headquarters in Sanction, trained his troops here, kept his slaves here, tortured his prisoners here.

The Chaos War and the departure of the gods that brought devastation to many parts of Ansalon delivered prosperity to Sanction. At first, it seemed that Sanction must be destroyed and that no one would rule it, for the lava flows spilling from the Lords of Doom threatened to bury the city. A man called Hogan Bight arrived to save Sanction from the mountains' wrath. Using powerful magicks that he never explained, he diverted the flow of lava, drove out the evil people who had long ruled the city. Merchants and others seeking to better their lives were invited in and, almost overnight, Sanction grew prosperous, as goods flowed into its wharves and docks.

Seeing its wealth, needing access to its ports, the Dark Knights had wanted Sanction back under their control, and now they had it.

With Qualinost destroyed, Silvanesti occupied, and Solamnia under her rulership, it might be truly said that those parts of Ansalon that were not under Mina's control were not worth controlling. She had come full circle, back to Sanction where her legend had begun.

Having been warned of Mina's march on their city, the citizens of Sanction, who had weathered the siege without any great hardship, heard the rumors of the advancing army of Dark Knights, and fearing that they would be enslaved, their homes looted, their daughters raped, their sons slain by their cruel conquerers, they took to their boats or their horse carts, putting out to sea or heading for the mountains.

Only a few remained behind: the poor who did not have the means to leave; the infirm, the elderly, the sick who could not leave; kender (a fact of nature); and those entrepreneurs who had no care for any god, who owed no allegiance to any government or cause except their own. These people lined the streets to watch the entry of the army, their expressions ranging from dull apathy to eager anticipation.

In the case of the poor, their lives were already so miserable that they had nothing to fear. In the case of the entrepreneurs, their eyes fixed greedily on two enormous, wooden, iron-bound chests that had been transported under heavy guard from Palanthas. Here was much of the wealth of the Dark Knights, wealth that the late Lord Targonne had so covetously amassed. The wealth was now to be shared with all those who had fought for Mina, or so the rumor ran.

Reinforce religious fervor with bags of steel coins— a wise move, Gerard thought, and one guaranteed to win her the hearts, as well as the souls, of her soldiers.

The army advanced along Shipbuilder's Road into a large marketplace. One of Gerard's fellow Knights, who had once visited Sanction, stated that this was known as the Souk Bazaar, and that it was usually so crowded with people that one scarcely had room enough to draw a breath, let alone walk. That was not true now. The only people around were a few enterprising hoodlums taking advantage of the commotion to raid the abandoned stalls.

Calling a halt at this central location, Mina proceeded to take control of the city. She dispatched guards under trustworthy officers to seize the warehouses, the taverns, the mageware shops, and the shops of the money-lenders. She sent another group of guards, led by the minotaur Galdar, to the impressive palace where lived the city's governor, the mysterious Hogan Bight. The guards had orders to arrest him, take him alive if he cooperated, kill him if he didn't. Hogan Bight continued to be a mystery, however, for Galdar returned to report that the man was nowhere to be found and no one could tell when they'd last seen him.

"The palace is empty and would make an ideal dwelling place for you, Mina," said Galdar. "Shall I order the troops to make it ready for your arrival?"

"The palace will be military headquarters," said Mina, "but not my dwelling place. The One God does not reside in grand palaces, and neither will I."

She glanced at the wagon carrying the body of Goldmoon in the amber coffin. Goldmoon's body had not withered, had not decayed. Frozen in the amber, she seemed forever young, forever beautiful. The wagon had been given an honored place in the procession, following directly after Mina, surrounded by an honor guard of her Knights.

"I will dwell in what was once called the Temple of Huerzyd but is now known as the Temple of the Heart. Detain any of the Mystics who remain in the temple. Put them somewhere secure, for their own safety. Treat them with respect and tell them that I look forward to meeting with them. You will escort the body of Goldmoon to the temple and carry the sarcophagus inside to be placed before the altar. You will feel at home, Mother," said Mina, speaking softly to the still, cold face of the woman imprisoned in amber.

Galdar did not appear particularly pleased at his assignment. He did not question Mina, however. The wagon and its guard of honor rolled out of the bazaar, heading for the temple, which was located in the northern part of the city.

Seated astride her irritable horse, Mina proceeded to issue commands. Her Knights crowded around her, eager to serve, hoping for a look, a word, a smile. Gerard held back, not wanting to get caught in the crush of men and horses. He needed to know what he was to do with the elf, but he wasn't in any hurry. He was glad to have this time to think, determine what his next move was going to be. He didn't like at all what was happening to Odila. Her talk of withering hands frightened him. Medallion or no medallion, he was going to find a way to get her out of here, if he had to bash her over the head and haul her out bodily.

Gerard suddenly felt a fierce determination to do something—anything—to fight this One God, even if he caused the One God less harm than a bee sting. One bee might not do much damage, but if there were hundreds of bees, thousands . . . He'd heard stories of dragons fleeing such swarms. There had to be—

"Hey, Gerard," called someone. "You've lost your prisoner."

Gerard came to himself with a jolt. The elf was no longer at his side. Gerard had no fear—or hope—that Silvanoshei would try to escape. He knew right where to look for him. Silvanoshei was urging his horse forward, trying to force his way through the armed circle of Knights surrounding Mina.

Cursing them both beneath his breath, Gerard spurred his horse. The Knights around Mina were aware of the elf and were deliberately blocking his passage. Silvanoshei set his jaw and continued to determinedly and stubbornly pursue his course. One of the Knights, whose horse was jostled by Silvanoshei's horse, turned to stare at him. The Knight was Clorant, his face bruised and swollen, his lip bloodied. The split lip pulled back in a grimace. Silvanoshei hesitated, then pushed ahead. Clorant tugged sharply on the reins, jerking his horse's head. The animal, annoyed, took a nip at Silvanoshei's horse, which bared its teeth. In the confusion, Clorant gave Silvanoshei a shove, trying to unseat him. Silvanoshei managed to cling to the saddle. He shoved back.

Gerard guided his steed through the melee and caught up with the elf, jostling Clorant's arm in passing.

"This is not a good time to interrupt Mina, Your Majesty," Gerard said in an undertone to the elf. "Maybe later." He reached for the reins of Silvanoshei's horse.

"Sir Gerard," called Mina. "Attend me. Bring His Majesty with you. The rest of you, make way."

At Mina's command, Clorant was forced to edge his horse backward, so that Gerard and Silvanoshei could ride past. Clorant's dark, grim gaze followed them. Gerard could feel it tickle the back of his neck as he rode to receive his orders.

Removing his helm, Gerard saluted Mina. Due to his fight with Clorant, Gerard's face was bruised, dried blood matted his hair. Most of the other Knights looked the same or worse, though, after the battle. Gerard was hoping Mina wouldn't notice.

She might not have noticed him, but she gazed intently at Silvanoshei, whose shirt was sliced open and stained with blood, his traveling cloak covered with dirt.

"Sir Gerard," Mina said gravely, "I entrusted His Majesty to you, to keep him safely out of the affray. I see you both bruised and bloodied. Did either of you take serious harm?"

"No, Madam," replied Gerard.

He refused to call her Mina, as did her other Knights. Like a medicine made of alum and honey, her name, sweet at first, left a bitter taste on his tongue. He said nothing more about the fight with Clorant and his fellow Knights. Neither did Silvanoshei. After assuring her that he was not injured, the elf fell silent. No one in the crowd of waiting Knights spoke. Here and there, a horse shifted beneath a restless rider. By now all Mina's Knights knew about the affray. Perhaps they had even been in on the conspiracy.

"What are your orders, Madam?" Gerard asked, hoping to let the matter drop.

"That can wait. What happened?" Mina persisted.

"A Solamnic patrol came out of nowhere, Madam," said Gerard evenly. He looked straight into the amber eyes. "I think they hoped to seize our supply wagon. We drove them away."

"His Majesty fought them, too?" asked Mina, with a half smile.

"When they saw he was an elf, they sought to rescue him, Madam."

"I didn't want to be rescued," Silvanoshei added.

Gerard's lips tightened. That statement was true enough.

Mina cast the young elf a cool glance, then turned her attention back to Gerard.

"I saw no bodies."

"You know Solamnics, Madam," he replied evenly. "You know what cowards they are. We rattled our swords at them, and they ran away."

"I *do* know Solamnics," Mina replied, "and contrary to what you believe, Sir Gerard, I have a great respect for them."

Mina's amber gaze swept over the line of Knights, unerringly picked out the four who had been involved. Her gaze fixed longest on Clorant, who tried to defy it, but ended up squirming and cringing. Finally, she turned her amber eyes back to Silvanoshei, another insect caught in the warm resin.

"Sir Gerard," said Mina, "do you know where to find the City Guard Headquarters?"

"No, Madam," said Gerard. "I have never been in Sanction. But I have no doubt I can locate it."

"There you will find secure prison cells. You will escort His Majesty to these cells and make certain that he is locked in one of them. See to his comfort. This is for your own protection, Your Majesty," Mina added. "Someone might try to 'rescue' you again, and the next time you might not have such a valiant defender."

Gerard glanced at Silvanoshei, then looked away. The sight was too painful. Her words might have been a dagger thrust in the elf's gut. His face drained of life. Even the lips lost their color. In the young man's livid face, the burning eyes were the only life.

"Mina," he said quietly, desperately. "I have to know one thing. Did you ever love me? Or have you just been using me?"

"Sir Gerard," said Mina, turning away. "You have your orders."

"Yes, Madam," he said. Taking the reins from the elf's hand, he started to lead his horse away.

"Mina," pleaded Silvanoshei. "I deserve at least that much. To know the truth."

Mina glanced back at him, over her shoulder.

"My love, my life is the One God."

Gerard led the elf's horse away.

The City Guard Headquarters turned out to be south of the West Gate by a few blocks. The two rode in silence through the streets that had been deserted when the army marched in, but were now filling rapidly with the soldiers of the army of the One God. Gerard had to watch where they were going to avoid riding down anyone, and their progress was slow. He glanced back in concern for Silvanoshei, saw his face set, his jaw clenched, his eyes staring down at the hands that gripped the pommel so tightly the knuckles were chalk white.

"Women." Gerard grunted. "It happens to all of us."

Silvanoshei smiled bitterly and shook his head.

Well, he's right, Gerard admitted. None of the rest of us had a god involved in our love-making.

They rode past the West Gate. Gerard had been harboring a vague notion that he and the elf might be able to escape during the confusion, but he discarded that idea immediately. The road was clogged with Mina's troops, and more remained on the field outside the city. Every man they passed cast Silvanoshei a dark, frowning glance. More than one muttered threats.

Mina is right, Gerard decided. Prison is probably the safest place for the young man. If any place is safe for Silvanoshei in Sanction.

The city guards had either fled the guardhouse or been killed. Mina had placed one of her Knights in charge. The Knight glanced without interest at Silvanoshei, listened with impatience to Gerard's insistence that the young man be placed under special guard. The Knight jerked a thumb in the direction of the cell block. A brief search turned up the keys.

Gerard escorted his prisoner to a cell in darkest corner of the block, hoping he would escape notice.

"I'm sorry about this, Your Majesty," said Gerard.

Silvanoshei shrugged, sat down on the stone block that passed for a bed. Gerard shut the cell door, locked it.

At the sound of key turning, Silvanoshei raised his head. "I should thank you for saving my life."

"I'll bet now you wished I'd let them kill you," said Gerard, sympathetic.

"Their swords would have been less painful," Silvanoshei agreed with a pale flicker of a smile.

Gerard glanced around. They were the only two in the cellblocks. "Your Majesty," he said quietly. "I can help you escape. Not now—there's something else I have to do first. But soon."

"Thank you, sir. But you'd be putting yourself in danger for nothing. I can't escape."

"Your Majesty," said Gerard, his voice hardening, "you saw her, you heard her. You have no chance with her! She doesn't love you. She's all wrapped up in this . . . this god of hers."

"Not only hers. My god, too," he said, speaking with an eerie calm. "The One God promised me that Mina and I would be together."

"Do you still believe that?"

"No," Silvanoshei said, after a moment. The word seemed wrenched from him. "No, I don't."

"Then be ready. I'll come back for you."

Silvansoshei shook his head.

"Your Majesty," said Gerard, exasperated, "do you know the reason Mina lured you here away from your kingdom? Because she knows that your people will not follow anyone but you. The Silvanesti are sitting around waiting for you to return to them. Go back and be their king, the king she fears!"

"Go back to be their king." Silvanoshei's mouth twisted. "Go back to my mother, you mean. Go back to ignominy and shame, tears and rebukes. I would sit in this prison cell the rest of my life—and we elves live a long, long time—rather than face that."

"Look, damn it, if it was just you, I'd let you rot here," Gerard said grimly. "But you're their king, like it or not. You have to think about your people."

"I am," said Silvanoshei. "I will."

Rising to his feet, he walked over to Gerard, tugging on a ring as he came. "You're a Solamnic Knight, as Mina said, aren't you? Why are you here? To spy on Mina?"

Gerard glowered, shrugged, didn't answer.

"You don't have to admit it," said Silvanoshei. "Mina saw into your heart. That's why she set you to guard me. If you're serious about wanting to help me—"

"I am, Your Majesty," said Gerard.

"Then take this." Silvanoshei handed through the cell bars a blue, glittering ring. "Somewhere out there—close by, I'm certain—you will find an elven warrior. His name is Samar. He has been sent by my mother to bring me back home. Give him this ring. He will recognize it. I've worn it since I was a child. When he asks you how you came by it, tell him you took it from my corpse."

"Your Majesty—"

Silvanoshei thrust the ring at him. "Take it. Tell him I am dead."

"Why would I lie? And why would he believe me?" Gerard asked, hesitating.

"Because he will want to believe you," said Silvanoshei. "And by this action, you will free me."

Gerard took the ring, which was a circlet of sapphires, small enough to fit a child's hand.

"How will I find this Samar?"

"I will teach you a song," said Silvanoshei. "An old elven children's song. My mother used it as a signal if ever she needed to warn me of danger. Sing the song as you ride. Samar will hear it, and he will be intensely curious as to how you—a human—would know this song. He will find you."

"And then slit my throat—"

"He'll want to interrogate you first," said Silvanoshei. "Samar is a man of honor. If you tell him the truth, he'll know you for a man of honor, as well."

"I wish you'd reconsider, Your Majesty," Gerard said. He was starting to like this young man, even as he deeply pitied him.

Silvanoshei shook his head.

"Very well," said Gerard, sighing. "How does this song go?"

Silvanoshei taught the song to Gerard. The words were simple, the melody melancholy. It was a song meant to teach a child to count. "*Five for the fingers on each hand. Four for the legs upon a horse.*'"

The last line he knew he would never forget.

"*One is one and all alone and evermore shall be so.*"

Silvanoshei went to the stone bed, lay down upon it, turned away his face.

"Tell Samar I am dead," he reiterated softly. "If it's any comfort to you, Sir Knight, you won't be telling a lie. You'll be telling him the truth."

II

To Free the Snared Bird

erard emerged from the prison to find that night had fallen. He looked up the street and down, even took a casual saunter behind the prison, and saw no one lurking in a doorway or hiding in the shadows.

"This is my chance," he muttered. "I can ride out of the gate, lose myself in the confusion of the troops setting up camp, find this Samar, and start over from there. That's what I'll do. Leaving now is logical. It makes sense. Yes, that's definitely what I'm going to do."

But even as he said this to himself, even as he told himself repeatedly that this was his best course of action, he knew very well that he wouldn't. He would go find Samar, he had to go—he had promised Silvanoshei he would, and that was a promise he planned to keep, even if he didn't plan to keep any of the rest of the promises he'd made to the young man.

First, he had to talk to Odila. The reason was, of course, that he hoped to persuade her to come with him. He had thought up some very fine arguments against this One God and he planned to use them.

The Temple of the Heart was an ancient building that predated the Cataclysm. Dedicated to the worship of the old gods of Light, the temple had been built at the foot of Mount Grishnor and was reputed to be the oldest structure in Sanction, probably built when Sanction was little more than a fishing village. Various rumors and legends surrounded the temple, including one that the foundation stone had been laid by one of the Kingpriests, who'd had the misfortune to be shipwrecked. Washing up on this shore, the Kingpriest had given thanks to Paladine for his survival. To show his gratitude, he built a temple to the gods.

After the Cataclysm, the temple might have suffered the same fate as many other temples during that time, when people took out their anger on the gods by attacking and destroying their temples. This temple remained standing, unscathed, mostly due to the rumor that the spirit of that same Kingpriest lingered here, refusing to allow anyone to harm his tribute to the gods. The temple suffered from neglect, but that was all.

Following the Chaos War, the vengeful spirit must have departed, for the Mystics of the Citadel of Light moved into the temple without encountering any ghosts.

A small, square, unimposing structure of white marble, the temple had a steeply pitched roof that soared up among the trees. Beneath the roof was a central altar chamber—the largest and most important room in the temple. Other rooms surrounded the altar and were there to support it: sleeping quarters for the priests, a library, and so forth. Two sets of double doors led into the temple from the front.

Deciding that he would make faster time in the crowded streets on foot, Gerard stabled his horse in a hostelry near the West Gate and walked north to where the temple stood on a hill, somewhat isolated from the city, overlooking it.

He found a few people gathered in front of the temple, listening to Mina telling them of the miracles of the One God. An elderly man frowned exceedingly, but most of the others appeared interested.

The temple flared with lights, both inside and out. Huge double doors were propped open. Under Galdar's command, the Knights were carrying Goldmoon's amber sarcophagus into the altar room. The head of the minotaur was easily seen, his horns and snout silhouetted against the flames of torches that had been placed in sconces on the walls. Mina kept close watch on the procedure, glancing often in the direction of the procession to make certain that the sarcophagus was being handled carefully, that her Knights were behaving with dignity and respect.

Pausing in the deep shadows of a night-shrouded tree to reconnoiter, and, hopefully, try to catch a glimpse of Odila, Gerard watched the amber sarcophagus move slowly and with stately formality into the temple. He heard Galdar issue a sharp rebuke at one point, saw Mina turn her head swiftly to look. She was so concerned that she lost the thread of her exhortation and was forced to think a moment to remember where she'd left off.

Gerard could never ask for a better time to talk to Odila than this, while Galdar was supervising the funeral detail and Mina was proselytizing. When a group of Knights walked toward the temple, carrying Mina's baggage, Gerard fell in behind them.

The Knights were in a good mood, talking and laughing over what a fine joke it was on the do-gooder Mystics that Mina had taken over their temple. Gerard couldn't see the humor himself, and he doubted very much if Mina would have been pleased had she overheard them.

The Knights entered through another set of double doors, heading for Mina's living quarters. Looking through an open door on his left into a blaze of candle light, Gerard saw Odila standing beside the altar, directing the placement of the amber sarcophagus on several wooden trestles.

Gerard hung back in the shadows, hoping for a chance to catch Odila alone. The Knights lumbered in with their burden, deposited it with much grunting and groaning and a yelp and a curse, as one of the men dropped his end of the coffin prematurely, causing it to pinch the fingers of another man's hand. Odila issued a sharp rebuke. Galdar growled a threat. The men pushed and shoved, and soon the crystal sarcophagus was in place.

Hundreds of white candles burned on the altar, probably placed there by Odila's hands. The reflection of the candles burned in the amber, so that it seemed Goldmoon lay in the midst of a myriad tiny flames. The light illuminated her waxen face. She looked more peaceful than Gerard remembered, if such a thing were possible. Perhaps, as Mina had said, Goldmoon was pleased to be home.

Gerard wiped his sleeve across his forehead. The candles gave off a surprising amount of heat. Gerard found a seat on a bench in the back of the altar room. He moved as quietly as he could, holding his sword to keep it from knocking against the wall. He couldn't see very well, having stared into the candle flames, and he bumped into someone. Gerard was about to make his excuses when he saw, with a shudder, that his companion was Palin. The mage sat unmoving on the bench, stared unblinking into the candle flames.

Touching the mage's flaccid arm was like touching a warm corpse. Feeling his gorge rise, Gerard moved hastily to another bench. He sat down, waited impatiently for the minotaur to leave.

"I will post a guard around the sarcophagus," Galdar stated.

Gerard muttered a curse. He hadn't counted on that.

"No need," Odila said. "Mina is coming to worship at the altar, and she has given orders that she is to be left alone."

Gerard breathed more freely, then his breathing stopped altogether. The minotaur was half-way out the door when he paused, sent a searching gaze throughout the altar room. Gerard froze in place, trying desperately to remember whether or not minotaurs have good night vision. It seemed to him that Galdar saw him, for the beady, bovine eyes stared straight at him. He waited tensely for Galdar to call to him, but, after a moment's scrutiny, the minotaur walked out.

Gerard wiped away the sweat that was now running down his face and dripping off his chin. Slowly and cautiously, he edged out from the rows of benches and walked toward the front of the altar. He tried to be quiet, but leather creaked, metal rattled.

Odila was swathed in candlelight. Her face was partially turned toward him, and he was alarmed to see how thin and wasted she had grown. Riding for weeks in the wagon, doing nothing but listening to Mina's harangues and force-feeding the mages had caused her fine muscle tone to diminish. She could probably still wield her sword, but she wouldn't last two rounds with a healthy, battle-hardened opponent.

She no longer laughed or spoke much, but went about her duties in silence. Gerard hadn't liked this god before. Now he was starting to actively hate the One God. What sort of god stamped out joy and was offended by laughter? No sort of god he wanted to have anything to do with. He was glad he'd come to talk to her, hoped to be able to convince her to abandon this and come away with him.

But even as the hope was born, it died within him. One look at her face as she bent over the candles and he knew he was wasting his time.

He was suddenly reminded of an old poacher's trick for snaring a bird. You attach berries at intervals to a long, thin cord tied to a stake. The bird eats the berries, one by one, ingesting the cord at the same time. When the bird reaches the end of the cord, it tries to fly away, but by now the cord is wound up inside its vitals, and it cannot escape.

One by one, Odila had consumed the berries attached to the lethal cord. The last was the power to work miracles. She was tied to the One God, and only a miracle—a reverse miracle—would cut her free.

Well, perhaps friendship was that sort of miracle.

325

"Odila—" he began.

"What do you want, Gerard?" she asked, without turning around.

"I have to talk to you," he said. "Please, just a moment. It won't take long."

Odila sat down on a bench near the amber sarcophagus. Gerard would have been happier sitting farther back, out of the light and the heat, but Odila wouldn't move. Tense and preoccupied, she cast frequent glances at the door, glances that were half-nervous, half-expectant.

"Odila, listen to me," said Gerard. "I'm leaving Sanction. Tonight. I came to tell you that and to try to convince you to leave with me."

"No," she said, glancing at the door. "I can't leave now. I have too much to do here before Mina comes."

"I'm not asking you to go on a picnic!" he said, exasperated. "I'm asking you to escape this place with me, tonight! The city is in confusion, what with soldiers marching in and out. No one knows what's going on. It'll be hours before some sort of order is established. Now's the perfect time to leave."

"Then go," she said, shrugging. "I don't want you around anyway."

She started to rise. He grabbed her arm, gripped her wrist tightly, and saw her wince with pain.

"You don't want me around because I remind you of what you used to be. You don't like this One God. You don't like the change that's come over you anymore than I do. Why are you doing this to yourself?"

"Because, Gerard," Odila said wearily, as if she'd gone over the same argument again and again, "the One God is a god. A god who came to this world to care for us and guide us."

"Where? Off the edge of a precipice?" Gerard demanded. "After the Chaos War, Goldmoon found her guide in her own heart. Love and caring, compassion, truth, and honor did not leave with gods of light. They are inside each of us. Those are our guides or they should be."

"At her death, Goldmoon turned to the One God," said Odila, glancing at the still, calm face entombed in amber.

"Did she?" Gerard demanded harshly. "I wonder about that. If she really did embrace the One God, why didn't the One God keep her alive to go around shouting her miracle to the world? Why did the One God feel it necessary to stop her mouth in death and lock her up in an amber prison?"

"She will be freed, Mina says," said Odila defensively. "On the Night of the New Eye, the One God will raise Goldmoon from the dead, and she will come forth to rule the world."

Gerard released her hand, let go of her. "So you won't come with me?"

Odila shook her head. "No, Gerard, I won't. I know you don't understand. I'm not as strong as you are. I'm all by myself in the dark forest, and I'm afraid. I'm glad to have a guide, and if the guide is not perfect, neither am I. Goodbye, Gerard. Thank you for your friendship and your caring. Go on your journey safely in the name of the—"

"One God?" he said grimly. "No, thanks."

Turning, he walked out of the altar room.

The first place Gerard went was to the army's central command post, located in the former Souk Bazaar, whose stalls and shops had been replaced by a small city of tents. Here, the contents of the strongboxes were being distributed.

Taking his place in line, Gerard felt a certain satisfaction in taking the Dark Knights' steel. He'd earned it, no question about that, and he would need money for his journey back to Lord Ulrich's manor or wherever the Knights were consolidating their forces.

After receiving his pay, he headed for the West Gate and freedom. He put Odila out of his mind, refused to let himself think about her. He removed most of his armor—the braces and greaves and his chain mail, but continued to wear the cuirass and helm. Both were uncomfortable, but he had to consider the possibility that sooner or later Galdar might grow tired of shadowing Gerard and just stab him in the back.

The bulk of the two towers of the West Gate loomed black against the red light that shone from the lava moat surrounding the city. The gates had been shut. The gate guards weren't about to open them until they'd had a good look at Gerard and heard his story—that he was a messenger dispatched to Jelek with word of their victory. The guards wished him a good journey and opened a wicket gate to let him ride through.

Glancing back to see the walls of Sanction lined with men, Gerard was once more profoundly and grudgingly impressed with Mina's leadership and her ability to impose discipline and order on her troops.

"She will grow in strength and in power every day she remains here," he remarked gloomily to himself as his horse cantered through the gate. Ahead of him was the harbor and beyond that the black expanse of New Sea. A whiff of salt air was a welcome relief from the continuous smell of sulfur and brimstone that lingered in the air of Sanction. "And how are we to fight her?"

"You can't."

A hulking figure blocked his path. Gerard recognized the voice, as his horse recognized the stench of minotaur. The horse snorted and reared, and Gerard had his hands full trying to remain on the animal's back, during which frantic few moments he lost any opportunity he might have had to either run the minotaur down or gallop away and leave him standing in the dust.

The minotaur drew closer, his bestial face faintly illuminated by the red glow of the lava that made Sanction's night perpetual twilight. Galdar grabbed hold of the horse's bridle.

Gerard drew his sword. He had no doubt that this was going to be their final confrontation, and he was not in much doubt about how it would end. He'd heard tales of how Galdar had once cut a man in two with a single stroke of his massive sword. One glance at the knotty muscles of the arms and the smooth, sleek muscles of the minotaur's hairy chest attested to the veracity of the storyteller.

"Look, Galdar," Gerard said, interrupting the minotaur as he was about to speak, "I've had a bellyful of sermons, and I'm fed up with being watched day and night. You know that I'm a Solamnic Knight sent here to spy on Mina. I know you know, so let's just end this right now—"

"I would like to fight you, Solamnic," said Galdar, and his voice was cold. "I would like to kill you, but I am forbidden."

"I figured as much," said Gerard, lowering his sword. "May I ask why?"

329

"You serve her. You do her bidding."

"Now, see here, Galdar, you and I both know that I'm not riding to do Mina's bidding—" Gerard began, then stopped, growing confused. Here he was, arguing for his own death.

"By *her*, I do not mean Mina," said Galdar. "I mean the One God. Have you never thought to find out the name?"

"Of the One God?" Gerard was becoming increasingly annoyed by this conversation. "No. To be honest, I never really gave a rat's—"

"Takhisis," said Galdar.

"—ass," said Gerard, and then fell silent.

He sat on his horse in the road in the darkness, thinking, it all makes sense. It all makes bloody, horrible, awful sense. No need to ask him if he believed the minotaur. Deep inside, Gerard had suspected this truth all along.

"Why are you telling me this?" he demanded.

"I am not allowed to kill you," Galdar said dourly, "but I can kill your spirit. I know your plans. You carry a message from that wretched elf king to his people, begging them to come save him. Why do you think Mina chose you to take the elf to prison, if not to be his 'messenger'? She *wants* you to bring his people here. Bring the entire elven nation. Bring the Knights of Solamnia—what is left of them. Bring them all here to witness the glory of Queen Takhisis on the Night of the New Eye."

The minotaur released the horse's bridle. "Ride off, Solamnic. Ride to whatever dreams of victory and glory you have in your heart and know, as you ride, that they are nothing but ash. Takhisis controls your destiny. All you do, you do in her name. As do I."

Giving Gerard an ironic salute, the minotaur turned and walked back to the walls of Sanction.

Gerard looked up at the sky. Clouds of smoke rolling from the Lords of Doom obliterated the stars and the moon. The night was dark above, fire-tinged below. Was it true that somewhere out there, Takhisis watched him? Knew all he thought and planned?

"I have to go back," Gerard thought, chilled. "Warn Odila." He started to turn his horse's head, then halted. "Maybe that's what Takhisis *wants* me to do. If I go back, perhaps she'll see to it that I lose my chance to talk with Samar. I can't do anything to help Odila. I'll ride on."

He turned his horse's head the other way, then stopped. "Takhisis wants me to talk to the elf. Galdar said as much. So maybe I shouldn't! How can I know what to do? Or does it even make any difference?"

Gerard stopped dead in his tracks.

"Galdar was right," he said bitterly. "He would have done me a favor by sticking a plain, ordinary, everyday sword in my gut. The blade he's left there now is poisoned, and I can never rid myself of it. What do I do? What *can* I do?"

He had only one answer, and it was the one he'd given Odila.

He had to follow what was in his heart.

12

The New Eye

s he stalked back toward the West Gate, Galdar was disappointed to find that he didn't feel as pleased with himself as he should have. He had hoped to infect the confident and self-assured Solamnic with the same sickness that infected him. He'd done what he'd set out to accomplish—the angry, frustrated expression on the Solamnic's face had proven that. But Galdar found he couldn't take any satisfaction from his victory.

What had he hoped? That the Solamnic would prove him wrong?

"Bah!" Galdar snorted. "He's caught in the same coil as the rest of us, and there's no way out. Not now. Not ever. Not even in death."

He rubbed his right arm, which had begun to ache persistently, and found himself wishing he could lose it again, so much did it pain him. Once he'd been proud of that arm, the arm that Mina had restored to him, the first miracle she'd ever performed in the name of the One God. Now he caught himself fingering his sword with some vague notion of hacking off the arm himself. He wouldn't, of course. Mina would be angry with him and, worse, she would be hurt and saddened. He could endure her anger, he'd felt its lash before. He could never do anything to hurt her. Most of the pent-up fury and resentment he felt toward Takhisis was based not on her treatment of him but the way she treated Mina, who had sacrificed everything, even her life, for her goddess.

Mina had been rewarded. She'd been given victory over her enemies, given the power to perform miracles. But Galdar knew Takhisis of old. The minotaur race had never thought very highly of the goddess, who was the consort of the minotaur god, Sargas, or Sargonnas, as the other races called him. Sargas had remained with his people to fight Chaos until the bitter end, when—so legend had it—he had sacrificed himself to save the minotaur race. Takhisis would never dream of sacrificing herself for anything. She expected sacrifices to be made to her, demanded them in return for her dubious blessings.

Perhaps that is what she has in mind for Mina. Galdar grew uneasy listening to Mina's constant talk of this "great miracle" Takhisis was going to perform on the Night of the New Eye. Takhisis never gave something for nothing. Galdar had only to feel the throbbing pain of the goddess's displeasure with him to know that. Mina was so trusting, so guileless. She could never understand Takhisis's deceitfulness, her treacherous and vindictive nature.

That, of course, was why Mina had been chosen. That and because she was beloved of Goldmoon.

Takhisis would not pass up a chance to inflict pain on anyone, most especially on Goldmoon, who had thwarted her in the past.

I could tell all this to Mina, Galdar thought as he entered the temple. I could tell her, but she wouldn't hear me. She hears only one voice these days.

The Temple of the Heart, now the Temple of the One God. How Takhisis must revel in that appellation! After an eternity of being one of many, now she was one and all powerful.

He shook his horned head gloomily.

The temple grounds were empty. Galdar went first to Mina's quarters. He did not truly expect to find her there, although she must be exhausted after the day's battle. He knew where she would be. He wanted to check to make certain that everything was prepared for her when she finally chose to go to bed.

He glanced into the room that had once been the room for the head of the Order, probably that old fool who'd scowled all through Mina's sermon. Galdar found all in readiness. Everything had been arranged for her comfort. Her weapons were here, as was her armor, carefully arranged on a stand. Her morning star had been polished, the blood cleaned from it and from her armor. Her boots were free of dirt and blood. A tray of food stood on a desk near the bed. A candle burned to light her way in the darkness. Someone had even thought of placing some late-blooming wild-flowers in a pewter cup. Everything in the room attested to the love and devotion her troops felt for her.

For her. Galdar wondered if she realized that. The men fought for her, for Mina. They shouted her name when she led them forth to battle. They shouted her name in victory.

Mina . . . Mina . . .

They did not shout, "For the One God." They did not shout, "For Takhisis."

"And I'll wager you don't like that," Galdar said to the darkness.

Could a god be jealous of a mortal?

This god could, Galdar thought, and he was suddenly filled with fear.

Galdar entered the altar room, stood blinking painfully while his eyes became accustomed to the light of the candles blazing on the altar. Mina was alone, kneeling before the altar in prayer. He could hear her voice, murmuring, halting, then murmuring again, as if she were receiving instructions.

The other Solamnic, the female Knight turned priestess, lay stretched out on a bench, asleep. She slept soundly on her hard bed. Mina's own cloak covered the female. Galdar could never remember her name.

Goldmoon, in her amber coffin, slept as well. The two mages sat in the back of the chamber, where'd they'd been planted. He could see their forms, shadowy in the candlelight. His gaze flicked over them quickly, went back to Mina. The sight of the wretched mages gave him the horrors, made the hair rise on his spine, ripple down his back.

Someday perhaps his own corpse would sit there quietly, staring at nothing, doing nothing, waiting for Takhisis's orders.

Galdar walked toward the altar. He tried to move quietly, out of respect for Mina, but minotaurs are not made for stealthy movement. His knee bumped a bench, his sword clanked and clattered at his side, his footfalls boomed, or so it seemed to him.

The female Solamnic stirred uneasily, but she was too deeply drowned in sleep to waken.

Mina did not hear him.

Walking up to stand behind her, he spoke to her quietly, "Mina."

She did not lift her head.

Galdar waited a moment, then said, "Mina" again and placed his hand gently on her shoulder.

Now she turned, now she looked around. Her face was pale and drawn with fatigue. Smudged circles of weariness surrounded her amber eyes, whose bright gleam was dimmed.

"You should go to bed," he told her.

"Not yet," she said.

"You were all over the battlefield," he persisted. "I couldn't keep up with you. Everywhere I looked, there you were. Fighting, praying. You need your rest. We have much to do tomorrow and in the days following to fortify the city. The Solamnics will attack us. Their spy rides to alert them even now. I let him go," Galdar growled, "as you commanded. I think it was a mistake. He's in league with the elf king. The Solamnics will make some deal with the elves, bring the might of both nations down on us."

"Most likely," said Mina.

She held out her hand to Galdar. He was privileged to help her rise to her feet. She retained his hand—his right hand—in her own, looked up into his eyes.

"All is well, Galdar. I know what I am doing. Have faith."

"I have faith in you, Mina," Galdar said.

Mina cast him a disappointed glance. Releasing his hand, she turned away from him to face the altar. Her look and her silence were her rebuke, that and the sudden gut-twisting pain in his arm. He clamped his lips shut, massaged his arm, and stubbornly waited.

"I have no more need of you, Galdar," Mina said. "Go to your bed."

"I do not sleep until you sleep, Mina. You know that. Or you should, after all this time together."

Her head bowed. He was astonished to see two tears glitter in the candlelight, slide down her cheeks. She whisked them both swiftly away.

"I know, Galdar," she said in muffled voice that tried to be gruff but failed, "and I do appreciate your loyalty. If only . . ." She paused, then, glancing back at him, she said, almost shyly, "Will you wait here with me?"

"Wait for what, Mina?"

"For a miracle."

Mina lifted her hands in a commanding gesture. The flames leaped and swelled, burning brighter and hotter. A wave of searing heat smote Galdar in the face, causing him to gasp for breath and lift his hand to shield himself.

A breath filled the chamber, blew on the flames, caused them to grow stronger, burn higher. Banners and tapestries graced with emblems sacred to the Mystics hung behind the altar. The flames licked the fringe of the tapestries. The fabric caught fire.

The heat grew in intensity. Smoke coiled around the altar and around Goldmoon's amber sarcophagus. The Solamnic female began to cough and choke and woke herself up. She stared in fearful amazement, jumped to her feet.

"Mina!" she cried. "We must get out of here!"

The flames spread rapidly from the banners to the wooden beams that supported the steep ceiling. Galdar had never seen fire move so fast, as if the wood and the walls had been soaked with oil.

"If your miracle is to burn down this temple, then the Solamnic is right," Galdar bellowed over the roar of the fire. "We must get out of here now, before the ceiling collapses."

"We are in no danger," Mina said calmly. "The hand of the One God protects us. Watch and wonder and glory in her power."

The gigantic wooden ceiling beams were now ablaze. At any moment, they would start to crumble and break apart, come crashing down on top of them. Galdar was just about to grab hold of Mina and carry her out bodily, when he saw, to his utter confusion, that the flames consumed the beams entirely. Nothing was left of them. No cinders fell, no fiery timbers came thundering down in a rush of sparks. The holy fire devoured the wood, devoured the ceiling, devoured whatever materials had been used to build the roof. The flames consumed and then went out.

Nothing was left of the temple roof, not even ashes. Galdar stared into the night sky that glittered with stars.

The corpses of the two mages sat on their bench, unseeing, uncaring. They could have perished in the flames and never made a sound, spoken no word of protest, done nothing to save themselves. At a sharply spoken command from Mina, the bodies of the mages rose to their feet and moved toward the altar. Walking without seeing where they were going, they came to a halt when Mina ordered them to stop—near Gold-moon's amber sarcophagus—and stood once more staring at nothing.

"Watch!" said Mina softly. "The miracle begins."

Galdar had seen many wondrous and terrible sights in his long life, particularly that part of it that revolved around Mina. He had never seen anything like this, and he stared, thunderstruck.

A hundred thousand souls filled the night sky. The ghostly mist of their hands, their faces, their diaphanous limbs blotted out the stars. Galdar stared, aghast, amazed, to see that in their ephemeral hands, the dead carried the skulls of dragons.

Reverently, gently, the souls of the dead lowered the first skull through the charred opening where the roof had been and placed the skull on the floor, before the altar.

The skull was enormous, that of a gold dragon—Galdar could tell by the few golden scales that clung to the bone and gleamed pathetically in the flickering candlelight. Though the altar room was large, the skull filled it.

The dead brought down another skull, that of a red dragon. The dead placed the skull of the red dragon down beside that of the gold.

Shouts and cries rose up from outside. Seeing the flames, people came running to the Temple. The shouts ceased as they gazed in shock at the wondrous and fearful sight of dragon skulls, hundreds of them, spiraling down out of the dark night, cradled in the arms of the dead.

Methodically, the dead piled the skulls one on top of the other, the largest skulls on the bottom to form a secure base, the skulls of smaller dragons piled on top of that. The mound of skulls rose higher and higher, stacking up well above what would have been the height of the steep-pitched roof.

Galdar's mouth went dry. His eyes burned, his throat constricted so that he had difficulty speaking.

"This is a skull totem from one of the dragon overlords!" he cried.

"*Three* of the dragon overlords to be precise," Mina corrected.

The totem increased in height, now taller than the tallest trees, and still the dead continued to bring more skulls to add to it.

"This is the totem of Beryllinthranox the Green and of Khellendros the Blue and of Malystryx the Red. As Malystryx stole the totems of the other two, so the dead steal hers."

Galdar's stomach shriveled. His knees weakened. He was forced to grab hold of the altar to remain standing. He was terrified, and he was not ashamed to admit to his terror.

"You have stolen Malys's totem? The dragon will be furious, Mina. She will find out who has taken the totem, and she will come here after you!"

"I know," said Mina calmly. "That is the plan."

"She will kill you, Mina!" Galdar gasped. "She will kill us all. I know this foul dragon. No one can stand up to her. Even her own kind are terrified of her."

"Look, Galdar," said Mina softly.

Galdar turned his reluctant gaze back to the pile of skulls that was now almost complete. One last skull, that of a small white dragon, was laid upon the top. The dead lingered for a moment, as if admiring their handiwork. A chill wind blew down from the mountainside, shredded the souls into wisps of fog, and dispersed them with a puff.

The eyes of dead dragons began to shine from their hollow eye sockets. It seemed to Galdar that he could hear voices, hundreds of voices, raised in a triumphant paean. A shadowy form took shape above the totem, coiled around it covetously. The shadowy form became clearer, more distinct. Scales of many colors gleamed in the candlelight. An enormous tail curled around the totem's base, the body of a giant dragon circled it. Five heads rose over the totem. Five heads attached to one body and that body attached to the totem.

The body lacked substance, however. The five heads were daunting, but they were not real heads, not as real as the skulls of the dead over which they hovered. The eyes of the dead dragons gleamed bright. Their light was almost blinding, and suddenly it lanced straight into the heavens.

The light of the totem blazed through the sky, and there, looking down upon them, was a single eye. The eye of the goddess.

White, staring, the eye gazed down at them, unblinking.

The body of the five-headed dragon grew more distinct, gained in substance and in strength.

"The power of the totem feeds the One God as the totem once fed Malys," Mina said. "With each passing moment, the One God comes closer to entering the world, joining the mortal and immortal. On the Night of the Festival of the New Eye, the One God will become the paradox, she will take a mortal form and imbue it with immortality. In that moment, she will rule over all that is in the heavens and all that is below. She will rule over the living and the dead. Her victory will be assured, her triumph complete."

She will take a mortal form. Galdar knew then why they'd been forced to cart the body of Goldmoon across Ansalon, haul it up mountains, and hoist it out of valleys.

Takhisis's final revenge. She would enter the body of the one person who had fought life-long against her, and she would use that body to seduce and enthrall and entrap the trusting, the innocent, the guileless.

He could hear outside the temple a hubbub of voices, raised in excitement, babbling and clamoring at the sight of this new moon in the heavens. The cry raised, "Mina! Mina!"

She would go out to them, bask in the light and warmth of their affection, far different from that chill, cold light. She would tell them that this was the work of the One God, but no one would pay any attention.

"Mina . . . Mina . . ."

She walked out the door of the ruined temple. Galdar heard the swelling cheer raised when she appeared, heard it reverberate off the sides of the mountains, echo to the heavens.

To the heavens.

Galdar looked up at the five heads of the ethereal dragon, swaying over the totem, consuming its power. The single eye burned, and he realized in that moment that he was closer to this goddess than Mina was or ever could be.

The trusting, the innocent, the guileless.

Galdar wanted his bed, wanted to sleep and forget all this in dark oblivion. He would break his own rule this night. Mina was with those who adored her. She had no need of him. He was about to depart, when he heard a moan.

The Solamnic female crouched on the floor, huddled within herself, staring up, appalled, at the monster that writhed and coiled above her.

She, too, had seen the truth.

"Too late," he said to her as he passed by on his way to his bed. "Too late. For all of us."

13

Restless Spirits

The bodies of the two mages stood where they had been told to stand, near the amber sarcophagus in the Temple of the Heart, now the Temple of the One God. The spirit of only one of the mages was there to watch the building of the totem. Dalamar's spirit had departed with the arrival of the skull-bearing dead. Palin continued to watch the totem grow, a monument to the strengthening power of Queen Takhisis. He had no idea where Dalamar had gone. The spirit of the dark elf was often absent, gone more than he was around.

Palin still found it disconcerting to be away from his body for any period of time, but had been venturing farther these past few days. He was growing increasingly alarmed, for he realized—as did all the dead—that Takhisis was very close to the time when she would make her triumphant entry into the world.

Palin watched the totem grow and, with it, Takhisis's power. Takhisis could take many forms, but when dealing with dragons, she preferred her dragon form. Five heads, each of a different color and species of dragon, emerged from a body of massive power and strength. The head of the red dragon was brutal, vicious. Flames flickered in the nostrils. The head of the blue was sleek, elegant, and deadly. Lightning crackled from between the razor-sharp fangs. The head of the black was cunning, sly, and dripped poison acid. The head of the white was cruel, calculating, and radiated a bone-numbing chill. The head of the green was devious and clever. Noxious fumes spewed from the gaping jaws.

This was Takhisis on the immortal plane, the Takhisis the dead served in dread terror, the Takhisis whom Palin hated and loathed and, despite himself, felt moved to worship. For in the eyes of the five dragons was the mind of the god, a mind that could span the vastness of eternity and see and understand the limitless possibilities and, at the same time, number all the drops in the swelling seas and count the grains of sand in the barren desert.

The sight of the Dark Queen hovering around the skulls of the dead dragons, receiving the accolades of the dead dragons, was too much for him to bear. Palin tore his spirit from his body and flitted restlessly out into the darkness.

He found it difficult to give up the habits of the living, and so he roamed the streets of Sanction in his spirit form as he might have done in his living form. He walked around buildings, when he might have passed through them. Physical objects were no barrier to a spirit, yet they blocked him. To walk through walls—to do something that was so completely against the laws of nature—would be to admit that he had lost any connection to life, to the physical part of life. He could not do that, not yet.

His spirit form did allow him easy passage through the streets that were clogged with people, everyone running to the newly proclaimed Temple of the One God to see the miracle. If he had been alive and breathing, Palin would have been swept up in the mob or run down, just as were two beggars floundering in the street. One, a lame man, had his crutch knocked out from under him. The other, a blind man, had lost his cane and was groping about helplessly with his hands, trying to find it.

Instinctively, Palin started to offer them help, only to remember what he was, remember there was no help he could give. Drifting nearer, Palin noted that the blind man looked familiar—the silver hair, the white robes. . . . The silver hair especially. He couldn't see the man's face, which was covered by bandages to hide the hideous wound that had robbed him of his sight. Palin knew the blind man, but he couldn't place him. The man was out of context, not where he was supposed to be. The Citadel of Light came to Palin's mind, and he suddenly recalled where he had seen this man before. This man, who was no man.

Using the eyes of the spirit world, Palin saw the true forms of the two beggars, forms that existed on the immortal plane and thus could not be banished, although they had taken other shapes in the mortal world. A silver dragon—Mirror—former guardian of the Citadel of Light stood side by side, wing-tip to wing-tip with a blue dragon.

Palin remembered then what it was to hope.

Dalamar's spirit was also abroad this night. The dark elf ventured much farther afield than Palin. Unlike Palin, Dalamar let no physical barrier impede him. Mountains were for him as insubstantial as clouds. He passed through the solid rock walls of Malys's lair, penetrated its labyrinthine chambers with the ease of blinking an eye or drawing a breath.

He found the great, red dragon sleeping, as he had been accustomed to finding her on previous occasions. Yet, this time, there was a difference. On his earlier visits, she'd slept deeply and peacefully, secure in the knowledge that she was supreme ruler of this world and there were none strong enough to challenge her. Now, her sleep was troubled. Her huge feet twitched, her eyes roved behind closed lids, her nostrils inflated. Saliva drooled from her jaw, and a growl rumbled deep in her chest. She dreamed—an unpleasant dream, seemingly.

That would be nothing, compared to her waking.

"Most Great and Gracious Majesty," Dalamar said.

Malys opened one eye, another sign that her slumber was not restful. Usually Dalamar had to speak to her several times or even summon one of her minions to come wake her.

"What do you want?" she growled.

"To make you aware of what is transpiring in the world while you sleep."

"Yes, go on," Malys said, opening the other eye.

"Where is your totem, Majesty?" Dalamar asked coolly.

Malys turned her massive head to look reassuringly upon her collection of skulls, trophies of her many victories, including those over Beryl and Khellendros.

Her eyes widened. Her breath escaped in a sizzling hiss. Rearing up with such force that she caused the mountain to quiver, she turned her head this way and that.

"Where is it?" she bellowed, lashing out with her tail. Granite walls cracked at the blows, stalactites crashed down from the ceiling, shattered on her red scales. She paid them no attention. "Where is the thief? Who has stolen it? Tell me!"

"I will tell you," Dalamar said, ignoring her fury, for she could do him no harm. "But I want something in exchange."

"Always the shrewd bargainer!" she hissed with a flicker of flame from out her teeth.

"You are aware of my present lamentable condition," said Dalamar, extending his hands to exhibit his ghostly form. "If you recover the totem and defeat the person who has unlawfully taken it, I ask that you use your magic to restore my soul to my living body."

"Granted," said Malys with a twitch of her clawed foot. Her head leaned forward. "Who has it?"

"Mina."

"Mina?" Malys repeated, baffled. "Who is this Mina and why has she taken my totem? *How* has she taken it? I smell no thief! No one has been in my lair! No thief could transport it!"

"Not even an army of thieves," Dalamar agreed. "An army of the dead could. And did."

"Mina . . ." Malys breathed the name with loathing. "Now I remember. I heard it said that she commanded an army of souls. What rubbish!"

"The 'rubbish' stole away the totem while you slept, Majesty, and they have rebuilt it in Sanction, in what was once known as the Temple of the Heart, but is now known as the Temple of the One God."

"This so-called One God again," snarled Malys. "This One God is starting to annoy me."

"The One God could do far more than annoy you, Majesty," said Dalamar coolly. "This One God was responsible for the destruction of Cyan Bloodbane, your cousin Beryl, and Khellendros the Blue—next to yourself, the three mightiest dragons in Krynn. This One God has encompassed the fall of Silvanesti, the destruction of Qualinost, the defeat of the Solamnic Knights in Solanthus, and now she has been victorious in Sanction. You alone stand in the way of her absolute triumph."

Malys glowered, silent, brooding. He had spoken harshly, and although she didn't like to hear it, she couldn't deny the truth.

"She steals my totem. Why?" Malys asked sullenly.

"It has not been your totem for a long time," Dalamar replied. "The One God has been subverting the souls of the dead dragons who once worshiped her. She has been using the power of their souls to fuel her own power. By stealing the totems of your cousin and Khellendros, you played into the One God's hands. You made the souls of the dead dragons more powerful still. Do not underestimate this goddess. Although she was weakened and near destruction when first she came to this world, she has recovered her strength, and she is now poised to lay claim to a prize she has long coveted."

"You speak as if you know this goddess," said Malys, eyeing Dalamar with contempt.

"I do know her," said Dalamar, "and so do you—by reputation. Her name is Takhisis."

"Yes, I've heard of her," said Malys, with a dismissive flick of a claw. "I heard she abandoned this world during the war with Father Chaos."

"She did not abandon it," said Dalamar. "She stole it and brought it here, as she had long planned to do with the aid of Khellendros. Did you never stop to think how this world suddenly came into being in this part of the universe? Did you never wonder?"

"No, why should I?" Malys returned angrily. "If food falls into the hands of a starving man, he does not question, he eats!"

"You dined exceedingly well, Majesty," Dalamar agreed. "It is a shame that afterward you did not take out the garbage. The souls of the dead dragons have recognized their queen, and they will do anything she requires. You are sadly outnumbered, Your Majesty."

"Dead dragons have no fangs." Malys sneered. "I face a puny god who has a child for a champion and who must rely on expired souls for her might. I will recover my totem and deal a death blow to this god."

"When does Your Majesty plan to attack Sanction?" Dalamar asked.

"When I am ready," Malys growled. "Leave me now."

Dalamar bowed low. "Your Majesty will not forget her promise—to restore my soul to my body. I could be of so much more use to you as one whole person."

Malys waved a claw. "I do not forget my promises. Now go."

Closing her eyes, she let her massive head sink to the floor.

Dalamar was not fooled. For all her appearance of nonchalance, Malys had been shaken to the core of her being. She might sham sleep, but inside the fires of her rage burned bright and hot.

Satisfied that he had done all he could—here, at least—Dalamar departed.

The totem grew inside the fire-ravaged Temple. Mina's Knights and soldiers cheered her and called her name. Takhisis's shadow hovered over the totem, but few could see her. They did not look for her. They saw Mina, and that was all they cared about.

In Sanction's streets, now almost completely emptied, the silver dragon Mirror groped about for his beggar's staff, that had been knocked out of his hands. "What is happening?" he asked his companion, who silently handed him his staff. "What is going on? I hear a tumult and a great cry."

"It is Takhisis," said Razor. "I can see her. She has revealed herself. Many of my brethren circle in the heavens, shouting her name. The dead dragons cry out to her. I hear the voice of my mate among them. Red, blue, white, black, green, living, dead—all swear their loyalty to her. She grows in power as I speak."

"Will you join them?" Mirror asked.

"I have been thinking long on what you said back in the cave of the mighty Skie," said Razor slowly. "How none of the calamities that have befallen this world would have happened if it had not been for Takhisis. I hated and detested Paladine and the other so-called gods of light. I cursed his name, and if I had a chance to kill one of his champions, I took that chance and gloried in it. I longed for the day when our queen might rule uncontested.

"Now that day has come, and I am sorry for it. She has no care for us." Razor paused, then said, "I see you smiling, Silver. You think 'care' is the wrong word. I agree. Those of us who followed the Dark Queen are not noted for being caring individuals. Respect. That is the word I want. Takhisis has no respect for those who serve her. She uses them until they are no longer of value to her, then she casts them aside. No, I will not serve Takhisis."

"But will he work actively against her?" a familiar voice whispered in Mirror's ear. "If you will vouch for him, I can use his help, as well as yours."

"Palin?" Mirror turned gladly in the direction of the voice. He reached out his hand toward the source of the voice, but felt no warm hand clasp his in return.

"I cannot see you or touch you, but I hear you, Palin," Mirror said. "And even your voice seems far away and distant, as though you speak from across a wide vale."

"So I do," said Palin. "Yet, together, perhaps we can cross it. I want you to help me destroy this totem."

Dalamar's spirit joined the river of souls flowing toward the Temple of the One, as other rivers flow toward the sea. His spirit paid no heed to the rest, but concentrated on his next objective. The other souls ignored him. They would not have heard him if he had spoken. They did not see him. They heard only one voice, saw only one face.

On arriving, Dalamar broke free of the torrent that spiraled around and around the totem of dragon skulls. The immense monument towered high in the air, visible for miles, or so said some of the thousands who stood staring at it in awe and admiration, exulting in Mina's victory over the hated red dragon, Malys.

Dalamar flicked the totem a glance. It was impressive, he had to admit. He then shifted his mind to more urgent matters. Guards stood posted at the temple doors. None with substantial bodies were being admitted inside the temple. His spirit flowed past the guards and into the altar room. He made certain that his body was safe, noted with some suprise that Palin's spirit was abroad this night.

Palin's departure was such an unusual occurrence that, despite the urgency of his errand, Dalamar paused to ponder where he might be, what the mage's soul could be up to. Dalamar wasn't concerned. He considered Palin as devious as a bowl of porridge.

"Still," Dalamar reminded himself, "he is Raistlin's nephew. And while porridge may be pale and lumpy, it is also thick and viscous. Much can be concealed beneath that bland surface."

The souls whirled in frenetic ecstasy around the totem, as thick as smoke rising from water-soaked wood. Millions of faces streamed past Dalamar any instant he chose to look. He continued on his way, moved ahead with the next stage of his plan.

Mina stood alone at the candle-lit altar. Her back to the totem, she stared, rapt, into the flames. The big minotaur was nearby. Where Mina was, the minotaur was.

"Mina, you are exhausted," Galdar pleaded. "You can barely stand. You must come to your bed. Tomorrow . . . who knows what tomorrow will bring? You should be rested."

"I thought you went to bed, Galdar," said Mina.

"I did," the minotaur growled. "I could not sleep. I knew I would find you here."

"I like to be here," said Mina in a dreamy voice. "Close to the One God. I can feel her holy presence. She folds me in her arms and lifts me up with her."

Mina raised her gaze upward into the night sky, now visible since the roof of the temple had been destroyed. "I am warm when I am with her, Galdar. I am warm and loved and fed and clothed and safe in her arms. When I come back to this world, I am cold and starving and thirsty. It is a punishment to be here, Galdar, when I would so much rather be up there."

Galdar made a rumbling sound in his throat. If he had doubts, he knew better than to speak them. He said only, "Yet, while you are down here, Mina, you have a job to do for the One God. You will not be able to do that job if you are sick with fatigue."

Mina reached out her hand, placed it on the minotaur's arm. "You are right, Galdar. I am being selfish. I will come to bed, and I will even sleep late in the morning."

Mina turned to look at the totem. Her amber eyes shone as if she still stared into the flames. "Isn't it magnificent?"

She might have said more, but Dalamar took care to enter her line of sight. He bowed low.

"I seek but a moment of your time, Mina," said Dalamar, bowing again.

"Go on ahead and make certain that my chamber is prepared, Galdar," Mina ordered. "Don't worry. I will come shortly."

Galdar's bestial eyes passed over the place where Dalamar's spirit hovered. Dalamar could never decide if the minotaur saw him or not. He didn't think so, but he had the feeling that Galdar knew his spirit was there. The minotaur's nose wrinkled, as though he smelled something rotten. Then with a grunting snort, Galdar turned away and left the altar room.

"What do you want?" Mina asked Dalamar. Her

tone was calm, composed. "Have you word of the magical device carried by the kender?"

"Alas, no, Mina," said Dalamar, "but I do have other information. I have dire news. Malys is aware that you are the one who has stolen her totem."

"Indeed," said Mina, smiling slightly.

"Malys will come to take it back, Mina. The dragon is furious. She sees you now as a threat to her power."

"Why are you telling me all this, wizard?" Mina asked. "Surely, you are not fearful for my safety."

"No, Mina, I am not," said Dalamar coolly. "But I am fearful for my own if something should happen to you. I will help you defeat Malys. You will need a wizard's help to fight against this dragon."

"How will you, in your sorry state, help me?" Mina asked, amused.

"Restore my soul to my body. I am one of the most powerful wizards in the history of Krynn. My help to you could be invaluable. You have no leader for the dead. You tried to recruit Lord Soth and failed."

The amber eyes flickered. She was displeased.

"Yes, I heard about that," Dalamar said. "My spirit travels the world. I know a great deal about what is transpiring. I could be of use to you. I could be the one to lead the dead. I could seek out the kender and bring him and the device to you. Burrfoot knows me, he trusts me. I have made a study of the Device of Time Journeying. I could teach you to use it. I could use my magic to help you fight the dragon's magic. All this I could do for you—but only as living man."

Dalamar saw himself reflected in the amber eyes— a wisp, more insubstantial than spider's silk.

"All this you will do for me and more, if I require it," Mina said, "not as living man but as living corpse."

She lifted her head proudly. "As for your help against Malys, I have no need of your aid. The One God supports me and fights at my side. I need no other."

"Listen to me, Mina, before you go," insisted Dalamar, as she was turning away. "In my youth, I came to your One God as a lover comes to his mistress. She embraced me and caressed me and promised me that one day we would rule the world, she and I. I believed her, I trusted in her. My trust was betrayed. When I was no longer of use to her, she cast me to my enemies. She will do the same to you, Mina. When that day comes, you will need an ally of my strength and power. A living ally, not a corpse."

Mina paused, glanced back at him. She wore a thoughtful look. "Perhaps there is something in what you say, wizard."

Dalamar watched her warily, not trusting this sudden about-face. "There is, I assure you."

"Your faith in the One God was betrayed. She might say the same of you, Dalamar the Dark. Lovers often quarrel, a silly quarrel, soon forgotten, neither of them remembering."

"I remember," said Dalamar. "Because of her betrayal, I lost everything I ever loved and valued. Do you think I would so readily forget?"

"She might say that you put all that you loved and valued above her," Mina said, "that she was the one forsaken. Still, after all this time, it doesn't matter who was at fault. She values your affection. She would like to prove she still loves you by restoring to you everything you lost and more."

"In return for what?" Dalamar asked warily.

"A pledge of your affection."

"And? . . ."

"A small favor."

"And what is this 'small' favor?"

"Your friend, Palin Majere—"

"He is not my friend."

"That makes this easier, then," Mina said. "Your fellow wizard conspires against the One God. She is aware of his plots and schemings, of course. She would have no trouble thwarting them, but she has much on her mind these days, and she would appreciate your help."

"What must I do?" Dalamar asked.

Mina shrugged. "Nothing much. Simply alert her when he is about to act. That is all. She will take care of the matter from there."

"And in return?"

"You will be restored to life. You will be given all you ask for, including the leadership of the army of souls, if that is what you want. In addition . . ." Mina smiled at him. The amber eyes smiled.

"Yes? In addition?"

"Your magic will be restored to you."

"*My* magic," Dalamar emphasized. "I do not want the magic she borrowed from the dead and then loaned to me. I want the magic that once lived inside me!"

"You want the god's magic. She promises."

Dalamar thought back to all the promises Takhisis had made him, all the promises she had broken. He wanted this so much. He wanted to believe.

"I will," he said softly.

14

The Ring and the Cloak

D ays, weeks, had passed since the Qualinesti elves had arrived in Silvanesti. How long they had been here, Gilthas could not say, for one day blended into another in the timeless woods. And though his people were content to allow one day to slide off time's silken strand and fall into the soft green grass, Gilthas was not. He grew increasingly frustrated. Alhana kept up the pretense that Silvanoshei was recovering inside his tent. She spoke of him to her people, giving details of what he said and what he ate and how he was slowly mending. Gilthas listened in shock to these lies, but, after a time, he came to the conclusion that Alhana actually believed them. She had woven the threads of falsehood into a warm blanket and was using that blanket to shield herself from the cold truth.

The Silvanesti listened to her and asked no questions— something else that was incomprehensible to Gilthas.

"We Silvanesti do not like change," explained Kiryn in response to Gilthas's frustration. "Our mages halted the changing of the seasons, for we could not bear to see the green of spring wither and die. I know you cannot understand this, Gilthas. Your human blood runs hot, will not let you sit still. You count the seconds because they are so short and slip away so fast. The human side of you revels in change."

"Yet change comes!" said Gilthas, pacing back and forth, "whether the Silvanesti will it or not."

"Yes, change has come to us," said Kiryn with a sad smile. "Its raging torrent has washed away much of what we loved. Now the waters are calmer, we are content to float on the surface. Perhaps we will wash up on some quiet shore, where no one will find us or touch us or harm us ever again."

"The Dark Knights are desperate," said Gilthas. "They are outnumbered, they have no food. Their morale is low. We should attack now!"

"What would be the outcome?" asked Kiryn, shrugging. "The Dark Knights are desperate, as you say. They will not go down without a fight. Many of our people would die."

"And many of the enemy would die," said Gilthas impatiently.

"The death of one human is as the crushing of an ant—there are so many left and so many more to come. The death of a single elf is like the falling of a mighty oak. None will grow up to take his place for hundreds of years, if then. So many of us have died already. We have so little left to us, and it is all precious. How can we waste it?"

"What if the Silvanesti knew the truth about

Silvanoshei?" Gilthas asked grimly. "What would happen then?"

Kiryn looked out into the green leaves of the never changing forest. "They know, Gilthas," he said quietly. "They know. As I said, they do not like change. It easier to pretend that it is always springtime."

Eventually, Gilthas had to quit worrying about the Silvanesti and start worrying about his own people. The Qualinesti were beginning to splinter into factions. One was led, unfortunately, by his wife. The Lioness sought revenge, no matter what the cost. She and those like her wanted to fight the humans in Silvanost, drive them out, whether the Silvanesti would join them or not. It fell to Gilthas to argue time and again that under no circumstances could the Qualinesti launch an attack against the lord city of their cousins. No good could come of this, he argued. It would lead to more years of bitter division between the two nations. He could see this so clearly that he wondered how others could be so blind.

"You are the one who is blind," said the Lioness angrily. "No wonder. You stare constantly into the darkness of your own mind!"

She left him, moved out of their tent, going to live among her Wilder elf troops. Gilthas grieved at this quarrel—the first since their marriage—but he was king first, not loving husband. Much as he longed to give in, he could not, in good conscience, permit her to have her way.

Another faction of Qualinesti was being seduced by the Silvanesti way of life. Their hearts bruised and aching, they were content to live in the dream-like state in the beautiful forest that reminded them of the forests of their homeland. Senator Palthainon, the leader of this faction, slavishly flattered the Silvanesti, dropping hints into their ears that Gilthas, because he was part human, was not the right ruler of the Qualinesti and could never be. Gilthas was erratic and wayward, as are all humans, and not to be trusted. If it had not been for the staunch and steadfast courage of Senator Palthainon, the Qualinesti would have never made it across the desert alive, and so on and so forth.

Some of the Qualinesti knew this to be untrue, and many argued in favor of their king, but the rest, while they applauded Gilthas's courage, would not have been sorry to see him go. He was the past, the pain, the gaping wound. They wanted to start to heal. As for the Silvanesti, they did not trust Gilthas to begin with, and Palthainon's whispers did not help.

Gilthas felt as though he had walked into a quagmire. Relentlessly, inch by agonizing inch, he was being sucked down into some nameless doom. His struggles caused him to sink further, his cries went unheeded. The end was approaching so slowly that no one else seemed to be aware of it. Only he could see it.

The stalemate continued. The Dark Knights hid in Silvanost, afraid to come out. The elves hid in the forest, unwilling to move.

Gilthas had taken to walking the forests alone these days. He wanted no company for his gloom-ridden thoughts, had even banished Planchet. Hearing a bestial cry from the air, he looked up, and his blood thrilled. A griffin, bearing a rider, circled above the trees, searching for a safe place to land. Change, for good or ill, was coming.

Gilthas hastened through the forest to where Alhana had established her camp, about thirty miles south of the border between Silvanesti and Blöde. The majority of the Silvanesti force was in this location, along with the refugees who had fled or been rescued from the capital city of Silvanost, and the Qualinesti refugees. Other elven forces were located along the Thon-Thalas River, with more lurking in the Bleeding Woods that surrounded Silvanost. Although scattered, the elven forces were in constant contact, using the wind, the creatures of woods and air, and runners to speed messages from one group to another.

Gilthas had wandered far from the campsite, and he was some time retracing his steps. When he arrived, he found Alhana in company with an elf who was a stranger to him. The elf was dressed as a warrior, and by the looks of his weathered face and travel-stained clothing, he had been on the road for many long months. Gilthas could tell by the warmth in Alhana's voice and the agitation in her manner that this elf was someone special to her. Alhana and the strange elf disappeared inside her shelter before Gilthas had a chance to make himself known.

Seeing Gilthas, Kiryn waved him over.

"Samar has returned."

"Samar . . . the warrior who went in search of Silvanoshei?"

Kiryn nodded.

"And what of Silvanoshei?" Gilthas looked in the direction of Alhana's tent.

"Samar came back alone," said Kiryn.

An agonized cry came from Alhana's shelter. The cry was quickly smothered and was not repeated.

Those waiting tensely outside glanced at each other and shook their heads. A sizeable crowd had formed in the small clearing. The elves waited in respectful silence, but they waited, determined to hear the news for themselves.

Alhana came out to speak to them, accompanied by Samar, who stood protectively at her side. Samar reminded Gilthas of Marshal Medan, a resemblance that would not have been appreciated by either one. Samar was an older elf, probably near the same age as Alhana's husband, Porthios. Years of exile and warfare had etched the delicate bone structure of the elven face into granite, sharp and hard. He had learned to bank the fire of his emotions so that he gave away nothing of what he was thinking or feeling. Only when he looked at Alhana did warmth flicker in his dark eyes.

Alhana's face, surrounded by the mass of black hair, was normally pale, the pure white of the lily. Now her skin was completely without color, seemed translucent. She started to speak, but could not. She shuddered, pain wracked her as if it might rend her bone by bone. Samar reached out a supportive arm. Alhana thrust him aside. Her face hardened into firm resolve. Mastering herself, she looked out upon the silent watchers.

"I give my words to the wind and to the rushing water," said Alhana. "Let them carry the words to my people. I give my words to the beasts of the forests and the birds of the air. Let them carry my words to my people. All of you here, go forth and carry my words to my people and to our cousins, the Qualinesti." Her gaze touched on Gilthas but only for an instant.

"You know this man—Samar, my most trusted commander and loyal friend. Many long weeks ago, I sent him on a mission. He has returned from that mission with news of importance." Alhana paused, moistened her lips. "In telling you what Samar has told me, I must make an admission to you. When I claimed that Silvanoshei, your king, was ill inside his tent, I lied. If you want to know why I told this lie, you have only to look about you. I told the lie in order keep our people together, to keep us unified and to keep our cousins united beside us. Because of the lie, we are strong, when we might have been terribly weakened. We will need to be strong for what lies ahead."

Alhana paused, drew in a shivering breath.

"What I tell you now is the truth. Shortly after the battle of Silvanost, Silvanoshei was captured by the Dark Knights. We tried to rescue him, but he was taken away from us in the night. I sent Samar to try to find out what had become of him. Samar has found him. Silvanoshei, our king, is being held prisoner in Sanction."

The elves made soft sounds, as of a breath of wind blowing through the branches of the willow, but said nothing.

"I will let Samar tell you his tale."

Even as Samar spoke to the people, he had a care for Alhana. He stood near her, ready to assist her if her strength failed.

"I met a Knight of Solamnia, a brave and honorable man." Samar's dark eyes swept the crowd. "For those who know me, this is high praise. This Knight saw Silvanoshei in prison and spoke to him, at peril of his own life. The Knight bore Silvanoshei's cloak and this ring."

Alhana held up the ring for all to see. "The ring is my son's. I know it. His father gave it to him when he was a child. Samar also recognized it."

The elves looked from the ring to Alhana, their expressions troubled. Several officers, standing near Kiryn, nudged him and urged him forward.

Kiryn advanced. "May I have permission to speak, gracious Queen?"

"You may, Cousin," said Alhana, regarding him with an air of defiance as if to say, "You may speak, but I do not promise to listen."

"Forgive me, Alhana Starbreeze," Kiryn said respectfully, "for doubting the word of such a great and renowned warrior as Samar, but how do we know we can trust this human Knight? Perhaps it is a trap."

Alhana relaxed. Apparently this wasn't the question she had been anticipating.

"Let Gilthas, ruler of the Qualinesti, son of the House of Solostaran, come forward."

Wondering what this had to do with him, Gilthas walked out of the crowd to make his bow to Alhana. Samar's stern gaze flicked over Gilthas, who had the impression of being weighed in the balance. Whether he came out the winner or the loser in Samar's estimation, the young king had no way of judging.

"Your Majesty," said Samar, "when you were in Qualinesti, did you know a Solamnic by the name of Gerard uth Mondar?"

"Yes, I did," said Gilthas, startled.

"You consider him a man of courage, of honor?"

"I do," said Gilthas. "He is all that and more. Is this the Knight of whom you spoke?"

"Sir Gerard said he heard that the king of the Qualinesti and survivors of that land were going to try to reach safe haven in our land. He expressed deep sorrow for your loss but rejoiced that you are safe. He asked to be remembered to you."

"I know this Knight. I know of his courage, and I can attest to his honor. You are right to trust his word. Gerard uth Mondar came to Qualinesti under strange circumstances, but he left that land a true friend carrying with him the blessing of our beloved Queen Mother Lauranalanthalasa. His was one of the last blessings my mother ever bestowed."

"If both Samar and Gilthas attest to the honor of this Knight, then I have no more to say against him," said Kiryn. Bowing, he returned to his place within the circle.

Over a hundred elves had gathered. They were quiet, said nothing, but exchanged glances. Their silence was eloquent. Alhana could proceed, and she did so.

"Samar has brought other information. We can now give a name to this One God. The One God came to us in the name of peace and love, but that turned out to be part of her despicable plan to ensnare and destroy us. And now we know why. The name of the One God is an ancient one. The One God is Takhisis."

Like a pebble dropped into still water, the ripples of this astounding news spread among the elves.

"I cannot explain to you how this terrible miracle came about," Alhana continued, her voice growing stronger and more majestic with every word. The elves were with her now. She had their full support. All questions about the human Knight were forgotten, overshadowed by the dark wings of an ancient foe. "But we do not need to know. At last, we can put a name to our enemy and it is an enemy that we can defeat, for we have defeated her in the past.

"The Solamnic Knight, Gerard, carries word of this to the Knights' Council," Samar added. "The Solamnics are forming an army to attack Sanction. He urges the elves to be part of this force, to rescue our king. What say you?"

The elves gave a cheer that caused the branches of the trees to shake. Hearing the commotion, more and more elves came running to the site, and they raised their voices. The Lioness arrived, her Wilder elves behind her. Her face was aglow, her eyes alight.

"What is this I hear?" she cried, sliding from her horse and racing to Gilthas. "Is it true? Are we going to war at last?"

He did not answer her, but she was too excited to notice. Turning from him, she sought out those soldiers among the Silvanesti. Before this, they would have never deigned to speak to a Wilder elf, but now they answered her eager questions with joy.

Alhana's officers clustered around her and around Samar, offering suggestions, making plans, discussing what routes that they would take and how fast they could possibly reach Sanction and who would be permitted to go and who would be left behind.

Gilthas alone stood silent, listening to the tumult. When he finally spoke, he heard his own voice, heard the human sound to it, deeper and harsher than the voices of the elves.

"We must attack," he said, "but our target should not be Sanction. Our target is Silvanost. When that city is secure, then we turn our eyes to the north. Not before."

The elves stared at him in shocked disapproval, as if he were a guest at a wedding who had gone berserk and smashed all the gifts. The only elf who paid any heed to him was Samar.

"Let us hear the Qualinesti king," he orderd, raising his voice over the angry rumblings.

"It is true that we have defeated Takhisis in the past," Gilthas told his glowering audience, "but we had the help of Paladine and Mishakal and the other gods of light. Now Takhisis is the One God, alone and supreme. Her defeat will not be easy.

"We will have to march hundreds of miles from our homeland, leaving our own land in the hands of the enemy. We will join a fight with humans to attack and try to win a human city. We will make sacrifices for which we will never be rewarded. I do not say that we should *not* join this battle against Takhisis," Gilthas added. "My mother, as all of you know, fought among humans. She fought to save human cities and human lives. She made sacrifices for which no one ever thanked her. This battle against Takhisis and her forces is a battle that I believe is worth fighting. I counsel only that we make certain we have a homeland to which to return. We have lost Qualinesti. Let us not lose Silvanesti."

Hearing his impassioned words, the Lioness's expression softened. She came to stand at his side.

"My husband is right," she said. "We should attack Silvanost and hold it secure before we send a force to rescue the young king."

The Silvanesti looked at them with hostile eyes. A half-human and a Wilder elf. Outsiders, aliens. Who were they to tell the Silvanesti and even the Qualinesti what to do? Prefect Palthainon stood beside Alhana, whispering in her ear, undoutedly urging her to pay no attention to the "puppet king." Gilthas found one ally among them—Samar.

"The king of our cousins speaks wisely, Your Majesty," said Samar. "I think we should heed his words. If we march to Sanction, we leave behind us an enemy who may well attack and slay us when our backs are turned."

"The Dark Knights are trapped in Silvanost like bees caught in a jar," replied Alhana. "They bumble about, unable to escape. Mina has no intention of sending reinforcements to the Dark Knights in Silvanost. If she was going to, she would have done so by now. I will leave a small force behind to keep up the illusion that a larger force has them surrounded. When we return, triumphant, we will deal with these Dark Knights, my son and I," she added proudly.

"Alhana," Samar began.

She cast him a glance, her violet eyes wine-dark and chill.

Samar said nothing more. Bowing, he took up his stance behind his queen. He did not look at Gilthas, nor did Alhana. The decision had been made, the matter closed.

Silvanesti and Qualinesti gathered eagerly around her, awaiting her commands. The two nations were united at last, united in their determination to march to Sanction. After a moment's worried look at her husband, the Lioness squeezed his hand for comfort, then she, too, hastened over to confer with Alhana Starbreeze.

Why couldn't they see? What blinded them?

Takhisis. This is her doing, Gilthas said to himself. Now free to rule the world unchallenged, she has seized hold of love's sweet elixir, stirred it with poison, and fed it to both the mother and her son. Silvanoshei's love for Mina turns to obsession. Alhana's love for her son muddles her thoughts. And how can we fight this? How can we fight a god when even love—our best weapon against her—is tainted?

15

The Rescue of a King

Elves could be dreamy and lethargic, spend all their daylight hours watching the unfolding of the petals of a rose or sit hushed and rapt beneath the stars for nights on end. But when they are stirred to action, the elves astonish their humans observers with their quickness of thought and of movement, their ability to make swift decisions and carry them through, their resolve and determination to overcome any and all obstacles.

If either Alhana or Samar slept in the next few days, Gilthas had no idea when. Day and night, the stream of people coming and going from her tree shelter never ceased. He himself was one of them, for as ruler of his people, he was included in all important decisions. He said very little, however, although Alhana graciously took pains to invite him to share his opinion. He knew quite well that his opinion was not valued. In addition, he had such small knowledge

371

of the lands through which they must pass that he was not much help anyway.

He was surprised to see how readily the Silvanesti and Qualinesti looked to Alhana, once an outcast, a dark elf, for leadership. His surprise ended when he heard her detail the outlines of her plan. She knew the mountainous lands through which they must march, for she had hidden her forces there for many years. She knew every road, every deer path, every cave. She knew war, and she knew the hardships and terrors of war.

No Silvanesti commander had such extensive knowledge of the lands they would traverse, the forces they might have to fight, and soon the most obdurate of them deferred to Alhana's superior knowledge and swore loyalty to her. Even the Lioness, who would lead her Wilder elves, was impressed.

Alhana's plan for the march was brilliant. The elves would travel north into into Blöde, land of their enemies, the ogres. This might appear to be suicidal, but many years ago, Porthios had discovered that the Khalkist mountain range split in two, hiding with its tall peaks a series of valleys and gorges nestled in the center. By marching in the valleys, the elves could use the mountains to guard their flanks. The route would be long and arduous, but the elven army would travel light and swift. They hoped to be safely through Blöde before the ogres knew they were there.

Unlike human armies, who must cart about blacksmith forges and heavily laden supply wagons, the elves wore no plate or chain armor, carried no heavy swords or shields. The elves relied on the bow and arrow, making good use of the skill for which elven archers are renowned. Thus the elven army could cover far greater distances than their human counterparts. The elves would have to travel swiftly, for within only a few short weeks the winter snows would start to fall in the mountains, sealing off the passes.

Much as he admired Alhana's plan of battle, every fiber in Gilthas's body cried out that it was wrong. As Samar had said, they should not march ahead, leaving the enemy in control behind. Gilthas grew so despondent and frustrated that he knew he must stop going to the meetings. Yet, the Qualinesti needed to be represented. He turned to the man who had been his friend for many years, a man who had, along with his wife, helped to lift Gilthas from the debilitating depression that had once sought to claim him.

"Planchet," said Gilthas, early one morning, "I am dismissing you from my service."

"Your Majesty!" Planchet stared, aghast and dismayed. "Have I done anything or said anything to displease you? If so, I am truly sorry—"

"No, my friend," said Gilthas, smiling a smile that came from the heart, not from diplomacy. He rested his arm on the shoulder of the man who had stood by his side for so long. "Do not protest the use of that word. I say 'friend,' and I mean it. I say adviser and mentor, and I mean that, too. I say father and councilor, and I mean those, as well. All these you have been to me, Planchet. I do not exaggerate when I say that I would not be standing here today if it were not for your strength and your wise guidance."

"Your Majesty," Planchet protested, his voice husky. "I do not deserve such praise. I have been but the gardener. Yours is the tree that has grown strong and tall—"

"—from your careful nurturing."

"And this is the reason I must leave His Majesty?" Planchet asked quietly.

"Yes, because now it is your time to nurture and watch over others. The Qualinesti need a military leader. Our people clamor to march to Sanction. You must be their general. The Lioness leads the Kagonesti. You will lead the Qualinesti. Will you do this for me?"

Planchet hesitated, troubled.

"Planchet," said Gilthas, "Prefect Palthainon is already trying to squirm his way into this position. If I appoint you, he will grumble and gripe, but he will not be able to stop me. He knows nothing of military matters, and you are a veteran with years of experience. You are liked and trusted by the Silvanesti. Please, for the sake of our people, do this for me."

"Yes, Your Majesty," Planchet replied at once. "Of course. I thank you for your faith in me, and I will try to be worthy of it. I know that Your Majesty is not in favor of this course of action, but I believe that it is the right one. Once we defeat Takhisis and drive her from the world, the shadow of dark wings will be lifted, the light will shine on us, and we will remove the enemy from both our lands."

"Do you truly think so, Planchet?" Gilthas asked in somber tones. "I have my doubts. We may defeat Takhisis, but we will not defeat that on which she thrives—the darkness in men's hearts. Thus I think we would be wise to drive out the enemy that holds our homes, secure our homeland and make it strong, then march out into the world."

Planchet said nothing, appeared embarrassed.

"Speak your thoughts, my friend," said Gilthas,

smiling. "You are now my general. You have an obligation to tell me if I am wrong."

"I would say only this, Your Majesty. It is these very isolationist policies that have brought great harm to the elves in the past, causing us to be mistrusted and misunderstood by even those who might have been our allies. If we fight alongside the humans in this battle, it will prove to them that we are part of the larger world. We will gain their respect and perhaps even their friendship."

"In other words," said Gilthas, smiling wryly, "I have always been one to languish in my bed and write poetry—"

"No, Your Majesty," said Planchet, shocked. "I never meant—"

"I know what you meant, dear friend, and I hope you are right. Now, you'll be wanted in the next military conference that is convening shortly. I have told Alhana Starbreeze of my decision to name you general, and she approves of it. Whatever decisions you make, you make them in my name."

"I thank you for your trust, Your Majesty," said Planchet. "But what will you do? Will you march with us or remain behind?"

"I am no warrior, as you well know, dear friend. What small skill I have with the sword I have you to thank for it. Some of our people cannot travel, those with children to care for, the infirm and the elderly. I am considering remaining behind with them."

"Yet, think, Your Majesty, Prefect Palthainon marches with us. Consider that he will attempt to insinuate himself into Alhana's trust. He will demand a part in any negotiations with humans, a race he detests and despises."

"Yes," said Gilthas wearily. "I know. You had best go now, Planchet. The meeting will convene shortly, and Alhana requires that everyone be prompt in their attendance."

"Yes, Your Majesty," said Planchet, and with one final, troubled glance at his young king, he departed.

Within a far shorter time than anyone could have imagined, the elves were prepared to march. They left behind a force as the home guard to watch over those who could not make the long trek north, but the force was small, for the land itself was their best defender—the trees that loved the elves would shelter them, the animals would warn them and carry messages for them, the caverns would hide them.

They left behind another small force to maintain the illusion that an elven army had the city of Silvanost surrounded. So well did this small force play its part that General Dogah, shut up in the walls of a city he'd come to loathe, had no idea that his enemy had marched away. The Dark Knights remained imprisoned inside their victory and cursed Mina, who had left them to this fate.

The kirath remained to guard the borders. Long had they walked within the gray desolation left behind by the shield. Now they rejoiced to see small green shoots thrusting up defiantly through the gray dust and decay. The kirath took this as a hopeful sign for their homeland and their people, who had themselves almost withered and died, first beneath the shield, then beneath the crushing boot of the Dark Knights.

Gilthas had made up his mind to stay behind. Two days before the march, Kiryn sought him out.

Seeing the elf's troubled face, Gilthas sighed inwardly.

"I hear you plan to remain in Silvanesti," Kiryn said. "I think you should change your mind and come with us."

"Why?" asked Gilthas.

"To guard the interests of your people."

Gilthas said nothing, interrogated him with a look. Kiryn flushed. "I was given this information in confidence."

"I do not want you to break a vow," said Gilthas. "I have no use for spies."

"I took no vow. I think Samar wanted me to tell you," said Kiryn. "You know that we march through the Khalkist Mountains, but do you know how we plan to make our way into Sanction?"

"I know so little of the territory—" Gilthas began.

"We will ally ourselves with the dark dwarves. March our army through their underground tunnels. They are to be well-paid."

"With what?" Gilthas asked.

Kiryn stared down at the leaf-strewn forest floor. "With the money you have brought with you from Qualinesti."

"That wealth is not mine," Gilthas said sharply. "It is the wealth of the Qualinesti people. All that we have left."

"Prefect Palthainon offered it to Alhana, and she accepted."

"If I protest, there will be trouble. My attendance on this ill-fated venture will not change that."

"No, but now Palthainon, as highest-ranking official, has charge of the wealth. If you come, you take your people's trust into your keeping. You may be forced to use it. There may not be another way. But the decision would be yours to make."

"So now it comes to this," Gilthas muttered when Kiryn had gone. "We pay off the darkness to save us. How far do we sink into darkness before we become the darkness?"

On the day the march began, the Silvanesti left their beloved woods with dry eyes that looked to the north. They marched in silence, with no songs, no blaring horns, no crashing cymbals, for the Dark Knights must never know that they were leaving, the ogres must not be warned of their coming. The elves marched in the shadows of the trees to avoid the eyes of watchful blue dragons, circling above.

When they crossed the border of Silvanesti, Gilthas paused to look behind him at the rippling leaves that flashed silver in the sunlight, a brilliant contrast to the gray line of decay that was the forest's boundary, the shield's legacy. He gazed long, with the oppressive feeling in his heart that once he crossed, he could never go back.

A week after the Silvanesti army had departed, Rolan of the kirath walked his regular patrol along the border. He kept his gaze fixed on the ground, noting with joy in his heart a small sign that nature was fighting a battle against the evil caused by the shield.

Although the shield's deadly magic was gone, the destruction wrought by its evil magic remained. Whatever plant or tree the shield had touched had died, so the borders of Silvanesti were marked by a gray, grim line of death.

Yet now, beneath the gray shroud of desiccated leaves and withered sticks, Rolan found tiny stalks of green emerging triumphantly from the soil. He could not tell yet what they were: blades of grass or delicate wildflowers or perhaps the first brave shoot of what would become a towering oak or a flame-colored maple. Maybe, he thought with a smile, this was some common, humble plant he tended—dandelion or catnip or spiderwort. Rolan loved this, whatever it might turn out to be. The green of life sprouting amidst death was an omen of hope for him and for his people.

Carefully, gently he replaced the shroud, which he now thought of as a blanket, to protect the frail young shoots from the harsh sunlight. He was about to move on when he caught whiff of a strange scent.

Rolan rose to his feet, alarmed. He sniffed the air, trying hard to place the peculiar odor. He had never smelled anything like it: acrid, animal. He heard distant sounds that he recognized as the crackling of breaking tree limbs, the trampling of vegetation. The sounds grew louder and more distinct, and above them came sounds more ominous: the warning cry of the hawk, the scream of the timid rabbit, the panicked bleat of fleeing deer.

The foul animal scent grew strong, overwhelming, sickening. The smell of meat-eaters. Drawing his sword, Rolan put his fingers to his lips to give the shrill, penetrating whistle that would alert his fellow kirath to danger.

Three enormous minotaurs emerged from the forest. Their horns tore the leaves, their axes left gashes in the tree limbs as they impatiently hacked at the underbrush that blocked their way. The minotaurs halted when they saw Rolan, stood staring him, their bestial eyes dark, without expression.

He lifted his sword, made ready to attack.

A bovine smell engulfed him. Strong arms grabbed him. He felt the prick of the knife just below his ear; swift, bitter pain as the knife slashed across his throat . . .

The minotaur who slew the elf dumped the body onto the ground, wiped the blood from his dagger. The minotaur's companions nodded. Another job well done. They proceeded through the forest, clearing a path for those who came behind.

For the hundreds who came behind. For the thousands.

Minotaur forces tramped across the border. Minotaur ships with their painted sails and galleys manned by slaves sailed the waters of the Thon-Thalas, traveling south to the capital of Silvanost, bringing General Dogah the reinforcements he had been promised.

Many kirath died that day, died as did Rolan. Some had the chance to fight their attackers, most did not. Most were taken completely by surprise.

The body of Rolan of the kirath lay in the forest he had loved. His blood seeped below the gray mantle of death, drowned the tiny green shoots.

16

Odila's Prayer, Mina's Gift

n the night, the eyes of the dead dragons within the skulls that made up the totem gleamed bright. The phantom of the five-headed dragon floated above the totem, causing those who saw it to marvel. In the night, in the darkness that she ruled, Queen Takhisis was powerful and reigned supreme. But, with the light of the sun, her image faded away. The eyes of the dead dragons flickered and went out, as did the candles on the altar, so that only wisps of smoke, blackened wicks, and melted wax remained.

The totem that appeared so magnificent and invulnerable in the darkness was by daylight a pile of skulls—a loathsome sight, for bits of scales or rotted flesh still clung to the bones. By day, the totem was a stark reminder to all who saw it of the immense power of Malys, the dragon overlord who had built it.

The question on everyone's lips was not *if* Malys would attack, but when. Fear of her coming spread through the city. Fearing massive desertions, Galdar ordered the West Gate closed. Although publicly Mina's Knights maintained a show of nonchalance, they were afraid.

When Mina walked the streets every day, she lifted fear from the hearts of all who saw her. When she spoke every night of the power of the One God, the people listened and cheered, certain that the One God would save them from the dragon. But when Mina departed, when the sound of her voice could no longer be heard, the shadow of red wings spread a chill over Sanction. People looked to the skies with dread.

Mina was not afraid. Galdar marveled at her courage, even as it worried him. Her courage stemmed from her faith in Takhisis, and he knew the goddess was not worthy of such faith. His one hope was that Takhisis needed Mina and would thus be loath to sacrifice her. One moment he had convinced himself she would be safe, the next he was convinced that Takhisis might use this means to rid herself of a rival who had outlasted her usefulness.

Compounding Galdar's fears was the fact that Mina refused to tell him her strategy for defeating Malys. He tried to talk to her about it. He reminded her of Qualinost. The dragon had been destroyed, but so had a city.

Mina rested her hand reassuringly on the minotaur's arm. "What happened to Qualinost will not happen to Sanction, Galdar. The One God hated the elves and their nation. She wanted to see them destroyed. The One God is pleased with Sanction. Here she plans to enter the world, to inhabit both the physical plane and the spiritual. Sanction and its people will be safe, the One God will see to that."

"But then what is your strategy, Mina?" Galdar persisted. "What is your plan?"

"To have faith in the One God, Galdar," said Mina, and with that, he had to be content, for she would say no more.

Odila was also worried about the future, worried and confused and distraught. Ever since the souls had built the totem and she had recognized the One God as Queen Takhisis, Odila had felt very much like one of the living dead mages. Her body ate and drank and walked and performed its duties, but she was absent from that body. She seemed to stand apart, staring at it uncaring, while mentally she groped in the storm-ridden darkness of her soul for answers, for understanding.

She could not bring herself to pray to the One God. Not any longer. Not since she knew who and what the One God was. Yet, she missed her prayers. She missed the sweet solace of giving her life into the hands of Another, some Wise Being who would guide Odila's steps and lead her away from pain to blissful peace. The One God had guided Odila's steps but not to peace. The One God had led her to turmoil and fear and dismay.

More than once Odila clasped the medallion at her throat and was prepared to rip it off. Every time her fingers closed around the medallion, she felt the metal's warmth. She remembered the power of the One God that had flowed through her veins, the power to halt those who had wanted to slay the elven king. Her hand fell away, fell limp at her side. One morning, watching the sun's red rays give a sullen glow to the clouds that hung perpetually over the Lords of Doom, Odila decided to put her faith to the test.

Odila knelt before the altar that was near the totem of dragon skulls. The room smelled of death and decay and warm, melting wax. The heat of the candles was a contrast to the cold draught that blew in from the gaping hole in the roof, whistled eerily through the teeth of the skulls. Sweat from the heat chilled on Odila's body. She wanted very much to flee this terrible place, but the medallion was warm against her cold skin.

"Queen Takhisis, help me," she prayed, and she could not repress a shudder at speaking that name. "I have been taught all my life that you are a cruel god who has no care for any living being, who sees us all as slaves meant to obey your commands. I have been taught that you are ambitious and self-serving, that you mock and denigrate those principles that I hold dear: honor, compassion, mercy, love. Because of what you are, I should not believe in you, I should not serve you. And yet . . ."

Odila lifted her eyes, gazed up into the heavens. "You are a god. I have witnessed your power. I have felt it thrill inside me. How can I choose *not* to believe in you? Perhaps . . ." Odila hesitated, uncertain. "Perhaps you have been maligned. Misjudged. Perhaps you *do* care for us. I ask this not for myself, but for someone who has served you faithfully and loyally. Mina faces terrible danger. I am certain that she intends to try to fight Malys alone. She has faith that you will fight at her side. She has put her trust in you. I fear for her, Queen Takhisis. Show me that my fears are unfounded and that you care for her, if you care for no one else."

She waited tensely, but no voice spoke. No vision came. The candle flames wavered in the chill wind that flowed through the altar room. The bodies of the mages sat upon their benches, staring unblinking into the flames. Yet, Odila's heart lightened, her burden of doubt eased. She did not know why and was pondering this when she became aware of someone standing near the altar.

Her eyes dazzled by the bright light of hundreds of candles, she couldn't see who was there.

"Galdar?" she said, at last making out the minotaur's hulking form. "I didn't hear you or see you enter. I was preoccupied with my prayers."

She wondered uneasily if he had overheard her, if he was going to berate her for her lack of faith.

He said nothing, just stood there.

"Is there something you want from me, Galdar?" Odila asked. He'd never wanted anything of her before, had always seemed to distrust and resent her.

"I want you to see this," he said.

In his hands, he carried an object bound in strips of linen, tied up with rope. The linen had once been white, but was now so stained by water and mud, grass and dirt that the color was a dull and dingy brown. The ropes had been cut, the cloth removed, but both appeared to have been clumsily replaced.

Galdar placed the object on the altar. It was long and did not seem particularly heavy. The cloth concealed whatever was inside.

"This came for Mina," he continued. "Captain Samuval sent it. Unwrap it. Look inside."

Odila did not touch it. "If it is a gift for Mina, it is not for me to—"

"Open it!" ordered Galdar, his voice harsh. "I want to know if it is suitable."

Odila might have continued to refuse, but she was certain now that Galdar had heard her prayer, and she feared that unless she agreed to this, he might tell Mina. Gingerly, her fingers trembling from her nervousness, Odila tugged at the knots, removed the strips of cloth. She was unpleasantly reminded of the winding cloths used to bind the bodies of the dead.

Her wonder grew as she saw what lay beneath, her wonder and her awe.

"Is it what Samuval claims it to be?" Galdar demanded. "Is it a dragonlance?"

Odila nodded wordlessly, unable to speak.

"Are you certain? Have you ever seen one before?" Galdar asked.

"No, I haven't," she admitted, finding her voice. "But I have heard stories of the fabled lances from the time I was a little girl. I always loved those stories. They led me to become a Knight."

Odila reached out her hand, ran her fingers along the cold, smooth metal. The lance gleamed with a silver radiance that seemed apart and separate from the yellow flames of the candles.

If all the lights in the universe were snuffed out, Odila thought, even the light of sun and moon and stars, the light of this lance would still shine bright.

"Where did Captain Samuval find such a treasure?" she asked.

"In some old tomb somewhere," said Galdar. "Solace, I think."

"Not the Tomb of the Heroes?" Odila gasped.

Snatching her hand back from the lance, she stared at Galdar in horror.

"I don't know," said Galdar, shrugging. "He didn't say what the tomb was called. He said the tomb brought him bad luck, for when the locals caught him and his men inside, they attacked in such numbers that he barely escaped with his life. He was even set upon by a mob of kender. This was one of the treasures he managed to bring along with him. He sent it to Mina with his regards and respect."

Odila sighed and looked back at the lance.

"He stole it from the dead," said Galdar, frowning. "He said himself it was bad luck. I do not think we should give it to Mina."

Before Odila could answer, another voice spoke from out of the darkness.

"Do the dead have need of this lance anymore, Galdar?"

"No, Mina," he said, turning to face her. "They do not."

The light of the lance shone bright in Mina's amber eyes. She took hold of it, her hand closing over it. Odila flinched when she saw Mina touch it, for there were some who claimed that the fabled dragonlances could be used only by those who fought on the side of light and that any others who touched them would be punished by the gods.

Mina's hand grasped the lance firmly. She lifted the lance from the altar, hefted it, regarded it with admiration.

"A lovely weapon," she said. "It seems almost to have been made for me." Her gaze turned to Odila. The amber eyes were warm as the medallion around Odila's throat. "An answer to a prayer."

Placing the lance upon the altar, Mina reverently knelt before it.

"We will thank the One God for this great blessing."

Galdar remained standing, looking stern. Odila sank down before the altar. Tears flowed down Odila's cheeks. She was grateful for Mina's sake that her prayer had been answered. Her tears were not for something found, however, but for something lost. Mina had been able to grip the lance, to lift it from the altar, to hold it in her hand.

Odila looked down at her own hands through her tears. The tips of the fingers that had touched the dragonlance were blistered and burned, and they hurt so that she wondered if she would ever again be free of the pain.

17

The Volunteer

Night had come again to Sanction. Night was always a relief to the inhabitants, for it meant that they'd survived another day. Night brought Mina out to speak them of the One God, speeches in which she lent them some of her courage, for when in her presence they were emboldened and ready for battle against the dragon overlord.

Having lived for centuries within the shadows of the Lords of Doom, the city of Sanction was essentially fireproof. Buildings were made of stone, including the roofs, for any other material, such as thatch, would have long ago burned away. True, it was said that the breath of dragons had the power to melt granite, but there was no defense against that, except to hope desperately that whoever spread the rumor was exaggerating.

Every soldier was being hastily trained in archery, for with a target this large, even the rankest amateur could hardly miss. They hauled catapults up onto the wall, hoping to fling boulders at Malys, and they trained their ballistae to shoot into the sky. These tasks accomplished, they felt they were ready, and some of the boldest called upon Malys to come and have done with it. Still, all were relieved when night fell and they'd lived through another day, never mind that dread came again with morning.

The blue dragon Razor, still forced to rove about Sanction in human guise, watched the preparations with the keen interest of a veteran soldier and told Mirror about them in detail, adding his own disapproval or approval, whichever seemed warranted. Mirror was more interested in the totem, in what it looked like, where it was positioned in the city. Razor had been supposed to reconnoiter, but he'd been wasting time among the soldiers.

"I know what you're thinking," Razor said suddenly, stopping himself in the midst of describing the precise workings of a catapult. "You're thinking that none of this will make any difference. None will have any effect on that great, red bitch. Well, you're right. And," he added, "you're wrong."

"How am I wrong?" Mirror asked. "Cities have used catapults before to defend against Malys. They've used archers and arrows, heroes and fools, and none have survived."

"But they have never had a god on their side," stated Razor.

Mirror tensed. A silver dragon, loyal to Paladine, he had long feared that Razor would revert to his old loyalties, to Queen Takhisis. Mirror had to proceed carefully. "So you are saying we should abandon our plan to help Palin destroy the totem?"

"Not necessarily," said Razor evasively. "Perhaps, reconsider, that is all. Where are you going?"

"To the temple," said Mirror. Shrugging off Razor's guiding hand, the blind silver dragon in human guise started off on his own, tapping his way with his staff. "To view the totem for myself, since you will not be my eyes."

"This is madness!" Razor protested, following after him with his fake limp. Mirror could hear the pounding of the crutch on the bricks. "You said before that Mina saw you in your beggar form on the road and immediately recognized you as the guardian of the Citadel of Light. She knows you by sight, both as a human and in your true form."

Mirror began to rearrange the bandages he wore wrapped about his damaged eyes, tugging them down so that they covered his face.

"It is a risk I must take. Especially if you are wavering in your decision."

Razor said nothing. Mirror could no longer hear the crutch thumping along beside him and assumed that he was going alone. He had only the vaguest idea where the temple was located. He knew only that it was on a hill overlooking the city.

So, he calculated, if I walk uphill, I am bound to find it.

He was startled to hear Razor's rasping breath in his ear. "Wait, stop. You've blundered into a cul-de-sac. I'll guide you, if you insist on going."

"Will you help me destroy the totem?" Mirror demanded.

"That I must think about," said Razor. "If we are going, we should go now, for the temple is most likely to be empty."

The two wended their way through the mazelike streets. Mirror was thankful for Razor's guidance, for the blind silver could have never found his way on his own.

What will Palin and I do if Razor decides to shift his allegiance? Mirror wondered. A blind dragon and a dead wizard out to defeat a goddess. Well, if nothing else, maybe Takhisis will get a bellyache from laughing.

The noise made by the crowds told Mirror they were close to the temple. And there was Mina, telling them of the wonders and magnificence of the One God. She was persuasive, Mirror had to admit. He had always liked Mina's voice. Even as a child, her tone had been mellow and low and sweet to hear.

As he listened, he was taken back to those days in the Citadel, watching Mina and Goldmoon together—the elderly woman in the sunset of her life, the child bright with the dawn. Now Mirror could not see Mina for the darkness, and not the darkness of his own blind eyes.

Razor led him past the crowd. The two proceeded quietly, not to draw attention to themselves, and entered the ruined temple that now stood as a monument to the dragon skull totem.

"Are we alone?" Mirror asked.

"The bodies of the two wizards sit in a corner."

"Tell me about them," said Mirror, his heart aching. "What are they like?"

"Like corpses propped up at their own funerals," said Razor dourly. "That is all I will say. Be thankful you cannot see them."

"What of their spirits?"

"I see no signs of them. All to the good. I have no use for wizards, living or dead. We don't need their meddling. Here, now. You stand before the totem. You can reach out and touch the skulls, if you want."

Mirror had no intention of touching anything. He had no need to be told he stood before the totem. Its magic was powerful, potent—the magic of a god. Mirror was both drawn to it and repelled by it.

"What does the totem look like?" he asked softly.

"The skulls of our brethren, stacked one on top of the other in a grotesque pyramid," Razor answered. "The skulls of the larger support the smaller. The eyes of the dead burn in the sockets. Somewhere in that pile is the skull of my mate. I can feel the fire of her life blaze in the darkness."

"And I feel the god's power residing within the totem," said Mirror. "Palin was right. This is the doorway. This is the Portal through which Takhisis will walk into the world at last."

"I say, let her," said Razor. "Now that I see this, I say let Takhisis come, if her help is needed to slay Malystryx."

Mirror could smell the flickering candles, if he could not see them. He could feel their heat. He could feel, as Razor felt, the heat of his own anger and his longing for revenge. Mirror had his own reasons for hating Malys. She had destroyed Kendermore, killed Goldmoon's dearly loved husband Riverwind and their daughter. Malys had murdered hundreds of people and displaced thousands more, driving them from their homes, terrorizing them as they fled for her own cruel amusement. Standing before the totem that Malys had built of the bones of those she had devoured, Mirror began to wonder if Razor might not be right.

Razor leaned near, whispered in his ear. "Takhisis has her faults, I admit that freely. But she is a god, and she is our god, of our world, and she's all we've got. You have to concede that."

Mirror conceded nothing.

"You can't see them," Razor continued relentlessly, "but there are the skulls of silver dragons in that totem. A good many of them. Don't you want to avenge their deaths?"

"I don't need to see them," said Mirror. "I hear their voices. I hear their death cries, every one of them. I hear the cries of their mates who loved them and the cries of the children who will never be born to them. My hatred for Malys is as strong as yours. To rid the world of this terrible scourge, you say I must choke down the bitter medicine of Takhisis's triumph."

Razor shrugged. "She is our god," he repeated. "Of our world."

A terrible choice. Mirror sat on the hard bench, trying to decide what to do. Lost in his thoughts, he forgot where he was, forgot he was in the camp of his enemies. Razor's elbow dug into his side.

"We have company," the blue warned softly.

"Who is it? Mina?" Mirror asked.

"No, the minotaur who is never far from her side. I told you this was a bad idea. No, don't move. It's too late now. We're in the shadows. Perhaps they won't take notice of us. Besides," the Blue added coolly, "we might learn something."

Indeed, Galdar did not notice the two beggars as he entered the altar room. At least, not immediately. He was preoccupied with his own worries. Galdar knew Mina's plan, or he thought he did. He hoped he was wrong, but his hope wasn't very strong, probably because he knew Mina so well.

Knew Mina and loved her.

All his life, Galdar had heard legends of a famous minotaur hero known as Kaz, who had been a friend of the famous Solamnic hero, Huma. Kaz had ridden with Huma in his battle against Queen Takhisis. The minotaur had risked his life for Huma many times, and Kaz's grief at Huma's death had been lifelong. Although Kaz had been on the wrong side of the war, as far as the minotaur were concerned, he was honored among his people to this day for his courage and valor in warfare. A minotaur admires a valiant warrior no matter which side he fights on.

As for his friendship with a human, few minotaurs could understand that. True, Huma had been a valiant warrior—for a human. Always that qualification was added. In minotaur legends, Kaz was the hero, saving Huma's life time and again, at the end of which, Huma is always humbly grateful to the gallant minotaur, who accepts the human's thanks with patronizing dignity.

Galdar had always believed these legends, but now he was starting to think differently. Perhaps, in truth, Kaz had fought with Huma because he loved Huma, just as Galdar loved Mina. There was something about these humans. They wormed their way into your heart.

Their puny bodies were so frail and fragile, and yet they could be tough and enduring as the last hero standing in the bloodstained arena of the minotaur circus.

They never knew when they were defeated, these humans, but fought on when they should have laid down and died. They led such pitifully short lives, but they were always ready to throw away these lives for a cause or a belief, or doing something as foolish and noble as rushing into a burning tower to save the life of a total stranger.

Minotaurs have their share of courage, but they are more cautious, always counting the cost before spending their coin. Galdar knew what Mina planned, and he loved her for it, even as his heart ached to think of it. Kneeling beside the altar, he vowed that she would not go into battle alone if there was any way he could stop her. He did not pray to the One God. Galdar no longer prayed to the One God, ever since he'd found out who she was. He never said a word to Mina about this—he would take his secret to the grave with him—but he would not pray to Queen Takhisis, a goddess whom he considered treacherous and completely without honor. The vow he made, he made within himself.

His prayer concluded, he rose stiffly from the altar. Outside, he could hear Mina telling the admiring crowds that they had no need to fear Malys. The One God would surely save them. Galdar had heard it all before. He no longer heard it now. He heard Mina's voice, her loved voice, but that was all. He guessed that was all most of those listening heard.

Galdar fidgeted near the altar, waiting for Mina, and it was then he saw the beggars. The altar room was crowded during the day, for the inhabitants of Sanction, mostly soldiers, came to make offerings to the One God or to gape at the totem or to try to catch a glimpse of Mina and touch her or beg her blessing. At night, they went to hear her, to hide themselves beneath the blanket of her courage. After that, they went to their posts or to their beds. Few worshipers came to the altar room at night, one reason Galdar was here.

This night, a blind man and a lame beggar sat on a bench near the altar. Galdar had no use for mendicants. No minotaur does. A minotaur would starve to death before he would dream of begging for even a crust. Galdar could not imagine what these two were doing in Sanction and wondered why they hadn't fled, as had many of their kind.

He eyed them more closely. There was something about them that made them different from other beggars. He couldn't quite think what it was—a quiet confidence, capability. He had the feeling that these were no ordinary beggars and he was about to ask them a few questions when Mina returned.

She was exalted, god-touched. Her amber eyes shone. Approaching the altar, she sank down, almost too tired to stand, for during these public meetings, she poured forth her whole soul, giving everything to those who listened, leaving nothing for herself. Galdar forgot the strange beggars, went immediately to Mina.

"Let me bring you some wine, something to eat," he offered.

"No, Galdar, I need nothing, thank you," Mina replied. She sighed deeply. She looked exhausted.

Clasping her hands, she said a prayer to the One God, giving thanks. Then, appearing refreshed and renewed, she rose to her feet. "I am only a little tired, that is all. There was a great crowd tonight. The One God is gaining many followers."

They follow you, Mina, not the One God, Galdar might have said to her, but he kept silent. He had said such things to her in the past, and she had been extremely angry. He did not want to risk her ire, not now.

"You have something to say to me, Galdar?" Mina asked. She reached out to remove a candle whose wick had been drowned in molten wax.

Galdar arranged his thoughts. He had to say this carefully, for he did not want to offend her.

"Speak what is in your heart," she urged. "You have been troubled for a long time. Ease your burden by allowing me to share it."

"You are my burden, Mina," said Galdar, deciding to do as she said and open his heart. "I know how you plan to fight Malys on dragonback. You have the dragonlance, and I assume that the One God will provide you with a dragon. You plan to go up alone to face her. I cannot allow you to do that, Mina. I know what you are about to say." He raised his hand, to forestall her protest. "You will not be alone. You will have the One God to fight at your side. But let there be another at your side, Mina. Let me be at your side."

"I have been practicing with the lance," Mina said. Opening her hand, she exhibited her palm, that was red and blistered. "I can hit the bull's-eye nine times out of ten."

"Hitting a target that stands still is much different from hitting a moving dragon," Galdar growled. "Two dragonriders are most effective in fighting aerial battles, one to the keep the dragon occupied from the front while the other attacks from the rear. You must see the wisdom in this?"

"I do, Galdar," said Mina. "True, I have been studying the combat in my mind, and I know that two riders would be good." She smiled, an impish smile that reminded him of how young she was. "A thousand riders would be even better, Galdar, don't you think?"

He said nothing, scowled at the flames. He knew where she was leading him, and he could not stop her from going there.

"A thousand would be better, but where would we find these thousand? Men or dragons?" Mina gestured to the totem. "Do you remember all the dragons who celebrated when the One God consecrated this totem? Do you remember them circling the totem and singing anthems to the One God? Do you remember, Galdar?"

"I remember."

"Where are they now? Where are the Reds and the Greens, the Blues and the Blacks? Gone. Fled. Hiding. They fear I will ask them to fly against Malys. And I can't blame them."

"Bah! They are all cowards," said Galdar.

He heard a sound behind him and glanced around. He'd forgotten the beggars. He eyed them closely, but if either of them had spoken neither seemed inclined to do so now. The lame beggar stared down at the floor. As for the blind beggar, his face was so swathed in bandages that it was difficult to tell if he had a mouth, much less whether he had used it. The only other two beings in the room were the wizards, and Galdar had no need to look at them. They never moved unless someone prodded them.

"I'll make you a bargain, Galdar," Mina said. "If you can find a dragon who will voluntarily carry you into battle, you can fly at my side."

Galdar grunted. "You know that is impossible, Mina."

"Nothing is impossible for the One God, Galdar," Mina told him, gently rebuking. She knelt down again before the altar, clasped her hands. Glancing up at Galdar, she added, "Join me in my prayers."

"I have already made my prayer, Mina," said Galdar heavily. "I have duties to attend to. Try to get some rest, will you?"

"I will," she said. "Tomorrow will be a momentous day."

Galdar looked at her, startled. "Will Malys come tomorrow, Mina?"

"She will come tomorrow."

Galdar sighed and walked out into the night. The night may bring comfort to others but not to him. The night brought only morning.

Mirror felt Razor's human body shift restlessly on the bench beside him. Mirror sat with his head lowered, taking care that Mina did not see him, although he suspected he could have leaped up and done a dance with bells and tambour and she would have been oblivious to him. She was with her One God. For now, she had no care or concern for what transpired on this mortal plane. Still, Mirror kept his head down.

He was troubled and at the same time relieved. Perhaps this was the answer.

"You would like to be the dragon that Galdar seeks, is that right?" Mirror asked in a quiet undertone.

"I would," Razor said.

"You know the risk you take," said Mirror. "Malys's weapons are formidable. Fear of her alone drove a nation of kender mad, so it is claimed by the wise. Her flaming breath is said to be hotter than the fires of the Lords of the Doom."

"I know all this," Razor returned, "and more. The minotaur will find no other dragon. Craven cowards, all of them. No discipline. No training. Not like the old days."

Mirror smiled, thankful that his smile was hidden beneath the bandages.

"Go, then," he said. "Go after the minotaur and tell him that you will fight by his side."

Razor was silent. Mirror could feel his astonishment.

"I cannot leave you," Razor said, after a pause. "What would you do without me?"

"I will manage. Your impulse is brave, noble, and generous. Such weapons are our strongest weapons against her." By *her*, Mirror did not mean Malys, but he saw no reason to clarify his pronoun.

"Are you certain?" Razor asked, clearly tempted. "You will have no one to guard you, protect you."

"I am not a hatchling," Mirror retorted. "I may not be able to see, but lack of sight does not hamper my magic. You have done your part and more. I am glad to have known you, Razor, and I honor you for your decision. You had best go after the minotaur. You two will need to make plans, and you will not have much time to make them."

Razor rose to his feet. Mirror could hear him, feel him moving at his side. The Blue's hand rested on Mirror's shoulder, perhaps for the last time.

"I have always hated your kind, Silver. I am sorry for that, for I have discovered that we have more in common than I realized."

"We are dragons," said Mirror simply. "Dragons of Krynn."

"Yes," said Razor. "If only we had remembered that sooner."

The hand lifted. Its warm pressure gone, Mirror felt the lack. He heard footsteps walking swiftly away, and he smiled and shook his head. Reaching out his hand, groping about, he found Razor's crutch, tossed aside.

"Another miracle for the One God," said Mirror wryly. Taking the crutch, he secreted it beneath the bench.

As he did so, Mina's voice rose.

"Be with me, my god," she prayed fervently, "and lead me and all who fight with me to glorious victory against this evil foe."

"How can I refuse to echo that prayer?" Mirror asked himself silently. "We are dragons of Krynn, and though we fought against her, Takhisis was our goddess. How can I do what Palin asks of me? Especially now that I am alone."

Galdar made the rounds, checking on the city's defenses and the state of Sanction's defenders. He found all as he expected. The defenses were as good as they were going to get, and the defenders were nervous and gloomy. Galdar said what he could to raise their spirits, but he wasn't Mina. He couldn't lift their hearts, especially when his own was crawling in the dust.

Brave words he'd spoken to Mina about fighting at her side against Malys. Brave words, when he knew perfectly well that when Malys came he'd be among those watching helplessly from the ground. Tilting his head, he scanned the skies. The night air was clear, except for the perpetual cloud that roiled out of the Lords of Doom.

"How I would love to astonish her," he said to the stars. "How I long to be there with her."

But he was asking the impossible. Asking a miracle of a goddess he didn't like, didn't trust, couldn't pray to.

So preoccupied was Galdar that it took him some time—longer than it should have—for him to realize he was being followed. This was such a strange occurrence that he was momentarily taken aback. Who could be following him and why? He would have suspected Gerard, but the Solamnic Knight had left Sanction long ago, was probably even now urging the Knights to rise up against them. Everyone else in Sanction, including the Solamnic female, was loyal to Mina. He wondered, suddenly, if Mina was having him followed, if she no longer trusted him. The thought made him sick to his stomach. He determined to know the truth.

Muttering aloud something about needing fresh air, Galdar headed for the temple gardens that would be dark and quiet and secluded this time of night.

Whoever was following him either wasn't very good at it or wanted Galdar to notice him. The footfalls were not stealthy, not padded, as would be those of a thief or assassin. They had a martial ring to them— bold, measured, firm.

Reaching a wooded area, Galdar stepped swiftly to one side, concealed himself behind the bole of a large tree. The footsteps came to a halt. Galdar was certain that the person must have lost him, was astonished beyond measure to see the man walk right up to him.

The man raised his hand, saluted.

Galdar started instinctively to return the salute. He halted, glowering, and rested his hand on his sword's hilt.

"What do you want? Why do you sneak after me like a thief?" Peering more closely at the person, Galdar recognized him and was disgusted. "You filthy beggar! Get away from me, scum. I have no money—"

The minotaur paused. His gaze narrowed. His hand tightened its grasp on the hilt, half-drew the sword from its sheath. "Weren't you lame before? Where is your crutch?"

"I left it behind," said the beggar, "because I no longer need it. I want nothing of you, sir," he added, his tone respectful. "I have something to give you."

"Whatever it is, I don't want it. I have no use for your kind. Begone and trouble me no more or I'll have you thrown in prison." Galdar reached out his hand, intending to shove the man aside.

The night shadows began to shimmer and distort. Tree branches cracked. Leaves and twigs and small limbs rained down around him. Galdar's hand touched a surface hard and solid as armor, but this armor wasn't cold steel. It was warm, living.

Gasping, Galdar staggered backward, lifted his astounded gaze. His eyes met the eyes of a blue dragon.

Galdar stammered something, he wasn't sure what.

The blue dragon drew in a huge breath and expelled it in satisfaction and immense relief. Fanning his wings, he luxuriated in a stretch and sighed again. "How I hate that cramped human form."

"Where . . . ? What . . . ?" Galdar continued to stammer.

"Irrelevant," said the dragon. "My name is Razor. I happened to overhear your conversation with your commander in the temple. She said that if you could find a dragon that would carry you into battle against Malys, you could fight at her side. If you truly meant what you said, warrior; if you have the courage of your convictions, then I will be your mount."

"I meant what I said," Galdar growled, still trying to recover from the shock. "But why would you do this? All your brethren have fled, and they are the sensible ones."

"I am"—the dragon paused, corrected himself with grave dignity—"I *was* the dragon attached to Marshal Medan. Did you know him?"

"I did," said Galdar. "I met him when he came to visit Lord Targonne in Jelek. I was impressed. He was a man of sense, a man of courage and of honor. A valiant Knight of the old school."

"Then you know why I do this," said Razor, with a proud toss of his head. "I fight in his name, in his memory. Let's be clear about that from the outset."

"I accept your offer, Razor," said Galdar, joy filling his soul. "I fight for the glory of my commander. You fight for the memory of yours. We will make this battle one of which they will sing for centuries!"

"I was never much for singing," said Razor dourly. "Neither was the Marshal. So long as we kill that red monstrosity, that is all I care about. When do you think she will attack us?"

"Mina says tomorrow," said Galdar.

"Then tomorrow I will be ready," said Razor.

18

Day's Dawning

A tremor shook the city of Sanction in the early hours before the dawn. The rippling ground dumped sleepers from their beds, sent the crockery spilling to floor, and set all the dogs in the city to barking. The quake jarred nerves that were already taut.

Almost before the ground had ceased to tremble, crowds began to gather outside the temple. Although no official word had been given or orders gone out, rumors had spread, and by now every soldier and Knight in Sanction knew that this was the day Malys would attack. Those not on duty (and even some who were) left their billets and their posts and flocked to the temple. They came out of a hunger to see Mina and hear her voice, hear her reassurance that all would be well, that victory would be theirs this day.

As the sun lifted over the mountains, Mina emerged from the temple. Customarily at her appearance a resounding cheer went up from the crowd. Not this day. Everyone stared, hushed and awed.

Mina was clad in glistening armor black as the frozen seas. The helm she wore was horned, the visor black, rimed with gold. On the breastplate was etched the image of a five-headed dragon. As the first rays of the sun struck the armor, the dragon began to shimmer eerily, shifting colors, so that some who saw it thought it was red, while others thought it was blue, and still others swore it was green.

Some in the audience whispered in excited voices that this was armor once worn by the Dragon Highlords, who had fought for Takhisis during the fabled War of the Lance.

In her gloved hand, Mina held a weapon whose metal burned like flame as it caught the rays of the rising sun. She lifted the weapon high above her head in a gesture of triumph.

At this, the crowd raised a cheer. They cheered long and loud, crying, "Mina, Mina!" The cheers rebounded off the mountains and thundered over the plains, shaking the ground like another tremor.

Mina knelt upon one knee, the lance in her hand. The cheering ceased as people joined her in prayer, some calling upon the One God, many more calling upon Mina.

Rising to her feet, Mina turned to face the totem. She handed the lance to a priestess of the One God, who stood beside her. The priestess was clad in white robes, and whispers went about that she was a former Solamnic Knight who had prayed to the One God and been given the dragonlance, which she had in turn given to Mina. The Solamnic held the lance steady, but her face was contorted by pain, and she often bit her lip as if to keep from crying out.

Mina placed her hands upon two of the enormous dragon skulls that formed the totem's base. She cried out words that no one could understand, then stepped back and raised her arms to the heavens.

A being rose from the totem. The being had the shape and form of an enormous dragon, and those standing near the totem tumbled back in terror.

The dragon's brown-colored scaly skin stretched taut over its skull, neck, and body. The skeleton could be seen clearly through the parchmentlike skin: the round disks of the neck and spine, the large bones of the massive rib cage, the thick and heavy bones of the gigantic legs, the more delicate bones of the wings and tail and feet. Sinews were visible and tendons that held the bones together. Missing were the heart and blood vessels, for magic was the blood of this dragon, vengeance and hatred formed the beating heart. The dragon was a mummified dragon, a corpse.

The wing membranes were dried and tough as leather, their span massive. The shadow of the wings spread over Sanction, doused the rays of the sun, turned dawning day to sudden night.

So horrible and loathsome was the sight of the putrid corpse hanging over their heads that the cheers for Mina died, strangled, in the throats of those who had raised them. The stench of death flowed from the creature, and with the stench came despair that was worse than the dragonfear, for fear can act as a spur to courage, while despair drains the heart of hope. Most could not bear to look at it, but lowered their heads, envisioning their own deaths, all of which were pain-filled and terrifying.

Hearing their cries, Mina took pity on them and gave to them from her own strength.

She began to sing, the same song they'd heard many times, but now with new meaning.

The gathering darkness takes our souls,
Embracing us in chilling folds,
Deep in a Mistress's void that holds
Our fate within her hands.

Dream, warriors, of the dark above
And feel the sweet redemption of
The Night's Consort, and of her love
For those within her bands.

Her song helped quell their fears, eased their despair. The soldiers called her name again, vowed that they would make her proud of them. Dismissing them, she sent them to do their duties with courage and with faith in the One God. The crowd left, Mina's name on their lips.

Mina turned to the priestess, who had been holding the lance all this time. Mina took the lance from her.

Odila snatched her hand away, hid her hand behind her back.

Mina raised the visor of her helm. "Let me see," she said.

"No, Mina," Odila mumbled, blinking back tears. "I would not burden you—"

Mina grabbed hold of Odila's hand, brought it forth to the light. The palm was bloodied and blackened, as if it had been thrust into a pit of fire.

Holding Odila's hand, Mina pressed her lips to it. The flesh healed, though the wound left terrible scars.

Odila kissed Mina and bade her good fortune in a soundless voice.

Holding the lance, Mina looked up to the death dragon. "I am ready," she said.

The image of an immortal hand reached out of the totem. Mina stepped upon the palm and the hand lifted her gently from the ground, carried her safely through the air. The hand of the goddess raised her higher than the treetops, higher than the skulls of the dragons stacked one atop the other. The hand halted at the side of the death dragon. Mina stepped off the hand, mounted the dragon's back. The corpse had no saddle, no reins that anyone could see.

Another dragon appeared on the eastern horizon, speeding toward Sanction. People cried out in fear, thinking that this must be Malys. Mina sat astride the death dragon, watched and waited.

As the dragon came in sight, cries of fear changed to wild cheering. The name "Galdar" flew from mouth to mouth. His horned head, silhouetted against the rising sun, was unmistakable.

Galdar held in his hand an enormous pike of the kind usually thrust into the ground to protect against cavalry charges. The pike's heavy weight was nothing to him. He wielded it with as much ease as Mina wielded the slender dragonlance. In his other hand, he held the reins of his mount, the blue dragon, Razor.

Galdar lifted the pike and shook it in defiance, then raised his voice and gave a mighty roar, a minotaur battle cry. An ancient cry, the words called upon the god Sargas to fight at the warrior's side, to take his body if he fell in the fray, and to smite him if he faltered. Galdar had no idea where the words came from as he shouted them. He supposed he must have heard this cry when he was a child. He was astonished to hear the words come from his mouth, but they were appropriate, and he was pleased with them.

Mina raised her visor to greet him. Her skin, in stark contrast to the black of the helm, was bone white. Her eyes shone with her own excitement. He saw himself in the amber mirror, and for the first time he was not a bug trapped in their molten gold. He was himself, her friend, her loyal comrade. He could have wept. Perhaps he did weep. If so, his battle lust burned away the tears before they could shame him.

"You will not go alone into battle this day, Mina!" Galdar roared.

"The sight of you gladdens my heart, Galdar," Mina shouted. "This is a miracle of the One God. It is among the first we will see this day, but not the last."

The blue dragon bared his teeth, a sparkle of lightning flickered from his clenched jaws.

Perhaps Mina was right. Truly, this did feel miraculous to Galdar, as wonderful a miracle as the tales of heroes of old.

Mina lowered her visor. A touch of her hand upon the corpse dragon caused it to lift its head, spread its wings, and soar into the sky, carrying her high above the clouds. The Blue glanced back at Galdar to ascertain his orders. Galdar indicated they were to follow.

The city of Sanction dwindled in size. The people were tiny black dots, then they disappeared. Higher the Blue climbed into the cold, clear air, and the world itself grew small beneath him. All was quiet, profoundly quiet and peaceful. Galdar could hear only the creak of the dragon's wings, then even that stopped as the beast took advantage of a thermal to soar effortlessly among the clouds.

All sounds of the world ceased, so that it seemed to Galdar that he and Mina were the only two left in it.

On the ground below, the people watched until they could no longer catch sight of Mina. Many still continued to watch, staring into the sky until their necks ached and their eyes burned. Officers began shouting orders, and the crowd started to disperse. Those on duty went to their posts, to take up positions on the walls. A vast number of people continued to crowd around the temple, talking excitedly of what they had seen, speaking of Malys's easy defeat and how from this day forth Mina and the Knights of the One God would be the rulers of Ansalon.

Mirror lingered near the totem, waiting for Palin's spirit to join him. The Silver did not wait long.

"Where is the blue dragon?" Palin asked immediately, alarmed by his absence.

Palin's words came to the Silver clearly, so clearly that Mirror could almost believe they were spoken by the living, except that they had a strange feel to them, a spidery feel that brushed across his skin.

"You have only to look in the sky above you to see where Razor has gone," said Mirror. "He fights his own battle in his own way. He leaves us to fight ours—whatever that may be."

"What do you mean? Are you having second thoughts?"

"That is the nature of dragons," said Mirror. "We do not rush into things headlong like you humans. Yes, I have been having second thoughts and third and fourth thoughts as well."

"This is nothing to joke about," said Palin.

"Too true," said Mirror. "Have you considered the consequences of your proposed actions? Do you know what destroying the totem will do? Especially destroying it as Malys attacks?"

"I know that this is the only opportunity we will have to destroy the totem," said Palin. "Takhisis has all her attention focused on Malys, as does everyone else in Sanction. If we miss this chance, we will not have another."

"What if, in destroying the totem, we give the victory to Malys?"

"Malys is mortal. She will not live forever. Takhisis will. I admit," Palin continued, "that I do not know what will be the consequences of the destruction of the totem. But I do know this. Every day, every hour, every second I am surrounded by the souls of the dead of Krynn. Their numbers are countless. Their torment is unspeakable, for they are driven by a hunger that can never be assuaged. She makes them promises she has no intention of keeping, and they know this, and yet they do her bidding in the pitiful hope that one day she will free them. That day will never come, Mirror. You know that, and I know it. If there is a chance that the totem's destruction will stop her from entering the world, then that is a chance we must take."

"Even if it means that we are all burned alive by Malys?" Mirror asked.

"Even if it means that," said Palin.

"Leave me a while," said Mirror. "I need to think this over."

"Do not think too long," Palin cautioned. "For while dragons think, the world moves under them."

Mirror stood alone, wrestling with his problem. Palin's words were meant to remind Mirror of the old days when the dragons of light lay complacent and sleepy in their lairs, ignoring the wars raging in the world. The dragons of light spoke smugly and learnedly of evil: evil destroys its own, good redeems its own, they said. Thus they spoke and thus they had slept and thus the Dark Queen stole their eggs and destroyed their children.

The wind shifted, blowing from the west. Mirror sniffed, caught the scent of blood and brimstone, faint, but distinct.

Malys.

She was far distant still, but she was coming.

Locked in his prison house of darkness, he heard the people around him talking glibly of the approaching battle. He could find it in his heart to pity them. They had no idea of the horror that was winging toward them. No idea at all.

Mirror groped his way past the totem, heading for the temple. He moved slowly, forced to tap out a clear path with his staff, bumping it into people's shins, knocking against trees, stumbling off the path and bumbling into flower gardens. The soldiers swore at him. Someone kicked him. He kept the rising sun on his left cheek and knew he was heading in the direction of the temple, but he should have reached it by now. He feared that he had veered off course. For all he knew, he could be headed up the mountain—or off it.

He cursed his own helplessness and came to a standstill, listening for voices and the clues they might give. Then a hand touched his outstretched hand.

"Sir, you appear to be lost and confused. Can I be of aid?"

The voice was a woman's, and it had a muffled, choked sound to it, as though she had been weeping. Her touch on his hand was firm and strong, he was startled to feel calluses on her palm, the same that could be felt on the hands of those who wielded a sword. Some female Dark Knight. Odd that she should trouble herself with him. He detected a Solamnic accent, though. Perhaps that was the reason. Old virtues are comfortable, like old clothes, and hard to part with.

"I thank you, Daughter," he said humbly, playing his role of beggar. "If you could lead me into the temple, I seek counsel."

"There we are alike, sir," said the woman. Linking her arm in his, she slowly guided his steps. "For I, too, am troubled."

Mirror could hear the anguish in her voice, feel it in the trembling of her hand.

"A burden shared is a burden halved," he said gently. "I can listen, if I cannot see."

Even as he spoke, he could hear, with his dragon soul, the beating of immense wings. The stench of Malys grew stronger. He had to make his decision.

He should break off this conversation and go about his own urgent business, but he chose not to. The silver dragon had lived long in the world. He did not believe in accidents. This chance meeting was no chance. The woman had been drawn to him out of compassion. He was touched by her sadness and pain.

They entered the Temple. He groped about with his hand, until he found what he sought.

"Stop here," he said.

"We have not reached the altar," said the woman. "What you touch is a sarcophagus. Only a little farther."

"I know," Mirror said, "but I would rather remain here. She was an old friend of mine, you see."

"Goldmoon?" The woman was startled, wary. "A friend of yours?"

"I came a long way to see her," he said.

Palin's voice whispered to him, soft and urgent. "Mirror, what are you doing? You cannot trust this woman. Her name is Odila. She was once a Solamnic Knight, but she has been consumed by darkness."

"A few moments with her. That's all I ask," Mirror replied softly.

"You may take all the time you want with her, sir," said Odila, mistaking his words. "Although the time we have is short before Malys arrives."

"Do you believe in the One God?" Mirror asked.

"Yes," said Odila, defiantly. "Don't you?"

"I believe in Takhisis," said Mirror. "I revere her, but I do not serve her."

"How is that possible?" Odila demanded. "If you believe in Takhisis and revere her, it follows that you must serve her."

"My reply takes the form of a story. Were you with Goldmoon when she died?"

"No," Odila said. Her voice softened. "No one but Mina was with her."

"Yet there were witnesses. A wizard named Palin Majere saw and heard their conversation, during which Takhisis revealed her true nature to Goldmoon. That was a moment of triumph for Takhisis. Goldmoon had long been her bitter enemy. How sweet it must have been for Takhisis to tell Goldmoon that it was she who gave Goldmoon the power of the heart, the power to heal and to build and to create. Takhisis told Goldmoon that this power of the heart stemmed not from the light but from the darkness. Takhisis hoped to convince Goldmoon to follow her. The goddess promised Goldmoon life, youth, beauty. All in return for her service, her worship.

"Goldmoon refused to accept. She refused to worship the goddess who had brought such pain and sorrow to the world. Takhisis was angry. She inflicted on Goldmoon the burden of her years, made her old and feeble and near death. The goddess hoped Goldmoon would die in despair, knowing that Takhisis had won the battle, that she would be the 'one god' for now and forever. Goldmoon's dying words were a prayer."

"To Takhisis?" Odila faltered.

"To Paladine," said Mirror. "A prayer asking for his forgiveness for having lost her faith, a prayer reaffirming her belief."

"But why did she pray to Paladine when she knew he could not answer?" Odila asked.

"Goldmoon did not pray for answers. She knew the answers. She had long carried the truth of his wisdom and his teachings in her soul. Thus, even though she might never again see Paladine or hear his voice or receive his blessings, he was with her, as he had always been. Goldmoon understood that Takhisis had lied. The good that Goldmoon had done came from her heart, and that good could never be claimed by darkness. The miracles would always come from Paladine, because he had never left her. He was always with her, always a part of her."

"It is too late for me," said Odila, despairing. "I am beyond redemption. See? Feel this." Grasping his hand, she placed his fingers on her palm. "Scars. Fresh scars. Made by the blessed dragonlance. I am being punished."

"Who punishes you, Daughter?" Mirror asked gently. "Queen Takhisis? Or the truth that is in your heart?"

Odila had no answer.

Mirror sighed deeply, his own mind at ease. He had his answer. He knew now what he must do.

"I am ready," he said to Palin.

19

Malys

aldar and Mina flew together, though not side by side. The blue dragon, Razor, kept his distance from the death dragon. He would not come near the foul corpse, did nothing to hide his disgust. Galdar feared that Mina might be offended by the Blue's reaction, but she did not seem to notice, and he came at last to realize that she saw nothing except the battle that lay ahead. All else, she had shut out of her mind.

As for Galdar, even though he was certain that his own death lay ahead of him, he had never been so happy, never been so much at peace. He thought back to the days when he'd been a one-armed cripple, forced to lick the boots of such scum as his former talon leader, the late and unlamented Ernst Magit. Galdar looked back along the path of time that had brought him to this proud moment, fighting alongside her, the one who had saved him from that bitter fate, the one who had restored his arm and, in so doing, restored his life. If he could give that life for her, to save her, that was all he cared about.

They flew high into the air, higher than Galdar had ever flown on dragonback before. Fortunately, he was not one of those who are cursed with vertigo. He did not enjoy flying on dragonback—the minotaur has not been born who enjoys it—but he did not fear it. The two dragons soared above the peaks of the Lords of Doom. Galdar looked down, fascinated, to see the fiery red innards of the mountains boiling and bubbling inside deep cavities of rock. The dragons flew in and out of the clouds of steam spewing from the mountains, keeping watch for Malys, hoping to see her first, hoping for the advantage of surprise.

The surprise came, but it was on them. Galdar and Mina and the dragons were keeping watch on the horizon when Mina gave a sudden shout and pointed downward. Malys had used the clouds herself to evade their watchfulness. She was almost directly below them and flying fast for Sanction.

Galdar had seen red dragons before and been awed by their size and their might. The red dragons of Krynn were dwarf dragons, compared to Malystrx. Her massive head could have swallowed him and his Blue in one snap of the jaws. Her talons were large enough to uproot mountains, and sharp as the mountain peaks. Her tail could flatten those peaks, obliterate them, make of them piles of dust. He stared at the dragon in dry-mouthed wonder, his hand clutching the pike so that his fingers ached.

Galdar had a sudden vision of the fire belching from Malys's belly, the dragonfire that could melt stone, consume flesh and bone in an instant, set the seas to boiling. He was about to order Razor to chase after her, but the dragon was an old campaigner and knew his business, probably better than Galdar. Swift and silent, Razor folded his wings to his sides and dived down upon his foe.

The death dragon matched Razor's speed, then outdid him. Mina lowered her visor. Galdar could not see her face, but he knew her so well that he had no need to. He could envision her: pale, fey. She and the death dragon were far ahead of him now. Galdar cursed and kicked at the Blue as if he were a horse, urging him to keep up. Razor did not feel the minotaur's kicks, nor did he need any urging. He was not going to be left behind.

The dragon flew so fast that the stinging wind brought tears to Galdar's eyes, forced his eyelids shut. Try as he might, he could not keep them open except for quick peeks now and then. Malys was a red blur through the tears that never had a chance to fall, for the wind whipped them away.

Razor did not slacken his speed. Despite the wind in Galdar's eyes, this maddened flight was exhilarating, just as the first wild charge in battle was exhilarating. Galdar gripped his pike, leveled it. The notion came to him that Razor meant to crash headlong into Malys, ram her as one ship rams another, and though that would mean Galdar's death, he had no care about that, no care for himself at all. A strange calm came over him. He had no fear. He wanted to deal death, to kill this beast. Nothing else mattered.

He wondered if Mina, gripping the dragonlance, had the same idea. He envisioned the two of them, dying together in blood and in fire, and he was exalted.

Malystryx's target was Sanction. She had the city in sight. She could see its buglike inhabitants, who were just now starting to feel the terror of her might. Malys did not fear attack from the air, for she never imagined that anyone—not even this Mina—would be so crazed as to fight her from dragonback. Happening to glance up for no other reason than to enjoy the prospect of the bright blue sky, Malys was shocked to the depth of her soul to see two dragonriders plummeting down on her.

She was so startled that for a moment she doubted her senses. That moment almost proved to be her last, for her foes were on her with a suddenness that took away her breath. An instinctive, banking move saved her, carried her out of their path. The attacking dragons were flying too fast to be able to halt. They sailed past her and began to pull up, both of them circling around for another attack.

Malys kept her eye on them, but she did not immediately fly to annihilate them. She held back, wary, watchful, waiting to see what they would do next. No need to exert herself. She had only to wait until the dragonfear, which she knew how to wield better than any other dragon who had ever existed on Krynn, caused these pitiful, lesser dragons to blanch and break, turn tail and flee. Once they had their backs to her, then she would slay them.

Malys waited, watched in glee to see the blue dragon falter in his flight, while his minotaur rider cowered on his back. Certain those two were not a threat, Malys turned her attention to the other dragon and its rider. She was annoyed to note that the other dragon had not halted in its banking turn, but was coming straight for her. Malys suddenly understood why her fear did not work on this one. She had seen enough dragon corpses to recognize one more.

So this One God could raise the dead. Malys was more irritated than impressed, for now she would have to rethink her battle strategy. This creaking, worm-eaten, grotesque monstrosity could not be defeated by terror and would not succumb to pain. It was already dead, so how could she kill it? This was going to be more work than she'd anticipated.

"First you use the souls of the dead to rob me," Malys roared. "Now you bring a moldering, mummified relic to fight me. What do you and this small and desperate god of yours expect me to do? Scream? Faint? I have no fear of the living or the dead. I have fed upon both. And I will soon feed upon you!"

Malys watched her enemies carefully, trying to guess what they would do, even as she plotted her next attack. She discounted the blue dragon. The creature was in a sad state. She could smell the reek of his dread and his rider was not much better. The rider of the dead dragon was different. Malys hovered before Mina, letting the human get a good look at the power of her foe. She could not possibly win. No god could save her.

Malys knew the impression she must make upon the human. The largest living being on all of Krynn, the red dragon was enormous, dwarfing all native dragons. A snap of Malys's massive jaws could sever the spine of the mummy dragon. A single claw was as large as this human who dared to challenge her. Beyond that, Malys wielded a magical power that had raised up mountains.

She opened her jaws, let the molten fire drool from her mouth, pool around her sharp fangs. She flexed the claws that were stained brown with blood, claws that had once pierced the scales of a gold dragon and ripped out the still-beating heart. She twitched the huge tail that could crack a red dragon's skull or break its neck, sending it plummeting to the ground while its hapless rider could do nothing but scream to see obliteration rushing up at him.

Few mortals had ever been able to withstand the horror of Malys's coming, and it seemed that Mina could not. She froze on the back of the mummified beast. She tried to keep her head up, but the terror of what she saw seemed to crush her, for she drooped and shrank, then lowered her head as if she knew death was coming and could not bear to look at it.

Malys was pleased and relieved. Opening her mouth, she drew in a breath of air that would mix with the brimstone in her belly and be unleashed in a gout of flame, cremating what was left of the corpse dragon and turn this minion of the so-called One God into a living torch.

Mina did not lower her head in fear. She lowered her head in prayer, and her god did not abandon her. Mina raised her head, looked directly at Malys. In her hand she held the dragonlance.

Silver light shone from the lance, light as sharp as the lance itself. The stabbing light struck Malys full in the eyes, for she'd been staring straight at it. Momentarily blinded, she choked upon the flaming breath, swallowed most of it. Thwarted in her attack she blinked her eyes, tried to rid them of the dazzling light.

"For the One God!" Mina cried.

Galdar knew they were finished. He hoped that they were finished. He longed for easeful death to end the fear that dissolved his organs so that he was literally drowning in his own terror. Beneath him, he could feel Razor shivering, hear the clicking of his teeth and feel tremor after tremor shake the Blue's body.

Then Mina called upon Takhisis, and the goddess answered. The dragonlance flared like a bursting star. Silver light shot through Galdar's darkness, channeled the fear into his muscles and his sinews and his brain. Razor let out a roar of defiance, and Galdar lifted his voice to match.

Mina gestured with the lance, and Galdar understood. They were not going to charge again, but would try another dive, attacking Malys from above. The red dragon, in her arrogance, had slowed her flight. They would wheel and attack her before she could recover.

The two dragons banked and began their dive. Malys gave one flap of her mighty wings, then another, and suddenly she was speeding straight at them with deadly intent. Her jaws gaped wide.

Razor anticipated the Red's attack. The Blue veered off, flipping over backward to avoid the blast of flame that came so close it singed the scales on his belly.

The world reeled beneath Galdar's horns. The minotaur's stomach rolled. Dangling upside down in the harness that held him to the saddle, he clung frantically to the pommel with one hand, his weapon with the other. The harness had been built for human dragonriders, not for a minotaur. Galdar could only hope that the straps held his weight.

Razor rolled out of his turn. Galdar was upright again, the world was back where it was supposed to be. He looked hastily about to see what had become of Mina. For a moment, he could not find her, and his heart nearly burst with fear.

"Mina!" he shouted.

"Below us!" Razor called out.

She was very far below them, flying close to the ground, flying underneath Malys, who was now caught between the two of them.

Malys's attention fixed on the Blue. A lazy flap of her wings and suddenly she was driving straight for them. Razor turned tail, beat his wings frantically.

"Fly, damn you!" Galdar snarled, although he could see that Razor was using every ounce of strength to try to outdistance the large red dragon.

Galdar looked back over his shoulder to see that the race was hopeless, lost before it could be won. Razor gasped for breath. His wings pumped. The muscles of the dragon's body flexed and heaved. Malys was barely even puffing. She seemed to fly effortlessly. Her jaws parted, fangs gleamed. She meant to snap the Blue's spine, dislodge his rider, send Galdar falling thousands of feet to his death on the rocks below.

Galdar gripped his pike.

"We're not going to make it!" he shouted at Razor. "Turn and close with her!"

The blue dragon wheeled. Galdar looked into Malys's eyes. He gripped the pike, prepared to launch it down her throat.

Malys opened her jaws, but instead of snapping at the Blue, she gave a gasp.

Mina had flown up underneath Malys. Wielding the dragonlance, Mina struck the Red in the belly. The lance sliced through the outer layer of red scales, ripped open a gash in the dragon's gut.

Malys's gasp was more astonishment than pain, for the lance had not done her serious damage. The shock and, worse than that, the insult angered her. She flipped in mid-air, tail over head, claws reaching and teeth gnashing.

The death dragon proved itself adept at maneuvering. Flying rapidly, ducking and dodging, it scrambled to keep clear of the red dragon's wild flailings. The death dragon dived. Galdar and his Blue rose and then banked for another attack.

Malys was growing weary of this battle, which was no longer fun for her. She could exert herself to some purpose when she tried, and now she stretched her wings and sought speed. She would catch this corpse and rend it bone from rotting bone, peel off its flesh and crush it into dust. And she would do the same to its rider.

Galdar had never seen anything move so fast. He and Razor flew after Malys, but they could not hope to catch up with her, not before she had slain Mina.

Malys breathed out a blast of flame.

Galdar screamed in defiance and kicked the flanks of the Blue. He might not be able to save Mina but he would avenge her.

Hearing the flame belch forth, the dead dragon lowered its head, nose down, and spread its leather wings. The ball of fire burst on its belly, spread along the wings. Galdar roared in rage, a roar that changed to a howl of glee.

The dragonlance gleamed in the flames. Mina lifted the lance, waved it to show Galdar she was safe. The death dragon's leathery wings and body shielded her from the fire. The maneuver was not without cost. The corpse's leather wings were ablaze. Tendrils of smoke snaked into the air. No matter that the corpse could neither feel pain nor die. Without the membrane of its wings, it could not remain airborne.

The death dragon began to lose altitude, flame dancing along the skeletal remains of its wings.

"Mina!" Galdar shouted in wrenching agony. He was helpless to save her.

Its wings consumed by the fire, the death dragon spiraled downward.

Certain that one foe was doomed, Malys turned her attention back to Galdar. The minotaur cared nothing about himself. Not anymore.

"Takhisis," he prayed. "I do not matter. Save Mina. Save her. She has given her all for you. Spare her life!"

In answer to his prayer, a third dragon appeared. This dragon was neither dead nor living. Shadowy, without substance, the five heads of this dragon flowed into the body of the dead dragon. The goddess herself had come to join in the battle.

The dead dragon's leathery wings began to shimmer with an eerie light. Even as flames continued to burn, the corpse pulled out of its death spiral only a short distance above the ground.

Galdar raised a mighty cheer and brandished his pike, hoping to draw Malys's attention from Mina.

"Attack!" he roared.

Razor needed no urging. He was already in a steep dive. The blue dragon bared his teeth. Galdar felt a rumbling in the dragon's belly. A bolt of lightning shot forth from the Blue's jaws. Crackling and sizzling, the lightning bolt struck Malys on the head. The concussive blast that followed nearly knocked Galdar from the saddle.

Malys jerked spasmodically as the electricity surged through her body. Galdar thought for a moment that the jolt had finished her, and his heart leaped in his chest. The lightning dissipated. Malys shook her head groggily, like a fighter who has received a blow to the nose, then she reared back, opened her jaws and came at them.

"Take me close!" Galdar cried.

Razor did as commanded. He swept in low over Malys's head. Galdar flung the pike with all his strength into the dragon's eye. He saw the pike pierce the eyeball, saw the eye redden and the dragon blink frantically.

Nothing more. And that blow had cost him dearly.

Razor's move had carried them too close to the dragon to be able to escape her reach. Galdar's strike had not taken Malys out of the battle, as he hoped. The huge pike looked puny, sticking out of Malys's eye. She felt it no more than he might feel an eyelash.

Her head reared up. She lunged at them, jaws snapping.

Galdar had one chance to save himself. He flung himself from the saddle, grabbed hold of Razor around the neck and held on. Malys drove her teeth into the blue dragon's body. The saddle disappeared in her maw.

Blood poured down Razor's flanks. The blue dragon cried out in pain and in fury as he struggled desperately to fight his attacker, lashing out with his forelegs and his hind legs, slapping at her with his tail. Galdar could do nothing but hang on. Splashed with the Blue's warm blood, Galdar clung to Razor's neck.

Malys shook the blue dragon like a dog shakes a rat

to break its spine. Galdar heard a sickening crunch of bone, and Razor gave a horrifying scream.

Mina looked up to see the blue dragon clasped in Malys's jaws. She could not see Galdar and assumed that he was dead. Her heart ached. Among all those who served her, he was most dear to her. Mina could see clearly the wound on the dragon's belly. A trail of glistening, dark red marred the fire-orange red of the scales. Yet, the wound was not mortal.

The dead dragon's wings were sheets of flame, and the flames were spreading to the body. Soon Mina would be sitting on a dragon made of fire. She felt the heat, but it was an annoyance, nothing more. She saw only her enemy. She saw what she must do to defeat the enemy.

"Takhisis, fight with me!" she cried and, raising her lance, she pointed upward.

Mina heard a voice, the same voice she had heard call to her at the age of fourteen. She had run away from home to seek out that voice.

"I am with you," said Takhisis.

The goddess spread her arms, and they became dragon wings. The burning wings of the death dragon lifted into the air, propelled by the wings of the goddess. Faster and faster they flew, the air fanning the flames on the dragon, whipping them so that the fire swirled about Mina. Her armor protected her from the flames but not from the heat. Imbued with the spirit of the god, she did not feel the burning, hot metal start to sear her skin. She saw clearly that victory must be theirs. The wounded underbelly of the red dragon came closer and closer. Malys's blood dripped down on Mina's upturned face.

And then, suddenly, Takhisis was gone.

Mina felt the absence of the goddess as a rush of chill air that snatched away her breath, left her suffocating, gasping. She was alone now, alone on a dragon that was disintegrating in fire. Her goddess had left her, and Mina did not know why.

Perhaps, Mina thought frantically, this is a test.

Takhisis had administered such tests before when Mina had first found the One God and offered to be her servant. Those tests had been hard, demanding that she prove her loyalty in blood, word, and deed. She had not failed one of them. None had been as hard as this one, though. She would not survive this one, but that made no difference, because, in death, she would be with her goddess.

Mina willed the death dragon that was now a dragon of fire to keep going, and either her will or the dragon's own momentum carried it up those last few feet.

The blazing dragon crashed into Malys's body with tremendous force. The blood dripping from the wound began to bubble and boil, so hot were the flames.

Lifting the dragonlance, Mina drove it with all her strength into the dragon's belly. The lance pierced through the weakened scales, opened a gaping wound in the flesh.

Engulfed in blood and in fire, Mina held fast to the lance and prayed to the goddess that she might now be found worthy.

Malys felt pain, a pain such as she'd never before experienced. The pain was so dreadful that she released her hold on the blue dragon. Her bellowings were horrible to hear. Galdar wished he could cover his ears so that he could blot out the sound. He had to endure it, though, for he dared not move or he would lose his hold and fall to his death. He and Razor were spiralling downward. The Lords of Doom that had been small beneath Galdar now towered over him. The jagged rocks of the mountainous terrain would make for a bone-crunching landing.

Razor had taken a mortal wound, but the dragon was still alive and with unbelievable courage was struggling desperately to remain in control. Although Razor knew he was doomed, he was fighting to save his rider. Galdar did what he could to help, hanging on and trying not move. Every flap of the dragon's wings must be agony, for Razor gasped and shuddered with the pain, but he was slowly descending. He searched with his dimming vision for a clear spot on which to land.

Clinging to the neck of the dying dragon, Galdar looked up to see Mina sitting astride wings of fire. The dragon's entire body was in flames. Flames raced up the dragonlance. The fiery dragon rammed Malys, struck her in the belly. Mina jabbed the dragonlance straight into the wound she'd already made. Malys's belly split wide open. A great, gushing rush of black blood poured out of the dragon.

"Mina!" Galdar cried out in anguish and despair, as a terrifying roar from Malys obliterated his words.

Malys screamed her death scream. She knew that death scream. She'd heard it often. She'd heard it from the Blue as she shattered his spine. Now it was her turn. The death scream rose, bubbling with agony and fury, from her throat.

Blinded by the dragon's blood, abandoned by her god, Mina yet held fast to the dragonlance. She thrust the lance up into the dreadful wound, guided the lance to pierce Malys's heart.

The red dragon died in that moment, died in midair. Her body plunged from the sky, smashed onto the rocks of the Lords of Doom below. She carried her slayer down with her.

20

Blinding Light

o pent up and excited were the defenders of Sanction that they gave a cheer when Malys's huge, red body emerged from shredded clouds.

The cheers sank, as did their courage, when the dragonfear washed over Sanction in a tidal wave that crushed hope and severed dreams and brought every person in the city face to face with the dread image of his own doom. The archers who were supposed to fire arrows at the gleaming red scales threw down their bows and fell to their bellies and lay there shivering and whimpering. The men at the catapults turned and fled their posts.

The stairs leading up to the battlements were clogged with the terrified troops so that none could go up and none could go down. Fights broke out as desperate men sought to save themselves at the expense of their fellows. Some were so maddened by the fear that they flung themselves off the walls. Those who managed to control their fear tried to calm the rest, but they were so few in number that they made little difference. One officer who tried to halt the flight of his panic-stricken men was struck down with his own sword, his body trampled in the rush.

Stone walls and iron bars were no barrier. A prisoner in the guard house near the West Gate, Silvanoshei felt the fear twist inside him as he lay on his hard bed in his dark cell, dreaming of Mina. He knew he was forgotten, but he could never forget her and he spent entire nights in hopeless dreams that she would walk through that cell door, walk with him again the dark and tangled path of his life.

The jailer had come to the cells to give Silvanoshei his daily food ration, when Malys's dragonfear washed over the city. The jailer's duty was onerous and boring, and he liked to brighten it by tormenting the prisoners. The elf was an easy target, and, although the jailer was forbidden to harm Silvanoshei physically, he could and did torment him verbally. The fact that Silvanoshei never reacted or responded did not faze the jailer, who imagined that he was having a devastating effect on the elf. In reality, Silvanoshei rarely even heard what the man said. His voice was one of many: his mother's, Samar's, his lost father's, and the voice that had made him so many promises and kept none. Real voices, such as the jailer's, were not as loud as these voices of his soul, were no more than the chattering of the rodents that infested his cell.

The dragonfear twisted inside Silvanoshei, caught in his throat, strangling and suffocating. Terror jolted him out of the nether world in which he existed, flung him onto the hard floor of reality. He crouched there, afraid to move.

"Mina save us!" moaned the jailer, shivering in the doorway. He made a lunge at Silvanoshei, caught hold of his arm with a grip that nearly paralyzed the elf.

The jailer broke into slobbering tears and clung to Silvanoshei as if he'd found an elder brother.

"What is it?" Silvanoshei cried.

"The dragon! Malys," the jailer managed to blurt out. His teeth clicked together so he could barely talk. "She's come. We're all going to die! Mina save us!"

"Mina!" Silvanoshei whispered. The word broke the shackling fear. "What has Mina to do with this?"

"She's going to fight the dragon," the jailer burbled, wringing his hands.

The prison erupted into chaos as the guards fled and the prisoners screamed and shouted and flung themselves against the bars in frantic efforts to escape the horror.

Silvanoshei pushed away the quivering, blubbering mound that had once been the jailer. The cell door stood open. He ran down the corridor. Men pleaded with him to free them, but he paid no heed to them.

Emerging outside, he drew in a deep breath of air that was not tainted with the stink of unwashed bodies and rat dung. Looking into the blue sky, he glimpsed the red dragon—a huge, bloated monster hanging in the heavens. His eager, searching gaze flicked past Malys without interest. Silvanoshei scanned the heavens and at last found Mina. His sharp elven eyesight could see better than most. He could see the tiny speck that gleamed silver in the sunlight.

Silvanoshei stood in the middle of the street, staring upward. People ran past him, dashed into him, shoved him and jostled him in their mindless panic.

He paid no attention, fended off hands, fought to keep his feet, and fought to keep his gaze fixed upon that small sparkle of light.

When Malys appeared, Palin discovered that there was one advantage to being dead. The dragonfear that plunged Sanction's populace into chaos had no effect upon him. He could look upon the great red dragon and feel nothing.

His spirit hovered near the totem. He saw the fire blaze in the eyes of the dead dragons. He heard their cries for revenge rise up to the heavens, rise up to Takhisis. Palin never doubted himself. His duty was clear before him. Takhisis must be stopped or at least slowed, her power diminished. She had invested much of that power into the totem, planning to use it as a doorway into the world, to merge the physical realm and the spiritual. If she succeeded she would reign supreme. No one—spirit or mortal—would be strong enough to fight her.

"You were right," said Mirror, who stood by Palin's side. "The city has gone mad with terror."

"It will wear off soon—" Palin began. He broke off abruptly.

Dalamar's spirit emerged from among the dragon skulls.

"The view of the battle is better from the box seats," Dalamar said. "You do not have feet, you know, Majere. You are not bound to the ground. Together you and I can sit at our ease among the clouds, watch every thrust and parry, see the blood fall like rain. Why don't you join me?"

"I have very little interest in the outcome," said Palin. "Whoever wins, we are bound to lose."

"Speak for yourself," Dalamar said.

To Palin's discomfiture, Dalamar's spirit was taking an unusual interest in Mirror.

Could Dalamar see both the man and the silver dragon? Could Dalamar have guessed their plan? If he knew, would he attempt to thwart them, or was he preoccupied with his own schemes? That Dalamar had schemes of his own, Palin did not doubt. Palin had never fully trusted Dalamar, and he had grown more wary of him these past few days.

"The battle goes well," Dalamar continued, his soul's gaze fixed on Mirror. "Malys is fully occupied, that much is certain. People are calming down. The dragonfear is starting to abate. Speaking of which, your blind beggar friend appears to be remarkably immune to dragonfear. Why is that, I wonder?"

What Dalamar said was true. The dragonfear was fading away. Soldiers who had been hugging the ground and screaming that they were all going to die were sitting up, looking sheepish and embarrassed.

If we are going to do this, we have to act now, realized Palin. What danger can Dalamar be to us? He can do nothing to stop them. Like me, he has no magic.

A roaring bellow boomed among the mountains. People in the street stared upward, began to shout and point to the sky.

"A dragon has drawn blood," said Mirror, peering upward. "Hard to say which, though."

Dalamar's spirit hung in the air. The eyes of his soul stared at them as if he would delve the depths of theirs. Then, suddenly, he vanished.

"The outcome of this fight means something to him, that is certain," said Palin. "I wonder which horse he is backing."

"Both, if he can find a way," said Mirror.

"Could he see your true form, do you think?" Palin asked.

"I believe that I was able to hide from him," said Mirror. "But when I begin to cast my magic, I can no longer do so. He will see me for what I am."

"Then let us hope the battle proves interesting enough to keep him occupied," said Palin. "Do you have fur and amber . . . ? Ah, sorry, I forgot," he added, seeing Mirror smile. "Dragons have no need of such tools for their spell casting."

Now that the battle had begun, the totem's magic intensified. Eyes in the skulls burned and glittered with a fury so potent it shone from ground to heaven. The single eye, the New Eye, gleamed white, even in the daylight. The magic of the totem was strong, drew the dead to it. The souls of the dead circled the totem in a pitiful vortex, their yearning a torment fed by the goddess.

Palin felt the pain of longing, a longing for what is lost beyond redemption.

"When you cast your spell," he said to Mirror, the longing for the magic an aching inside him, "the dead will swarm around you, for yours is a magic they can steal. The sight of them is a terrible one, unnerving—"

"So there is at least one advantage to being blind," Mirror remarked, and he began to cast the spell.

Dragons, of all the mortal beings on Krynn, are born with the ability to use magic. Magic is inherent to them, a part of them like their blood and their shining scales. The magic comes from within.

Mirror spoke the words of magic in the ancient language of dragons. Coming from a human throat, the words lacked the rich resonance and rolling majesty that the silver dragon was accustomed to hearing, sounded thin and weak. Small or large, the words would accomplish the goal. The first prickles of magic began to sparkle in his blood.

Wispy hands plucked at his scales, tore at his wings, brushed across his face. The souls of the dead now saw him for what he was—a silver dragon—and they surged around him, frantic for the magic that they could feel pulsing inside his body. The souls reached out to him with their wispy hands and pleaded with him. The souls clung to him and hung from him like tattered scarves. The dead could do him no harm. They were an annoyance, like scale mites. But scale mites did nothing more than raise an irritating itch. Scale mites did not have voices that cried out in desperation, begging, beseeching. Hearing the despair in the voices, Mirror realized he had spoken truly. There was an advantage to being blind. He did not have to see their faces.

Even though the magic was inherent to him, he still had to concentrate to cast the spell, and he found this difficult. The fingers of the souls raked his scales, their voices buzzed in his ears.

Mirror tried to concentrate on one voice—his voice. He concentrated on the words of his own language, and their music was comforting and reassuring. The magic burned within him, bubbled in his blood. He sang the words and opened his hands and cast the magic forth.

Although Dalamar guessed that his fellow mage was up to something, he had discounted Palin as a threat. How could he be? Palin was as impotent as

Dalamar when it came to magic. True, Dalamar would not let that stop him. He had schemed and connived so that whichever way the bread landed, he'd still have the butter side up.

Yet, there was something strange about that blind beggar. Probably the fellow was or fancied himself a wizard. Probably Palin had concocted some idea that they could work together, although what sort of magical rabbit they would be able to pull out of their joint hats was open to debate. If they were able to come up with a rabbit at all, the souls of the dead would grab it and rip it apart.

Satisfied, Dalamar felt it safe to leave Palin and his blind beggar to bumble about in the darkness while he went to witness first hand the gladiatorial contest between Malys and Mina. Dalamar was not overly interested in which one won. He viewed the battle with the cold, dispassionate interest of the gambler who has all his bets covered.

Malys breathed blazing fire on the corpse dragon, the leather wings erupted into flames. Malys chortled, thinking she was the victor.

"Don't count your winnings yet," Dalamar advised the red dragon, and he was proven right.

Takhisis advanced onto the field of battle. Reaching out her hand, she touched the death dragon. Her spirit flowed into the body of the burning corpse, saving Mina, her champion.

At that moment, Dalamar's soul heard the sound of a voice chanting. He could not understand the words, but he recognized the language of dragons, and he was alarmed to realize by the cadence and the rhythm that the words were magic. His spirit fled the battle, soared back to the temple. He saw a spark of bright light and realized immediately that he had made a mistake—perhaps a fatal mistake.

As Dalamar the Dark had misjudged the uncle, so had he misjudged the nephew. Dalamar saw in an instant what Palin planned.

Dalamar recognized the blind beggar as Mirror, guardian of the Citadel of Light, one of the few silver dragons who had dared remain in the world after all the others had so mysteriously fled. He saw the dead surrounding Mirror, trying to feed off the magic he was casting, but the dragon would be poor pickings. The dead might leech some of the magic, but they would not seriously impede Mirror's spellcasting. Dalamar knew immediately what the two were doing, knew it as well as if he had plotted it with them.

Dalamar looked back to the battle. This was Takhisis's moment of victory, the moment she would avenge herself on this dragon who had dared moved in to take over her world. The Dark Queen had been forced to endure Malys's taunts and gibes in seething silence. She had been forced to watch Malys slay her minions and use their power—that should have been her power.

At last, Takhisis had grown strong enough to challenge Malys, to wrench away the souls of the dead dragons, who now worshiped their queen and gave their power to their queen. Dragons of Krynn, their souls were hers to command.

Long had Takhisis watched and worked and waited for this moment when she would remove the last obstacle to stand in her way of taking full and absolute control of her world. Concentrating on the foe in front, Takhisis was oblivious to the danger creeping up on her from behind.

Dalamar could warn Takhisis. He had but to say one word and she would run to protect her totem. She could not afford to do otherwise. She had worked hard to create the door for her entry and she was not about to have it slammed shut in her face. There would be other days to fight Malys, other champions to fight Malys if she lost Mina.

Dalamar hesitated.

True, Takhisis had offered him rich reward—a return to his body and the gifting of the magic to go with it.

Dalamar reached out with his soul and touched the past, touched the memory that was all that was left to him: the memory of the magic. He would do anything, say anything, betray, destroy anyone for the sake of the magic.

The thought that he must abase himself before Takhisis was galling to him. Once years ago, when the magic had been his to command, he had been open in his defiance of the Dark Queen. Nuitari, her son, had no love for his mother and could always be counted upon to defend his worshipers against her. Nuitari was gone now. The power the dark god of magic had lavished on his servant was gone.

Dalamar must now abase himself before the Dark Queen, and he knew that Takhisis would not be generous in her victory over him. Yet, for the magic, he could do even this.

Takhisis straddled the world, watching the battle in which she took such a keen interest. Her champion was winning. Mina flew straight up at Malys, the gleaming dragonlance in her hand.

Dalamar knelt in the dust and bowed his head low and said humbly, "Your Majesty . . ."

Mirror could not see the magic, but he could feel it and hear it. The spell flowed from his fingers as bolts of jagged, blue lightning that crackled and sizzled. The air smelled of brimstone. He could see the blazing bolts in his mind's eye, see them striking a skull, dancing from that skull to another, from the skull of a gold to the skull of a red, from that skull to the skull touching it, and round and round, jumping from one to the next, in a blazing, fiery chain.

"Is the spell cast?" Mirror cried.

"It is cast," said Palin, watching in awe.

He wished Mirror could see this sight. The lightning sizzled and danced. Blue-white, the bolts jumped from one skull to the next, so fast that the eye could not follow them. As the lightning struck each skull, that skull began to glow blue-white, as though dipped in phosphorus. Thunder boomed and blasted, shaking the ground, shaking the totem.

Power built in the totem, the magic shuddered in the air. The voices of the dead fell silent as the voices of the living raised in a terrible clamor, screaming and crying out. Feet pounded, some running toward the totem, others running away.

Watching Mirror cast the spell, Palin recited to himself the words of magic that for him held no meaning, but which were imprinted on his soul. His body sat unmoved, uncaring, on a bench in the temple. Exultant, his soul watched lightning leap from skull to skull, setting each afire.

The magic reverberated, hummed, grew stronger and stronger. The white-hot fire burned bright. The intense heat drove back those gathered around the totem. The skulls of the dragons now had eyes of white flame.

In the heavens, thunder rolled. The New Eye glared down on them.

Dark clouds, thick and black, shot through with bolts of orange and red, bubbled and boiled and frothed. Tendrils of destruction twisted down from the storm, raising dust clouds and uprooting trees. Hail pelted, smashed into the ground.

"Do your damndest, Takhisis," cried Palin to the thundering, angry voice of the storm. "You are too late."

The black clouds blanketed Sanction with darkness and rain and hail. A gust of wind blew on the totem. Torrential rains deluged the city, trying desperately to douse the magic.

The rain was like oil on the fire. The wind fanned the flames. Mirror could not see the fire, but he could feel the searing heat. He staggered backward, stumbling over benches, backed into the altar. His groping hands found purchase, cool and smooth. He recognized by touch the sarcophagus of Goldmoon, and it seemed to him that he could hear her voice calm and reassuring. Mirror crouched beside the sarcophagus, though the heat grew ever more intense. He kept his hand upon it protectively.

A ball of fire formed in the center of the totem, shining bright as a lost star fallen to the ground. Light, bright and white as starlight, began to shine within the eyes of the dragons. The light grew brighter and brighter until none of the living could look at it, but were forced to cover their eyes.

The fire grew in strength and intensity, burning purely and radiantly, its luminous brilliance so dazzling that Mirror could see it through his blindness, saw bursting, blue-white flame and the petals of flame drifting up into the heavens. The rain had no effect on the magical fire. The wind of the goddess's fury could not diminish it.

The light shone pure white at its heart. The skulls of the dragons shattered, burst apart. The totem teetered and swayed, then fell in upon itself, dissolving, disintegrating.

The New Eye stared into the white heart of the blaze. Blood-red, the Eye fought to maintain its gaze, but the pain proved too much.

The Eye blinked.

The Eye vanished.

Darkness closed over Mirror, but he no longer cursed it, for the darkness was blessed, safe and comforting as the darkness from which he'd been born. His trembling hand ran over the smooth, cool surface of the sarcophagus. There came a ringing sound as of shattering glass, and he felt cracks in the surface, felt them spread through the amber like winter ice melting in the spring sun.

The sarcophagus broke apart, the bits and pieces falling around him. He felt a soft touch on his hand that was like ashes drifting on the wind.

"Goodbye, dear friend," he said.

"The blind beggar!" a voice like thunder rumbled. "Slay the blind beggar. He has destroyed the totem! Malys will kill us! Malys will kill us all."

Voices cried out in anger. Footsteps pounded. Fists began to pummel him.

A rock struck Mirror and another.

Palin watched, exultant, as the totem fell. He saw the sarcophagus destroyed and, though he could not find Goldmoon's spirit, he rejoiced that her body would no longer be held in thrall, that she would no longer be a slave of Takhisis.

He would be called to account. He would be made to pay. He could not avoid it, could not hide, for though her eye might have been blinded, Takhisis was still master. Her presence in the world had not been banished, merely diminished. He remained a slave, and there was nowhere he could hide that her dogs would not sniff him out, hunt him down.

He waited to accept his fate, waited near the crumbling ruins of the totem, waited beside the pitiful shell of flesh that was his body. The dogs were not long in coming.

Dalamar appeared, materializing out of the smoking ruins of the burning skulls.

"You should not have done this, Palin. You should not have interfered. Your soul faces oblivion. Darkness eternal."

"What is to be your reward for your service to her?" Palin asked. "Your life? No"—he answered his own question—"you cared little for your life. She gave you back the magic."

"The magic is life," said Dalamar. "The magic is love. The magic is family. The magic is wife. The magic is child." .

Inside the temple, Palin's body sat on the hard bench, stared unseeing at the candle flames that wavered, fearful and helpless, in the storm winds that swept through the room.

"How sad," he said, as his spirit started to ebb, water receding from the shoreline, "that only at the end do I know what I should have known from the start."

"Darkness eternal," Dalamar echoed.

"No," said Palin softly, "for beyond the clouds, the sun shines."

Rough hands seized hold of Mirror. Angry, panicked voices clamored in his ear, so many at once that he could not possibly understand them. They mauled him, pulled him this way and that, as they screeched and argued between themselves about what to do with him. Some wanted to hang him. Others wanted to rend him apart where he stood.

The silver dragon could always slough off this puny human guise and transform into his true shape. Even blind, he could defend himself against a mob. He spread his arms that would become his silver wings and lifted his head. Joy filled him even as danger closed in on him. In a moment, he would be himself, shining silver in the darkness, riding the winds of the storm.

Shackles clamped over his wrists. He almost laughed, for no iron forged of man could hold him. He tried to shake them off, but the shackles would not fall, and he realized that they were not forged of iron, but of fear. Takhisis made them and she clamped them on him. Strive as he might, he could not transform himself. He was chained to his human body, shackled to this two-legged form, and in that form, blind and alone, he would die.

Mirror fought to escape his captors, but his thrashings only goaded them to further torment. Rocks and fists struck him. Pain shot through him. Blow after blow rained down on him. He slumped to the ground.

He heard, as in a dream of pain, a strong, commanding voice speak out. The voice was powerful, and it quelled the clamor.

"Back away!" Odila ordered. Her voice was cold and stern and accustomed to being obeyed. "Leave him alone or know the wrath of the One God!"

"He used some sort of magic to destroy the totem!" a man cried. "I saw him!"

"He's done away with the moon!" cried another. "Done something foul and unnatural that will curse us all!"

Other voices joined in the accusing clamor, demanded his death.

"The magic he used is the magic of the One God," Odila told them. "You should be down on your knees, praying for the One God to save us from the dragon, not maltreating a poor beggar!"

Her strong, scarred hands took firm hold of him, lifted him up.

"Can you walk?" she whispered to him, low and urgent. "If so, you must try."

"I can walk," he told her.

A trickle of warm blood seeped down into the bandages he wore around his eyes. The pain in his head eased, but he felt cold and clammy and nauseous. He staggered to his feet. Her arms wrapped around him, supported his faltering steps.

"Good," Odila whispered in his ear. "We're going to walk backward." Taking a firm grip on him, she suited her action to her words. He stumbled with her, leaning on her.

"What is happening?" he asked.

"The mob is holding back for the moment. They feel my power, and they fear it. I speak for the One God, after all." Odila sounded amused, reckless, joyful. "I want to thank you," she said, her voice softening. "I was the one who was blind. You opened my eyes."

"Let's go after him," someone shouted. "What's stopping us? She's not Mina! She's just some traitor Solamnic."

Odila let go of Mirror, moved to stand defensively in front of him. He heard a roar as the mob surged forward.

"A traitor Solamnic with a club, not a sword," Odila said to him. He heard the splintering of wood, guessed that she had smashed up one of the benches. "I'll hold them off as long as I can. Make your way behind the altar. You'll find a trapdoor—"

"I have no need for trapdoors," Mirror said. "You will be my eyes, Odila. I will be your wings."

"What the—" she began, then she gasped. He heard her drop the club.

Mirror spread his arms. Fear was gone. The Dark Queen had no power over him. He could see, once again, the radiant light. As it had destroyed the totem, so it burned away the shackles that bound him. His human body, so frail and fragile, small and cramped, was transformed. His heart grew and expanded, blood pulsed through massive veins, fed his strong taloned legs and an enormous silver-scaled body. His tail struck the altar, smashed it, sent the candles tumbling to the floor in a river of melted wax.

The mob that had surged forward to kill a blind beggar fell all over itself trying to escape a blind dragon.

"No saddle, Sir Knight," he told Odila. "You'll have to hang on tight. Grasp my mane. You'll need to lean close to my head to be able to tell me where we are going. What of Palin?" he asked, as she caught hold of his mane and pulled herself up on his back. "Can we take him with us?"

"His body is not there," Odila reported.

"I feared as much," said Mirror quietly. "And the other one? Dalamar."

"He is there," said Odila. "He sits alone. His hands are stained with blood."

Mirror spread his wings.

"Hold on!" he shouted.

"I'm holding," said Odila. "Holding fast."

In her hand was the medallion that bore on it the image of the five-headed dragon. The medallion burned her scarred fingers. The pain was minor compared to the pain that seared her when she touched the dragonlance. Clasping the medallion, Odila tore it off.

The silver dragon gave a great leap. His wings caught the winds of the storm, used them to carry him aloft.

Odila brought the medallion to her lips. She kissed it, then, opening her fingers, she let the medallion fall. The medallion spiraled down into the pile of dust that was now all that remained of Malys's monument to death.

Mina's followers witnessed the breathtaking battle. They cheered to see Malys fall, gasped in horror as Mina fell in flames along with her foe.

Desperately they waited to see her rise again from the fire, as she had done once before. Smoke drifted up from the mountain, but it brought no Mina with it.

Silvanoshei had watched with the rest. He started walking. He would go to the temple. Someone there would have news. As he walked, as the blood flowed and his stiff muscles warmed, he came gradually to realize that not only was he still alive, he was free.

People milled about in the streets, shocked and confused. Some wept openly. Some simply wandered aimlessly, not knowing what to do next, waiting for someone to come and tell them. Some spoke of the battle, reliving it, relating over and over what they had seen, trying to make it real. People jabbered about the moon and that it was gone and so was the One God, if the One God had ever been, and that now Mina was gone too. No one paid any attention to Silvanoshei. Everyone was too caught up in his own despair to care about an elf.

I could walk out of Sanction, Silvanoshei said to himself, and no one would lift a finger to stop me.

He had no thought of leaving Sanction, however. He could not leave, not until he knew for certain what had become of Mina. Arriving at the temple, he found a huge throng of people gathered around the totem and he joined them, staring in dismay at the pile of ashes that had once been the glory of Queen Takhisis.

Silvanoshei stared into the ashes and he saw what he had been, saw what he might have been.

He saw the events that had led him to this point, saw them with his soul that never sleeps, always watches. He saw the terrible night the ogres attacked. He saw himself— consumed with hatred for his mother and for the life she had forced him to lead, consumed with fear and guilt when it seemed that she might die at the hands of the ogres. He saw himself running through the darkness to save her, and he saw himself proud to think that he would be the one to save his people. He saw the lightning bolt that sent him tumbling into unconsciousness. He saw himself falling down the hill to land at the base of the shield and then he saw what he had not been able to see with mortal eyes. He saw the dark hand of the goddess lift the shield so that he could enter.

Staring into the darkness, he saw the darkness staring back at him, and he realized that he had looked into the Dark Queen's eyes many times before, looked into them without blinking or turning away.

He heard again words that Mina had said to him on that first night they had come together. Words that he had tossed aside as nonsense, meaningless, without importance.

You do not love me. You love the god you see in me.

Everything his mother yearned for, he had been given. She had wanted to rule Silvanesti. He was the king of Silvanesti. She had longed to be loved by the people. They loved him. That was his revenge, and it had been sweet. But that was only part of the revenge. The best part was that he had thrown it all away. Nothing he could have done had the power to hurt his mother more.

If the goddess had used him, it was because Takhisis had gazed deeply into the eyes of his soul and had seen one eye wink.

21

The Dead and Dying

azor's strength gave out while they were still airborne. He could no longer move his wings, and he began to twist downward in an uncontrolled dive. Galdar had the terrifying image of sheersided, jagged rocks stabbing upward. Razor crashed headlong into a small grove of pine trees.

For a heart-stopping moment, all Galdar could see was a blur of orange rocks and green trees, blue dragon scales and red blood. He squinched his eyes tight shut, gripped the dragon with all the strength of his massive body, buried his head in the dragon's neck. Buffeted and jolted, he heard the rending and snapping of limbs and bones, smelled and tasted the sharp odor of pine needles and the iron-tinged smell of fresh blood. A branch struck him on the head, nearly ripping off his horn. Another smote him on the back of his shoulder. Shattered branches tore at his legs and arms.

Suddenly, abruptly, they slammed to a halt.

Galdar spent a long moment doing nothing except gasping for breath and marveling that he was still alive. Every part of him hurt. He had no idea if he was seriously wounded or not. He moved, gingerly. Feeling no sharp, searing pain, he concluded that no bones were broken. Blood dribbled down his nose. His ears rang, and his head throbbed. He felt Razor give a shuddering sigh.

The dragon's head and upper portion of his shattered body rested in the pine trees that had broken beneath his weight. Disentangling himself from a nest of twisted, snapped branches, Galdar slid down off the dragon's back. He had the woozy impression that the blue dragon was resting in a cradle of pine boughs. The lower half of the dragon's body—the broken wings and tail—trailed behind him onto the rocks, leaving a smear of blood.

Galdar looked swiftly about for Malys's carcass. He saw it, off in the distance. Her corpse was easy to located. In death, she made her final mountain—a glistening, red mound of bloody flesh. Smoke and flame drew his eye. Fire consumed the death dragon, the flames spreading to the scrub pine. Farther down in the valley lay Sanction, but he couldn't see the city. Dark thunderclouds swirled beneath him. Where he stood, the sun shone brightly, so brightly that it had apparently eclipsed that New Eye, for he could not see it.

He did not take time to search for it. His main concern was Mina. He was frantic with worry about her and wanted nothing more than to go off immediately to search for her. But the minotaur owed his life to the heroics of the blue dragon. The least Galdar could do was to stay with him. No one, minotaur or dragon, should die alone.

Razor was still alive, still breathing, but his breaths were pain-filled and shallow. Blood flowed from his mouth. His eyes were starting to grow dim, but they brightened at the sight of Galdar.

"Is she . . ." The blue dragon choked on his own blood, could not continue.

"Malys is dead," Galdar said, deep and rumbling. "Thank you for the battle. A glorious victory that will be long remembered. You die a hero. I will honor your memory, as will my children and my children's children and their children after."

Galdar had no children, nor was there any likelihood he would ever have any. His words were the ancient tribute given to a warrior who has fought valiantly and died with honor. Yet Galdar spoke them from the depth of his soul, for he could only imagine what terrible agony these last few moments were for the dying dragon.

The blue dragon gave another shudder. His body went limp.

"I did my duty," he breathed, and died.

Galdar lifted his head and gave a howl of grief that echoed among the mountains—a final, fitting tribute. This done, he was free at last to follow his aching heart, to find out what had happened to Mina.

I should not be worried, he told himself. I have seen Mina survive poisoning, emerge whole and unscarred from her own flaming funeral pyre. The One God loves Mina, loves her as perhaps she has never before loved a mortal. Takhisis will protect her darling, watch over her.

Galdar told himself that, told himself repeatedly, but still he worried.

He scanned the rugged rocks around the carcass of the dragon. Chunks of flesh and gore were splattered about a wide area, the rocks were slippery with the mess. He hoped to see Mina come striding toward him, that exalted glow in her eyes. But nothing moved on the rocky outcropping where the dragon had fallen. The birds of the air had fled at her coming, the animals gone to ground. All was silent, except for a fierce and angry wind that hissed among the rocks with an eerie, whistling sound.

The rocks were difficult enough to navigate without the blood and blubber. Climbing was slow going, especially when every movement brought the pain of some newly discovered injury. Galdar found his pike. The weapon was covered with blood, and the blade was broken. Galdar was pleased to retrieve it. He would give it to Mina as a memento.

Search as he might, he could not find her. Time and again, he roared out, "Mina!" The name came back a hundredfold, careening off the sides of the mountains, but there was no answering call. The echoes faded away into silence. Climbing up and over a jumble of boulders, Galdar came at last to Malys's carcass.

Looking at the wreckage of the gigantic red dragon, Galdar felt nothing, not elation, not triumph, nothing except weariness and grief and a wonder that any of them had come out of this confrontation alive.

"Perhaps Mina didn't," said a voice inside him, a voice that sent shudders through him.

"Mina!" He called again, and he heard, in answer, a groan.

Malys's red-scaled and blood-smeared flank moved.

Alarmed, Galdar lifted the broken pike. He looked hard at the dragon's head, that lay sideways on the rocks, so that only one eye was visible. That eye stared, unseeing, at the sky. The neck was twisted and broken. Malys could not be alive.

The groan was repeated and a weak voice called out, "Galdar!"

With a cry of joy, Galdar flung down the pike and bounded forward. Beneath the belly of the dragon he saw a hand, covered with blood and moving feebly. The dragon had fallen on top of Mina, pinning her beneath.

Galdar put his shoulder to the fast cooling mass of blubber and heaved. The dragon's carcass was heavy, weighing several hundred tons. He might as well have tried to shift the mountain.

He was frantic with worry now, for Mina's voice sounded weak. He put his hands on the belly that had been slit wide open. Entrails spewed out; the stench was horrible. He gagged, tried to stop breathing.

"I can barely lift this, Mina," he called to her. "You must crawl out. Make haste. I can't hold it for long."

He heard something in reply but could not understand, for her voice was muffled. He gritted his teeth and bent his knees and, sucking in a great breath of air, he gave a grunt and heaved upward with all his might. He heard a scrabbling sound, a pain-filled gasping for breath, and a muffled cry. His muscles ached and burned, his arms grew wobbly. He could hold on no longer. With a loud shout of warning, he dropped the mass of flesh and stood gasping for breath amid the putrid remains. He looked down to find Mina lying at his feet.

Galdar was reminded of a time when Mina had been invited to bless a birthing. Galdar hadn't wanted to be there, but Mina had insisted and, of course, he'd obeyed. Looking down at Mina, Galdar remembered vividly the tiny child, so frail and fragile, covered in blood. He knelt by Mina's side.

"Mina," he said, helpless, afraid to touch her, "where are you hurt? I cannot tell if this is your blood or the dragon's."

Her eyes opened. The amber was bloodshot, rimmed with red. She reached out her hand, grasped Galdar's arm. The move caused her pain. She gasped and shivered but still managed to cling to him.

"Pray to the One God, Galdar," she said, her voice no more than a whisper. "I have done something . . . to displease her . . . Ask her . . . to forgive . . ."

Her eyes closed. Her head lolled to one side. Her hand slipped from his arm. His own heart stopping in fear, Galdar put his hand on her neck to feel for her pulse. Finding it, he gave a great sigh of relief.

He lifted Mina in his arms. She was light as he remembered that newborn babe to have been.

"You great bitch!" Galdar snarled. He was not referring to the dead dragon.

Galdar found a small cave, snug and dry. The cave was so small that the minotaur could not stand to his full height, but was forced to crouch low to enter. Carrying Mina inside, he laid her down gently. She had not regained consciousness, and although this scared him, he told himself this was good, for otherwise she would die of the pain.

Once in the cave, he had time to examine her. He stripped away her armor, tossed it outside to lie in the dust. The wounds she had sustained were terrible. The end of her leg bone protruded from the flesh, that was bloody, purple, and grotesquely swollen. One arm no longer looked like an arm, but like something hanging in a butcher's stall. Her breathing was ragged and caught in her throat. Every breath was a struggle, and more than once he feared she lacked the strength to take another. Her skin was burning hot to the touch. She shivered with the cold that brings death.

He no longer felt the pain of his own wounds. Whenever he made a sudden move and a sharp jab reminded him, he was surprised, wondered vaguely where it came from. He lived only for Mina, thought only of her. Finding a stream a short distance from the cave, he rinsed out his helm, filled it with water, carried it back to her.

He laved her face and touched her lips with the cool liquid, but she could not drink. The water trickled down her blood-covered chin. Up here in these rocks he would find no herbs to treat her pain or bring down her fever. He had no bandages. He had a rough sort of battlefield training in healing, but that was all, and it was not much help. He should amputate that shattered leg, but he could not bring himself to do it. He knew what it was for a warrior to live as a cripple.

Better she should die. Die in the glorious moment with the defeat of the dragon. Die as a warrior victorious over her foe. She was going to die. Galdar could do nothing to save her. He could do nothing but watch her life bleed away. He could do nothing but be by her side so that she would not die alone.

Darkness crept into the cave. Galdar built a fire inside the cavern's entrance to keep her warm. He did not leave the cavern again. Mina was delirious, fevered, murmuring incoherent words, crying out, moaning. Galdar could not bear to see her suffer, and more than once, his hand stole to his dagger to end this swiftly, but he held back. She might yet regain consciousness, and he wanted her to know, before she died, that she died a hero and that he would always love and honor her.

Mina's breathing grew erratic, yet she struggled on. She fought very hard to live. Sometimes her eyes opened and he saw the agony in them and his heart wrenched. Her eyes closed again without showing any signs of recognition, and she battled on.

He reached out his hand, wiped the chill sweat from her forehead.

"Let go, Mina," he said to her, tears glimmering on his eyelids. "You brought down your enemy—the largest, most powerful dragon ever to inhabit Krynn. All nations and people will honor you. They will sing songs of your victory down through the ages. Your tomb will be the finest ever built in Ansalon. People will travel from all over the world to pay homage. I will lay the dragonlance at your side and the put the monstrous skull of the dragon at your feet."

He could see it all so clearly. The tale of her courage would touch the hearts of all who heard it. Young men and women would come to her tomb to pledge themselves to lives of service to mankind, be it as warrior or healer. That she had walked in darkness would be forgotten. In death, she was redeemed.

Still, Mina fought on. Her body twitched and jerked. Her throat was ragged and raw from her screams.

Galdar could not bear it. "Release her," he prayed, not thinking what he was doing or saying, his only thought of her. "You've done with her! Release her!"

"So this is where you have her hidden," said a voice.

Galdar drew his dagger, twisted to his feet, and emerged from the cave all in one motion. The fire stole away his night vision. Beyond the crackling flames, all was darkness. He was a perfect target, standing there in the firelight, and he moved swiftly. Not too far away. He would never leave Mina, let them do what they might to him.

He blinked his eyes, tried to pierce the shadows. He had not heard the sound of footfalls or the chink of armor or the ring of steel. Whoever it was had come upon him by stealth, and that boded no good. He made certain to hold his dagger so it did not reflect the firelight.

"She is dying," he said to whoever was out there. "She has not long to live. Honor her dying and allow me to remain with her to the end. Whatever is between us, we can settle that afterward. I pledge my word."

"You are right, Galdar," said the voice. "Whatever is between us, we will settle at a later date. I gave you a great gift, and you returned my favor with treachery."

Galdar's throat constricted. The dagger slid from the suddenly nerveless right hand, landed on the rocks at his feet with a clash and a clatter. A woman stood at the mouth of the cave. Her figure blotted out the light of the fire, obliterated the light of the stars. He could not see her face with his eyes, for she had yet to enter the world in her physical form, but he saw her with the eyes of his soul. She was beautiful, the most beautiful thing he had ever seen in his life. Yet her beauty did not touch him, for it was cold and sharp as a scythe. She turned away from him. She walked toward the entrance to the cave.

Galdar managed with great effort to move his shaking limbs. He dared not look into that face, dared not meet those eyes that held in them eternity. He had no weapon that could fight her. No such weapon existed in this world. He had only his love for Mina, and perhaps that was what gave him courage to place his own body between Queen Takhisis and the cave.

"You will not pass," he said, the words squeezed out of him. "Leave her alone! Let go of her! She did what you wanted and without your help. You abandoned her. Leave it that way."

"She deserves to be punished," Takhisis returned, cold, disdainful. "She should have known the wizard Palin was treacherous, secretly plotting to destroy me. He nearly succeeded. He destroyed the totem. He destroyed the mortal body that I had chosen for my residence while in the world. Because of Mina's negligence, I came close to losing everything I have worked for. She deserves to punished! She deserves death and worse than death! Still—" Takhisis's voice softened— "I will be merciful. I will be generous."

Galdar's heart almost stopped with fear. He was panting and shaking, yet he did not move.

"You need her," said Galdar harshly. "That's the only reason you're saving her." He shook his horned head. "She's at peace now, or soon will be. I won't let you have her."

Takhisis moved closer.

"I keep you alive, minotaur, for only one reason. Mina asks me to do so. Even now, as her spirit is wrenched from its shell of flesh, she begs me to be merciful toward you. I indulge her whim, for now. The day will come, however, when she will see that she no longer has need of you. Then, what lies between you and me will be settled."

Her hand lifted him up by the scruff of his neck and tossed him carelessly aside. He landed heavily among the sharp rocks and lay there, sobbing in anger and frustration. He pounded his left hand into the rocks, pounded it again and again so that it was bruised and bloody.

Queen Takhisis entered the cavern, and he could hear her crooning softly, sweetly, "My child . . . My beloved child . . . I do forgive you. . . ."

22

Lost in the Maze

Gerard was determined to reach the Knights' Council with the urgent news of the return of Queen Takhisis as quickly as possible. He guessed that once she had built her totem and secured Sanction, the Dark Queen would move swiftly to secure the world. Gerard had no time to waste.

Gerard had found the elf, Samar, without difficulty. As Silvanoshei had predicted, the two men, though of different races, were experienced warriors and, after a few tense moments, suspicion and mistrust were both allayed. Gerard had delivered the ring and the message from Silvanoshei, though the Knight had not been exactly honest in relating the young king's words. Gerard had not told Samar that Silvanoshei was captive of his own heart. Gerard had made Silvanoshei a hero who had defied Mina and been punished for it. Gerard's plan was for the elves to join the Solamnics in the attempt to seize Sanction and halt the rise of Takhisis.

Gerard trusted that the elves would want to free their young king, and although Gerard had received the distinct impression that Samar did not much like Silvanoshei, Gerard had managed to impress the dour warrior with the true story of Silvanoshei's courage in the fight with Clorant and his fellow Knights. Samar had promised that he would carry the matter to Alhana Starbreeze. He had little doubt that she would agree to the plan. The two had parted, vowing to meet each other again as allies on the field of battle.

After bidding farewell to Samar, Gerard rode to the sea coast. Standing on a cliff that overlooked the crashing waves, he stripped off the black armor that marked him as a Knight of Takhisis, and one by one he hurled the pieces into the ocean. He had the distinct satisfaction of seeing, in the pre-dawn light, the waves lift the black armor and slam it against the jutting rocks.

"Take that and be damned to you," Gerard said. Mounting his horse, clad only in leather breeches and a well-worn woolen shirt, he set off west.

He hoped that with fair weather and good roads he might reach Lord Ulrich's manor in ten days. Gerard soon glumly revised his plan, hoped to reach the manor house in ten years, for at that point everything began to go strangely wrong. His horse threw a shoe in a region where no one had ever heard of a blacksmith. Gerard had to travel miles out of his way, leading his lame horse, to find one. When he did come across a blacksmith, the man worked so slowly that Gerard wondered if he was mining the iron and then forging it.

Days passed before his horse was shod and he was back in the saddle, only to discover that he was lost. The sky was cloudy and overcast. He could see neither sun nor stars, had no idea which direction he was heading. The land was sparsely populated. He rode for hours without seeing a soul. When he did come upon someone to ask directions, everyone in the land appeared to have suddenly gone stupid, for no matter what route he was told to take, the road always landed him in the middle of some impenetrable forest or stranded him on the banks of some impassable river.

Gerard began to feel as if he were in one of those terrible dreams, where you know the destination you are trying to reach, but you can never quite seem to reach it. At first he was annoyed and frustrated, but after days and days of wandering he began to feel uneasy.

Galdar's poisoned sword lodged in Gerard's gut.

"Am I making the decisions or is Takhisis?" he asked himself. "Is she determining my every move? Am I dancing to her piping?"

Constant rain soaked him. Cold winds chilled him. He had been forced to sleep outdoors for the past few nights, and he was just asking himself drearily what was the use of going on, when he saw the lights of a small town shining in the distance. Gerard came upon a road house. Not much to look at, it would provide a roof over his head, hot food and cold drink and, hopefully, information.

He led his horse to the stable, rubbed the animal down and saw to it that the beast was fed and resting comfortably. This done, he entered the road house. The hour was late, the innkeeper had gone to bed and was in a foul mood at being wakened. He showed Gerard to the common room, indicated a place on the floor. As the Knight spread out his blanket, he asked the innkeeper for the name of the town.

The man yawned, scratched himself, muttered irritably, "The town is Tyburn. On the road to Palanthas."

Gerard slept fitfully. In his dreams, he wandered about inside a house, searching for the door and never finding it. Waking long before morning, he stared at the ceiling and realized that he was now completely and thoroughly lost. He had the feeling the innkeeper was lying about the town's name and location, although why he should lie was a mystery to Gerard, except that he now suspected everyone he met of lying.

He went down to breakfast. Sitting in a rickety chair, he poked at a nameless mass that a scullery maid termed porridge. Gerard had lost his appetite. His head ached with a dull, throbbing pain. He had no energy, although he'd done nothing but ride about aimlessly the day before. He had the choice of doing that again today or going back to his blanket. Shoving aside the porridge, he walked over to the dirty window, rubbed off a portion of soot with his hand, and peered out. The drizzling rain continued to fall.

"The sun has to shine again sometime," Gerard muttered.

"Don't count on it," said a voice.

Gerard glanced around. The only other person in the inn was a mage, or at least that's what Gerard presumed, for the man was clad in reddish brown robes—the color of dried blood—and a black, hooded cloak. The mage sat in a small alcove as near the fire burning in the large stone hearth as he could manage. He was ill, or so Gerard assumed, for the mage coughed frequently, a bad-sounding cough that seemed to come from his gut. Gerard had noticed him when he first entered, but because he was a mage, Gerard had left his fellow traveler to himself.

Gerard hadn't thought he'd spoken loudly enough to be heard on the other side of the room, but apparently what this inn lacked in amenities it made up for in acoustics.

He could make some polite rejoinder or he could pretend he hadn't heard. He decided on the latter. He was in no mood for companionship, especially companionship that appeared to be in the last stages of consumption. He turned back to continue staring out the window.

"She rules the sun," the mage said. His voice was weak, with a whispering quality to it that Gerard found eerily compelling. "Although she no longer rules the moon." He gave what might have been a laugh, but it was interrupted by a fit of coughing. "She will soon rule the stars if she is not stopped."

Finding this conversation disturbing, Gerard turned around. "Are you speaking to me, sir?"

The mage opened his mouth, but was halted by another fit of coughing. He pressed a handkerchief to his lips, drew in a shuddering breath. "No," he rasped, irritated, "I am speaking for the joy of spitting up blood. Talking is not so easy for me that I waste my breath on it."

The shadow of the hood concealed the mage's face. Gerard glanced about. The maid had vanished back into a smoke-filled kitchen. Gerard and the mage were the only two in the room. Gerard moved closer, determined to see the man's face.

"I refer, of course, to Takhisis," the mage continued. He fumbled in the pocket of his robes. Drawing out a small, cloth pouch, he placed it on the hob. A pungent smell filled the room.

"Takhisis!" Gerard was astounded. "How did you know?" he asked in a low voice, coming to stand beside the mage.

"I have known her long," said the mage in his whispering voice, soft as velvet. "Very long, indeed." He coughed again briefly and motioned with his hand. "Fetch the kettle and pour some hot water into that mug."

Gerard didn't move. He stared at the hand. The skin had a gold tint to it, so that it glistened in the firelight like sunlit fish scales.

"Are you deaf as well as doltish, Sir Knight?" the mage demanded.

Gerard frowned, not liking to be insulted and not liking to be ordered about, especially by a total stranger. He was tempted to bid this mage a cold good morning and walk out. The mage's conversation interested him, however. He could always walk out later.

Lifting the kettle with a pair of tongs, Gerard poured out the hot water. The mage dumped the contents of the pouch into the mug. The smell of the mixture was noxious, caused Gerard to wrinkle his nose in disgust. The mage allowed the tea to steep and the water to cool before he drank it.

Gerard found a chair, dragged it over.

"Do you know where I am, sir? I've been riding for days without benefit of sun or stars or compass to guide me. Everyone I ask tells me something different. This innkeeper tells me that this road leads to Palanthas. Is that right?"

The mage sipped at his drink before he answered. He kept his hood pulled low over his head, so that his face was in shadow. Gerard had the impression of keen, bright eyes, with something a bit wrong with them. He couldn't make out what.

"He is telling the truth as far as it goes," said the mage. "The road leads to Palanthas—eventually. One might say that all roads that run east and west lead to Palanthas—eventually. What you should be more concerned with now is that the road leads to Jelek."

"Jelek!" Gerard exclaimed. Jelek—the headquarters of the Dark Knights. Realizing that his alarm might give him away, he tried to pass it off with a shrug. "So it leads to Jelek. Why should that concern me?"

"Because at this moment twenty Dark Knights and a few hundred foot soldiers are bivouacked outside of Tyburn. They march to Sanction, answering Mina's call."

"Let them camp out where they will," said Gerard coolly. "I have nothing to fear from them."

"When they find you here, they will arrest you," said the mage, continuing to sip at his tea.

"Arrest me? Why?"

The mage lifted his head, glanced at him. Again, Gerard had the impression there was something wrong with the man's eyes.

"Why? Because you might as well have 'Solamnic Knight' stamped in gold letters on your forehead."

"Nonsense," said Gerard with a laugh, "I am but a traveling merchant—"

"A merchant without goods to sell. A merchant who has a military bearing and close-cropped hair. A merchant who wears a sword in the military manner, counts cadence when he walks, and rides a trained war-horse." The mage snorted. "You couldn't fool a six-year-old girlchild."

He went back to drinking his tea.

"Still, why should they come here?" Gerard asked lightly, though his nervousness was increasing.

"The innkeeper knew you for a Solamnic Knight the moment he saw you." The mage finished his tea, placed the empty mug upon the hob. His cough had noticeably improved. "Note the silence from the kitchen? The Dark Knights frequent this place. The innkeeper is in their pay. He left to tell them you were here. He will gain a rich reward for turning you in."

Gerard looked uneasily toward the kitchen that had grown strangely quiet. He shouted out loudly for the innkeeper.

There was no response.

Gerard crossed the room and flung open the wooden door that led to the cooking area. He startled the scullery maid, who confirmed his fears by giving a shriek and fleeing out the back door.

Gerard returned to the common room.

"You are right," said Gerard. "The bastard has run off, and the maid screamed as though I was likely to slit her throat. I had best be going." He held out his hand. "I want to thank you, sir. I'm sorry, but I never asked your name or gave you mine. . . ."

The mage ignored the outstretched hand. He took hold of a wooden staff that had been resting against the chimney and used it to support himself as he regained his feet.

"Come with me," the mage ordered.

"I thank you for your warning, sir," said Gerard firmly, "but I must depart and swiftly—"

"You will not escape," said the mage. "They are too close. They rode out with the dawn, and they will be here in minutes. You have only one chance. Come with me."

Leaning on the staff, which was decorated with a gold dragon claw holding a crystal, the mage led the way to stairs that went to the upper floor. His motions were quick and fluid, belying his frail appearance. His nondescript robes rustled around his ankles. Gerard hesitated another moment, his gaze going to the window. The road was empty. He could hear no sounds of an army, no drums, no stamp of marching feet.

Who is this mage that I should trust him? Just because he seems to know what I am thinking, just because he spoke of Takhisis . . .

The mage paused at the foot of the staircase. He turned to face Gerard. The strange eyes glittered from the shadows.

"You spoke once of following your heart. What is in your heart now, Sir Knight?"

Gerard stared, his tongue stuck to the roof of his mouth.

"Well?" said the mage impatiently. "What is in your heart?"

"Despair and doubt," said Gerard at last, his voice faltering, "suspicion, fear . . ."

"Her doing," said the mage. "So long as these shadows remain, you will never see the sun." He turned, continued walking up the stairs.

Gerard heard sounds now, sounds of men shouting orders, sounds of jingling harness and the clash of steel. He ran for the stairs.

The lower level contained the kitchen, an eating room, and a large common room where Gerard had passed the night. The upper level contained separate rooms for the convenience of better-paying guests, as well as the innkeeper's private quarters, protected by a door that was locked and bolted.

The mage walked straight up to this door. He tried the handle, which wouldn't budge, then touched the lock with the crystal of his staff. Light flared, half blinding Gerard, who stood blinking and staring at blue stars for long moments. When he could see, the mage had pushed open the door. Tendrils of smoke curled out from the lock.

"Hey, you can't go in there—" Gerard began.

The mage cast him a cold glance. "You are starting to remind me of my brother, Sir Knight. While I loved my brother, I can truthfully say of him that there were times he irritated me to death. Speaking of death, yours is not far off." The mage pointed with his staff into the room. "Open that wooden chest. No, not that one. The one in the corner. It is not locked."

Gerard gave up. In for a copper, in for a steel as the saying went. Entering the innkeeper's room, he knelt beside the large wooden chest the mage had indicated. He lifted the lid, stared down at an assortment of knives and daggers, the odd boot, a pair of gloves, and pieces of armor: bracers, grieves, epaulets, a cuirass, helms. All of the armor was black, some stamped with the emblem of the Dark Knights.

"Our landlord is not above stealing from his guests," said the mage. "Take what you need."

Gerard dropped the lid of the chest with a bang. He stood up, backed off. "No," he said.

"Disguising yourself as one of them is your only chance. There is not much there, to be sure, but you can cobble something together, enough to pass."

"I just rid myself of an entire suit of that accursed stuff—'

"Only a sentimental fool would be that stupid," the mage retorted, "and thus I am not surprised to hear that you did it. Put on what armor you can. I'll loan you my black cloak. It covers a multitude of sins, as I have come to know."

"Even if I am disguised, it won't matter anyway," Gerard said. He was tired of running, tired of disguises, tired of lying. "You said the innkeeper told them about me."

"He is an idiot. You have a quick wit and a glib tongue." The mage shrugged. "The ruse may not work. You may still hang. But it seems to me to be worth the risk."

Gerard hesitated a moment longer. He may have been tired of running, but he wasn't yet tired of living. The mage's plan seemed a good one. Gerard's sword, a gift from Marshal Medan, would be recognized. His horse still bore the trappings of a Dark Knight, and his boots were like those worn by the Dark Knights.

Feeling more and more as if he were caught in a terrible trap in which he was continually running out the back only to find himself walking in the front, he grabbed up what parts of the armor he thought might fit him, began hastily buckling them onto various parts of his body. Some were too big and others painfully small. He looked, when he finished, like an armored harlequin. Still, with the black cloak to cover him, he might just pull it off.

"There," he said, turning around. "How do I—"

The mage was gone. The black cloak he had promised lay on the floor.

Gerard stared about the room. He hadn't heard the mage depart, but then he recalled that the man moved quietly. Suspicion crept into Gerard's mind, but he shrugged it off. Whether the strange mage was for him or against him didn't much matter now. He was committed.

Gerard picked up the black cloak, tossed it over his shoulder, and hastened from the landlord's room. Reaching the stairs, he looked out a window, saw a troop of soldiers drawn up outside. He resisted the urge to run and hide. Clattering down the stairs, he walked out door to the road house. Two soldiers, bearing halberds, shoved him rudely in their haste to enter.

"Hey!" Gerard called out angrily. "You damn near knocked me down. What is the meaning of this?"

Abashed, the two halted. One touched his hand to his forehead. "I beg pardon, Sir Knight, but we're in a hurry. We've been sent to arrest a Solamnic who is hiding in this inn. Perhaps you have seen him. He is wearing a shirt and leather breeches, tries to pass himself off as a merchant."

"Is that all you know of him?" Gerard demanded. "What does he look like? How tall is he? What color hair does he have?"

The soldiers shrugged, impatient. "What does that matter, sir. He's inside. The innkeeper told us we would find him here."

"He *was* in there," said Gerard. "You just missed him." He nodded his head. "He rode off that way not fifteen minutes ago."

"Rode off!" The soldier gaped. "Why didn't you stop him?"

"I had no orders to stop him," said Gerard coldly. "The bastard is none of my concern. If you make haste, you can catch him. Oh, and by the way, he's a tall, handsome man, about twenty-five years old, with jet-black hair and a long black mustache. What are you standing there staring at me for like a pair of oafs? Be off with you."

Muttering to themselves, the soldiers dashed out the door and down the street, not even bothering to salute. Gerard sighed, gnawed his lip in frustration. He supposed he should be grateful to the mage who had saved his life, but he wasn't. At the thought of yet more lying, dissembling, deceiving, of being always on his guard, always fearful of discovery, his spirits sank. He honestly wondered if he could do it. Hanging might be easier, after all.

Removing his helm, he ran his fingers through his yellow hair. The black cloak was heavy. He was sweating profusely, but dared not discard it. In addition, the cloak had a peculiar smell—reminding him of rose petals combined with something else not nearly as sweet or as pleasant. Gerard stood in the doorway, wondering what to do next.

The soldiers were escorting a group of prisoners. Gerard paid little attention to the poor wretches, beyond thinking he might have been one of them.

The best course of action, he decided, would be to ride away during the confusion. If anyone stops me, I can always claim to be a messenger heading somewhere with something important.

He stepped out into the street. Glancing up in the sky, he noted with pleasurable astonishment that the rain had ceased, the clouds departed. The sun shone brightly.

A very strange sound, like the bleat of a pleased goat, caused him to turn around.

Two pairs of gleaming eyes stared at him over the top of a gag. The eyes were the eyes of Tasslehoff Burrfoot, and the bleat was the glad and cheerful bleat of Tasslehoff Burrfoot.

The Tasslehoff Burrfoot.

23

In Which It Is Proven That Not All Kender Look Alike

The sight of Tasslehoff there, right in front of him, affected Gerard like a lightning blast from a blue dragon, left him dazed, paralyzed, incapable of thought or action. He was so amazed he simply stared. Everyone in the world was searching for Tasslehoff Burrfoot—including a goddess—and Gerard had found him.

Or rather, more precisely, this troop of Dark Knights had found the kender. Tasslehoff was among several dozen kender who were being herded to Sanction. Every single one of them probably claimed to be Tasslehoff Burrfoot. Unfortunately, one of them really was.

Tasslehoff continued to bleat through the gag, and now he was trying his best to wave. One of the guards, hearing the unusual sound, turned around. Gerard quickly clapped his helm over his head, nearly slicing off his nose in the process, for the helm was too small.

"Whoever's making that noise, stop it!" the guard shouted. He bore down on Tasslehoff, who—not watching where he was going—stumbled over his manacles and tumbled to the street. His fall jerked two of the kender who were chained to him off their feet. Finding this a welcome interlude in an otherwise dull and boring march, the other kender jerked themselves off their feet, with the result that the entire line of some forty kender was cast into immediate confusion.

Two guards, wielding flails, waded in to sort things out. Gerard strode swiftly away, almost running in his eagerness to leave the vicinity before something worse happened. His brain hummed with a confusion of thoughts, so that he moved in a kind of daze without any real idea of where he was going. He blundered into people, muttered excuses. Stepping into a hole, he wrenched his ankle and almost fell into a water trough. At last, spotting a shadowy alley, he ducked into it. He drew in several deep breaths. The cool air soothed his sweat-covered brow, and he was at last able to catch his breath and sort out the tangle.

Takhisis wanted Tasslehoff, she wanted the kender in Sanction. Gerard had a chance to thwart her, and in this, Gerard knew he followed the dictates of his own heart. The shadow lifted. The seeds of a plan were already sprouting in his mind.

Giving a mental salute to the wizard and wishing him well, Gerard headed off to put his plan, which involved finding a knight Gerard's own height and weight and, hopefully, head size, into action.

The Dark Knights and their foot soldiers set up camp in and around the town of Tyburn, bedded down for the night. The commander and his officers took over the road house, not much of a triumph, for its food was inedible and its accommodations squalid. The only good thing that could be said of the ale was that it made a man pleasantly light-headed and helped him forget his problems.

The commander of the Dark Knights drank deeply of the ale. He had a great many problems he was glad to drown, first and foremost of which was Mina, his new superior.

The commander had never liked nor trusted Lord Targonne, a small-minded man who cared more for a bent copper than he did for any of the troops under his command. Targonne did nothing to advance the cause of the Dark Knights but concentrated instead on filling his own coffers. No one in Jelek had mourned Targonne's death, but neither did they rejoice at Mina's ascension.

True, she was advancing the cause of the Dark Knights, but she was advancing at such a rapid pace that she had left most of them behind to eat her dust. The commander had been shocked to hear that she had conquered Solanthus. He wasn't sure that he approved. How were the Dark Knights to hold both that city and Solanthus and the Solamnic lord city of Palanthas?

This blasted Mina never gave a thought to guarding what she'd taken. She never gave a thought to supply lines stretched too thin, men overworked, the dangers of the populace rising in revolt.

The commander sent letters explaining all this to Mina, urging her to slow down, build up her forces, consolidate her winnings. Mina had forgotten someone else, too—the dragon overlord Malys. The commander had been sending conciliatory messages to the dragon, maintaining that the Dark Knights had no designs on her rulership. All this new territory they were conquering was being taken in her name, and so forth. He'd heard nothing in response.

Then, a few days ago, he had received orders from Mina to pull out of Jelek and march his forces south to help reinforce Sanction against a probable attack by a combined army of elves and Solamnics. He was to set forth immediately, and while he was at it, he was to round up and bring along any kender he happened to come across.

Oh, and Mina thought it quite likely that Malys was also going to attack Sanction. So he was to be prepared for that eventuality, as well.

Even now, rereading the orders, the commander felt the same shock and outrage he'd experienced reading them the first two dozen times. He had been tempted to disobey, but the messenger who had delivered the message made it quite clear to the commander that Mina and this One God of hers had a long reach. The messenger provided several examples of what had happened to commanders who thought they knew better than Mina what course of action to take, starting with the late Lord Targonne himself. Thus the commander now found himself on the road to Sanction, sitting in this wretched inn, drinking tepid ale, of which to say it tasted like horse piss was to give it a compliment it didn't deserve.

This day had gone from bad to worse. Not only had the kender slowed up their progress by tangling themselves in their chains—a tangle that had taken hours to sort out—the commander had lost a Solamnic spy, who'd been tipped off to their coming. Fortunately, they now had a good description of him. With his long black hair and black mustache, he should be easy to apprehend.

The commander was drowning his problems in ale when he looked up to see yet another messenger from Mina come walking through the door. The commander would have given all of his wealth to hurl the mug of ale at the man's head.

The messenger came to stand before him. The commander glowered balefully and did not invite him to be seated.

Like most messengers, who needed to travel light, this one was clad in black leather armor covered by a thick black cloak. He removed his helm, placed it under his arm, and saluted.

"I come in the name of the One God."

The commander snorted in his ale. "What does the One God want with me now? Has Mina captured Ice Wall? Am I supposed to march there next?"

The messenger was an ugly fellow with yellow hair, a pockmarked face, and startling, blue eyes. The blue eyes stared at the commander, obviously baffled.

"Never mind." The commander sighed. "Deliver your message and be done with it."

"Mina has received word that you have captured several kender prisoners. As you may know, she is searching for one kender in particular."

"Burrfoot. I know," said the commander. "I have forty or so Burrfoots out there. Take your pick."

"I will do that, with your permission, sir," said the messenger respectfully. "I know this Burrfoot by sight. Because the matter of his capture is so very urgent, Mina has sent me to look over your prisoners to see if I can find him among them. If he is, I'm to carry him to Sanction immediately."

The commander looked up in hope. "You wouldn't like to take all forty, would you?"

The messenger shook his head.

"No, I didn't think so. Very well. Go look for the blasted thief." A thought occurred to him. "If you do find him, what am I supposed to do with the rest?"

"I have no orders regarding that, sir," said the messenger, "but I would think you might as well release them."

"Release them . . ." The commander stared more closely at the messenger. "Is that blood on your sleeve? Are you wounded?"

"No, sir," said the messenger. "I was attacked by bandits on the road."

"Where? I'll send out a patrol," said the commander.

"No need to bother, sir," said the messenger. "I resolved the matter."

"I see," said the commander, who thought he noted blood on the leather armor, too. He shrugged. None of his concern. "Go search for this Burrfoot, then. You, there. Escort this man immediately to the pen where we keep the kender. Give him any assistance he requires." Raising his mug, he added, "I drink to your success, sir."

The messenger thanked the commander and departed.

The commander ordered another ale. He mulled over what to do with the kender. He was considering lining them all up and using them for target practice, when he heard a commotion at the door, saw yet another messenger.

Groaning inwardly, the commander was about to tell this latest nuisance to go roast himself in the Abyss, when the man shoved back his hat, and the commander recognized one of his most trusted spies. He motioned him forward.

"What news?" he asked. "Keep your voice down."

"Sir, I've just come from Sanction!"

"I said keep your voice down. No need to let everyone know our business," the commander growled.

"It won't matter, sir. Rumor follows fast on my heels. By morning, everyone will know. Malys is dead. Mina killed the dragon."

The crowd in the alehouse fell silent, everyone too stunned to speak, each trying to digest this news and think what it might mean to him.

"There's more," said the spy, filling the vacuum with his voice. "It is reported that Mina is dead, too."

"Then who is in charge?" the commander demanded, rising to his feet, his ale forgotten.

"No one, sir," said the spy. "The city is in chaos."

"Well, well." The commander chuckled. "Perhaps Mina was right, and prayers are answered after all. Gentlemen," he said, looking around at his officers and staff, "no sleep for us tonight. We ride to Sanction."

One down, thought Gerard to himself, tramping off behind the commander's aide. One to go.

Not the easiest, either, he thought gloomily. Hoodwinking a half-drunken commander of the Dark Knights had been goblin-play compared to what lay ahead—extricating one kender from the herd. Gerard could only hope that the Dark Knights, in their infinite wisdom, had seen fit to keep the kender gagged.

"Here they are," said the aide, holding up a lantern. "We have them penned up. Makes it easier."

The kender, huddled together like puppies for warmth, were asleep. The night air was cold, and few had cloaks or other protection from the chill. Those who did shared with their fellows. In repose, their faces looked pinched and wan. Obviously the commander wasn't wasting food on them, and he certainly wasn't concerned about their comfort.

The kenders' manacles were still attached, as were their leg irons and—Gerard breathed a hefty sigh of relief—their gags were still in place. Several soldiers stood guard. Gerard counted five, and he suspected there might be more he couldn't see.

At the bright light, the kender lifted their heads and blinked sleepily, yawning around the gags.

"On your feet, vermin," order the Knight. Two of the soldiers waded into the pen to kick the kender into wakefulness. "Stand up and look smart. Turn toward the light. This gentleman wants to see your dirty faces."

Gerard spotted Tasslehoff right away. He was about three-quarters of the way down the line, gaping and peering about and scratching his head with a manacled hand. Gerard had to make a show of inspecting every single kender, however, and this he did, all the while keeping one eye on Tas.

He looks old, Gerard realized suddenly. I never noticed that before.

Tas's jaunty topknot was still thick and long. Gray streaks were noticeable here and there, however, and the wrinkles on his face were starkly etched in the strong light. Still, his eyes were bright, his bearing bouncy, and he was watching the proceedings with his usual interest and intense curiosity.

Gerard walked down the line of kender, forcing himself to take his time. He wore a leather helm to conceal his face, afraid that Tas would recognize him again and make a glad outcry. His scheme did not work, however, for Tasslehoff shot one inquisitive look through the eyeslits of the helm, saw Gerard's bright blue eyes, and beamed all over. He couldn't speak, due to the gag, but he gave a wriggle expressive of his pleasure.

Coming to a halt, Gerard stared hard at Tas, who—to Gerard's dismay—gave a broad wink and grinned as wide as the gag would permit. Gerard grabbed hold of the kender's topknot and gave it a good yank.

"You don't know me," he hissed out from behind the helm.

"OfcourseIdont," mumbled the gagged Tas, adding excitedly, "Iwassosurprisedtoseeyouwherehave-youbeen—"

Gerard straightened. "This is the kender," he said loudly, giving the topknot another yank.

"This one?" The aide was surprised. "Are you sure?"

"Positive," said Gerard. "Your commander has done an outstanding job. You may be certain that Mina will be most pleased. Release the kender immediately into my custody. I'll take full responsibility for him."

"I don't know . . ." The aide hesitated.

"Your commander said I was to have him if I found him," Gerard reminded the man. "I've found him. Now release him."

"I'm going to go bring back the commander," said the aide.

"Very well, if you want to disturb him. He looked pretty relaxed to me," Gerard said with a shrug.

His ploy didn't work. The aide was one of those loyal, dedicated types who would not take a crap without asking for permission. The aide marched off. Gerard stood in the pen with the kender, wondering what to do.

"I overplayed my hand," Gerard muttered. "The commander could decide that the kender is so valuable he'll want to take him himself to claim the reward! Blast! Why didn't I think of that?"

Tasslehoff had, meanwhile, managed to work the gag loose, dislodging it with such ease that Gerard could only conclude he'd kept it on for the novelty.

"*I don't know you,*" said Tasslehoff loudly and gave another conspiratorial wink that was guaranteed to get them both hung. "What's your name?"

"Shut up," Gerard shot out of the corner of his mouth.

"I had a cousin by that name," observed Tas reflectively.

Gerard tied the gag firmly in place.

He eyed the two guards, who were eyeing him back. He'd have to act quickly, couldn't give them a chance to cry out or start a racket. The old ruse of pretending to find scattered steel coins on the ground might work. He was just about to gasp and stare and point in astonishment, readying himself to whack the two in the head when they came over to look, when a commotion broke out behind him.

Torchlight flared up and down the road. People began shouting and rushing about. Doors slammed and banged. Gerard's first panicked thought was that he'd been discovered and that the entire army was turning out to seize him. He drew his sword, then realized that the soldiers weren't running toward him. They were running away from him, heading for the road house. The two guards had lost interest in him entirely, were staring and muttering, trying to figure out what was going on.

Gerard heaved a sigh. This alarm had nothing to do with him. He forced himself to stand still and wait.

The aide did not return. Gerard muttered in impatience.

"Go find out what's going on," he ordered.

One guard ran off immediately. He stopped the first person he came to, then turned and pounded back their direction.

"Malys is dead!" he shouted. "And so is that Mina girl! Sanction is in turmoil. We're marching there straight away."

"Malys dead?" Gerard gaped. "*And* Mina?"

"That's the word."

Gerard stood dazed, then came to his senses. He'd served in the army a good many years, and he knew that rumors were a copper a dozen. This might be true—he hoped it was—but it might not be. He had to act under the assumption that it wasn't.

"That's all very well, but I still need the kender," he said stubbornly. "Where's the commander's aide?"

"It was him I talked to." The guard fumbled at his belt. Producing a ring of keys, he tossed them to Gerard. "You want the kender? Here, take 'em all."

"I don't want them all!" Gerard cried, aghast, but by that time, the two guards had dashed off to join the throng of troops massing in the road.

Gerard looked back to find every single kender grinning at him.

Freeing the kender did not prove easy. When they saw that Gerard had the keys, the kender set up a yell that must have been heard in Flotsam and surged around him, raising their manacled hands, each kender demanding that Gerard unlock him or her first. Such was the tumult that Gerard was nearly knocked over backward and lost sight of Tasslehoff in the mix.

Bleating and waving his hand, Tasslehoff battled his way to the front of the pack. Gerard got a good grip on Tas's shirt and began to work at the locks on the chains on his hands and feet. The other kender milled about, trying to see what was going on, and more than once jerked the chains out of Gerard's grip. He cursed and shouted and threatened and was even forced to shove a few, who took it all in good humor. Eventually—he was never to know how—he managed to set Tasslehoff free. This done, he tossed the keys into the midst of the remaining kender, who pounced on them gleefully.

Gerard grabbed the bedraggled, disheveled, straw-covered Tasslehoff and hurried him off, keeping one eye on Tas and the other on the turmoil among the troops.

Tas ripped off his gag. "You forgot to remove it," he pointed out.

"No, I didn't," said Gerard.

"I am so glad to see you!" Tas said, squeezing Gerard's hand and stealing his knife. "What have you been doing? Where have you been? You'll have to tell me everything, but not now. We don't have time."

He came to a halt, began fumbling about for something in his pouch. "We have to leave."

"You're right, we don't have time for talk." Gerard retrieved his knife, grabbed Tas by the arm and hustled him along. "My horse is in the stable—"

"Oh, we don't have time for the horse either," said Tasslehoff, wriggling out of Gerard's grasp with the ease of an eel. "Not if we're going to reach the Knights'

Council in time. The elves are marching, you see, and they're about to get into terrible trouble and—well, things are happening that would take too long to explain. You'll have to leave your horse behind. I'm sure he'll be all right, though."

Tas pulled out an object, held it to the moonlight. Jewels sparkled on its surface, and Gerard recognized the Device of Time Journeying.

"What are you doing with that?" he asked uneasily.

"We're going to use it to travel to the Knights' Council. At least, I *think* that's where it's going to take us. It's been acting funny these past few days. You wouldn't believe the places I've been—"

"Not me," said Gerard, retreating.

"Oh, yes, you," said Tasslehoff, nodding his head so vigorously that his topknot flipped over and struck him in the nose. "You have to come with me because they won't believe *me*. I'm just a kender. Raistlin says they'll believe you, though. When you tell them about Takhisis and the elves and all—"

"Raistlin?" Gerard repeated, trying desperately to keep up. "Raistlin who?"

"Raistlin Majere. Caramon's brother. You met him in the road house this morning. He was probably mean and sarcastic to you, wasn't he? I knew it." Tas sighed and shook his head. "Don't pay any attention. Raistlin always talks like that to people. It's just his way. You'll get used to it. We all have."

The hair on Gerard's arms prickled. A chill crept up his back. He remembered hearing Caramon's stories about his brother—the red robes, the tea, the staff with the crystal, the mage's barbed tongue . . .

"Stop talking nonsense," said Gerard in a decided tone. "Raistlin Majere is dead!"

"So am I," said Tasslehoff Burrfoot. He smiled up at Gerard. "You can't let a little thing like that stop you."

Reaching out, Tas took hold of the Knight's hand. Jewels flashed, and the world dropped out from under Gerard's feet.

24

The Decision

When Gerard was young, a friend of his had concocted a swing for their entertainment. His friend suspended a wooden board, planed smooth, between two ropes and tied the ropes to a high tree branch. The lad then persuaded Gerard to sit in the swing while he turned him round and round, causing the ropes to twist together. At that point, his friend gave the swing a powerful shove and let loose. Gerard went spinning in a wildly gyrating circle that ended only when he pitched out of the swing and landed facedown on the grass.

Gerard experienced exactly the same sensation with the Device of Time Journeying, with the notable exception that it didn't dump him facedown. It might as well have, though, for when his feet touched the blessed grass, he didn't know if he was up or down, on his head or his heels. He staggered about like a drunken gnome, blinking, gasping, and trying to get his bearings. Wobbling about beside him, the kender also looked rattled.

"As many times as I've done that," said Tasslehoff, mopping his forehead with a grimy sleeve, "I never seem to get used to it."

"Where are we?" Gerard demanded, when the world had ceased to spin.

"We *should* be attending a Knights' Council," said Tasslehoff, dubious. "That's where we wanted to go, and that's the thought I thought in my head. But whether we're at the *right* Knights' Council is another question. We might be at Huma's Knights' Council, for all I know. The device has been acting very oddly." He shook his head, glanced about. "Does anything look familiar?"

The two had been deposited in a heavily forested tract of land on the edge of a stubbly wheat field that had long since been harvested. The thought came to Gerard that he was lost yet again, and this time a kender had lost him. He had no hope that he would ever be found and was just about to say so when he caught a glimpse of a large stone building reminiscent of a fortress or a manor. Gerard squinted, trying to bring the flag fluttering from the battlements into focus.

"It looks like the flag of Lord Ulrich," said Gerard, astonished. He looked all around him more closely now and thought that he recognized the landscape. "This *could* be Ulrich manor," he said cautiously.

"Is that where we're supposed to be?" Tas asked.

"It's where they were holding the Knights' Council the last time I was here," said Gerard.

"Well done," said Tasslehoff, giving the device a pat. He dropped it back carelessly into his pouch and stared expectantly at Gerard.

"We should hurry," he said. "Things are happening."

"Yes, I know," said Gerard, "but we can't just say we dropped out of the sky." He cast an uneasy glance upward.

"Why not?" Tas was disappointed. "It makes a great story."

"Because no one will believe us," Gerard stated. "I'm not sure I believe us." He gave the matter some thought. "We'll say that we rode from Sanction and my horse went lame and we had to walk. Got that?"

"It's not nearly as exciting as dropping out of the sky," Tas said. "But if you say so," he added hurriedly, seeing Gerard's eyebrows meet together in the middle of his forehead.

"What is the horse's name?" he asked, as they started off across the field, the stubble crunching beneath their feet.

"What horse?" Gerard muttered, absorbed in his thoughts that continued to whirl, even though he was, thankfully, on solid ground.

"Your horse," said Tas. "The one that went lame."

"I don't have a horse that went lame . . . Oh, that horse. It doesn't have a name."

"It *has* to have a name," said Tas severely. "All horses have names. I'll name it, may I?"

"Yes," said Gerard in a rash moment, thinking only to shut the kender up so he could try to sort out the puzzle of the strange mage and the extremely fortuitous and highly coincidental discovery of the kender in exactly the right place, in exactly the right time.

A walk of about a mile brought them to the manor house. The Knights had transformed it into an armed camp. Sunlight glinted off the steel heads of pikes. The smoke of cook fires and forge fires smudged the sky. The green grass was trampled with hundreds of feet and dotted with the colorful striped tents of the Knights. Flags representing holdings from Palanthas to Estwilde flapped in the brisk autumn wind. The sounds of hammering, metal on metal, rang through the air. The Knights were preparing to go to war.

After the fall of Solanthus, the Knights had sent out the call to defend their homeland. The call was answered. Knights and their retainers marched from as far as Southern Ergoth. Some impoverished Knights arrived on foot, bringing with them nothing but their honor and their desire to serve their country. Wealthy Knights brought their own troops, and treasure boxes filled with steel to hire more.

"We're going to see Lord Tasgall, Knight of the Rose and head of the Knights' Council," said Gerard. "Be on your best behavior, Burrfoot. Lord Tasgall doesn't tolerate any nonsense."

"So few people do," said Tas sadly. "I really think it might be a better world all the way around if more people did. Oh, I've thought of your horse's name."

"Have you?" Gerard asked absently, not paying attention.

"Buttercup," said Tasslehoff.

"That is my report," said Gerard. "The One God has a name and a face. Five faces. Queen Takhisis. How she managed to achieve this miracle, I cannot say."

"I can," Tasslehoff interrupted, leaping to his feet.

Gerard shoved the kender back into his chair.

"Not now," he said, for the fortieth time. He continued speaking. "Our ancient enemy has returned. In the heavens, she stands alone and unchallenged. In this world, though, there are those who are willing to give their lives to defeat her."

Gerard went on to tell of his meeting with Samar, spoke of the promise of that warrior that the elves would ally themselves with the Knights to attack Sanction.

The three lords glanced at each other. There had been much heated debate among the leadership as to whether the Knights should try to recapture Solanthus before marching to Sanction. Now, with Gerard's news, the decision was almost certainly going to be made to launch a major assault on Sanction.

"We received a communiqué stating that the elves have already begun their march," said Lord Tasgall. "The road from Silvanesti is long and fraught with peril—"

"The elves are going to be attacked!" Tasslehoff sprang out of his chair again.

"Remember what I said about the nonsense!" Gerard said sternly, shoving the kender back down.

"Does your friend have something to say, Gerard?" asked Lord Ulrich.

"Yes," said Tasslehoff, standing up.

"No," said Gerard. "That is, he always has something to say, but not anything we need to listen to."

"We have no guarantee that the elves will even arrive in Sanction," Lord Tasgall continued, "nor can we say *when* they will arrive. Meanwhile, according to reports we have been receiving from Sanction, all is in confusion there. Our spies confirm the rumor that Mina has vanished and that the Dark Knights are engaged in a leadership struggle. If we judge by events of the past, someone will rise to take her place, if that has not happened already. They will not be leaderless for long."

"At least," said Lord Ulrich, "We don't have to worry about Malys. This Mina managed to do what none of us had the guts to do. She fought Malys and killed her." He raised a silver goblet. "I drink to her. To Mina! To courage."

He gulped down the wine noisily. No one else raised a glass. The others appeared embarrassed. The Lord of the Rose fixed a stern gaze upon Lord Ulrich, who—by his flushed features and slurred words—had taken too much wine already.

"Mina had help, my lord," said Gerard gravely.

"You might as well call the goddess by name," said Lord Siegfried in dire tones. "Takhisis."

Lord Tasgall looked troubled. "It is not that I doubt the veracity of Sir Gerard, but I cannot believe—"

"Believe it, my lord," called Odila, entering the hall.

She was thin and pale, her white robes covered in mud and stained with blood. By her appearance, she had traveled far and slept and eaten little.

Gerard's gaze went to her breast, where the medallion of her faith had once hung. Its place was empty.

Gerard smiled at her, relieved. She smiled back. Her smile was her own, he was thankful to see. A bit tremulous, perhaps, and not quite as self-assured or self-confident as when he had first met her, but her own.

"My lords," she said, "I bring someone who can verify the information presented to you by Sir Gerard. His name is Mirror, and he helped rescue me from Sanction."

The lords looked in considerable astonishment at the man Odila brought forward. His eyes were wrapped in bandages that only partially concealed a terrible wound that had left him blind. He walked with a staff, to help him feel his way. Despite his handicap, he had an air of quiet confidence about him. Gerard had the feeling he'd seen this man somewhere before.

The Lord of the Rose made a stiff bow to the blind man, who, of course, could not see it. Odila whispered something to Mirror, who bowed his head. Lord Tasgall turned his complete attention to Odila. He regarded her sternly, his face impassive.

"You come to us a deserter, Sir Knight," he said. "It has been reported you joined with this Mina and served her, did her bidding. You worshiped the One God and performed miracles in the name of the One God, a god we now learn is our ancient foe, Queen Takhisis. Are you here because you have recanted? Do you claim to have discarded your faith in the god you once served? Why should we believe you? Why should we think that you are anything more than a spy?"

Gerard started to speak up in her defense. Odila rested her hand on his arm, and he fell silent. Nothing he could say would do any good, he realized, and it might do much harm.

Odila bent down on one knee before the lords. Although she knelt before them, she did not bow her head. She looked at all of them directly.

"If you expect shame or contrition from me, my lords, you will be disappointed. I am a deserter. That I do not deny. Death is the punishment for desertion, and I accept that punishment as my due. I offer only in my defense that I went in search of what we all are seeking. I went in search of a power greater than my own, a power to guide me and comfort me and give me the knowledge that I was not alone in this vast universe. I found such a power, my lords. Queen Takhisis, our god, has returned to us. I say 'our' god, because she is that. We cannot deny it.

"Yet I say to you that you must go forth and fight her, my lords. You must fight to halt the spread of darkness that is fast overtaking our world. But in order to fight her, you must arm yourselves with your faith. Reverence her, even as you oppose her. Those who follow the light must also acknowledge the darkness, or else there is no light."

Lord Tasgall gazed at her, his expression troubled. Lord Siegfried and Lord Ulrich spoke softly together, their eyes on Odila.

"Had you made a show of contrition, Lady, I would not have believed you," said Lord Tasgall at last. "As it is, I must consider what you say and think about it. Rise, Odila. As to your punishment, that will be determined by the council. In the meantime, I am afraid that you must be confined—"

"Do not lock her away, my lord," urged Gerard. "If we are going to attack Sanction, we are going to need all the experienced warriors we can muster. Release her into my care. I guarantee that I will bring her safely to trial, as she did me when I was on trial before you in Solanthus."

"Will this suit you, Odila?" asked the Lord of the Rose.

"Yes, my lord." She smiled at Gerard, whispered to him in an undertone. "It seems our destiny to be shackled together."

"My lords, if you're going to attack Sanction, you could probably use the help of some gold and silver dragons," Tasslehoff stated, jumping to his feet. "Now that Malys is dead, all the red dragons and the blue dragons and the black and the green will come to Sanction's defense—"

"I think you had better remove the kender, Sir Gerard," said the Lord of the Rose.

"Because the gold and silver dragons *would* come," Tasslehoff shouted over his shoulder, squirming in Gerard's grasp. "Now that the totem is destroyed, you see. I'd be glad to go fetch them myself. I have this magical device—"

"Tas, be quiet!" said Gerard, his face flushed with the exertion of trying to retain a grip on the slippery kender.

"Wait!" the blind man called out, the first words he'd spoken. He had been standing so quietly that everyone in the hall had forgotten his presence.

Mirror walked toward the sound of the kender's voice, his staff impatiently striking and knocking aside anything that got in his way. "Don't remove him. Let me talk to him."

The Lord of the Rose frowned at this interruption, but the man was blind, and the Measure was strict in its admonition that the blind, the lame, the deaf, and the dumb were to be treated with the utmost respect and courtesy.

"You may speak to this person, of course, sir. Seeing that you are sadly afflicted and lack sight, I think it only right to tell you, however, that he is naught but a kender."

"I am well aware that he is a kender, my lord," said Mirror, smiling. "That makes me all the more eager to speak to him. In my opinion, kender are the wisest people on Krynn."

Lord Ulrich laughed heartily at this odd statement, to receive another reproving glance from Lord Tasgall. The blind man reached out a groping hand.

"I'm here, sir," said Tas, catching hold of Mirror's hand and shaking it. "I'm Tasslehoff Burrfoot. *The* Tasslehoff Burrfoot. I tell you that because there's a lot of me going around these days, but I'm the only real one. That is, the others are real, they're just not really me. They're themselves, if you take my meaning, and I'm myself."

"I understand," said blind man solemnly. "I am called Mirror and *I* am, in reality, a silver dragon."

Lord Tasgall's eyebrows shot up to his receding hairline. Lord Ulrich sputtered in his wine. Lord Siegfried snorted. Odila smiled reassuringly at Gerard and nodded complacently.

"You say that you know where the silver and gold dragons are being held prisoner?" Mirror asked, ignoring the Knights.

"Yes, I know," Tasslehoff began, then he halted. Having been termed one of "the wisest people on Krynn," he felt called upon to tell the truth. "That is, the device knows." He patted his pouch where the Device of Time Journeying was secreted. "I could take you there, if you wanted," he offered, without much hope.

"I would like to go with you very much," said Mirror.

"You would?" Tasslehoff was astonished, then excited. "You would! That's wonderful. Let's go! Right now!" He fumbled about in his pouch. "Could I ride on your back? I love flying on dragons. I knew this dragon once. His name was Khirsah, I think, or something like that. He took Flint and I riding, and we fought a battle, and it was glorious."

Tas halted his fumbling, lost in reminiscences. "I'll tell you the whole story. It was during the War of the Lance—"

"Some other time," Mirror interrupted politely. "Speed is imperative. As you say, the elves are in danger."

"Oh, yes." Tas brightened. "I'd forgotten about that." He began once again to fumble in his pouch. Retrieving the device, Tas took hold of Mirror by the hand. The kender held the device up over his head and began to recite the spell.

Waving to the astonished Knights, Tas cried, "See you in Sanction!"

He and Mirror began to shimmer, as if they were oil portraits that someone had left out in the rain. At the last moment, before he had disappeared completely, Mirror reached out, seized hold of Odila, who reached out to take hold of Gerard.

In an eyeblink, all four of them vanished.

"Good grief!" exclaimed the Lord of the Rose.

"Good riddance," sniffed Lord Siegfried.

25

Into the Valley

The elven army marched north, made good time. The warriors rose early and slept late, speeding their march with songs and tales of the old days that lightened their burdens and gladdened their hearts.

Many of the Silvanesti songs and stories were new to Gilthas, and he delighted in them. In turn, the stories and songs of the Qualinesti were new to their cousins, who did not take so much delight in them, since most were concerned with the Qualinesti's dealing with lesser races such as humans and dwarves. The Silvanesti listened politely and praised the singer if they could not praise the song. The one song the Silvanesti did not sing was the song of Lorac and the dream.

When the Lioness traveled among them, she sang the songs of the Wilder elves, and these, with their stories of floating the dead down rivers and living wild and half-naked in the treetops, succeeded in shocking the sensibilities of both Qualinesti and Silvanesti, much to the amusement of the Wilder elves. The Lioness and her people were rarely among them, however. She and her Wilder elves acted as outriders, guarding the army's flanks from surprise attacks, and riding in advance of the main body to scout out the best routes.

Alhana seemed to have shed years. Gilthas had thought her beautiful when he'd first met her, but her beauty had a frost upon it, as a late-blooming rose. Now, she walked in autumn's bright sunshine. She was riding to save her son, and she could ride with honor, for she believed that Silvanoshei had redeemed himself. He was being held prisoner, and if he had landed himself in this predicament by his near fatal obsession with this human girl, her mother's heart could conveniently forget that part of the tale.

Samar could not forget it, but he kept silent. If what Sir Gerard had told him about Silvanoshei proved true, then perhaps this hard experience would help the young fool grow into a wise man, worthy of being king. For Alhana's sake, Samar hoped so.

Gilthas marched with his own misgivings. He had hoped that once they were on the road, he could cast off his dark fears and forebodings. During the day he was able to do so. The singing helped. Songs of valor and courage reminded him that there had been heroes of old, who had overcome terrible odds to drive back the darkness, that the elven people had undergone greater trials than this and had not only survived, but thrived. In the night, however, trying to sleep while missing the comfort of his wife's arms around him, dark wings hovered over him, blotted out the stars.

One matter worried him. They heard no news from Silvanesti. Admittedly, their route would be difficult for a runner to follow, for Alhana had not been able to tell the runners exactly where to find them. She had sent back runners of her own to act as guides, however, while every chipmunk would be able to give news of their passing. Time passed without word. No new runners came, and their own runners did not return.

Gilthas mentioned this to Alhana. She said sharply that the runners would come when they came and not before and it was not worth losing sleep and wasting one's energy worrying about it.

The elves traveled north at a prodigious pace, eating up the miles, and soon they had entered the southern portion of the Khalkist Mountains. They had long ago crossed the border into ogre lands, but they saw no signs of the ancient enemy, and it seemed that their strategy—to march along the backbone of the mountains, hiding themselves in the valleys—was working. The weather was fine, with cool days that were cloudless and sunny. Winter held back her heavy snow and frost. There were no mishaps on the trail, none fell seriously ill.

If there had been gods, it might have been said that they smiled upon the elves, so easy was this portion of their march. Gilthas began to relax, let the warm sun melt his worries as it melted the light dusting of snowflakes that sometimes fell in the night. Exhaustion from the long day's march and the crisp mountain air forced sleep upon him. He slept long and deeply and woke refreshed. He could even remind himself of the old human adage, "No news is good news," and find some comfort in that.

Then came the day that Gilthas would remember for the rest of his life, remember every small detail, for on that day life changed forever for the elves of Ansalon.

It began as any other. The elves woke with the first gray light of dawn. Packing up their bedrolls with practiced haste, they were on the march before the sun had yet lifted up over the mountaintops. They ate as they walked. Food was harder to come by in the mountains where vegetation was sparse, but the elves had foreseen this and filled their packs with dried berries and nutmeats.

They were still many hundred miles from Sanction, but all spoke confidently of their journey's end, which seemed no more than a few weeks away. The dawn was glorious. The Qualinesti elves sang their ritual song to welcome the sun, and this morning the Silvanesti joined in. The sun and the marching burned away night's chill. Gilthas marveled at the beauty of the day and of the mountains. He could never feel at home among mountains, no elf could, but he could be moved and awed by their stark grandeur.

Then, behind him came the pounding of horse's hooves. Ever after, when he heard that sound, he was swept back in time to this fateful day. A rider was pushing the horse to the limit, something unusual on the narrow, rocky trails. The elves continued to march, but many cast wondering glances over their shoulders.

The Lioness rode into view, the sun lighting her golden hair so that it seemed she was bathed in fire. Gilthas would remember that, too.

He reined in his horse, his heart filled suddenly with dread. He knew her, knew the grim expression

on her face. She rode past him, heading for the front
of the column. She said nothing to him, but cast him
a single glance as she galloped by, a glance that sent
him spurring after her. He saw now that there were
two people on the horse. A woman sat behind the
Lioness, a woman clad in the green, mottled clothing of a Silvanesti runner. That was all Gilthas
noticed about her before the Lioness's mad charge
carried her around a bend in the narrow trail and
out of his sight.

He rode after her. Elves were forced to scatter in
all directions or be ridden down. Gilthas had a brief
glimpse of staring eyes and concerned faces. Voices
cried out, asking what was going on, but the words
whipped past him and he did not respond. He rode
recklessly, fear driving him.

He arrived in time to see Alhana turn her horse's
head, stare back in astonishment at the Lioness, who
was shouting in her crude Silvanesti for the queen to
halt. The runner dismounted, sliding off the back of
the horse before the Lioness could stop the plunging
animal. The runner took a step, then collapsed onto
the ground. The Lioness slid off her horse, knelt
beside the fallen runner. Alhana hastened to her,
accompanied by Samar. Gilthas joined them, gesturing to Planchet, who marched at the head of the
column with the Silvanesti commanders.

"Water," Alhana commanded. "Bring water."

The runner tried to speak, but the Lioness wouldn't
permit her, not until she had drunk something.
Gilthas was close enough now to see that the runner
was not wounded, as he had feared, but weak from
exhaustion and dehydration. Samar offered his own
waterskin, and the Lioness gave the runner small

sips, encouraging her with soothing words. After a draught or two, the runner shook her head.

"Let me speak!" she gasped. "Hear me, Queen Alhana! My news is . . . dire. . . ."

Among humans, a crowd would have gathered around the fallen, ears stretched, anxious to see and hear what they could. The elves were more respectful. They guessed by the commotion and the hurry that the news this runner bore was probably bad news, but they kept their distance, patiently waiting to be told whatever they needed to know.

"Silvanesti has been invaded," said the runner. She spoke weakly, dazedly. "Their numbers are countless. They came down the river in boats, burning and looting the fishing villages. So many boats. None could stop them. They entered Silvanesti, and even the Dark Knights feared them, and some fled. But they are allies now. . . ."

"Ogres?" Alhana asked in disbelief.

"Minotaurs, Your Majesty," said the runner. "Minotaurs have allied with the Dark Knights. The numbers of our enemies are vast as the dead leaves in autumn."

Alhana cast Gilthas one burning-eyed glance, a glance that seared through flesh and bone and struck him in the heart.

You were right, the glance said to him. *And I was wrong*.

She turned her back on him, on them all, and walked away. She repulsed even Samar, who would have gone to her.

"Leave me," she commanded.

The Lioness bent over the runner, giving her more water. Gilthas was numb. He felt nothing. The news was too enormous to comprehend. Standing there, trying to make sense of this, he noticed that the runner's feet were bruised and bloody. She had worn out her boots, run the last miles barefoot. He could feel nothing for his people, but her pain and heroism moved him to tears. Angrily, he blinked them away. He could not give in to grief, not now. He strode forward, determined to talk to Alhana.

Samar saw Gilthas coming and made a move as if to intercept him. Gilthas gave Samar a look that plainly said the man could try, but he might have a tough time doing it. After a moment's hesitation, Samar backed off.

"Queen Alhana," said Gilthas.

She lifted her face, that was streaked with tears. "Spare me your gloating," she said, her voice low and wretched.

"This is no time to speak of who was right and who was wrong," Gilthas said quietly. "If we had stayed to lay siege to Silvanesti, as I counseled, we would all probably be dead right now or slaves in the belly of a minotaur galley." He rested his hand gently on her arm, was shocked to feel her cold and shivering. "As it is, our army is strong and intact. It will take some time for the armies of our enemies to entrench themselves. We can return and attack, take them by surprise—"

"No," said Alhana. She clasped her arms around her body, set her teeth and, through sheer effort of will, forced herself to stop shaking. "No, we will continue on to Sanction. Don't you see? If we help the human armies conquer Sanction, they will be honor-bound to help us free our homeland, drive out the invaders."

"Why should they?" he asked sharply. "What reason would humans have to die for us?"

"Because we will help them fight for Sanction!" Alhana stated.

"Would we be doing that if your son were not being held prisoner inside Sanction's walls?" Gilthas demanded.

Alhana's skin, cheeks, lips were all one, all ashen. Her dark eyes seemed the only living part of her, and they were smudged with shadow.

"We Silvanesti will march to Sanction," she said. She did not look at him. She stared southward, as if she could see through the mountains and into her lost homeland. "You Qualinesti may do what you like."

Turning from him, she said to Samar. "Summon our people. I must speak to them."

She walked away, tall, straight-backed, shoulders squared.

"Do you agree with this?" Gilthas demanded of Samar as he started to follow her.

Samar cast Gilthas a look that might have been a backhanded blow across the face, and Gilthas realized he had been wrong to ask. Alhana was Samar's queen and his commander. He would die before he questioned any decision she made. Gilthas had never before felt so utterly frustrated, so helpless. He was filled with raging anger that had no outlet.

"We have no homeland," he said, turning to Planchet. "No homeland at all. We are exiles, people without a country. Why can't she see that? Why can't she understand?"

"I think she does," said Planchet. "For her, attacking Sanction is the answer."

"The wrong answer," said Gilthas.

Elven healers came to tend to the runner, treating her wounds with herbs and potions, and they shooed the Wilder elf away. The Lioness walked over to join him.

"What are we doing?"

"Marching to Sanction," Gilthas said grimly. "Did the runner have any news of our people?"

"She said that there were rumors they had managed to escape Silvanesti, flee back into the Plains of Dust."

"Where they will most certainly *not* be welcome." Gilthas sighed deeply. "The Plainspeople warned us of that."

He stood, troubled. He wanted desperately to return to his people, and he realized now that the anger he was feeling was aimed at himself. He should have followed his instincts, remained with his people, not marched off on this ill-fated campaign.

"I was wrong, as well. I opposed you. I am sorry, my husband," said the Lioness remorsefully. "But don't punish yourself. You could not have stopped the invasion."

"At least I could be with our people now," he said bitterly. "Sharing their trouble, if nothing else."

He wondered what he should do. He longed to go back, but the way would be hard and dangerous, and the odds were he would never make it alone. If he took away Qualinesti warrriors, he would leave Alhana's force sadly depleted. He might cause dissension in the ranks, for some Silvanesti would certainly want to return to their homes. At this time, more than any other, the elves needed to be united.

A shout rang from the rear, then another and another, all up and down the line. Alhana stopped in the midst of her speech, turned to look. The cries were coming from every direction now, thundering down on them like the rocks of an avalanche.

"Ogres!"

"What direction?" the Lioness called out to one of her scouts.

"All directions!" he cried and pointed.

Their line of march had carried the elves into a small, narrow valley, surrounded by high cliffs. Now, as they looked, the cliffs came alive. Thousands of huge, hulking figures appeared along the heights, stared down at the elves, and waited in silence for the order to start the killing.

26

The Judgment

The gods of Krynn met once again in council. The gods of light stood opposite the gods of darkness, as day stands opposite night, with the gods of neutrality divided evenly in between. The gods of magic stood together, and in their midst was Raistlin Majere.

Paladine nodded, and the mage stepped forward.

Bowing, he said simply, "I have been successful."

The gods stared in wordless astonishment, all except the gods of magic, who exchanged smiles, their thoughts in perfect accord.

"How was this accomplished?" Paladine asked at last.

"My task was not easy," Raistlin said. "The currents of chaos swirl about the universe. The magic is wayward and unwieldy. I no more set my hand upon it than it slides through my fingers. When the kender used the device, I managed to seize hold of him and wrench him back into the past, where the winds of chaos blow less fiercely. I was able to keep Tas there long enough for him to have a sense of where he was before the magic whipped away from me and I lost him. I knew where to look for him, however, and thus, when next he used the device, I was ready. I took him to a time we both recognized, and he began to know me. Finally, I carried him to the present. Past and present are now linked. You have only to follow the one, and it will lead you to the other."

"What do you see?" Paladine asked Zivilyn.

"I see the world," said Zivilyn softly, tears misting his eyes. "I see the past, and I see the present, and I see the future."

"Which future?" asked Mishakal.

"The path the world walks now," Zivilyn replied.

"Then it is not possible to alter it?" Mishakal asked.

"Of course, it is possible," said Raistlin caustically. "We may all yet cease to exist."

"You mean that the blasted kender is not yet dead?" Sargonnas growled.

"He is not. The power of Queen Takhisis has grown immense. If you are to have any hope of defeating her, Tasslehoff has yet one important task to accomplish with the Device of Time Journeying. If he accomplishes this task—"

"—he must be sent back to die," said Sargonnas.

"He will be given the choice," Paladine corrected. "He will not be forced back or sent against his wishes. He has freedom of will, as do all living beings upon Krynn. We cannot deny that to him, just because it suits our convenience."

"Suits our convenience!" Sargonnas roared. "He could destroy us all!"

"If that is the risk we run for our beliefs," said Paladine, "then so be it. Your queen, Sargonnas, disdained free will. She found it easier to rule slaves. You opposed her in that. Would your minotaurs worship a god who made them slaves? A god who denied them their right to determine their own fate, a right to find honor and glory?"

"No, but then my minotaurs have sense. They are not brainless kender," muttered Sargonnas, but he muttered it into his fur. "That brings us to the next question, however. Providing this kender does not yet get us all killed"—he cast a baleful glance at Paladine—"what punishment do we mete out to the goddess whose name I will never more speak? The goddess who betrayed us?"

"There can be only one punishment," said Gilean, resting his hand upon the book.

Paladine looked around. "Are we all agreed?"

"So long as the balance is maintained," said Hiddukel, the keeper of the scales.

Paladine looked at each of the gods. Each, in turn, nodded. Last, he looked at his mate, his beloved Mishakal. She did not nod. She stood with her head bowed.

"It must be," said Paladine gently.

Mishakal lifted up her eyes, looked long and lovingly into his. Then, through her tears, she nodded.

Paladine rested his hand upon the book. "So be it," he said.

27

Tasslehoff Burrfoot

asslehoff's life had been made up of glorious moments. Admittedly, there had been some bad moments, too, but the glorious moments shone so very brightly that their radiance overwhelmed the unhappy moments, causing them to fade back into the inner recesses of his memory. He would never forget the bad times, but they no longer had the power to hurt him. They only made him a little sad.

This moment was one of the glorious moments, more glorious than any moment that had come before, and it kept improving, with each coming moment shining more gloriously than the next.

Tas was now growing accustomed to traveling through space and time, and while he continued to feel giddy and disoriented every time the device dumped him out at a destination, he decided that such a sensation, while not suited to everyday use, made for an exhilarating change. This time, after landing and stumbling about a bit and wondering for an exciting instant if he was going to throw up, the wooziness receded, and he was able to look around and take note of his surroundings.

The first thing he saw was an immense silver dragon, standing right beside him. The dragon's eyes were horribly wounded by a jagged scar that slashed across them, and Tas recognized the blind man who had spoken to him in the Knights' Council. The dragon, like Tas, appeared to have taken the journey through time in stride, for he was fanning his wings gently and turning his head this way and that, sniffing the air and listening. Either traveling through time did not bother dragons, or being blind kept one from getting dizzy. Tas wondered which it was and made a mental note to ask during a lull in the proceedings.

His other two companions were not faring quite as well. Gerard had not liked the journey the first time, so he could be excused for really not liking it the second time. He swayed on his feet and breathed heavily.

Odila was wide-eyed and gasping and reminded Tas of a poor fish he'd once found in his pocket. He had no idea how the fish had come to be there, although he did have a dim sort of memory that someone had lost it. He'd managed to restore the fish to water, where, after a dazed moment, it had swum off. The fish had the same look that Odila had now.

"Where are we?" she gasped, clinging to Gerard with a white-knuckled grip.

He looked grimly at the kender. One and all, they looked grimly at the kender.

"Right were we're supposed to be," Tas said confidently. "Where the Dark Queen has kept the gold and silver dragons prisoners." Gripping the device tightly in his hand, he added a soft, "I hope!" that didn't come out all that softly and rather spoiled matters.

Tas had never been anywhere like this before. All around him was gray rock and nothing except gray rock as far as the eye could see. Sharp gray rocks, smooth gray rocks, enormous gray rocks, and small gray rocks. Mountains of gray rock, and valleys of the same gray rock. The sky above him was black as the blackest thing he'd ever seen, without a single star, and yet he was bathed in a cold white light. Beyond the gray rock, on the horizon, shimmered a wall of ice.

"I feel stone beneath my feet," said Mirror, "and I do not smell vegetation, so I assume the land in which we have arrived is bleak and barren. I hear no sounds of any kind: not the waves breaking on the shore, not the wind rushing through the trees, no sound of bird or animal. I sense that this place is desolate, forbidding."

"That about sums it up," said Gerard, wiping sweat from his forehead with the back of his hand. "Add to that description the fact that the sky above us is pitch black, there is no sun, yet there is light; the air is colder than a troll's backside, and this place appears to be surrounded by what looks like a wall made of icicles, and you have said all there is to say about it."

"What he didn't say," Tas felt called upon to point out, "is that the light makes the wall of ice shimmer with all sorts of different colors—"

"Rather like the scales of a many-colored dragon?" Mirror asked.

"That's it!" Tas cried, enthused. "Now that you come to mention it, it does look like that. It's lovely in a sort of cold and unlovely way. Especially how the colors shift whenever you look at them, dancing all along the icy surface . . ."

"Oh, shut up!" ordered Gerard.

Tas sighed inwardly. As much he liked humans, traveling with them certainly took a lot of joy out of the journey.

The cold was biting. Odila shivered, wrapped her robes around her more closely. Gerard stalked over to the ice wall. He did not touch it. He looked it up and down. Drawing his dagger, he jabbed the weapon's point into the wall.

The blade shattered. Gerard dropped the knife with an oath, wrung his hand in pain, then slid his hand beneath his armpit.

"It's so damn cold it broke the blade! I could feel the chill travel through the metal and strike deep into my bone. My hand is still numb."

"We can't survive long in this," Odila said. "We humans will perish of the cold, as will the kender. I can't speak for the dragon."

Tas smiled at her to thank her for including him.

"As for me," said Mirror, "my species is cold-blooded. My blood will thicken and grow sluggish. I will soon lose my ability to fly or even to think clearly."

"And except for you," said Gerard grumpily, looking around the barren wasteland on which they stood, "I don't see a single dragon."

Tasslehoff was forced to admit that he was feeling the chill himself and that it was causing very unpleasant sensations in his toes and the tips of his fingers. He thought with regret back to a fur-lined vest he'd once owned, and he wondered whatever became of it. He wondered also what had become of the dragons, for he was absolutely positive—well, relatively certain—that this was the place where he'd been told he would find them. He peered under a few gray rocks with no luck.

"You better take us back, Tas," said Odila, as best she could for her teeth clicking together.

"He can't take us back," said Mirror, and the dragon was oddly complacent. "This place was constructed as a prison for dragons. It has frozen the magic in my blood. I doubt if the magic of the device will work either."

"We're trapped here!" Gerard said grimly. "To freeze to death!"

Tasslehoff drew himself up. This was a glorious moment, and while admittedly it didn't look or feel very glorious (he'd lost all feeling in his toes), he knew what he was doing.

"Now, see here," he said sternly, eyeing Gerard. "We've been through a lot together, you and I. If it wasn't for me, you wouldn't be where you are today. That being the case," he added hurriedly, before Gerard could reply, "follow me."

He turned around, bravely confident, ready to proceed forward, without having the least idea where he was going.

A voice said softly, distinctly, in his ear, "Over the ridge."

"Over the ridge," said Tasslehoff. Pointing at the first ridge of gray rock that he saw, he marched off that direction.

"Should we go after him?" Odila asked.

"We don't dare lose him," said Gerard.

Tas clamored among the gray stones, dislodging small rocks that slid and slithered out from under him and went clattering and bounding down behind him, seriously impeding Odila and Gerard, who were attempting to climb up after him. Glancing back, Tas saw that Mirror had not moved. The silver dragon continued to stand where he had landed, fanning his wings and twitching his tail, probably to try to keep his blood stirring.

"He can't see," said Tasslehoff, stung by guilt. "And we've left him behind, all alone. Don't worry, Mirror!" he called out. "We'll come back for you."

Mirror said something in response, something that Tas couldn't quite hear clearly, what with all the noise that Odila and Gerard were making dodging rocks, but it seemed to him that he heard, "The glory of this moment is yours, kender. I will be waiting."

"That's the great thing about dragons," Tas said to himself, feeling warm all over. "They always understand."

Topping the ridge, he looked down, and his breath caught in his throat.

As far as the eye could see were dragons. Tasslehoff had never seen so many dragons in one place at one time. He had never imagined that there were so many gold and silver dragons in the world.

The dragons slumbered in a cold-induced torpor. They pressed together for warmth, heads and necks entwined, bodies lying side by side, wings folded, tails wrapped around themselves or their brother dragons. The strange light that caused rainbows to dance mockingly in the ice wall stole the colors from the dragons, left them gray as the rocky peaks that surrounded them.

"Are they dead?" Tas asked, his heart in his throat.

"No," said the voice in his ear, "they are deeply asleep. Their slumber keeps them from dying."

"How do I wake them?"

"You must bring down the ice wall."

"How do I do that? Gerard's knife broke when he tried it."

"A weapon is not what is needed."

Tas thought this over, then said doubtfully, "Can I do it?"

"I don't know," the voice said. "Can you?"

"By all that is wonderful!" Gerard exclaimed. Pulling himself up to the top of the ridge, he now stood beside Tasslehoff. "Would you look at that!"

Odila said nothing. She stood long moments, gazing down at the dragons, then she turned and ran back down the ridge. "I will go tell Mirror."

"I think he knows," said Tasslehoff, then he added, politely, "Excuse me. I have something to do."

"Oh, no. You're not going anywhere!" Gerard cried and made a snatch at Tasslehoff's collar.

He missed.

Tasslehoff began running full tilt, as fast as he could run. The climb had warmed his feet. He could feel his toes—essential for running—and he ran as he had never run before. His feet skimmed over the ground. If he stepped on a loose rock that might have sent him tumbling, he didn't touch it long enough to matter. He fairly flew down the side of the ridge.

He gave himself to the running. The wind buffeted his face and stung his eyes. His mouth opened wide. He sucked in great mouthfuls of cold air that sparkled in his blood. He heard shouts, but their words meant nothing in the wind of his running. He ran without thought of stopping, without the means of stopping. He ran straight at the ice wall.

Wildly excited, Tas threw back his head. He opened his mouth and cried out a loud "Yaaaa" that had absolutely no meaning but just felt good. Arms spread wide, mouth open wide, he crashed headlong into the wall of shimmering ice.

Rainbow droplets fell all around him. Sparkling in a radiant silver light, the droplets plopped down on his upturned face. He raced through the curtain of water that had once been a wall of ice, and he continued to run, out of control, running, madly running, and then he saw that just ahead of him, almost at his feet, the gray rock ended abruptly and there was nothing below it except black.

Tas flailed his arms, trying to stop. He struggled with his feet, but they seemed to have minds of their own, and he knew with certainty that he was going to sail right off the edge.

My last moment, but a glorious one, he thought.

He was falling, and silver wings flew above him. He felt a claw seize hold of his collar (not a new sensation, for it seemed that someone was always seizing hold of his collar), except that this was different. This was a most welcome seize.

Tas hung suspended over eternity.

He gasped for breath that he couldn't seem to find. He was dizzy and light-headed. Tilting back his head, he saw that he dangled from the claw of a silver dragon, a silver dragon who turned his sightless eyes in the general direction of the kender.

"Thank goodness you kept yelling," said Mirror, "and thank goodness Gerard saw your peril in time to warn me."

"Are they free?" Tasslehoff asked anxiously. "The other dragons?"

"They are free," said Mirror, veering slowly about, returning to what Tas could see now was nothing more than an enormous island of gray rock adrift in the darkness.

"What are you and the other dragons going to do?" Tas asked, starting to feel better now that he was over solid ground.

"Talk," said Mirror.

"Talk!" Tasslehoff groaned.

"Don't worry," said Mirror. "We are keenly aware of the passing of time. But there are questions to be asked and answered before we can make any decision." His voice softened. "Too many have sacrificed too much for us to ruin it all by acting rashly."

Tas didn't like the sound of that. It made him feel extremely sad, and he was about to ask Mirror what he meant, but the dragon was now lowering the kender to the ground. Gerard caught hold of Tasslehoff in his arms. Giving him a hug, he set him on his feet. Tas concentrated on trying to breathe. The air was warmer, now that the ice wall was gone. He could hear wings beating and the dragons' voices, deep and resonant, calling out to each other in their ancient language.

Tas sat on the gray rocks and waited for his breathing to catch up with him and for his heart to realize that he'd quit running and that it didn't need to beat so frantically. Odila went off with Mirror to serve as his guide, and he soon heard the silver dragon's voice rising in joy at finding his fellows. Gerard remained behind. He didn't tromp about, as usual, peering into this and investigating that. He stood looking down at Tas with a most peculiar expression on his face.

Maybe he has a stomach ache, Tas thought.

As for Tasslehoff, since he didn't have breath enough to talk, he spent some time thinking.

"I never quite looked at it that way," he thought to himself.

"What did you say?" Gerard asked, squatting down to be level with the kender.

Tas made up his mind. He could talk now and he knew what he had to say. "I'm going back."

"We're all going back," Gerard stated, adding, with an exasperated glance in the direction of the dragons, "eventually."

"No, I don't mean that," said Tas, having trouble with a lump in his throat. "I mean I'm going back to die." He managed a smile and a shrug. "I'm already dead, you know, so it won't be such a huge change."

"Are you sure about this, Tas?" Gerard asked, regarding the kender with quiet gravity.

Tas nodded. "'Too many have sacrificed too much . . .' that's what Mirror said. I thought about that when I ran off the edge of the world. If I die here, I said to myself, where I'm not supposed to, everything dies with me. And then, do you know what happened, Gerard? I felt scared! I've never been scared before." He shook his head. "Not like that."

"The fall would be enough to scare anyone," said Gerard.

"It wasn't the fall," Tas said. "I was scared because I knew if everything died, it would all be my fault. All the sacrifices that everybody has made down through history: Huma, Magius, Sturm Brightblade, Laurana, Raistlin . . ." He paused, then said softly, "Even Lord Soth. And countless others I'll never know. All their suffering would be wasted. Their joys and triumphs would be forgotten."

Tasslehoff pointed. "Do you see that red star? The one there?"

"Yes," said Gerard. "I see it."

"The kender tell me that people in the Fifth Age believe Flint Fireforge lives in that star. He keeps his forge blazing so that people will remember the glory of the old days and that they will have hope. Do you think that's true?"

Gerard started to say that he thought the star was just a star and that a dwarf could never possibly live in a star, but then, seeing Tas's face, the Knight changed his mind.

"Yes, I think it's true."

Tas smiled. Rising to his feet, he dusted himself off, looked himself over, twitched his clothes and his pouches into place. After all, if he was going to be stepped on by Chaos, he had to look presentable.

"That red star is the very first star I'm going to visit. Flint will be glad to see me. I expect he's been lonely."

"Are you going now?" Gerard asked.

"'No time like the present,'" Tas said cheerfully. "That's a time-travel joke," he added, eyeing Gerard. "All us time travelers make time-travel jokes. You're supposed to laugh."

"I guess I don't feel much like laughing," Gerard said. He rested his hand on Tas's shoulder. "Mirror was right. You are wise, perhaps the very wisest person I know, and certainly the most courageous. I honor you, Tasslehoff Burrfoot."

Drawing his sword, Gerard saluted the kender, the salute one true Knight gives to another.

A glorious moment.

"Goodbye," Tasslehoff said. "May your pouches never be empty."

Reaching into his pouch, he found the Device of Time Journeying. He looked at it, admired it, ran his

527

fingers over the jewels that sparkled more brightly than he ever remembered seeing them sparkle before. He caressed it lovingly, then, looking out at the red star, he said, "I'm ready."

"The dragons have finally reached a decision. They're about ready to return to Krynn," said Odila. "And they want us to go with them." She glanced about. "Where's the kender? Have you lost him again?"

Gerard wiped his nose and his eyes and thought, smiling, of all the times he'd wished he could have lost Tasslehoff Burrfoot.

"He's not lost," Gerard said, reaching out to take hold of Odila's hand. "Not anymore."

At that moment, a shrill voice spoke from the darkness.

"Hey, Gerard, I almost forgot! When you get back to Solace, be sure to fix the lock on my tomb. It's broken."

28

The Valley of Fire and Ice

The ogres did not attack immediately. They had laid their ambush well. The elves were trapped in the valley, their advance blocked, their retreat cut off. They weren't going anywhere. The ogres could start the assault at a time of their own choosing, and they chose to wait.

The elves were prepared to do battle now, the ogres reasoned. Courage pumped in their veins. Their enemy had come upon them so suddenly and unexpectedly that the elves had no time for fear. But let the day linger on, let the night come. Let them lie sleepless on their blankets and stare at the bonfires ringed around them. Let them count the numbers of their enemies, and let fear multiply those numbers, and by next day's dawning, elf stomachs would shrivel and elf hands shake, and they would puke up their courage on the ground.

The elves moved immediately to repel the enemy attack, moved with discipline, without panic, taking cover in stands of pine trees and brush, behind boulders. Elven archers sought higher ground, picked out their targets, took careful aim and waited for the order to fire. Each archer had an adequate store of arrows, but those would soon be spent, and there would be no more. They had to make every shot count, although the archers could see for themselves that they might spend every arrow they possessed and still not make a dent in the numbers of the enemy.

The elves were ready. The ogres did not attack. Understanding their strategy, Samar ordered the elves to stand down. The elves tried to eat and sleep, but without much success. The stench of the ogres, that was like rotting meat, tainted their food. The light of their fires crept beneath closed eyelids. Alhana walked among them, speaking to them, telling them stories of old to banish their fears and lift their hearts. Gilthas did the same thing, talking to his people, bolstering their spirits, speaking words of hope that he did not himself believe, that no rational person could believe. Yet, it seemed to bring comfort to the people and, oddly, to Gilthas himself. He couldn't understand it, for he had only to look all around to see the fires of his enemies outnumbering the stars. He supposed, cynically, that hope was always the last man standing.

The person Gilthas most sought to comfort refused to be comforted. The Lioness disappeared shortly after bringing the elven runner into camp. She galloped away on her horse, ignoring Gilthas's shout. He searched the camp for her, but no one who had seen her, not even among her own people. He found her at last, long after darkness. She sat on a boulder, far from the main camp. She stared out into the night, and although Gilthas knew that she must have heard him approach, for she could hear a sparrow moving in the woods twenty feet away, she did not turn to look at him.

No need to tell her that she was placing herself in danger of being picked off by some ogre raider. She knew that better than he.

"How many of your scouts are missing?" he asked.

"My fault!" she said bitterly. "My failure! I should have seen something, heard something to keep us from this peril!" She gestured toward the mountain peaks. "Look at that. Thousands of them! Ogres, who shake the ground with their feet and splinter trees and stink like warm cow dung. And I did not see them or hear them! I might as well be blind, deaf, and dumb with my nose cut off for all the good I am!"

After a pause, she added harshly. "Twenty are missing. All of them friends, loyal and dear to me."

"No one blames you," said Gilthas.

"I blame myself!" the Lioness said, her voice choked.

"Samar says that the some of the ogres have grown powerful in magic. Whatever force blocks our magic and causes it to go awry works in the ogres' favor. Their movements were cloaked by sorcery. You could not possibly be faulted for failing to detect that."

The Lioness turned to face him. Her hair was wild and disheveled, hung ragged about her face. The tracks of her tears left streaks of dirt on her cheeks. Her eyes burned.

"I thank you for trying to comfort me, my husband, but my only comfort is the knowledge that my failure will die with me."

His heart broke. He had no words to say. He held out his arms to her, and she lunged into them, kissed him fiercely.

"I love you!" she whispered brokenly. "I love you so much!"

"And I love you," he said. "You are my life, and if that life ends this moment, I count it blessed for having you in it."

He stayed with her, far from camp, all through the night, waiting for those who would never return.

The ogres attacked before dawn, when the sky was pale with the coming of morning. The elves were ready. None had been able to sleep. Each knew in his heart that he would not survive to see the noontide.

The hulking ogres began the assault by rolling boulders down the sides of the cliffs. The boulders were enormous, the size of houses, and here was proof of a goddess's magic, for although ogres are huge, averaging over nine feet in height, and massively built, not even the most powerful ogre was strong enough to wrench those gigantic rocks out of the ground and fling them down the mountainside. The voices of the ogre mages could be heard chanting the magic that was a gift from Queen Takhisis. .

The boulders careened into the valley, forcing the elves who had taken refuge among the rocks to flee and sending elven archers leaping for the lives. The dying screams of those crushed by the rocks echoed among the mountains, to be answered with gleeful hoots by the ogres.

A few angry or panicked elven archers wasted arrows, shooting before the enemy was in range. Samar angrily rebuked those who did, reiterated the command to wait for his orders. Gilthas was no archer. He gripped his sword and waited grimly for the charge. He wasn't very good with his weapon, but he'd been improving—so Planchet told him—and he hoped he would be good enough to at least take a few of the enemy with him and make the spirit of his father and mother proud.

Gilthas was strangely conscious of his mother this morning. He had the feeling that she was beside him, and once he thought he heard her voice and felt her touch. The feeling was so intense that he actually turned to look to see if she stood near him. What he saw was the Lioness, who smiled at him. They would fight together, here at the end, and lie together in death as they had lain together in life.

The ogres were black upon the mountain tops. They raised their spears and shook them, giving the elves a clear view of their fate, and then the ogres gave a cheer that rebounded down the mountain.

The elves gripped their weapons and waited for the onslaught. Gilthas and the Lioness stood among the command group, gathered around Queen Alhana and the elven standards of both the Qualinesti and the Silvanesti.

Finally we are united, only when we face annihilation and it is too late. Gilthas quickly put the bitter thought out of his mind. What was done was done.

Having cleared their way, the ogres began to move inexorably down the mountain, their numbers so great that they blackened the mountain side. The entire ogre nation must be here, Gilthas realized.

He reached out, clasped hold of the Lioness's hand. He would fill his soul with love and let that love carry him to wherever it was souls went.

Samar gave the order to prepare to fire. The elven archers nocked their arrows and took aim. Samar raised his hand, but he did not drop it.

"Wait!" he cried. His eyes squinted as he tried to see more clearly. "What is that, my queen? Am I seeing things?"

Alhana stood on a knoll, from which she could have a view of the battlefield and direct the battle, such as it would be. She was calm, beautiful as ever. More beautiful, if that were possible, fell and deadly. She shaded her eyes with her hands, stared into the east and the sun that had just now lifted above the mountaintops. "The forces near the mountaintop have slowed," she reported coolly, no emotion in her voice, neither elation nor despair. "Some are actually turning around."

"Something has them frightened," cried the Lioness. Lifting her gaze skyward, she pointed. "There! Blessed *E'li!* There!"

Light flared above them, light so brilliant that it seemed to catch the sun and drag its bright rays into the valley, banishing the shadows. At first, Gilthas thought that some miracle had brought the sun to the elves, but then he realized that the light was reflected light—the sun's rays shining off the scales of the belly of a golden dragon.

The Gold dived low, aiming for the side of the mountain that was thick with ogres. At the sight of the resplendent dragon, the marching ranks of the enemy dissolved into a jumbled mess. Mad with terror, the ogres ran up the mountainside and down and even sideways in their panicked effort to escape.

The dragon blasted the hillside with a fiery breath. Jammed together in knots of fear, the ogres died by the hundreds. Their agonized screams echoed among the rocks, screams so horrible that some of the elves covered their ears to blot out the sound.

The Gold sailed up and over the mountain. Smaller silver dragons flew in behind, breathing killing hoarfrost that froze the fleeing ogres, froze their blood, froze their hearts and their flesh. Hard and cold as rock, the bodies toppled over, rolled down into the valley. More golden dragons flew to the attack, so that the sky was aflame with the glitter of their scales. The ogre army that had been racing down gleefully upon their trapped enemy was now in full retreat. The dragons followed them, hunted them down wherever they tried to hide.

The ogres had sent thousands of their people into this fight that was supposed to lop off the head of the elven army and rip out its heart. United under the command of the ogre titans, trained into a disciplined fighting force, the ogres had tracked the elven march with cunning patience, waited for them to enter this valley.

The ogres lost a great many in the battle that day, but their nation was not destroyed, as some elves and humans would later claim. The ogres knew the land, they knew where to find caves in which to hide until the dragons departed. Skulking in the darkness, they licked their wounds and cursed the elves and vowed revenge. The ogres were now firmly allied with the minotaur nation. Penned up on northern islands, its burgeoning population spilling out into the ocean, the minotaurs had long eyed the continent of Ansalon as an area ripe for expansion. Although the ogres had been defeated this day, they would remain firm in their alliance with the minotaurs. A day of reckoning was yet to come.

Those ogres who dashed into the valley and accosted the elves were mad with fury, forgot their training, sought only to kill. The elves dispatched these with ease, and soon the battle was over. The ogres named the battlefield the Valley of Fire and Ice and proclaimed it accursed. No ogre would set foot there ever after.

The tide of battle had turned so swiftly that Gilthas could not comprehend they were safe, could not adjust to the fact that death was not advancing on him with club and spear. The elves were cheering now and singing anthems of joy to welcome the dragons, who wheeled overhead, the sun blazing off their glistening scales.

Two silver dragons broke free of the pack. They circled low, searching for a smooth and level patch of ground on which to land. Alhana and Samar advanced to meet them, as did Gilthas. He marveled at Alhana. He was shaking with the reaction of the sudden release of fear, the sudden return of life and of hope. She faced this reversal in fortune with the same cool aplomb that she had faced certain destruction.

The silver dragons settled to the ground—one of them with swooping, graceful movements, and the other landing as awkwardly as a young dragon fresh from the egg. Gilthas wondered at that, until he saw that this second dragon was maimed, his eyes disfigured and destroyed.

The dragon flew blind, under the guidance of his rider, a Solamnic Knight. Long black braids streamed down from beneath her shining helm. She saluted the queen, but did not dismount. She remained seated on the dragon, her sword drawn, keeping watch as other dragons hunted down and destroyed the remnants of the ogre army. The rider of the second dragon waved his hand.

"Samar!" he shouted.

"It is the Knight, Gerard!" exclaimed Samar, shocked out of his usual stoic complacency. "I would know him anywhere," he added, as Gerard ran toward them. "He is the ugliest human you are ever likely to see, Your Majesty."

"He looks very beautiful to me," said Alhana.

Gilthas heard tears in her voice, if he did not see them on her face, and he began to understand her better. She was frost without, fire within.

Gerard's face brightened when he saw Gilthas, and he came hastening forward to greet the Qualinesti king. Gilthas gestured obliquely with his head. Gerard took the hint and looked to Alhana. He halted dead in his tracks, stared at her, rapt. Too awestruck by beauty to remember his manners, he gaped, his mouth wide open.

"Sir Gerard," she said. "You are a most welcome sight."

Only then, at the sound of her voice, did he recall that he was in the presence of royalty. He sank down on one knee, his head bowed.

"Your servant, Madam."

Alhana extended her hand. "Rise, please, Sir Gerard. I am the one who should kneel to you, for you have saved my people from certain destruction."

"No, Madam, not me," said Gerard, flushing red, looking about as ugly as it was possible for a human to look. "The dragons came to your aid. I just went along for the ride and . . ." He seemed about to add something, but changed his mind.

Turning to Gilthas, Gerard bowed deeply. "I am overjoyed to see that you are alive and well, Your Majesty." His voice softened. "I was deeply grieved to hear of the death of your honored mother."

"Thank you, Sir Gerard," said Gilthas, clasping the Knight by the hand. "I find it strange that the paths of our lives cross once again—strange, yet fortuitous."

Gerard stood awkwardly, his keen blue eyes going from one to the other, searching, seeking.

"Sir Gerard," said Alhana, "you have something else to say. Please, speak without fear. We are deeply in your debt."

"No, you're not, Your Majesty," he said. His speech and manner were clumsy and awkward, as humans must always look to elves, but his voice was earnest and sincere. "I don't want you to think that. It's for this very reason I hesitate to speak, yet"—he glanced toward the sun—"time advances and we stand still. I have dire news to impart, and I dread to speak it."

"If you refer to the minotaur seizure of our homeland, we have been made aware of that," said Alhana.

Gerard stared at her. His mouth opened, shut again.

"Perhaps I can help," she said. "You want us to fulfill the promise Samar made and ride with you to attack Sanction. You fear that we will feel pressured into doing this by the fact that you came to our rescue."

"Lord Tasgall wants me to assure you that the Knights will understand if you feel the need to return to fight for your homeland, Madam," said Gerard. "I can say only that our need is very great. Sanction is guarded by armies of both the dead and the living. We fear that Queen Takhisis plans to try to rule both the mortal world and the immortal. If that happens, if she succeeds, darkness will encompass all of us. We need your help, Madam, and that of your brave warriors if we are to stop her. The dragons have offered to carry you there, for they will also join the battle."

"Have you had news? Is my son Silvanoshei still alive?" Alhana asked, her facing paling.

"I do not know, Madam," Gerard replied evasively. "I hope and trust so, but I have no way of knowing."

Alhana nodded, and then she did something unexpected. She turned to Gilthas. "You know what my answer must be, Nephew. My son is a prisoner. I would do all in my power to free him." Her cheeks stained with a faint flush. "But, as king of your people, you have the right to speak your thoughts."

Gilthas might have felt pleased. He might have felt vindicated. But he had been awake all night. He felt only bone tired.

"Sir Gerard, if we aid the Knights in the capture of Sanction, can we expect the Knights to aid us in the retaking of our homeland?"

"That is up to the Knights' Council, Your Majesty," Gerard replied, uncomfortable. As if aware that his answer was a poor one, he added with conviction, "I do not know what the other Knights would do, Your Majesty, but I willingly pledge myself to your cause."

"I thank you for that, sir," said Gilthas. He turned to Alhana. "I was opposed to this march at the beginning. I made no secret of that. The doom I foresaw has fallen. We are exiles now, without a homeland. Yet as this gallant Knight states, if we foreswear the promise Samar made to aid the Knights in their fight, Queen Takhisis will triumph. Her first act would be to destroy us utterly, to annihilate us as a people. I agree. We must march on Sanction."

"You have our answer, Sir Gerard," Alhana declared. "We are one—the Qualinesti and the Silvanesti—and we will join with the other free people of Ansalon to fight and destroy the Queen of Darkness and her armies."

Gerard said what was proper. He was obviously relieved and now eager to be gone. The dragons circled above them, the shadows of their wings sliding gracefully over the ground. The elves greeted the dragons with glad cries and tears and blessings, and the dragons dipped their proud heads in response to the salutes.

The silver dragons and the gold began to swoop down into the valley, one or two at a time. The elven warriors mounted on the backs of the dragons, crowding as many on as possible. Thus had the elves ridden into battle during the days of Huma. Thus had they ridden to battle during the War of the Lance. The air was charged with a sense of history. The elves began to sing again, songs of glory, songs of victory.

Alhana, mounted on a golden dragon, took the lead. Raising her sword into the air, she shouted an elven battle cry. Samar lifted his sword, joined in. The Gold carried the queen of the Silvanesti into the air and flew off over the mountains toward the west, toward Sanction. The blind silver dragon departed, guided by his human rider.

Gilthas volunteered to remain to the last, to make certain that the dead were given proper rites, their bodies cremated in dragonfire, since there was no time to bury them and no way they could be returned to their homeland. His wife stayed with him.

"The Knights will not come to our aid, will they?" said the Lioness abruptly, as the last dragon stood ready to bear them away.

"The Knights will not come," Gilthas said. "We will die for them, and they will sing our praises, but when the battle is won, they will return to their homes. They will not come to die for us."

Together, he and the Lioness and the last of the Qualinesti warriors took to the skies. The songs of the elves were loud and joyful and filled the valley with music.

Then all that was left was the echoes.

Then those faded away, leaving only silence and smoke.

29

The Temple of Duerghast

aldar had not seen Mina since her triumphant return to Sanction. His heart was sore as his body, and he used his wounds as an excuse to remain in his tent, refusing to see or speak to anyone. He was considerably surprised that he was still alive, for Takhisis had good reason to hate him, and she was not merciful to those who had turned on her. He guessed that Mina had much to do with the fact that he was not lying in a charred lump alongside Malys's carcass.

Galdar had not stayed to listen to the conversation between Takhisis and Mina. His fury was such that he could have torn down the mountain, stone by stone, with his bare hands, and fearing that his fury would hurt Mina, not help her, he stalked away to rage in solitude. He returned to the cave only when he heard Mina call for him.

He found her well, whole. He was not surprised. He expected nothing less. Nursing his bruised and bloodied hand—he had taken out his anger on the rocks—he regarded her in silence, waited for her to speak.

Her amber eyes were cold and hard. He could still see himself frozen inside them, a tiny figure, trapped.

"You would have let me die," she said, accusing.

"Yes," he replied steadily. "Better that you should have died with your glory fresh upon you than live a slave."

"She is our god, Galdar. If you serve me, you serve her."

"I serve you, Mina," Galdar said, and that was the end of the conversation.

Mina might have dismissed him. She might have slain him. Instead, she started off on the long trek down the Lords of Doom. He went with her. She spoke to him only once more, and that was an offer to heal his injuries. He declined. They walked to Sanction in silence and they had not talked since.

The joy at Mina's return was tumultuous. There had been those who were sure she was dead and those who were sure she lived, and so high was the level of anxiety and fear that these two factions came to blows. Mina's Knights argued among themselves, her commanders bickered and quarreled. Rumors flew about the streets, lies became truth, and truth degenerated into lies. Mina returned to find a city of anarchy and chaos. The sound of her name was all that it took to restore order.

"Mina!" was the jubilant cry at the gate as she appeared. "Mina!"

The name rang wildly throughout the city like the joyous sound of wedding bells, and she was very nearly overrun and smothered by those who cried out how thankful they were to see her alive. If Galdar had not wordlessly swept her up in his arms and mounted her on his strong shoulders for everyone to see, she might well have been killed by love.

Galdar could have pointed out that it was Mina they cheered, Mina they followed, Mina they obeyed. He said nothing, however, and she said nothing either. Galdar heard the tales of the destruction of the totem, of the appearance of a silver dragon who had attacked the totem and who had, in turn, been attacked and blinded by Mina's valiant troops. He heard of the perfidy and treachery of the Solamnic priestess who had joined forces with the silver dragon and how they had flown off together.

Lying on his cot, nursing his injuries, Galdar recalled the first time he'd seen the lame beggar, who had turned out to be a blue dragon. He had been in company with a blind man with silver hair. Galdar pondered this and wondered.

He went to view the wreckage. The pile of ash that had been the skulls of hundreds of dragons remained untouched, undisturbed. Mina would not go near it. She did not return to the altar room. She did not return to her room in the temple, but moved her things to some unknown location.

In the altar room, the candles had all melted into a large pool of wax colored dirty gray by the swirling ashes. Benches were overturned, some blackened from the fire. The odor of smoke and magic was all pervasive. The floor was covered with shards of amber, sharp enough to puncture the sole of a boot. No one dared enter the temple, which was said to be imbued with the spirit of the woman whose body had been imprisoned in the amber sarcophagus and was now a pile of ashes.

"At least one of us managed to escape," Galdar told the ashes, and he gave a soldier's salute.

The body of one of the wizards was gone, as well. No one could tell Galdar what had happened to Palin Majere. Some claimed to have seen a figure cloaked all in black carry it off, while others swore that they had seen the wizard Dalamar tear it apart with his bare hands. At Mina's command, a search was made for Palin, but the body could not be found, and finally Mina ordered the search ended.

The body of the wizard Dalamar remained in the abandoned temple, staring into the darkness, apparently forgotten, his hands stained with blood.

There was one other piece of news. The jailer was forced to admit that during the confusion of Malys's attack, the elf lord Silvanoshei had escaped his prison cell and had not been recaptured. The elf was thought to be still in the city, for they had posted look-outs for him at the exits, and no one had seen him.

"He is in Sanction," Mina said. "Of that, you may be certain."

"I will find him," said the jailer with an oath. "And when I do, I will bring him straight to you, Mina."

"I am too busy to deal with him," said Mina sharply. "If you find him, kill him. He has served his purpose."

Days passed. Order was restored. The elf was not found, nor did anyone really bother to look for him. Rumors were now whispered that Mina was having the ancient Temple of Duerghast, that had long been left to lie in ruins, reconstructed and refurbished. In a month's time, she would be holding a grand ceremony in the temple, the nature of which was secret. It would be the greatest moment in the history of Krynn, one that would be long celebrated and remembered. Soon, everyone in Sanction was saying that Mina was going to be rewarded with godhood.

The day Galdar first heard this, he sighed deeply. On that day, Mina came to see him.

"Galdar," she called outside his tent post. "May I come in?"

He gave a growl of acquiescence, and she entered.

Mina had lost weight—with Galdar not around, no one was there to persuade her to eat. Nor was anyone urging her to sleep, apparently, for she looked worn, exhausted. Her eyes blinked too often, her fingers plucked aimlessly at the buckles of her leather armor. Her skin was pale, except for a hectic, fevered stain on her cheeks. Her red hair was longer than he had ever known her to wear it, curled fretfully about her ears and straggled down her forehead. He did not rise to greet her, but remained sitting on his bed.

"They say you keep to your quarters because you are unwell," Mina said, regarding him intently.

"I am doing better," he said, refusing to meet her amber eyes.

"Are you able to return to your duties?"

"If *you* want me." He laid emphasis on the word.

"I do." Mina began to pace the tent, and he was startled to see her nervous, uneasy. "You've heard the talk that is going around. About my becoming a god."

"I've heard it. Let me guess, Her Dark Majesty isn't pleased."

"When she enters the world in triumph, Galdar, then there will be no question of whom the people will worship. It's just that . . ." Mina paused, helpless to explain, or perhaps loath to admit to the explanation.

"You are not to blame, Mina," said Galdar, relenting and taking pity on her. "You are here in the world. You are something the people can see and hear and touch. You perform the miracles."

"Always in her name," Mina insisted.

"Yet you never stopped them from calling out *your* name," Galdar observed. "You never told them to shout for the One God. It is always 'Mina, Mina.' "

She was silent a moment, then said quietly, "I do not stop it because I enjoy it, Galdar. I cannot help it. I hear the love in their voices. I see the love in their eyes. Their love makes me feel that I can accomplish anything, that I can work miracles . . ."

Her voice died away. She seemed to suddenly realize what she had said.

That I can work miracles.

"I understand," Mina said softly. "I see now why I was punished. I am amazed the One God forgave me. Yet, I will make it up to her."

She abandoned you, Mina! Galdar wanted to shout at her. If you had died, she would have found someone else to do her bidding. But you didn't die, and so she came running back with her lying tale of "testing" and "punishing."

The words burned on his tongue, but he kept his mouth shut on them, for if he spoke them, Mina would be furious. She would turn from him, perhaps forever, and he was the only friend she had now, the only one who could see clearly the path that lay ahead of her. He swallowed the words, though they came nigh to choking him.

"What is this I hear of you restoring the old Temple of Duerghast?" Galdar asked, changing the subject.

Mina's face cleared. Her amber eyes glimmered with a glint of her former spirit. "That is where the ceremony will be held, Galdar. That is where the One

God will make manifest her power. The ceremony will be held in the arena, and it will be magnificent, Galdar! Everyone will be there to worship the One God—her foes included."

Galdar's choked-down words were giving him a bellyache. He felt sick again, and he remained sitting on the bed, saying nothing. He couldn't look at her, couldn't return her gaze, couldn't bear to see himself, that tiny being, held fast in the amber. Mina came to him, touched his hand. He kept his face averted.

"Galdar, I know that I hurt you. I know that your anger was really fear—fear for me." Her fingers closed fast over his hand. "You are the only one who ever cared about me, Galdar. About *me*, about Mina. The others care only for what I can do for them. They depend on me like children, and like children I must lead them and guide them.

"I cannot depend on them. But I can depend on you, Galdar. You flew into certain death with me, and you were not afraid. I need you now. I need your strength and your courage. Don't be angry with me anymore." She paused, then said, "Don't be angry with *her*."

His thoughts went back to the night he'd seen Mina emerge from the storm, heralded by thunder, born of fire. He remembered the thrill when she touched his hand, this hand, the hand that was her gift. He had so many memories of her, each one linked with another to form a golden chain that bound them together. He lifted his head and looked at her, saw her human, small and fragile, and he was suddenly very much afraid for her.

He was so afraid that he could even lie for her.

"I am sorry, Mina," he said gruffly. "I was angry at—"

He paused. He had been going to say "Takhisis," but he was loath to speak her name. He temporized. "I was angry at the One God. I understand now, Mina. Accept my apology."

She smiled, released his hand. "Thank you, Galdar. You must come with me to see the temple. There is still much work to be done to make ready for the ceremony, but I have lighted the altar and—"

Horns blared. Rumbling drumbeats rolled over her words.

"What is this?" Mina asked, walking to the tent flap and peering out, irritated. "What do they think they are doing?"

"That is the call to arms, Mina," said Galdar, alarmed. He hastily grabbed up his sword. "We must be under attack."

"That cannot be," she returned. "The One God sees all and hears all and knows all. I would have been warned. . . ."

"Nevertheless," Galdar pointed out, exasperated, "that *is* the call to arms."

"I don't have time for this," she said, annoyed. "There is too much work to be done in the temple."

The drumbeat grew louder, more insistent.

"I suppose I will have to deal with it." She stalked out of the tent, walking with haste, her irritation plain to be seen.

Galdar strapped on his sword, snatched up the padded leather vest that served him for armor, and hastened after her, fastening buckles as he ran.

The streets were awash in confusion, with some people staring stupidly in the direction of the walls, as if they could divine what was going on by just looking, while others were loudly demanding answers from

549

people who were just as confused as they were. The levelheaded raced to their quarters to grab their weapons, reasoning that they'd arm themselves first and find out who they were fighting later.

Galdar opened up a path through the panic-clogged streets. His voice bellowed for people to make way. His strong arms picked up and tossed aside those who didn't heed his command. Mina followed closely behind him, and at the sight of her, the people cheered and called her name.

"Mina! Mina!"

Glancing back, Galdar saw her still annoyed by the interruption, still determined that this was nothing. They reached the West Gate. Just as the huge doors were thundering shut, Galdar caught a glimpse of one of their scouts—a blue dragon, who had landed outside the walls. The dragon's rider was talking to the Knight commanding the gate.

"What is going on? What is happening?" Mina demanded, shoving her way through the crowd to reach the officer. "Why did you sound the alarm? Who gave the order?"

Knight and rider both swung toward Mina. Both began talking at once. Soldiers and Knights crowded around her, adding to the chaos by trying to make their own voices heard.

"An army led by Solamnic Knights is on its way to Sanction, Mina," said the dragonrider, gasping for breath. "Accompanying the Knights is an army of elves, flying the standards of both Qualinesti and Silvanesti."

Mina cast an irate glance at the Knight in charge of the gate. "And for this you sound the alarm and start a panic? You are relieved of your command. Galdar, see that this man is flogged." Mina turned back to the dragonrider. Her lip curled. "How far away is this army? How many weeks' march?"

"Mina," the rider said, swallowing. "They are not marching. They ride dragons. Gold and silver dragons. Hundreds of them—"

"Gold dragons!" a man cried out, and before Galdar could stop him, the fool had dashed off, shouting out the news in a panicked voice. It would be all over the city in minutes.

Mina stared at the rider. Blood drained from her face, seemed to drain from her body. She had looked more alive when she was dying. Fearing she might collapse, Galdar put his hand out to steady her. She pushed him away.

"Impossible," she said through pale lips. "The gold and silver dragons have departed this world, never to return."

"I am sorry to contradict you, Mina," the rider said hesitantly, "but I saw them myself. We"—he gestured outside the walls, where his Blue stood, her flanks heaving, her wings and head drooping with exhaustion—"we were caught off-guard, nearly killed. We barely made it here alive."

Mina's Knights gathered tensely around her.

"Mina, what are your orders?"

"What is your command, Mina?"

Her pale lips moved, but she spoke to herself. "I must act now. The ceremony cannot wait."

"How far away are the dragons?" Galdar asked the rider.

The man glanced up fearfully at the sky. "They were right behind me. I am surprised you cannot see them yet—"

"Mina," said Galdar, "send out an order. Summon the red dragons and the blue. Many of Malys's old minions still remain close by. Summon them to fight!"

"They won't come," said the dragonrider.

Mina shifted her gaze to him. "Why not?"

He gestured with a jerk of his thumb over his shoulder to his own blue dragon. "They won't fight their own kind. Maybe later, the old animosities will return, but not now. We're on our own."

"What do we do, Mina?" her Knights demanded, their voices harsh and filled with fear. "What are your orders?"

Mina did not reply. She stood silent, her gaze abstracted. She did not hear them. She listened to another voice.

Galdar knew well whose voice she heard, and he meant that this time she should hear his. Grabbing her arm, Galdar gave her a shake.

"I know what you're thinking, and we can't do it, Mina," Galdar said. "We can't hold out against this assault! Dragonfear alone will unman most of our troops, make them unfit for battle. The walls, the moat of fire—these won't stop dragons."

"We have the army of the dead—"

"Bah!" Galdar snorted. "Golden dragons have no fear of the souls of dead humans or dead goblins or any of these other poor wretches whose spirits the One God has imprisoned. As for the Solamnics, they have fought the dead before, and this time they will be prepared to face the terror."

"Then what do you advise, Galdar?" Mina asked, her voice cold. "Since you are so certain we cannot win."

"I advise we get the hell out of here," Galdar said bluntly, and her Knights loudly echoed his opinion.

"If we leave now, we can evacuate the city, escape into the mountains. This place is honeycombed with tunnels. The Lords of Doom have protected us before, they'll protect us again. We can retreat back to Jelek or Neraka."

"Retreat?" Mina glared at him, tried to wrench her arm from his grasp. "You are a traitor to even speak those words!"

He held onto her with grim determination. "Let the Solamnics have Sanction, Mina. We took it away from them once. We can take it away from them again. We still own Solamnia. Solanthus is ours, as is Palanthas."

"No, we don't," Mina said, struggling to free herself. "I ordered most of our forces to march here, to come to Sanction to be witness to the glory of the One God."

Galdar opened his mouth, snapped it shut.

"I did not think there would be dragons!" Mina cried out.

He saw the image of himself in her eyes growing smaller and smaller. He loosed his hold on her.

"We will not retreat," she stated.

"Mina—"

"Listen to me, every one of you." She gathered them together with a glance, all the tiny figures frozen in the amber eyes. "We must hold this city at all costs. When the ceremony is complete and the One God enters this world, no force on Krynn will be able to stand against her. She will destroy them all."

The officers stared at her, not moving. Some flinched and cast glances skyward. Galdar felt a twinge of fear twist his gut—the dragonfear, distant yet, but fast approaching.

"Well, what do wait for?" Mina demanded. "Return to your posts."

No one moved. No one cheered. No one spoke her name.

"You have your orders!" Mina shouted, her voice ragged. "Galdar, come with me."

She turned to leave. Her Knights did not move. They blocked her path with their bodies. She bore no weapon. She had not thought to bring one.

"Galdar," said Mina. "Kill any man who tries to stop me."

Galdar laid his hand on the hilt of his sword.

One by one, the Knights stepped aside, cleared a path.

Mina walked among them, her face cold as death.

"Where are you going?" Galdar demanded, following after her.

"To the temple. We have much to do and little time to do it."

"Mina," he said, his voice low and urgent in her ear, "you can't leave them to face this alone. For love of you, they will find the courage to stand and fight even golden dragons, but if you are not here—"

Mina halted.

"They do not fight for love of me!" Her voice trembled. "They fight for the One God!" She turned around to face her Knights. "Hear my words. You fight this battle for the One God. You must hold this city in the name of the One God. Any man who flees before the enemy will know the wrath of the One God."

Her Knights lowered their heads, turned away. They did not march proudly back to their posts, as they might once have done. They slunk back sullenly.

"What is the matter with them?" Mina asked, dismayed, confused.

"Once they followed you for love, Mina. Now they

obey you as the whipped dog obeys—in fear of the lash," said Galdar. "Is this what you want?"

Mina bit her lip, seemed to waver in her decision, and Galdar hoped that she might refuse to heed the voice. That she would do what she knew to be honorable, knew to be right. She would remain loyal to her men, who had remained loyal to her through so much.

Mina's jaw set. The amber eyes hardened. "Let the curs run. I don't need them. I have the One God. I am going to the temple to prepare for the ceremony. Are you coming?" she demanded of Galdar. "Or are you going to run away, too?"

He looked into the amber eyes and could no longer see himself. He could no longer see anyone. Her eyes were empty.

She did not wait for his answer. She stalked off. She did not look to see if he was following. She didn't care, one way or the other.

Galdar hesitated. Looking back at the West Gate, he saw the Knights gathered in knots, talking in low voices. He doubted very much if they were determining a strategy for battle. A babble of screams and cries rose from the streets as word spread that hundreds of golden and silver dragons were bearing down on Sanction. No one was acting to quell the terror. Each man thought only of himself now, and he had only one thought in his mind—to survive. Soon there would be rioting, as men and women devolved into wild beasts, bit and clawed and fought to save their own hides. In their miserable panic, they might well destroy themselves before the armies of their enemies ever arrived.

If I stay here on the walls, I might rally a few, Galdar thought. I might find some who would brave the horror and fight alongside me. I would die well. I would die with honor.

He watched Mina walking away, walking alone, except for that shadowy five-headed figure that hovered over her, surrounded her, cut her off from everyone who had ever loved her or admired her or cared about her.

"You great bitch!" Galdar muttered. "You won't get rid of me that easily."

Gripping his sword, he hastened after Mina.

Mina was wrong when she told Galdar that he was the only one who had ever cared for her. Another cared, cared deeply. Silvanoshei hurried after her, shoving and pushing his way through the crowds that now milled about in panic in the streets, trying to keep her in sight.

He had stayed in Sanction to hear some word of Mina. Silvanoshei's joy when he heard she was alive was heartfelt, even as her return plunged him once more into danger. People suddenly remembered having seen an elf walking about Sanction.

He was forced to go into hiding. A kender obligingly introduced Silvanoshei to the system of tunnels that criss-crossed beneath Sanction. Elves abhor living beneath the ground, and Silvanoshei could remain in the tunnels for only short periods of time before he was driven to the surface by a desperate need for air. He stole food to keep himself alive, stole a cloak with a hood and a scarf to wrap around his face, hide his elven features.

He lurked about the ruins of the totem, hoping to find a chance to talk to Mina, but he never saw her there. He grew fearful, wondered if she'd left the city or if she had fallen ill. Then he overheard a chance bit of gossip to the effect that she had moved out of the Temple of the Heart and had taken up residence in another temple, the ruined Temple of Duerghast that stood on the outskirts of Sanction.

Built to honor some false god dreamed up by a demented cult, the temple was notorious for having an arena where human sacrifices were sent to die for the entertainment of a cheering crowd. During the War of the Lance, Lord Ariakas had appropriated the temple, using its dungeons to torture and torment his prisoners.

The temple had an evil reputation, and there had been talk in recent days, during the reign of Hogan Bight, of razing it. Tremors had caused gigantic cracks to open in the walls, weakening the structure to the point where no one felt safe even going near it. The citizens of Sanction had decided to let the Lords of Doom complete the destruction.

Then came the news that Mina was planning to rebuild the temple, transform it into a place of worship of the One God.

The Temple of Duerghast lay on the other side of the moat of lava that surrounded Sanction. The temple could not be reached overland, not without bridging the moat. Therefore, Silvanoshei reasoned, Mina would be forced to enter the temple via one of the tunnels. He traipsed about the tunnel system, losing himself more than once, and at last found what he was searching for—a tunnel that ran beneath the curtain wall on the southern side of the city.

Silvanoshei had been planning to explore this tunnel when the alarm was raised. He saw the dragon-rider fly overhead and land outside the West Gate.

Guessing that Mina would come to take charge of the situation, Silvanoshei concealed himself in the crowds of people who were eager to see Mina. He pressed as close as he dared, hoping against hope just to catch a glimpse of her.

Then he saw her, surrounded by her Knights, speaking to the dragonrider. Suddenly one man broke from the group and raced into the crowd, shouting out that silver and gold dragons were coming, dragons ridden by Solamnic Knights. People swore and cursed and started to push and shove. Silvanoshei was jostled and nearly knocked down. Through it all, he fought to keep his eyes on her.

The news of dragons and Knights meant little to Silvanoshei. He thought of it only in terms of how this would affect Mina. He was certain she would lead the battle, and he feared that he would have no opportunity to talk to her. He was astonished beyond measure to see her turn around and walk off, abandoning her troops.

Their loss was his blessing.

Her voice carried to him clearly. "I am going to the temple to prepare for the ceremony."

At last, maybe he could find a way to speak to her.

Silvanoshei entered the tunnel he had found, hoping that his calculations were correct and that it led beneath the moat of fire to the Temple of Duerghast. Hope almost died when he found that the tunnel roof had partially collapsed. He made his way past the chunks of rock and soil, continued on, and eventually found a ladder that led to the surface.

He climbed swiftly, had sense enough to slow as he neared the top. A wooden trapdoor kept the tunnel opening concealed from those above. As he pushed against the door, his hand broke through the rotting wood. A cascade of dirt and splinters fell down around him. Cautiously, he peered out of the hole in the trap-door. Bright sunshine half-blinded him. He blinked his eyes, waited for them to become accustomed to the light.

The Temple of Duerghast stood only a short dis-tance away.

To reach the temple, he would have to cross a space of open ground. He would be visible from the walls of Sanction. Silvanoshei doubted if anyone would see him or pay attention to him. All eyes would be turned skyward.

Silvanoshei wormed his way out of the hole and ran across the open patch of ground, hid himself in a shadow cast by the temple's outer wall. Constructed of black granite blocks, the temple's curtain wall was built in the shape of a square. Two towers guarded the front entrance. Circling around the wall, hugging the building, he searched for some way inside. He came to one of the towers, and here he found two doors, one at either end of the wall.

Heavy slabs of iron controlled by winches served for gates. Although they were covered with rust, the iron gates remained in place and would probably still be standing when the rest of the temple fell down around them. He could not enter there, but he could enter through a part of the outer wall that had collapsed into a pile of rubble. The climb would be difficult, but he was nimble. He was certain he could manage.

He started toward the wall, then halted, frozen in the shadows. He had caught movement out of the corner of his eye.

Someone else had come to the Temple of Duerghast. A man stood before it, gazing at it. The man stood in the open, the sunshine pouring down on him. Silvanoshei must have been blind to have missed seeing him. Yet, he could have sworn that there had been no one there when he came around the corner.

Judging by his looks, the man was not a warrior. He was quite tall, above average height. He wore no sword, carried no bow slung across his shoulder. He was clad in brown woolen hose, a green and brown tunic, and tall leather boots. A cowl, brown in color, covered his head and shoulders. Silvanoshei could not see the man's face.

Silvanoshei fumed. What was this simpleton doing here? Nothing, by the looks of it, except gawking at the temple like a kender on holiday. He had no weapon, he wasn't a threat, yet Silvanoshei was reluctant to have the man see him. Silvanoshei was determined to talk to Mina, and for all he knew this man might be some sort of guard. Or perhaps this stranger was also waiting to speak to her. He had the look of someone waiting.

Silvanoshei wished the man away. Time was passing. He had to get inside. He had to talk to Mina. Still the man did not move.

At last, Silvanoshei decided he could wait no longer. He was a swift runner. He could outdistance the man, if the stranger gave chase, lose himself in the temple confines before the man figured out what had happened. Silvanoshei drew in a breath, ready to run.

The man turned his head. Drawing back his cowl, he looked straight at Silvanoshei.

The man was an elf.

Silvanoshei stared, riveted, unmoving. For a pet-rifying moment, he feared that Samar had tracked him down, but he recognized immediately that this was not Samar.

At first glance, the elf appeared young, as young as Silvanoshei. His body had the strength, the lithesome grace of youth. A second glance caused Silvanoshei to rethink his first. The elf's face was unmarred by time, yet in his expression held a gravity that was not youth-ful, had nothing to do with youth's hope and high spirits and joyful expectations. The eyes were bright as the eyes of youth, but their brilliance was shadowed, tempered by sorrow. Silvanoshei had the odd impres-sion that this man knew him, but he could not place the strange elf at all.

The elf looked at Silvanoshei, then he looked away, turned his gaze back to the temple.

Silvanoshei took advantage of the elf's shift in attention to sprint to the opening in the wall. He climbed swiftly, one eye on the strange elf, who never moved. Silvanoshei dropped down over the side of the wall. He peered back through the rubble to see the elf still standing there, waiting.

Putting the stranger from his mind, Silvanoshei entered the ruined temple and set off in search of Mina.

30

For Love of Mina

ina fought her way through the crowded streets of Sanction. Her movement was hampered by the people who, at the sight of her, surged forward to touch her. They cried out to her in fear of the coming dragons. They begged her to save them.

"Mina, Mina!" they shouted, and the din was hateful to her.

She tried to block it out, tried to ignore them, tried to free herself from their clutching, clinging hands, but with every step she took, they gathered around her more thickly, calling out her name, repeating it over and over as a frantic litany against fear.

Another called her name. The voice of Takhisis, loud and insistent, urging her to make haste. Once the ceremony was complete, once Takhisis had entered the world and united the spiritual realm with the physical, the Dark Queen could take any form she chose, and in that form she would fight her enemies.

Let the foul Golds and the craven Silvers go up against the five-headed monster that she could become. Let the puny armies of the Knights and the elves battle the hordes of the dead that would rise up at her command.

Takhisis was glad that the wretched mage and his tool, the blind Silver, had freed the metallic dragons. She had been furious at the time, but now, in her calmer moments, she remembered that she was the only god on Krynn. Everything worked to her own ends, even the plots of her enemies.

Do what they might, they could never harm her. Every arrow they fired would turn to their own destruction, target their own hearts. Let them attack. This time she would destroy them all—knights, elves, dragons—destroy them utterly, wipe them out, crush them so that they would never rise up against her again. Then she would seize their souls, enslave them. Those who had fought her in life would serve her in death, serve her forever.

To accomplish this, Takhisis needed to be in the world. She controlled the door on the spiritual realm, but she could not open the door on the physical. She needed Mina for that. She had chosen Mina and prepared her for this one task. Takhisis had smoothed Mina's way, had removed Mina's enemies. Takhisis was so close to achieving her overweening ambition. She had no fear that the world might be snatched from her at the last moment. She was in control. No other challenged her. She was impatient, however. Impatient to begin the battle that would end in her final triumph.

She urged Mina to make haste. Kill these wretches, she commanded, if they will not get out of your way.

Mina grabbed a sword and raised it in the air. She no longer saw people. She saw open mouths, felt clutching hands. The living surrounded her, plucking at her, shrieking and gibbering, pressing their lips against her skin.

"Mina, Mina!" they cried, and their cries changed to screams and the hands fell away.

The street emptied, and it was only when she heard Galdar's horrified roar and saw the blood on her sword and on her hands and the bleeding bodies lying in the street that she realized what she had done.

"She commands me to hurry," Mina said, "and they wouldn't get out of my way."

"They are out of your way now," Galdar said.

Mina looked down at the bodies. Some she knew. Here was a soldier who had been with her since the siege of Sanction. He lay in a pool of blood. Her sword had run him through. She had some dim memory of him pleading with her to spare him.

Stepping over the dead, she continued on. She kept hold of the sword, though she had no skill in the use of such a weapon and she grasped it awkwardly, her hand gummed with blood.

"Walk ahead of me, Galdar," she ordered. "Clear the way."

"I don't know where we're going, Mina. The temple ruins lie outside the wall on the other side of the moat of fire. How do you get there from here?"

Mina pointed with the sword. "Stay on this street, follow the curtain wall. Directly across from the Temple of Duerghast is a tower. Inside the tower, a tunnel leads beneath the wall and underneath the moat to the temple."

They proceeded on, moving at a dead run.

"Make haste," Takhisis commanded.

Mina obeyed.

The first enemy dragons came into view, flying high over the mountains. The first waves of dragon-fear began to affect Sanction's defenders. Sunlight glittered on gold and silver scales, glinted off the armor of the dragonriders. Only in the great wars of the past had this many dragons of light come together to aid humans and elves in their cause. The dragons flew in long lines—the swift-flying Silvers in the lead, the more ponderous Golds in the rear.

A strange sort of mist began to flow up over the walls, seep into the streets and alleyways. Galdar thought it odd that fog should arise suddenly on a sunny day, and then he saw suddenly that the mist had eyes and mouths and hands. The souls of the dead had been summoned to do battle. Galdar looked up through the chill mist, looked up into the blue sky. Sunlight flashed off the belly of a silver dragon, argent light so bright that it burned through the mists like sunshine on a hot summer day.

The souls fled the light, sought the shadows, slunk down alleyways or sought shelter in the shade cast by the towering walls.

Dragons do not fear the souls of dead humans, dead goblins, dead elves.

Galdar envisioned the blasts of fire breathed by the gold dragons incinerating all those who manned the walls, melting armor, fusing it to the living flesh as the men inside screamed out their lives in agony. The image was vivid and filled his mind, so that he could almost smell the stench of burning flesh and hear the death cries. His hands began to shake, his mouth grew dry.

"Dragonfear," he told himself over and over. "Dragonfear. It will pass. Let it pass."

He looked back at Mina to see how she was faring. She was pale, but composed. The empty amber eyes stared straight ahead, did not look up to the skies or to the walls from which men were starting to jump out of sheer panic.

The Silvers flew overhead, flying rapidly, flying low. These were the first wave and they did not attack. They were spreading fear, evoking panic, doing reconnaissance. The shadows of the gleaming wings sliced through the streets, sending people running mad with terror. Here and there, some mastered their fear, overcame it. A lone ballista fired. A couple of archers sent arrows arcing upward in a vain attempt at a lucky shot. For the most part, men huddled in the shadows of the walls and drew in shivering breaths and waited for it all to go away, just please go away.

The fear that descended on the population worked in Mina's favor. Those who had been clogging the streets ran terrified into their homes or shops, seeking shelter where no shelter existed, for the fire of the Golds could melt stone. But at least they left the streets. Mina and Galdar made swift progress.

Arriving at one of the guard towers that stood along Sanction's curtain wall, Mina yanked open a door at the tower's base. The tower was sparsely inhabited, most of its defenders had fled. Those who were left, hearing the door bang open, peered fearfully down the spiral stairs. One called out in a cracked voice, "Who goes there?"

Mina did not deign to answer, and the soldiers did not dare come down to find out. Galdar heard their footsteps retreat farther down the battlements.

He grabbed a torch, fumbled to light it from a slow-match burning in a tub. Mina took the torch from him and led the way down a series of dank stone stairs to what appeared to be a blank wall, through which she walked without hesitation. Either the wall was illusion, or the Dark Queen had caused the solid stone to dissolve. Galdar didn't know, and he had no intention of asking. He gritted his teeth and barged in after her, fully expecting to dash his brains out against the rock.

He entered a dark tunnel that smelled strongly of brimstone. The walls were warm to the touch. Mina had ranged far ahead of him, and he had to hurry to catch up. The tunnel was built for humans, not minotaurs. He was forced to run with his shoulders hunched and his horns lowered. The heat increased. He guessed that they were passing directly under the moat of fire. The tunnel looked to be ancient. He wondered who had built it and why, more questions he was never going to have answered.

The tunnel ended at yet another wall. Galdar was relieved to see that Mina did not walk through this wall. She entered a small door. He squeezed in after her, a tight fit, to find himself in a prison cell.

Rats screeched and chittered at the light, scrambled to escape. The floor was alive with some sort of crawling insects that swarmed into the nooks and crevices of the crumbing stone walls. The cell door hung on a single rusted hinge.

Mina left the cell, that opened up into a corridor. Galdar caught a glimpse of other rooms extending off the main hall and he knew where he was—the Temple of Duerghast.

Thinking back to what he had heard about this temple, he guessed that these were the torture chambers where once the prisoners of the dragonarmy were "questioned." The light of his torch did not penetrate far into the shadows, for which he was grateful.

He hated this place, wished himself away from it, wished himself anywhere but here, even in the city above, though that city might be crawling with gold dragons. The screams of the dying echoed in these dark corridors, the walls were wet with tears and blood.

Mina looked neither to the right nor the left. The light of her torch illuminated a flight of stairs, leading upward. Climbing those stairs, Galdar had the feeling he was clawing his way back from death. They reached ground level, the main part of the temple.

Cracks had opened in the walls, and Galdar was able to catch a whiff of fresh air. Though it smelled strongly of sulfur from the moat of fire, the smell up here was better than what he'd smelled below. He drew in a deep breath.

Rays of dust-clouded sunlight filtered through the cracks. Galdar started to douse the torch, but Mina stopped him.

"Keep it lit," she told him. "We will need it where we are going."

"Where are we going?" he asked, fearing she would say the altar room.

"To the arena."

She led the way through the ruins, moving swiftly and without hesitation. He noted that piles of rubble had been cleared aside, opening up previously clogged corridors.

"Did you do this work yourself, Mina?" Galdar asked, marveling.

"I had help," she replied.

He guessed the nature of that help and was sorry he'd asked.

Unlike humans, Galdar was not disgusted to hear a temple had an open-air arena where people would come to witness blood sports. Such contests are a part of a minotaur's heritage, used to settle everything from family feuds to marital disputes to the choosing of a new emperor. He had been surprised to find that humans considered such contests barbaric. To him, the malicious, backstabbing political intrigue in which humans indulged was barbaric.

The arena was open to the air and was visible from the highest walls of Sanction. Galdar had noted it before with some interest as being the only arena he'd ever seen in human lands. The arena was built into the side of the mountain. The floor was below ground level and filled with sand. Rows of benches, carved into the mountain's slope, formed a semicircle around the floor. The arena was small by minotaur standards, and was in a state of ruin and decay. Wide cracks had opened up among the benches, holes gaped in the floor.

Galdar followed Mina through dusty corridors until they came to a large entryway that opened out onto the arena. Mina walked through the entryway. Galdar followed and went from dusty daylight to darkest night.

He stopped dead, blinking his eyes, suddenly afraid that he'd been struck blind. He could smell the familiar odors of the outdoors, including the sulfur of the moat of fire. He could feel the wind upon his face.

He should be feeling the warmth of the sun on his face, as well, for only seconds before he had been able to see sunshine and blue sky through the cracks in the ceiling. Looking up, he saw a black sky, starless, cloudless. He shuddered all over, took an involuntary step backward.

Mina grabbed hold of his hand. "Don't be afraid," she said softly. "You stand in the presence of the One God."

Considering their last meeting together, Galdar did not find reassuring the knowledge that he was in Takhisis's presence. He was more determined than ever to leave. He had made a mistake in coming here. He had come out of love for Mina, not love for Takhisis. He did not belong here, he was not welcome.

Stairs led from the ground floor into the arena.

Mina let go of his hand. She was in haste, already hurrying down the stairs, certain he would follow. The words to say goodbye to her clogged in his throat. Not that there were any words that would make a difference. She would hate him for what he was going to do, detest him. Nothing he could say would change that. He turned to leave, turned to go back into the sunlight, even though that meant the dragons and death, when he heard Mina give a startled cry.

Acting instinctively, fearing for her life, Galdar drew his sword and clattered down the stairs.

"What are you doing here, Silvanoshei? Skulking about in the shadows like an assassin?" Mina demanded.

Her tone was cold, but her voice trembled. The light of the torch she held wavered in her shaking hand. She'd been caught off-guard, taken unawares.

Galdar recognized Mina's besotted lover, the elf king. The elf's face was deadly pale. He was thin and wan, his fine clothes tattered, ragged. He no longer had that wasted, desperate look about him, however. He was calm and composed, more composed than Mina.

The word "assassin" and the young man's strange composure caused Galdar to lift his sword. He would have brought it down upon the young elf's head, splitting him in two, but Mina stopped him.

"No, Galdar," she said, and her voice was filled with contempt. "He is no threat to me. He can do nothing to harm me. His foul blood would only defile the sacred soil on which we stand."

"Be gone then, scum," said Galdar, reluctantly lowering his weapon. "Mina gives you your wretched life. Take it and leave."

"Not before I say something," said Silvanoshei with quiet dignity. "I am sorry, Mina. Sorry for what has happened to you."

"Sorry for me?" Mina regarded him with scorn. "Be sorry for yourself. You fell into the One God's trap. The elves will be annihilated, utterly, finally, completely. Thousands have already fallen to my might, and thousands more will follow until all who oppose me have perished. Because of you, because of your weakness, your people will be wiped out. And *you* feel sorry for *me?*"

"Yes," Silvanoshei said. "I was not the only one to fall into the trap. If I had been stronger, I might have been able to save you, but I was not. For that, I am sorry."

Mina stared at him, the amber of her eyes hardening around him, as if she would squeeze the life out of him.

He stood steadfast, his eyes filled with sorrow.

Mina turned away in contempt. "Bring him," she ordered Galdar. "He will be witness to the end of all that he holds dear."

"Mina, let me slay him—" Galdar began.

"Must you always oppose me?" Mina demanded, rounding on him angrily. "I said bring him. Have no fear. He will not be the only witness. All the enemies of the One God will be here to see her triumph. Including you, Galdar."

Turning, she entered the door that led into the arena.

The hackles rose on the back of Galdar's neck. His hands were wet with sweat.

"Run," he said abruptly to the elf. "I will not stop you. Go on, get out of here."

Silvanoshei shook his head. "I stay as do you. We both stay for the same reason."

Galdar grunted. He stood in the doorway, debating, though he already knew what he would do. The elf was right. They both stayed for the same reason.

Gritting his teeth, Galdar stalked through the door and entered the arena. Glancing back to see if the elf king was following, Galdar was astonished to see another elf standing behind Silvanoshei.

Ye gods, the place is crawling with them! Galdar thought.

The elf looked fixedly at Galdar, who had the sudden uneasy feeling that this elf with the young face and the old eyes could read the thoughts of his head and of his heart.

Galdar didn't like this. He didn't trust this new elf, and he hesitated, wondering if he should go back to deal with him.

The elf stood calmly, waiting.

All the enemies of the One God will be here to witness her triumph.

Assuming that this was just one more, Galdar shrugged and entered the arena. He was forced to follow the light of Mina's torch, for he could not see her in the darkness.

31

The Battle of Sanction

he silver dragons flew low over Sanction, not bothering to use their lethal breath weapons, relying on fear alone to drive away the enemy. Gerard had flown on dragonback before, but he'd never flown into battle, and he had often wondered why any person would risk his neck fighting in the air when he could be standing on solid ground. Now, experiencing the exhilaration of a diving rush upon Sanction's defenses, Gerard realized that he could never again go back to the heave and crush and heat of battle on land.

He yelled a Solamnic war cry as he and his Silver dived down upon the hapless defenders, not because he thought they would hear him, but for the sheer joy of the flight and the sight of his enemy fleeing before him in screaming panic. All around him, the other Knights yelled and shouted. Elven archers seated on the backs of golden dragons loosed their arrows into the throngs of soldiers trying desperately to escape the glittering death that circled above them.

The river of souls swirled around Gerard, seeking to stop him, seeking to wrap their chill arms around him, submerge him, blind him. But the army of the dead was leaderless now. They had no one to give them orders, no one to direct them. The wings of the golden and silver dragons sliced through the river of souls, shredding them like the rays of the sun shred the morning mists that drift along the riverbank. Gerard saw the clutching hands and pleading mouths of the souls whirl about him. They no longer inspired terror. Only pity.

He looked away, looked back to the task at hand, and the dead vanished.

When most of the defenders had been swept from the walls, the dragons landed in the valleys that surrounded Sanction. The elven and human warriors who had been riding on their backs dismounted. They formed into ranks, began to march upon the city, while Gerard and the other dragonriders continued to patrol the skies.

The Silvanesti and Qualinesti placed their flags on a small knoll in the center of the valley. Alhana would have liked to lead the assault on Sanction, but she was the titular ruler of the Silvanesti nation and reluctantly agreed with Samar that her place was in the rear, there to give orders and guide the attack.

"I will be the one to rescue my son," she said to Samar. "I will be the one to free him from his prison."

"My Queen—" he began, his expression grave.

"Do not say it, Samar," Alhana commanded. "We will find Silvanoshei alive and well. We will."

"Yes, Your Majesty."

He left her, standing on the hill, the colors of their tattered flag forming a faded rainbow above her head.

Gilthas stood beside her. Like Alhana, he would have liked to be among the warriors, but he knew that an inept and unpracticed swordsman is a danger to himself and everyone unfortunate enough to be near him. Gilthas watched his wife race to battle. He could pick her out of a crowd of thousands by her wild, curling mass of hair and by the fact that she would always be in the vanguard along with her Kagonesti warriors, shouting their ancient war cries and brandishing their weapons, challenging the enemy to quit skulking behind the walls and come out and fight.

He feared for her. He always feared for her, but he knew better than to express that fear to her or to try to keep her safe by his side. She would take that as an insult and rightly so. She was a warrior with a warrior's heart and a warrior's instincts and a warrior's courage. She would not be easy to kill. His heart reached out to her, and as if she felt his love touch her, she turned her head, lifted her sword, and saluted him.

He waved back, but she did not see him. She had turned her face toward battle. Gilthas could do nothing now but await the outcome.

Lord Tasgall led the Knights of Solamnia from the back of a silver dragon. He still smarted from the defeat of Solanthus. Remembering Mina's taunts from the walls as she stood victorious in the city, he was looking forward to seeing her once again upon a wall—her head on a pike on that wall.

A few of the enemy had managed to overcome the dragonfear and were mounting a defense. Archers regained the battlements, launched a volley of arrows at the silver dragon carrying Lord Tasgall. A golden dragon spotted the volley, breathed on it, and the arrows burst into flame. Lord Tasgall guided his silver dragon into the heart of Sanction.

The armies in the valley marched up to the moat of fire that guarded the city. The silver dragons breathed their frost-breath on the moat, cooling the lava and causing it to harden into black rock. Steam rose into the air, providing cover for the advancing armies as a few staunch defenders began to fire at them from the towers.

Elven archers halted to fire, sending wave after wave of arrows at the enemy. Under cover of the fire, Lord Ulrich led his men-at-arms in a rush upon the walls. A few catapults were still in operation, sent a boulder or two crashing down, but they were fired in panicked haste. Their aim was off. The boulders bounded harmlessly away. The soldiers flung grappling hooks up over the walls, began to scale them.

A few daring bands of elven archers dropped down off the backs of the low-circling dragons, landing on the roofs of the houses inside Sanction. From this vantage point, they fired their arrows into the backs of the defenders, wreaking further havoc.

They had not been able to bring with them a battering ram to smash open the gates, but as it turned out, they had no need. A golden dragon settled in front of the West Gate and, paying small heed to the arrows being fired at her from the battlements, breathed a jet of flame on the gates. The gates disintegrated into flaming cinders. With a triumphant cry, the humans and elves stormed into Sanction.

Once inside the city, the battle became more intense, for the defenders, faced now with certain death, lost their fear of the dragons and fought grimly. The dragons could do little to assist, afraid of harming their own forces.

Still, Gerard guessed that it would not be long before the day was theirs. He was about to order his dragon to set him down, so that he could join the fighting when he heard Odila shout his name.

As the blind silver dragon, Mirror, could not join in the assault, he and Odila had volunteered to act as scouts, directing the attackers to places they were needed. Calling out to Gerard, she pointed northward. A large force of black-armored Knights of Neraka and foot soldiers had managed to escape the city and were retreating toward the Lords of Doom. They were not in panicked flight but marched in ragged ranks.

Loath to let them escape, knowing that once they were in the mountains, they would be impossible to ferret out, Gerard urged his own dragon to fly to intercept them. A flash of metal from one of the mountain passes caught his eye.

Another army was marching out of the mountains to the east. These soldiers marched in rigid order, moving swiftly down the mountainside like some enormous, deadly, shining-scaled snake.

Even from this distance, Gerard recognized the force for what it was—an army of draconians. He could see the wings on their backs, wings that lifted them up and carried them easily over any obstacle in their way. Sunlight shone on their heavy armor, gleamed off their helms and their scaled skin.

Draconians were coming to Sanction's rescue. A thousand or more. The army of escaping Dark Knights saw the draconians heading in their direction and broke into cheers so loud that Gerard could hear them from the air. The retreating army of Dark Knights shifted about, intending to regroup and return to the attack with their new allies.

The draconians moved rapidly, racing down the sides of the mountains. They would soon be over Sanction's walls, and once they were in the city, the dragons could do nothing to stop them for fear of harming the Knights and elves fighting in the streets.

Gerard's Silver was preparing to dive to the attack, when, staring in astonishment, Gerard bellowed an order for his dragon to halt.

Wheeling smartly, the draconians smashed into the astonished ranks of Dark Knights that had, only moments before, been hailing the draconians as friends.

The draconians made short work of the beleagured Knights. The force crumbled under the attack, and as Gerard watched, it disintegrated. The job done, the draconians reformed again into orderly ranks and marched on toward Sanction.

Gerard had no idea what was going on. How was it possible that draconians should be allies of Solamnics and elves? He wondered if he should try to halt their march, or if he should allow the draconians to enter the city. Common sense voted for one, his heart held out for the other.

The decision was taken out of his hands, for the next instant, the city of Sanction, the snaking lines of marching draconians, the silver wings, head, and mane of the dragon on which he rode dissolved before his eyes.

Once again, he experienced the dizzying, stomach-turning motion of a journey through the corridors of magic.

Gerard found himself seated on a hard stone bench under a night-black sky, staring down into an arena that was illuminated by a chill, white light. The light had no source that he could see at first, but then he realized with a shudder that it emanated from the souls of the countless dead who overflowed the arena, so that it seemed to him that he and the arena and everyone in it floated upon a vast, unquiet ocean of death.

Gerard looked around to see Odila, staring, open-mouthed. He saw Lord Tasgall and Lord Ulrich seated together, with Lord Siegfried some distance off. Alhana Starbreeze occupied a seat, as did Samar, both staring about in anger and bewilderment. Gilthas was present, with his wife, the Lioness, and Planchet.

Friend and foe alike were here. Captain Samuval sat in the stands, looking dismayed and baffled. Two draconians sat there, one a large bozak wearing a golden chain around his neck, the other a sivak in full battle regalia. The bozak looked stern, the sivak uneasy. More than one person in that crowd had been snatched bodily from the fray. Their faces flushed and hot, spattered with blood, they stared about in amazed confusion. The body of the wizard Dalamar was here, sitting on a bench, staring at nothing.

The dead made no sound, and neither did the living. Gerard opened his mouth and tried to call out to Odila, only to discover that he had no voice. An unseen hand stopped his tongue, pressed him down into his seat so that he could not move except as the hand guided him. He could see only what he was meant to see and nothing more.

The thought came to him that he was dead, that he'd been struck down by an arrow in the back, perhaps, and that he'd been taken to this place where the dead congregated. His fear subsided. He could feel his heart beating, hear the blood pounding in his ears. He could clench his hands into fists, dig his nails into his flesh and feel pain. He could shuffle his feet. He could feel terror, and he knew then that he wasn't dead. He was a prisoner, brought here against his will for some purpose that he could only assume was a horrible one.

Silent and unmoving as the dead, the living were constrained to stare down into the eerily lit arena.

The figure of a dragon appeared. Ephemeral, insubstantial, five heads thrust hideously from a single neck. Immense wings formed a canopy that covered the arena, blotting out hope. The huge tail coiled around all who sat in the dread shadow of the wings. Ten eyes stared in all directions, looking forward and behind, seeing into every heart, searching for the darkness within. Five mouths gnawed hungrily, finding the darkness and feeding upon it.

The five mouths opened and gave forth a silent call that split the eardrums of all listening, so that they gritted their teeth against the pain and fought back tears.

At the call, Mina entered the arena.

She wore the black armor of the Knights of Neraka. The armor did not shine in the eerie light but was one with the darkness of the dragon's wings. She wore no helm, and her face glimmered ghostly white. She carried in her hand a dragonlance. Behind her, almost lost in the shadows, stood the minotaur, faithful guard at her back.

Mina faced the silent crowd in the stands. Her gaze encompassed both the dead and the living.

"I am Mina," she called out. "The chosen of the One God."

She paused, as if waiting for the cheers to which she'd become accustomed. None spoke, not the living, not the dead. Their voices stolen, they watched in silence.

"Know this," Mina resumed, and her voice was cold and commanding. "The One God is the One God for now and forever. No others will come after. You will worship the One God now and forever. You will serve the One God now and forever, in death as in life. Those who serve faithfully will be rewarded. Those who rebel will be punished. This day, the One God makes manifest her power. This day, the One God enters the world in physical form and thus joins together the immortal with the mortal. Free to move between both of them at will, the One God will rule both."

Mina lifted up the dragonlance. Once lovely to look upon, the shining silver lance glimmered cold and bleak, its point stained black with blood.

"I give this as proof of the One God's power. I hold in my hand the fabled dragonlance. Once a weapon of the enemies of the One God, the dragonlance has become her weapon. The dragon Malystryx died on the point of the dragonlance, died by the will of the One God. The One God fears nothing. In token of this, I shatter the dragonlance."

Grasping the lance in both hands, Mina brought it down upon her bent knee. The lance snapped as if it were a long-dead and dried-up stick, broken in twain. Mina tossed the pieces contemptuously over her shoulder. The pieces landed on the sandy floor of the arena. Their silver light flickered briefly, valiantly. The dragon's five heads spat upon them, the dragon's breath smothered them. Their light diminished and died.

The living and the dead watched in silence.

Galdar watched in silence.

He stood behind Mina, guarding her back, for somewhere in the darkness lurked that strange elf, not to mention the wretch, Silvanoshei. Galdar had not much fear of the latter, but he was determined that no one should get past him. No one would accost Mina in this, her hour of triumph.

This will be her hour, Galdar told himself. She will be honored. Takhisis can do no less for her. He told himself that repeatedly, yet fear gnawed at him.

For the first time, Galdar witnessed the true power of Queen Takhisis. He watched in awe to see the stadium fill with people, taken prisoner in the midst of their lives and brought here to watch her victorious entry into the mortal realm. He looked in awe at her dragon form, her vast wingspan blotting out the light of hope, bringing eternal night to the world.

He realized then that he had discounted her, and his soul sank to its knees before her. He was a rebellious slave, one who had tried foolishly to rise above his place. He had learned his lesson. He would be a slave always, even after death. He could accept his fate because here, in the presence of the Dark Queen's full might and majesty, he understood that he deserved nothing else.

But not Mina. Mina was not born to be a slave. Mina was born to rule. She had proven herself, proven her loyalty. She had walked through blood and fire and never blanched, never swerved in her unwavering belief. Let Takhisis do with him what she would, let her devour his very soul. So long as Mina was honored and rewarded, Galdar would be content.

"The foes of the One God are vanquished," Mina cried. "Their weapons are destroyed. None can stop her triumphant entry into the world."

Mina raised up her hands, her amber eyes lifted to the dragon. "Your Majesty, I have always adored you, worshiped you. I pledged my life to your service, and I stand ready to honor that pledge. Through my fault, you lost the body of Goldmoon, the body you would have inhabited. I offer my own. Take my life. Use me as your vessel. Thus, I prove my faith!"

Galdar gasped, appalled. He wanted to stop this madness, wanted to stop Mina, but though he roared his protest, his words came out a silent scream that no one heard.

The five heads gazed down on Mina.

"I accept your sacrifice," said Queen Takhisis.

Galdar lunged forward and stood still. He raised his arm and it didn't move. Bound by darkness, he could do nothing but watch to see all he had ever loved and honored destroyed.

Clouds, black and ghastly and shot with lightning, rolled down from the Lords of Doom. The clouds boiled around the Dragon Queen, obscuring her from view. The clouds swirled and churned, raised a whipping wind that buffeted Galdar with bruising force, drove him to his knees.

Mina's prayer, Mina's faith unlocked the prison door.

The storm clouds transformed into a chariot, drawn by five dragons. Standing in the chariot, her hand on the reins, was Queen Takhisis, in woman's form.

She was beautiful, her beauty fell and terrible to look upon. Her face was cold as the vast, frozen wastelands to the south, where a man perishes in an instant, his breath turning to ice in his lungs. Her eyes were the flames of the funeral pyre. Her nails were talons, her hair the long and ragged hair of the corpse. Her armor was black fire. At her side, she wore a sword perpetually stained with blood, a sword used to sever the souls from their bodies.

Her chariot hung in the air, the wings of the five dragons fanning, keeping it aloft. Takhisis left the chariot, descended to the arena floor. She trod on the lightning bolts, the storm clouds were her cloak, trailing behind her.

Takhisis walked toward Mina. The five dragons lifted their heads, cried out a paean of triumph.

Galdar could not move, he could not save her. The wind beat at him with such force that he could not even lift his head. He cried out to Mina, but his voice was whipped away by the raging wind, and his cry went unheard.

Mina smiled a tremulous smile. "My Queen," she whispered.

Takhisis stretched out her taloned hand.

Mina stood, unflinching.

Takhisis reached for Mina's heart, to make that heart her own. Takhisis reached for Mina's soul, to snatch it from her body and cast it into oblivion. Takhisis reached out to fill Mina's body with her own immortal essence.

Takhisis reached out, but her hand could not touch Mina.

Mina looked startled, confused. Her body began to tremble. She reached out her hand to her Queen, but could not touch her.

Takhisis glared. The eyes of flame filled the arena with the hideous light of her anger.

"Disobedient child!" she cried. "How dare you oppose me?"

"I do not!" Mina gasped, shivering. "I swear to you—"

"She does not oppose you. I do," said a voice.

The strange elf walked past Galdar.

The wind of the Dark Queen's fury howled around the elf and struck at him. Her lightning flared over him and sought to burn him. Her thunder boomed and tried to crush him. The elf was bowed by the winds, but he kept walking. He was knocked down by the lightning, but he rose again and kept walking. Undaunted, unafraid, he came to stand before the Queen of Darkness.

"Paladine! My dear brother!" Takhisis spat the words. "So you have found your misplaced world." She shrugged. "You are too late. You cannot stop me."

Amused, she waved her hand toward the gallery. "Find a seat. Be my guest. I am glad you came. Now you can witness my triumph."

"You are wrong, Sister," the elf said, his voice silver, ringing. "We can stop you. You know how we can stop you. It is written in the book. We all agreed."

The flame of the Dark Queen's eyes wavered. The taloned fingers twitched. For an instant, her crystalline beauty was marred with doubt, anxiety. Only for an instant. Her doubts vanished. Her beauty was restored.

She smiled.

"You would not do that to me, Brother," Takhisis said, regarding him with scorn. "The great and puissant Paladine would never make the sacrifice. "

"You misjudge me, Sister. I already have."

The elf thrust his hand into a pouch he wore at his side and drew out a small knife, a knife that had once belonged to a kender of his acquaintance.

Paladine drew the knife across the palm of his hand.

Blood oozed from the wound, dripped onto the floor of the arena.

"The balance must be maintained," he said. "I am mortal. As are you."

Storm clouds, dragons, lightning, chariot, all disappeared. The sun shone bright in the blue sky. The seats in the gallery were suddenly empty, except for the gods.

They sat in judgment, five on the side of light: Mishakal, gentle goddess of healing; Kiri-Jolith, beloved of the Solamnic Knights; Majere, friend of Paladine, who came from Beyond; Habakkuk, god of the sea; Branchala, whose music soothes the heart.

Five took the side of darkness: Sargonnas, god of vengeance, who looked unmoved on the fall of his consort; Morgion, god of disease; Chemosh, lord of the undead, angered at her intrusion in what had once been his province; Zeboim, who blamed Takhisis for the death of her loved son, Ariakan; Hiddukel, who cared only that the balance be maintained.

Six stood between: Gilean, who held the book; Sirrion, god of nature; Shinare, his mate, god of commerce; Reorx, the forger of the world; Chislev, goddess of the woodland; Zivilyn, who once more saw past, present and future.

The three children, Solinari, Nuitari, Lunitari, stood together, as always.

One place, on the side of light, was empty.

One place, on the side of darkness, was empty.

Takhisis cursed them. She screamed in rage, crying out with one voice now, not five, and her voice was the voice of a mortal. The fire of her eyes that had once scorched the sun dwindled to the flicker of the candle flame that may be blown out with a breath. The weight of her flesh and bone dragged her down from the ethers. The thudding of her heart sounded loud in her ears, every beat telling her that some day that beating would stop and death would come. She had to breathe or suffocate. She had to work to draw one breath after the other. She felt the pangs of hunger that she had never known and all the other pains of this weak and fragile body. She, who had traversed the heavens and roamed among the stars, stared down with loathing at the two feet on which she now must plod.

Lifting her eyes, that were gritty with sand and burning with fury, Takhisis saw Mina, standing before her, young, strong, beautiful.

"You did this," Takhisis raved. "You connived with them to bring about my downfall. You wanted them to sing your name, not my own!"

Takhisis drew her sword and lunged at Mina. "I may be mortal, but I can still deal death!"

Galdar gave a bellowing roar. He leaped to stop the blow, jumped in front of Mina to shield her with his body, raised his sword to defend her.

The Dark Queen's blade swept down in a slashing

arc. The blade severed Galdar's sword arm, hacked it off below the shoulder.

Arm, hand, sword fell at his feet, lay there in a widening pool of his own blood. He fell to his knees, fought the pain and shock that were trying to rob him of his senses.

The Dark Queen lifted her sword and held it poised above Mina's head.

Mina said softly, "Forgive me," and stood braced for the blow.

His own life ebbing away, Galdar was about to make a desperate lunge, when something smote him from behind. Galdar looked up with dimming eyes to see Silvanoshei standing over him.

The elf king held in his hand the broken fragment of the dragonlance. He threw the lance, threw it with the strength of his anguish and his guilt, threw it with the strength of his fear and his love.

The lance struck Takhisis, lodged in her breast.

She stared down in shock to see the lance protruding from her flesh. Her fingers moved to touch the bright, dark blood welling from the terrible wound. She staggered, started to fall.

Mina sprang forward with a wild cry of grief and love. She clasped the dying queen in her arms.

"Don't leave me, Mother," Mina cried. "Don't leave me here alone!"

Takhisis ignored her. Her eyes fixed upon Paladine, and in them her hatred burned, endless, eternal.

"If I have lost everything, so have you. The world in which you took such delight can never go back to the way it was. I have done that much, at least."

Blood frothed upon the queen's lips. She coughed, struggled to draw a final breath. "Someday you will

know the pain of death. Worse than that, Brother"—
Takhisis smiled, grimly, derisively, as the shadows
clouded her eyes—"you will know the pain of life."

Her breath bubbled with blood. Her body shuddered, and her hands fell limp. Her head lolled back
on Mina's cradling arm. The eyes fixed, stared into
the night she had ruled so long and that she would
rule no more.

Mina clasped the dead queen to her breast, rocked
her, weeping. The rest, Galdar, the strange elf, the
gods, were silent, stunned. The only sound was Mina's
harsh sobs. Silvanoshei, white-lipped and ashen-
faced, laid a hand upon her shoulder.

"Mina, she was going to kill you. I couldn't let her. . . ."

Mina lifted her tear-ravaged face. Her amber eyes
were hot, liquid, burned when they touched his flesh.

"I wanted to die. I would have died happily, grate-
fully, for I would have died serving her. Now, I live
and she is gone and I have no one. No one!"

Her hand, wet with the blood of her queen, grasped
Takhisis's sword.

Paladine sought to intercede, to stop her. An unseen
hand shoved him off balance, sent him tumbling into
the sand. A voice thundered from the heavens.

"We will have our revenge, Mortal," said Sargonnas.

Mina plunged the sword into Silvanoshei's stomach.

The young elf gasped, stared at her in astonishment.

"Mina . . ." His pallid lips formed the word. He had
no voice to speak it. His face contorted in pain.

Furious, grim-faced, Mina thrust harder, drove the
sword deeper. She let him hang, impaled on the blade,
for a long moment, while she looked at him, let the
amber eyes harden over him. Satisfied that he was
dying, she yanked the sword free.

Silvanoshei slid down the blade that was smeared with his blood and crumpled into the sand.

Clutching the bloody sword, Mina walked over to Paladine, who was slowly picking himself up off the floor of the arena. Mina gazed at him, absorbed him into the amber. She tossed the sword of Takhisis at his feet.

"You *will* feel the pain of death. But not yet. Not now. So my Queen wished it, and I obey her last wishes. But know this, wretch. In the face of every elf I meet, I will see your face. The life of every elf I take will be your life. And I will take many . . . to pay for the one."

She spat at him, spat into his face. She turned to the gods, regarded them in defiance. Then Mina knelt beside the body of her queen. She kissed the cold forehead. Lifting the body in her arms, Mina carried her dead from the Temple of Duerghast.

All was silent in the arena, silent except for Mina's departing footfalls. Galdar laid down his head in the sand that was warm from the sunshine. He was very tired. He could rest now, though, for Mina was safe. She was safe at last.

Galdar closed his eyes and began the long journey into darkness. He had not gone far, when he found his path blocked.

Galdar looked up to see an enormous minotaur. The minotaur stood tall as the mountain on which the red dragon had perished. His horns brushed the stars, his fur was jet black. He wore a leather harness, trimmed in pure, cold silver.

"Sargas!" Galdar whispered. Clutching his bleeding stump, he stumbled to his knees and bowed his head. His horns touched the ground.

"Rise, Galdar," said the god, his voice booming across the heavens. "I am pleased with you. In your need, you turned to me."

"Thank you, great Sargas," said Galdar, not daring to rise, tentatively lifting his head.

"In return for your faith, I restore your life," said Sargas. "I give you your life and your sword arm."

"Not my arm, great Sargas," Galdar pleaded, the pain burning hot in his breast. "I accept my life, and I will live it to honor you, but the arm is gone and I do not want it back."

Sargas was displeased. "The minotaur nation has at last thrown off the fetters that have bound us for so many centuries. We are breaking out of the islands where we have long been imprisoned and moving to take our rightful place upon this continent. I need gallant warriors such as yourself, Galdar. I need them whole, not maimed."

"I thank you, great Sargas," said Galdar humbly, "but, if it is all the same to you, I will learn to fight with my left hand."

Galdar tensed, waited in fear of the god's wrath. Hearing nothing, Galdar risked a peep.

Sargas smiled. His smile was grudging, but it was a smile. "Have it your way, Galdar. You are free to determine your own fate."

Galdar gave a long, deep sigh. "For that, great Sargas," he said, "I do truly thank you."

Galdar blinked his eyes, lifted his muzzle from the wet sand. He couldn't remember where he was, couldn't imagine what he was doing lying here, taking a nap, in the middle of the day. Mina would need him. She would be angry to find him lazing about. He jumped to his feet and reached instinctively for the sword that hung at his waist.

He had no sword. No hand to grasp it. His severed arm lay in the sand at his feet. He looked at where the arm had been, looked at the blood in the sand, and memory returned.

Galdar was healthy, except for his missing right arm. The stump was healed. He turned to thank the god, but the god was gone. All the gods were gone. No one remained in the arena except the body of the elf king and the strange elf with the young face and the ancient eyes.

Slowly, clumsily, fumbling with his left hand, Galdar picked up his sword. He shifted the sword belt so that he wore it now on his right hip, and, after many clumsy tries, he finally managed to return the sword to its sheath. The weapon didn't feel natural there, wasn't comfortable. He'd get used to it, though. This time, he'd get used to it.

The air was not as warm as he had remembered it. The sun dipped down behind the mountain, casting shadows of coming night. He would have to hurry, if he was going to find her. He would have to leave now, while there was still daylight left.

"You are a loyal friend, Galdar," said Paladine, as the minotaur stalked past him.

Galdar grunted and trudged on, following the trail of her footprints, the trail of her queen's blood.

For love of Mina.

32

The Age of Mortals

The fight for the city of Sanction did not last long. By nightfall, the city had surrendered. It would have probably surrendered much sooner, but there was no one willing to make the decision.

In vain, the Dark Knights and their soldiers called out Mina's name. She did not answer, she did not come, and they realized at last that she was not going to come. Some were bitter, some were angry. All felt betrayed. Knowing that they if they survived the battle they would be executed or imprisoned, a few Knights fought on. Most fought because they were trapped or cornered by the advancing enemy.

Some had decided to act on Galdar's advice and tried to find refuge in the caves of the Lords of Doom. These formed the force that had run into the army of draconians. Thinking that they had found an ally, the Dark Knights had been prepared to halt their retreat, turn around to try to retake the city. Their shock when the draconians smashed into them had been immense but short-lived.

Who these strange draconians were and why they came to the aid of elves and Solamnics would never be known. The draconian army did not enter Sanction. They held their position outside the city until they saw the flag of the Dark Knights torn down and the banners of the Qualinesti, the Silvanesti, and the Solamnic nation raised in its stead.

A large bozak draconian, wearing armor and a golden chain around his neck, marched forward, together with a sivak, wearing the trappings of a draconian high commander. The sivak called the draconian troops to attention. He and the bozak saluted the banners. The draconian troops clashed their swords against their shields in salute. The sivak gave the order to march, and the draconians wheeled and departed, heading back into the mountains.

Someone recalled hearing of a group of draconians who had taken control of the city of Teyr. It was said that these draconians had no love for the Dark Knights. Even if this was true, Teyr was a long march from Sanction, and no one could say how the draconians had managed to arrive at the critical time. Since no one ever saw the draconians again, this mystery was never solved.

When the victory in Sanction had been achieved, many of the golden and silver dragons departed, heading for the Dragon Isles or wherever they made their homes. Before they left, each dragon lifted up and carried away a portion of the ashes from the totem, taking them for a proper burial on the Dragon Isles. The Golds and Silver took all the remains, even though mingled among them were the ashes of Reds and Blues, Whites, Greens, and Blacks. For they were all dragons of Krynn.

"And what about you, sir?" Gerard asked Mirror. "Will you go back to the Citadel of Light?"

Gerard, Odila, and Mirror stood outside the West Gate of Sanction, watching the sunrise on the day after the battle. The sunrise was glorious, with bands of vibrant reds and oranges darkening to purple and deeper into black as day touched the departing night. The silver dragon faced the sun as if he could see it— and perhaps, in his soul, he could. He turned his blind head toward the sound of Gerard's voice.

"The Citadel will have no more need of my protection. Mishakal will make the temple her own. As for me, my guide and I have decided to join forces."

Gerard stared blankly at Odila, who nodded.

"I am leaving the Knighthood," she said. "Lord Tasgall has accepted my resignation. It is best this way, Gerard. The Knights would not have felt comfortable having me among their ranks."

"What will you do?" Gerard asked. They had been through so much, he had not expected to part with her so soon.

"Queen Takhisis may be gone," Odila said somberly, "but darkness remains. The minotaurs have seized Silvanesti. They will not be content with that land and may threaten others. Mirror and I have decided to join forces." She patted the silver dragon's neck. "A dragon who is blind and a human who was once blind—quite a team, don't you think?"

Gerard smiled. "If you're headed for Silvanesti, we may run into each other. I'm going to try to establish an alliance between the Knighthood and the elves."

"Do you truly believe the Knights' Council will agree to help the elves recover their land?" Odila asked skeptically.

"I don't know," Gerard said, shrugging, "but I'm damn sure going to make them think about it. First, though, I have a duty to perform. There's a broken lock on a tomb in Solace. I promised to go fix it."

An uncomfortable silence fell between them. Too much was left to say to be said now. Mirror fanned his wings, clearly eager to be gone. Odila took the hint.

"Goodbye, Cornbread," she said, grinning.

"Good riddance," said Gerard, grinning back.

Odila leaned close, kissed him on the cheek. "If you ever again take a bath naked in a creek, be sure and let me know."

She mounted the silver dragon. He dipped his sightless head in salute, spread his wings, and lifted gracefully into the air. Odila waved.

Gerard waved back. He watched them as they dwindled in size, remained watching until long after they had vanished from his sight.

Another goodbye was said that day. A farewell that would last for all eternity.

In the arena, Paladine knelt over the body of Silvanoshei. Paladine closed the staring eyes. He cleansed the blood from the young elf's face, composed the limbs. Paladine was tired. He was not accustomed to this mortal body, to its pains and aches and needs, to the range and intensity of emotions: of pity and sorrow, anger and fear. Looking into the face of the dead elven king, Paladine saw youth and promise, all lost, all wasted. He paused in his labor, wiped the sweat from his forehead, and wondered how, with such sorrow and heaviness in his heart, he could go on. He wondered how he could go on alone.

Feeling a gentle touch upon his shoulder, he looked to see a goddess, beautiful, radiant. She smiled down upon him, but there was sadness in her smile and the rainbows of unshed tears in her eyes.

"I will carry the young man's body to his mother," Mishakal offered.

"She was not witness to his death, was she?" Paladine asked.

"She was spared that much, at least. We freed all those who had been brought here forcibly by Takhisis to view her triumph. Alhana did not see her son die.

"Tell her," said Paladine quietly, "that he died a hero."

"I will do that, my beloved."

A kiss as soft as a white feather brushed the elf's lips.

"You are not alone," Mishakal said to him. "I will be with you always, my husband, my own."

He wanted very much for this to be so, willed that it should be so. But there was a gulf between them, and he saw that gulf grow wider with every passing moment. She stood upon the shore, and he floundered among the waves, and every wave washed him farther and farther away.

"What has become of the souls of the dead?" he asked.

"They are free," she said and her voice was distant. He could barely hear her. "Free to continue their journey."

"Someday, I will join them, my love."

"On that day, I will be waiting," she promised.

The body of Silvanoshei vanished, born away on a cloud of silvery light.

Paladine stood for a long time alone, stood in the darkness. Then he made his solitary way out of the arena, walked alone into the world.

The children of the gods, Nuitari, Lunitari, Solinari, entered the former Temple of the Heart. The body of the wizard Dalamar sat upon a bench, staring at nothing.

The gods of magic took their places before the dark and abandoned altar.

"Let the wizard, Raistlin Majere, come forth."

Raistlin emerged from the darkness and ruins of the temple. The hem of his black velvet robe scattered the amber shards that still lay upon the floor of this temple, for no one could be found who dared touch the accursed remnants of the sarcophogus that had imprisoned the body of Goldmoon. He trod upon them, crushed the amber beneath his feet.

In his arms, Raistlin held a body, shrouded in white.

"Your spirit is freed," said Solinari sternly. "Your twin brother awaits you. You promised to leave the world. You must keep that promise."

"I have no intention of remaining here," Raistlin returned. "My brother awaits, as do my former companions."

"They have forgiven you?"

"Or I have forgiven them," Raistlin returned smoothly. "The matter is between friends and none of your concern." He looked down at the body he held in his arms. "But this is."

Raistlin laid the body of his nephew at the feet of the gods. Then, drawing back his hood, he faced the three siblings.

"I ask one last boon of you, of all of you," said Raistlin. "Restore Palin to life. Restore him to his family."

"And why should we do this?" Lunitari demanded.

"His steps strayed onto the path that I once walked," said Raistlin. "He saw his mistake at the end, but he could not live to redeem it. If you give him back his life, he will be able to retrace his wandering footsteps and find the way home."

"As you could not," said Lunitari gently.

"As I could not," said Raistlin.

"Brothers?" Lunitari turned to Solinari and Nuitari. "What do you say to this?"

"I say that there is another matter to be decided, as well," said Nuitari. "Let the wizard Dalamar come forth.

The elf's body sat unmoving on the bench. The spirit of the wizard stood behind the body. Wary, tense, Dalamar approached the gods.

"You betrayed us," said Nuitari, accusing.

"You sided with Takhisis," said Lunitari, "and we nearly lost the one chance we had to return to the world."

"You betrayed our worshiper Palin," said Solinari sternly. "By her command, you murdered him."

Dalamar looked from one shining god to the next and when he spoke, his soul's voice was soft and bitter. "How could you possibly understand? How would you know what it feels like to lose everything?"

"Perhaps," said Lunitari, "we understand better than you think."

Dalamar kept silent, made no response.

"What is to be done with him?" Lunitari asked. "Is he to be given back his life?"

"Unless you give me back the magic," Dalamar interposed, "don't bother."

"I say we do not," said Solinari. "He used the dead to work his black arts. He does not deserve our mercy."

"I say we do," said Nuitari coolly. "If you restore Palin to life and offer him the magic, you must do the same for Dalamar. The balance must be maintained."

"What do you say, Cousin?" Solinari asked Lunitari.

"Will you accept my judgment?" she asked.

Solinari and Nuitari eyed each other, then both nodded.

"This is my decree. Dalamar shall be restored to life and the magic, but he must leave the Tower of High Sorcery he once occupied. He will henceforth be barred from entry there. He must return to the world of the living and be forced to make his way among them. Palin Majere will also be restored to life. We will grant him the magic, if he wants it. Are these terms satisfactory to you both, Cousins?"

"They are to me," said Nuitari.

"And to me," said Solinari.

"And are they satisfactory to you, Dalamar?" Lunitari asked.

Dalamar had what he wanted, and that was all he cared about. As for the rest, he would return to the world. Someday, perhaps, he would rule the world.

"They are, Lady," he said.

"Are these satisfactory to you, Raistlin Majere?" Lunitari asked.

Raistlin bowed his hooded head.

"Then both requests are granted. We grant life, and we gift you with the magic."

"I thank you, lords and lady," Dalamar said, bowing again. His gaze lingered for a moment on Nuitari, who understood perfectly.

Raistlin knelt beside the body of his nephew. He drew back the white shroud. Palin's eyes opened. He gazed around in shocked bewilderment, then his gaze fixed on his uncle. Palin's shock deepened.

"Uncle!" he gasped. Sitting up, he tried to reach out to take his uncle's hand. His fingers, flesh and bone and blood, slid through Raistlin's hand that was the ephemeral hand of the dead.

Palin stared at his hand, and the realization came to him that he was alive. He looked at his hands, so like the hands of his uncle, with their long, delicate fingers, and he could move those fingers, and they would obey his commands.

"I thank you," Palin said, lifting his head to see the gods in their radiance around him. "I thank you, Uncle." He paused, then said, "Once you foretold that I would be the greatest mage ever to live upon Krynn. I do not think that will come to pass."

"We had much to learn, Nephew," Raistlin replied. "Much to learn about what was truly important. Farewell. My brother and our friends await." He smiled. "Tanis, as usual, is impatient to be gone."

Palin saw before him a river of souls, a river that flowed placidly, slowly among the banks of the living. Sunlight shone upon the river, starlight sparkled in its fathomless depths. The souls of the dead looked ahead of them into a sea whose waves lapped upon the shores of eternity, a sea that would carry each on new journeys. Standing on the shore, waiting for his twin, was Caramon Majere.

Raistlin joined his twin. The brothers raised their hands in farewell, then both stepped into the river and rode upon its silvery waters that flow into the endless sea.

Dalamar's spirit flowed into his body. The magic flowed into his spirit. The blood burned in his veins, the magic burned in his blood, and his joy was deep and profound. Lifting his head, he looked up into the sky.

The one pale moon had vanished. Two moons lit the sky, one with silver fire, the other with red. As he watched in awe and thankfulness, the two converged into a radiant eye. The black moon stared out from the center.

"So they gave you back your life, as well," said Palin, emerging from the shadows.

"*And* the magic," Dalamar returned.

Palin smiled. "Where will you go?"

"I do not know," said Dalamar carelessly. "The wide world is open to me. I intend to move out of the Tower of High Sorcery. I was prisoner there long enough. Where do you go?" His lip curled slightly. "Back to your loving wife?"

"If Usha will have me," said Palin, his tone and look somber. "I have much to make up to her."

"Do not be too long about it. We must meet soon to discuss the reconvening of the Orders," said Dalamar briskly. "There is work to be done."

"And there will be other hands to do it," said Palin.

Dalamar stared at him, now suddenly aware of the truth. "Solinari offered you the magic. And you refused it!"

"I threw away too much of value because of it," said Palin. "My marriage. My life. I came to realize it wasn't worth it."

You fool! The words were on Dalamar's lips, but he did not say them aloud, kept them to himself. He had no idea where he was going, and there would be no one to welcome him when he got there.

Dalamar looked up at the three moons. "Perhaps I will come to visit you and Usha sometime," he said, knowing he never would.

"We would be honored to have you," Palin replied, knowing he would never see the dark elf again.

"I had best be going," Dalamar said.

"I should be going, too," said Palin. "It is a long walk back to Solace."

"I could speed you through the corridors of magic," Dalamar offered.

"No, thank you," said Palin with a wry smile. "I had best get used to walking. Farewell, Dalamar the Dark."

"Farewell, Palin Majere."

Dalamar spoke the words of magic, felt them bubble and sparkle on his lips like fine wine, drank deeply of them. In an instant, he was gone.

Palin stood alone, thoughtful, silent. Then he looked up at the moons, which were for him now nothing but moons, one silver and one red.

Smiling, his thoughts turning to home, he matched his feet to the same direction.

The Solamnic Knights deployed their forces on Sanction's battlements, started hasty work repairing the West Gate and shoring up the holes that had been made in Sanction's walls. Scouts from the ranks of the Knights and those of the elves were sent to search for Mina. Silver dragons flying the skies kept watch for her, but no one found her. Dragons brought word of enemy forces marching toward Sanction, coming from Jelek and from Palanthas. Sooner or later, they would hear word that Sanction had fallen, but how would they react? Would they turn and flee for home, or would they march on to try to retake it? And would Mina, bereft of her god-given power, return to lead them, or would she remain in hiding somewhere, licking her wounds?

None would ever know where the body of Queen Takhisis lay buried—if she had been buried at all. Down through the years, those who walked on the side of darkness would search for the tomb, for the legend sprang up that her unquiet spirit would grant gifts to those who found her final resting place.

The most enduring mystery was what became known as the Miracle of the Temple of Duerghast. People from all parts of Sanction, all parts of Ansalon, all parts of the world, had been snatched abruptly from their lives by the Dark Queen and brought to the arena in the Temple of Duerghast to witness her triumphant entry into the world. Instead, they witnessed an epoch.

Those who saw firsthand the death of Queen Takhisis retained the images of what they saw and heard forever, feeling it branded into their souls as the brand burns the flesh. The shock and pain were searing, at first, but eventually the pain faded away, as the body and mind worked to heal themselves.

At first, some missed the pain, for without it, what proof was there that this had all been real? To make it real, to insure that it had been real, some talked of what they had seen, talked volubly. Others kept their thoughts locked away inside and would never speak of the event.

As with those on Krynn who had witnessed other epochs—the chaotic travels of the Gray Gem, the fall of Istar, the Cataclysm—they passed their stories of the Miracle from one generation to the next. To future generations living on Krynn, the Fifth Age would begin with the theft of the world at the moment of Chaos's defeat. But the Fifth Age would only come to be widely called the Age of Mortals on the day when the Judgment of the Book took away the godhood of one god and accepted the sacrifice of the other.

Silvanoshei was to be laid to rest in the Tomb of the Heroes in Solace. This was not to be his final burial place. His grieving mother, Alhana Starbreeze, hoped to one day take him home to Silvanesti, but that day would be long in coming. The minotaur nation poured in troops and supplies and were firmly entrenched in that formerly fair land.

Captain Samuval and his mercenaries continued to raid throughout the elven lands of Qualinesti. The Dark Knights drove out or killed the few elves who remained and claimed the land of Qualinesti as their own. The elves were exiles now. The remnants of the two nations argued over where to go, what to do.

The elven exiles camped in the valley outside of Sanction, but they were not at home there, and the Solamnic Knights, now the rulers of Sanction, urged them politely to consider moving somewhere else. The Knights' Council discussed allying with the elves to drive the minotaurs out of Silvanesti, but there was some question in regard to the Measure, and the matter was referred to scholars to settle, which they might confidently be expected to do in ten or twenty years.

Alhana Starbreeze had been offered the rulership of the Silvanesti, but, her heart broken, she had refused. She suggested that Gilthas rule in her stead. The Qualinesti wanted this, most of them. The Silvanesti did not, though they had no one else to recommend. The two quarreling nations came together once more, their representatives traveling together to the funeral of Silvanoshei.

A golden dragon bore the body of Silvanoshei to the Tomb of the Heroes. Solamnic Knights, riding silver dragons, formed a guard of honor, led by Gerard uth Mondar. Alhana accompanied the body of her son, as did his cousin Gilthas.

He was not sorry to leave the quarrels and intrigues behind. He wondered if he had the strength to go back. He did not want the kingship of the elven nations. He did not feel he was the right person. He did not want the responsibility of leading a people in exile, a people without a home.

Standing outside the tomb, Gilthas watched as a procession of elves carried the body of Silvanoshei, covered in a shroud of golden cloth, to its temporary resting place. His body was laid in a marble coffin, covered over with flowers. The shards of the broken dragonlance were placed in his hands.

The tomb would be the final resting place of Goldmoon. Her ashes were mingled with the ashes of Riverwind. The two of them together at last.

An elf dressed in travel-stained clothes of brown and green came to stand beside Gilthas. He said nothing but watched in solemn reverence as the ashes of Goldmoon and Riverwind were carried inside.

"Farewell, dear and faithful friends," he said softly.

Gilthas turned to him.

"I am glad to have this chance to speak to you, E'li—" he began.

The elf halted him. "That is my name no longer."

"What, then, should we call you, sir?" Gilthas asked.

"So many names I have had," said the elf. "E'li among the elves, Paladine among the humans. Even Fizban. That one, I must admit, was my favorite. None of them serve me now. I have chosen a new name."

"And that is—" Gilthas paused.

"Valthonis," said the elf.

"'The exile?'" Gilthas translated, puzzled. Sudden understanding rushed upon him. He tried to speak but could not manage beyond saying brokenly, "So you will share our fate."

Valthonis laid his hand upon Gilthas's shoulder. "Go back to your people, Gilthas. They are both your people, the Silvanesti and the Qualinesti. Make them one people again, and though they are a people in exile, though you have no land to call your own, you will be a nation."

Gilthas shook his head.

"The task before you is not an easy one," Valthonis said. "You will work hard and painstakingly to join together what others will endeavor to tear apart. You will be beset with failure, but never give up hope. If that happens, you will know defeat."

"Will you be with me?" Gilthas asked.

Valthonis shook his head. "I have my own road to walk, as do you, as does each of us. Yet, at times, our paths may cross."

"Thank you, sir," said Gilthas, clasping the elf's hand. "I will do as you say. I will return to my people. All my people." He sighed deeply, smiled ruefully. "Even Senator Palthainon."

Gerard stood at the entrance to the tomb, waiting for the last of the mourners to leave. The ceremony was over. Night had fallen. The crowds who had gathered to watch began to drift away, some going to the Inn of the Last Home, where Palin and Usha joined with his sisters, Laura and Dezra, to comfort all who mourned, giving them smiles and good food and the best ale in Ansalon.

As Gerard stood there, he thought back to all that had happened since that day, so long ago, when he had first heard Tasslehoff's voice shouting from inside the tomb. The world had changed, and yet it had not.

There were now three moons in the sky instead of one. Yet the sun that rose every morning was the same sun that had ushered in the Fifth Age. The people could look up into the sky again and find the constellations of the gods and point them out to their children. But the constellations were not the same as they had once been. They were made up of different stars, held different places in the heavens. Two could not be found, would never be found, would never be seen above Krynn again.

"The Age of Mortals," Gerard said to himself. The term had a new significance, a new meaning.

He looked inside the tomb to see one last person still within—the strange elf he had first seen in the arena. Gerard waited respectfully, patiently, fully prepared to give this mourner all the time he needed.

The elf said his prayers in silence, then, with a final loving farewell, he walked over to Gerard.

"Did you fix the lock?" he asked, smiling.

"I did, sir," said Gerard. He shut the door to the tomb behind him. He heard the lock click. He did not immediately leave. He was also loath to say goodbye.

"Sir, I was wondering." Gerard paused, then plunged ahead. "I don't know how to say this, but did Tasslehoff—Did he . . . did he do what he meant to do?"

"Did he die when and where he was meant to die?" the elf asked. "Did he defeat Chaos? Is that what you mean?"

"Yes, sir," said Gerard. "That's what I mean."

In answer, the elf lifted his head, looked into the night sky. "There once used to be a red star in the heavens. Do you remember it?"

"Yes, sir."

"Look for it now. Do you see it?"

"No, sir," said Gerard, searching the heavens. "What happened to it?"

"The forge fire has gone out. Flint doused the flame, for he knew he was no longer needed."

"So Tasslehoff found him," said Gerard.

"Tasslehoff found him. He and Flint and their companions are all together again," said the elf. "Flint and Tanis and Tasslehoff, Tika, Sturm, Goldmoon and Riverwind. They wait only for Raistlin, and he will join them soon, for Caramon, his twin, would not think of leaving without him."

"Where are they bound, sir?" Gerard asked.

"On the next stage of their souls' journey," said the elf.

"I wish them well," said Gerard.

He left the Tomb of the Last Heroes, bade the elf farewell, and, pocketing the key, turned his steps toward the Inn of the Last Home. The warm glow that streamed from its windows lit his way.

An Excerpt from

THE MINOTAUR WARS
VOLUME I
NIGHT OF BLOOD

**Volume One of the new
Dragonlance trilogy**

The Minotaur Wars

Richard A. Knaak

Chapter I

Night of Blood

Zokun Es-Kalin, first cousin of the emperor, Ship Master of the House of Kalin's merchant fleet. . . .

* * * * *

They found Zokun at his estate on the wooded, northern edge of the imperial capital of Nethosak. He was fast asleep in his plush, down-filled bed. Although in command of a mighty fleet of some two hundred ships, he himself had not gone to sea for years and had no desire to do so. Zokun preferred the rewards of power to the work, and many of his tasks were handled by well-trained subordinates who knew their proper place in the imperium.

A bottle of rich and heady briarberry wine, one of the finest wines produced in the empire and coveted even by the lesser races beyond, stood empty next to three others previously drained. A slim, brown form beside the fat, snoring minotaur leader turned over in her sleep. This was not his mate, Hila, but a younger female who hoped soon to take Hila's place.

And so she did, dying along with the Ship Master. The helmed assassins dispatched her with one stroke—

compared to the four needed to gut her drunken lover. Both perished swiftly.

No servants heard them cry out. None of Zokun's family came to his aid. Most of the former had been rounded up and taken away. The latter, including Hila, had been slain at exactly the same time as the venerable Ship Master and his mistress.

* * * * *

The feminine hand took the long quill pen, dipped it in a rich, red ink, and drew a line through Zokun's name. The wielder of the quill took care not to spill any of the ink on her silky gold and sable robes. She moved the pen to another name below—the name of one Grisov Es-Neros, councilor to the emperor and patriarch of the house most closely allied with that of Kalin.

* * * * *

Grisov was a scarred, thin minotaur whose fur was almost snow white. His snout had a wrinkled, deflated appearance, and over the years his brow had enveloped his eyes. Despite his grizzled countenance, the patriarch was hardly infirm. His reflexes were still those of the young champion of the Great Circus he had been years before the bloody war against the aquatic Magori. His well-schooled, well-paid healers encouraged him to sleep at a proper hour, but Grisov continued to take his late-night walks, a cherished tradition to him and others in this area of Nethosak. Grisov liked to survey his fiefdom, reminding himself that, as long as Chot was kept in power, the children of Neros would profit. He had no qualms about what part he had played over the years in propping up the emperor; the strongest and most cunning always triumphed.

The street did not seem as well tended as when he was young. Grisov recalled immaculate streets of white marble with nary a sign of refuse. These days, all sorts of trash could be found littering the avenues. Bits and pieces of old food, broken ale bottles, and rotting vegetation offended the patriarch's sensibility. One large piece of trash, a snoring, drunken sailor, was snuggled against the high, spiked wall of the abode of one Grisov nephew, a wastrel who lived off the hard work of his uncle.

It was all the fault of the young generation. The young could be blamed for everything. They had never learned the discipline of their elders.

Two able warriors clad in thigh-length, leather-padded metal kilts, colored sea-blue and green—the official clan colors—accompanied the robed minotaur. Each carried a long, double-edged axe shined to a mirror finish and etched with the Neros symbol—a savage wave washing over rocks—in the center of the head. Grisov thought the guards a nuisance, but at least this pair knew not to speak unless spoken to. The guards knew his routine well, knew what stops their master would make, knew what comments he would murmur and how they ought to respond.

Yet, there was one change in the routine this night. Grisov had no intention of letting drunkards invade his domain.

"Kelto, see that piece of garbage on his way. I'll not have him sully this street!"

"Aye, patriarch." With a look of resignation, the young warrior headed toward the snoring sailor.

A whistling sound made the patriarch's ears stiffen. Recognition of what that sound presaged dawned just a second later—a second too late.

A gurgling noise made the elder warrior turn to see his guard transfixed, a wooden shaft piercing his throat.

As the hapless warrior fell, Grisov turned to Kelto— only to find that one sprawled on the ground, his blood already pooling on the street.

Peering around, the elder minotaur discovered that the drunken sailor had vanished.

A decoy.

Grisov reached for his sword and cried, "Villains! Cowards! Come to me, you dishonorable —"

Two bolts struck him from opposite directions, one piercing a lung, the other sinking deep into his back. Blood spilled over his luxurious blue robe, overwhelming the green Neros symbol on his chest.

With a short gasp, the patriarch dropped his blade and collapsed beside his guards.

* * * * *

A young minotaur clad in plain, ankle-length robes of white trimmed with red approached the senior priestess, bringing a silver flask of wine for the empty chalice sitting next to the pile of parchments. The priestess looked up briefly, then flicked her eyes toward the half-melted candle by which she checked her lists. The servant glanced that way but saw nothing. The servant finished refilling the goblet then quickly backed away.

"Tyra de-Proul?" asked the senior priestess. She was a chestnut-colored female, still attractive in the eyes of her kind. Her words were whispered to the open air. She fixed her gaze in the general direction of a lengthy silk tapestry depicting a white, almost ghostlike bird ascending to the starry heavens. "You are certain?" the priestess asked the emptiness.

A moment later, her ears twitched in clear satisfaction. She nodded, then looked over the lists. Many lines were already crossed out, but she soon located the one she desired.

A smile crossed her visage as she brought the quill down. "Another page complete."

* * * * *

On the island of Kothas, sister realm to Mithas and a two-day journey from the capital, Tyra de-Proul stirred from sleep. Her mate had been due to return this evening from his voyage to Sargonath, a minor minotaur colony located on the northeastern peninsula of Ansalon, but he had not yet arrived. Feeling pensive, Tyra pushed back her thick, gray mane and rose.

Jolar's ship might just be late. That shouldn't bother her at all, yet some vague dread insisted on disturbing her asleep.

The tall, athletic female poured some water. As appointed administrator of the emperor's interests, Tyra made constant sea trips between the imperial capital and this island's principal city of Morthosak. Jolar's lateness could readily be attributed to any number of innocent causes, even foul weather.

A muffled sound beyond her door brought her to full attention. At this hour, no one in the house other than the sentries should be awake, and the sentries knew to make their rounds without causing clamor of any sort.

Tyra seized her sword and scabbard, then headed toward the door. Weapon drawn, she opened it—

And was stunned to see a frantic struggle taking place between Jolar and three helmed minotaurs at the foot of the steps.

One of the intruders had a hand over her mate's muzzle, but Jolar twisted free and shouted, "Flee, Tyra! The house is under siege! There is no —"

He gasped, a dagger in his side. Jolar fell to the floor.

Like all minotaurs, Tyra had been trained from childhood first and foremost as a warrior. As a young female, she had helped fight back the vile Magori when the crustaceans rose from the sand and surf, the destruction of all minotaurs their sole desire. Never in her life had she turned from a battle, whether on the field or in the political arena.

With a savage cry, Tyra threw herself down the steps, her sword cutting the air as she descended.

The nearest foe stumbled against her mate's corpse. Tyra thrust the blade through the helmed assassin's unprotected throat. Before he had even dropped to the floor, she did battle with the second, a young female who moved with the haughtiness of one who thought that before her stood merely a decrepit elder. The imperial representative caught the intruder's blade and twisted it to the side. She kicked at her opponent and watched with satisfaction as the latter went flying back into a nearby wall, knocked unconscious.

In the dim illumination, she made out two dead bodies in the lower hall. One also wore a helm, but the other Tyra recognized even though he lay muzzle down.

Mykos. Her eldest son. In three days he would have become the newest addition to the Imperial Guard. General Rahm Es-Hestos, the commander of the emperor's elite, had personally recommended Mykos, a moment of great pride for his mother.

An axe had done him in. His blood still pooled beside his hacked torso.

Tyra screamed, swinging anew at the last of her attackers. He continued to back away from her.

"Stand still so I can smite the head from your body, you dishonorable dog! My mate—my children—demand your blood!"

Still edging away, her opponent said nothing.

Too late did the obvious occur to the outraged minotaur. Tyra de-Proul wheeled quickly, but not quickly enough.

The female assassin whom she thought had been knocked unconscious stabbed the imperial representative through the heart.

"Stupid old cow," the assassin muttered.

Tyra slipped to the floor and joined her mate in death.

* * * * *

So many names crossed out. So few remaining.

She looked over the pages, noting the survivors. Some looked to be of no major consequence, but a handful tugged at her, urgently.

A chill wind suddenly coursed through the stone chamber that served as her private sanctum. She quickly protected the candle.

My Lady Nephera . . . came a voice in her head, a voice rasping and striving for breath.

Nephera glanced beyond the candle, seeing only glimpses of a shadowy figure at the edge of her vision. At times, she could make out details—such as a hooded cloak—and within the cloak a minotaur unusually gaunt of form. Of the eyes that stared back at her, she sometimes made out the whites, but this monstrous phantasm had no pupils.

The cloak hung in damp tatters with glimpses of pale flesh beneath. Whenever this particular visitor appeared, the smell of the sea always seemed to accompany him—the sea as the eternal graveyard.

As she reached for a grape from the bowl set by her side—the only sustenance she would permit herself this glorious night—the elegantly clad High Priestess of the Temple of the Forerunners waited for the ominous figure to speak again.

The shade's decaying mouth did not move, but once more Lady Nephera heard a grating voice. *Four of the Supreme Circle now join me in death.*

She knew three names already, but the addition of a fourth pleased her. "Who? Name all four so that I can be certain!"

General Tohma, Boril, General Astos . . .

All names she had. "Who else?"

Kesk the Elder.

"Ah, excellent." Pulling free one of the parchments, Nephera located the name and gave it a swift, inky stroke—as lethal to the council member in question as the axes and swords that had actually killed him. The elimination of the highest-ranking members of the Supreme Circle, the august governing body under the emperor, gave her immense satisfaction. They, more than most, she held responsible for all that had happened to her and her husband—and to the empire.

Thinking of her mate, the Forerunner priestess scowled. "My husband's hand-picked warriors move quick, but not quick enough. This should be finished by now!"

Send out your own? responded the gaunt shadow. *Your trusted Protectors, mistress?*

She would have dearly loved to do so, but Hotak had insisted otherwise. This had to be done without the temple. The military might of the empire would not look with favor on her husband if it appeared that the Forerunners influenced his actions.

"No. We shall leave this to my husband. The triumph

must be his and his alone." Lady Nephera picked up the stack of parchments, her intense black gaze burning into each name. "Still, the temple will have its say."

* * * * *

Throughout the length and span of the empire, the Night of Blood continued relentlessly.

On Mito, three days' journey east of the imperial capital, the governor of the most populated island colony rushed forth to greet two massive vessels that had sailed into port. An honor guard had quickly been arranged, for who but an important dignitary would arrive without warning and with such a show of force? The captain of the first vessel marched a squad of helmed warriors down to salute the assembled well wishers—and then executed the governor where he stood.

On the island of Duma, the home of General Kroj, commander of the empire's southern forces and hero of the battles of Turak Major and Selees, became the scene of a pitched battle. The fight went on until dawn, when the barriers of the general's estate were finally broken down by his own troops, who joined the attackers. Kroj committed ritual suicide with a dagger even as helmed fighters burst down the door to his study. They would find his family already dead, their throats slit by Kroj just prior to his own demise.

In Mithas, Edan Es-Brog, the high priest of the Temple of Sargonnas, would be discovered dead in his sleep, a mixture of poisons in his evening potion.

Veria de-Goltyn, Chief Captain of the eastern fleet, drowned as she sought to escape her burning ship. Her own captains had been paid to turn on her.

Konac, imperial tax master, was stabbed more than a

dozen times at the door of the emperor's coffers. A stronger figure than his rotund appearance indicated, Konac would outlast his guards and two assassins, making it to just within a few yards of the Imperial Guard's headquarters before dying. No one within heard his final choked warning.

A massive fleet, organized quickly and secretly over the course of weeks and combining the might of over three dozen turncoat generals and captains, spread out over the expanse of minotaur interests. Some of them had been on their journeys for days already. Before the night would conclude, twenty-two colonial governors, their principal officers, and hundreds of loyal subordinates would be executed. All but a handful of the major territories and settlements within a week's reach of the main island would be under the iron control of Hotak's followers.

* * * * *

All of this, Lady Nephera saw as it happened. She had eyes everywhere. She knew more than her husband's lackeys. Even the emperor, with his complex and far-reaching network of messengers and spies, knew but a fraction of what the high priestess knew.

Thinking of the emperor, Nephera turned her brooding eyes to one particular page, reading the only name still listed. No furious stain of ink expunged this name's existence, yet by her estimate, only minutes remained before she would have the ultimate pleasure.

The high priestess read the name over and over, picturing the puffy, overfed countenance, the vain, ambitious, clownish visage.

Chot Es-Kalin.

* * * * *

In his younger days, the massive, graying minotaur had been the scourge of the Circus, the unbeatable champion to whom all had deferred in admiration. Chot the Terrible, he was called. Chot the Invincible! Over the span of his life and decades-long rule, scores of would-be rivals had fallen to his bloody battle-axe. No minotaur had ever held the title of emperor for so many years.

"More wine, my lord?"

Chot studied the slim, dark-brown female lounging next to him on the vast silk-sheeted bed. She had not only the energy of youth but the beauty as well. Chot's last mate had died over a decade ago, and since that time he had preferred such enticing visitors to a regular companion. The much-scarred emperor knew that this added to the list of grievances his political foes spouted about him, but he did not care. His foes could do nothing so long as he accepted the imperial challenges and faced down his opponents in the Great Circus.

They could do nothing so long as each of their champions fell dead at his feet.

He shifted his great girth and handed his mistress the empty goblet. Years of living the glory of an emperor had taken some toll on his body, but Chot still considered himself the ultimate warrior, the envy of other males, and the desire of all females.

"Is that enough, my lord?" his companion said as she topped off his drink.

"Enough, Maritia." Chot took a gulp of the rich, red liquid, then looked the female warrior over, savoring the curve of her lithe form. Some female minotaurs looked too much like males. Chot preferred curves. A female should look like a female, especially when she had been granted the glorious company of her emperor.

His bed companion replaced the squat wine bottle on

the carved, marble table. The well-cleaned remains of a roasted goat sat atop a silver tray next to the bottle, and beside that stood a wooden bowl filled with exotic fruit shipped to the capital from one of the farthest and most tropical colonies.

Maritia leaned forward, rubbing the soft tip of her muzzle against him. Curiously, the image of her father suddenly flashed into his mind. Chot had recently solved the problem of her insufficiently loyal and increasingly irritating father by sending him far, far away on a mission of some import—and some danger as well. If he succeeded, his glory would reflect on Chot. If he died in combat—a more likely outcome—so much the better.

Chot belched, and the world briefly swam around him. The emperor rolled onto his back, snorting. Enough entertainment for tonight. Time he got some sleep.

There was a fuzzy sound in the distance.

"What's that?" he rumbled, trying to rise.

"I heard nothing, my lord," replied Maritia. She rubbed her graceful hand over his matted brown and gray fur.

Chot relaxed again. It would be a shame when he had to banish her, but she would never forgive him anyway once she found out what he had done to her father.

"Sleep, my lord," Maritia cooed. "Sleep forever."

He jarred awake—in time to see the dagger poised above his head.

Drunken, tired, and out of shape, Chot nonetheless reacted with swiftness. He caught her wrist and managed to twist the blade free. The dagger clattered on the marble floor.

"What in the name of Argon's Chain do you think you're doing?" he roared, his head pounding.

In response, she raked her long, sharp nails across the side of his muzzle.

Roaring, Chot released the fool. Maritia scrambled away from the bed as the emperor put a hand to his bloody face.

"Vixen!" Legs protesting, the immense minotaur rose. "You little cow!"

She glared at the last insult, one of the worst things anyone could call a minotaur. Chot stood a head taller and still carried much muscle under his portly girth, but the female seemed strangely unafraid.

The emperor snorted. Maritia would learn fear.

Then he heard the same fuzzy noise as earlier, only closer.

"What's that?" he mumbled, forgetting her for the moment. "Who's fighting out there?"

"That would be your Imperial Guard, my lord," Maritia said, pronouncing his title as if it were excrement. "They are busy falling to the swords and axes of your enemies."

"What's that?" Chot struggled to think clearly. His guards. He had to call his guards. "Sentries! Attend me!"

Maritia smirked. "They are otherwise detained, my lord."

The emperor's stomach suddenly churned. Too much wine, too much goat. Chot put one hand on the bed. "I must think. I must think."

"Think all you like, but my father should be here shortly."

"Your . . . father?" Battling against the nausea and the pounding headache, Chot froze. "Hotak's here? Impossible. I sent him to the mainland weeks ago!"

"And despite your treachery, he's returned. Returned to demand the justice due to him, due the entire imperium!"

With a roar, Chot lunged for her. Maritia eluded his grasp. The emperor turned, seized his favorite axe, and swung wildly. He came nowhere near the treacherous female, though he did drive her back.

"Assassin! Traitor! Traitors!"

Maritia attempted to retrieve her dagger, but Chot swung again. The heavy blade of the twin-edged axe buried itself in his bed, cutting through expensive sheets, through the rich, down padding, and even through the oak frame.

As the bed collapsed in a heap, the emperor stumbled back. Through bleary eyes he glared at Hotak's daughter.

"Slay me if you can," Maritia sneered. "But you'll not live more than a few minutes longer." Her ears twitched toward the window behind Chot. "You hear that?"

Keeping his gaze on the female at all times, Chot stepped back to the balcony. He glanced over his shoulder just long enough to see that the palace grounds swarmed with dark figures heading toward the building.

"Father will be here very soon now," Maritia called to him.

"Then he'll find you begging him to save your life . . . cow!"

Chot stumbled toward her, reaching clumsily with one hand while with the other he threatened her with the axe. Maritia dodged readily, leading Chot a merry chase through the room, mocking his growing rage, and taunting him with her derision.

He swung more wildly. Rounded crystalline vases, minotaur statuettes of emerald, tapestries of spun gold, marble icons of dragons and other fearsome beasts—the treasures he had accumulated through his lengthy reign—scattered in shards.

His own body finally rebelled. Even as fists began to pound upon the door, Chot the Invincible fell against the broken bed, his head spinning, his insides a maelstrom.

"Chot the Magnificent," he heard Maritia mutter. "Rather you should be called Chot the Pathetic."

"I'll . . . I'll . . ." The emperor could say no more.

He heard her open the door, heard the sounds of armed and armored figures marching into his chamber.

"And this is supposed to be the supreme warrior, the epitome of what our people seek to be?"

The emperor fought to raise his head.

They wore the traditional silver helms. Nose guards ran along their muzzles. Their breastplates were also silver, with the ancient symbol of the condor clutching the axe emblazoned on the chest in deep crimson. Well-worn, padded-metal kilts with red tips at the bottom and open-toed sandals bound at the ankles completed their outfits.

These were his soldiers, warriors of the legions—and they had dared such treachery!

In the forefront of the traitorous band stood their leader. Although otherwise clad as his companions, he also wore the richly crested helmet reserved for the highest generals of the empire. The crest, made of thick, excellent horsehair, hung far back. Over his shoulders hung a long, flowing crimson cape.

Dark brown of fur, slightly over seven feet, well-muscled, and with very angular features for one of his race, the leader glared down at his lord with distaste. A pommel-handled sword hung in the scabbard at his side; a large battle-axe was in his grip.

"Chot Es-Kalin," announced the newcomer, nearly spitting out the name.

"Hotak de-Droka," responded the emperor. The de before the clan name indicated House Droka had its roots on the island of Kothas, considered, especially by those who bore the more regal Es, the lesser of the two kingdoms making up the heart of the empire.

627

Hotak looked to his daughter. His expression turned even grimmer. "You've sacrificed far too much, daughter."

"But it wasn't so terrible a sacrifice, father," she responded, turning back to smile coldly at Chot. "Only passing minutes."

"You . . . damned vixen!" Chot struggled to rise. If he could just get his hands around her throat —

The emperor fell to his hands and knees again. "I feel sick," he murmured.

General Hotak kicked at Chot's side. The immense, graying minotaur dropped flat, moaning.

Hotak snorted. He took a step toward his emperor. "Chot Es-Kalin. Chot the Invincible. Chot the Terrible." The one-eyed commander raised his weapon high. In the light cast by the torches of his followers, the symbol of the rearing horse etched into the axe head seemed to flare to life. "Chot the *Fool*. Chot the *Lying*. Chot the *Treacherous*. Time to put your misery and our shame to an end."

Chot could not think. He could not stand. He could no longer even raise a finger. This had to be a mistake! How could this happen?

"I am Chot," he mumbled, looking down in utter bewilderment. He felt the contents of his stomach finally coming up. "I am your *emperor*."

"No more," said Hotak. "No more."

The axe came down.

When it was over, the general handed the bloody weapon to one of his aides then removed his helmet. Dark brown hair with a touch of gray flowed behind his head. Nodding toward the body, Hotak commanded, "Remove that blubbery carcass for burning. Make sure nothing remains. As for the head . . . see to it that there's a high pole set up at the very entrance to the palace grounds.

Make certain that anyone who passes by will be able to see it from some distance. Understood?"

"Aye, General—aye, my lord!" the warrior said, correcting himself.

General Hotak de-Droka looked at the soldier, then at his daughter. Maritia smiled and went down on one knee.

One by one, the rest of those who followed him knelt before he who had slain Chot the Terrible, knelt before the new emperor of the minotaur race.

The Minotaur Wars

Richard A. Knaak

A new trilogy featuring the minotaur race that continues the story from the *New York Times* best-selling War of Souls trilogy!

Now available in paperback!
NIGHT OF BLOOD
Volume One

As the War of Souls spreads, a terrible, bloody coup led by the ambitious General Hotak and his wife, the High Priestess Nephera, over-takes the minotaur empire. With legions of soldiers and the unearthly magic of the Fore-runners at his command, the new emperor turns his sights towards Ansalon. But not all his enemies lie dead...

New in hardcover!
TIDES OF BLOOD
Volume Two

Making a bold pact with the ogres, and with the assurances of the mysterious warrior-woman Mina sweetly ringing in his ears, the minotaur emperor Hotak decides to invade Ansalon. But betrayal comes from the least expected quarters, and an escaped slave called Faros, the last of the blood of the lawful emperor, stirs up a fresh, vengeance-driven rebellion.

Follow Mina from the War of Souls into the chaos of post-war Krynn.

AMBER AND ASHES
The Dark Disciple, Volume I
Margaret Weis

With Paladine and Takhisis gone, the lesser gods
vie for primacy over Krynn. Recruited to a new
faith by a god of evil, Mina leads a religion of
the dead, and kender and a holy monk are all
that stand in the way of the dark stain
spreading across Ansalon.

**First in a new series from *New York Times*
best-selling author Margaret Weis.**

August 2004

The Ergoth Trilogy

Paul B. Thompson & Tonya C. Cook

Explore the history of the ancient DRAGONLANCE® world!

THE WIZARD'S FATE
Volume Two

The old Emperor is dead, sending shock
waves throughout the Ergoth Empire. Dark
forces gather as two brothers vie bitterly for the
throne. Key to the struggle for succession are
the rogue sorcerer Mandes and peasant general
Lord Tolandruth—sworn enemies of one
another—and the noble lady Tol loves, whose
first loyalty is to her husband, the Crown Prince.

A HERO'S JUSTICE
Volume Three

The Ergoth Empire has been invaded on two
fronts, and the teeming horde streaming across
the plain is no human army. As the warriors
of Ergoth reel back, defeated and broken, the
cry goes up far and wide, "Where is Lord
Tolandruth?!" Banished by Emperor Ackal V, no
one had seen Tol in more than six years. To save
Ergoth, Egrin Raemel's son rides forth to find Tol
and forge an alliance between a kender queen,
an aging beauty, and a lost and brilliant general.

December 2004

A WARRIOR'S JOURNEY
Volume One
Available Now